PINOT NOIR

AN INTERNATIONAL BANKING
SPY THRILLER

A LOUISE MOSCOW NOVEL
BOOK 2

LORRAINE EVANOFF

PINOT NOIR
AN INTERNATIONAL BANKING SPY THRILLER

First Edition: October 2019
ISBN: 978-1-698374-17-8
United States Copyright Office Case Number: 1-8022495281

To join my mailing list for new releases, please sign up here:
www.louisemoscownovel.com/newsletter

To my husband Robert Lane Levy

ACKNOWLEDGMENTS

To Patrick "Ubercritic" McDonald for your affirmations, and invaluable edits. To Karen Widess for your fastidious and insightful proofreading. To my family and friends for your enthusiastic support. To my mom for the brilliant title suggestion for Book 2. To LuAnn Kulpaka for your continued encouragement and remarkable creativity.

"Seek not outside yourself. For all your pain comes simply from a futile search for what you want, insisting where it must be found. Do you prefer that you be right or happy?"

A Course in Miracles (T-29.VII.1)

PROLOGUE

October 19, 1994

It was all over very quickly.

In many ways the Federal Reserve is the most powerful of U.S. government agencies. Although it does not have the power to subpoena or bring indictments under U.S. law, it is politically independent and therefore can move swiftly, unilaterally, and with decisive force within its own domain.

At 1:00 p.m. on July 5, 1991, a worldwide financial scandal erupted with regulators in eight countries shutting down the Bank of Credit and Commerce International (BCCI), charging it with fraud, drug money laundering, and illegal infiltration into the U.S. banking system. The scandal had raised significant questions about why American regulators, who had long had evidence of problems at the bank, failed to act quickly. Officials who worked under George Bush including John Sununu, chairman of the Senate Judicial Committee Joe Biden, and the CIA had refused to follow up on reports of corruption. Only after Senator John Kerry had enlisted New York County official Jack Blum to investigate were charges brought.[1]

Investigators had characterized the scandal as the largest financial fraud in history. As much as $20 billion that had been officially on the bank's books vanished when bank regulators around the world shut down BCCI's operations and accused it of fraud. Ultimately, more than $12 billion was believed to have been lost by depositors.

In June 1994, thirteen BCCI officials were tried in an Abu Dhabi court. Twelve were convicted and sentenced to jail and civil damages of $9 billion. On October 19, 1994, BCCI's chief executive – and Louise Moscow's former boss – Swaleh Naqvi, 62, was sentenced to 11 years in prison and ordered to pay restitution of more than $255 million for his role in the bank fraud that

---

[1] From the author's first novel in the Louise Moscow series, *Foliage: An International Banking Spy Thriller*

eluded regulators around the world for a decade.

For more than 20 years, Naqvi, a native of Pakistan, had been second in command after Aga Hasan Abedi, the founder of BCCI. Abedi had started BCCI in 1972 with the goal of developing a Third World Bank that would gain international respect. Both Naqvi and Abedi had been indicted by Federal and New York grand juries on charges of fraud, theft and money-laundering. Abedi was too ill in Pakistan for American officials to extradite him. But Naqvi was handed over to the US authorities to help them in their own BCCI investigations.

In addition to charges of bribing foreign officials and bankers, Naqvi had been indicted on charges of helping the Medellin cartel to launder millions of dollars in cocaine profits in the 1980's. The bank had long been identified as the leading financial institution for the illegal drug-smuggling activities of Panama's former leader, Gen. Manuel Noriega, and as a vehicle for concealing and moving illegal cocaine profits for the Medellin drug cartel. Even the CIA finally acknowledged that it had used the bank for routine activities, which it has never spelled out.

Louise Moscow was a key witness during the tense hearings. She had been sequestered under witness protection shortly after the bank was seized in 1991, to ensure her testimony would be heard. Under protective custody Louise had been given a new identity: Karen Baker, a schoolteacher living in Arlington Heights, Illinois, complete with a government-issued U.S. birth certificate and passport. She had assimilated into an entirely new background story with no public appearance by Louise Moscow until the trial.

The hearings had been held in secret with armed guards at the doors. Now the trial was over, Naqvi was found guilty, and it was sentencing day.

The U.S. District judge addressed Naqvi, "In addition to your sentence, you swear to continue to cooperate with United States government officials who are trying to unravel how BCCI had come to illegally own four U.S. banks."

"Yes, your Honor," Naqvi calmly replied. "I promise to continue to cooperate with government officials." As he was taken into custody, Naqvi gave Louise a faint conciliatory smile.

Louise had willingly fulfilled her star-witness responsibilities throughout the trial. Nonetheless, she was saddened to see her former boss – who had always treated her well – in this subjugated state. She breathed a sigh of relief and turned to leave, flanked by her bodyguard, a tall imposing black man named Big Steve, and FBI agent Michael Fuentes. The courtroom emptied and Louise walked toward the exit. In the hallway, suddenly two hulking men brazenly approached and stared menacingly at her. She stopped, Big Steve on her right, and Michael on her left.

"Have you met my friends, Big Steve and Michael Fuentes?" Louise defiantly asked the two men. Michael and Steve both placed their hands over their concealed sidearms in silent warning. The two thugs nodded slowly and smirked, then turned and walked out of the courthouse.

"That was a threat," Michael said under his breath.

They continued out of the courthouse and Big Steve opened the rear door of the Lincoln Town Car. Louise and Michael got in the back and Big Steve got in behind the steering wheel then drove off. Louise sat quietly, fuming. People like those thugs only fueled her anger. She was not one to cower, for better or worse.

"You know those guys were from the Black Network, don't you Louise?" Michael asked rhetorically. "I'm going to recommend to George Moscow that your security be increased."

Louise took a deep breath, then her frustration flared. "There's no way I'm living in protective custody anymore. It's going on four years."

Michael reached for his locked briefcase. "Do I need to show you the dossier your father and I compiled on your connections to the case? You are a direct witness to criminal behavior by powerful people all over the world. There's no telling what you know that could link any number of people to other crimes not under investigation. We don't even know half of what your historical knowledge could mean to others in the world of banking and finance. In the US there is no statute of limitations on fraud. There's no way you're returning to Chicago with no security detail."

"What did you have in mind? Should I marry a Big Steve and have him move in?"

"Something like that." Michael said. Big Steve shot him a sardonic look in the rearview mirror. "I'll tell George we're going to plan B."

"What the hell is plan B?" Louise's voice conveyed dread.

"Louise, we have to reach a compromise." George Moscow, a New York City detective in charge of white-collar fraud, and Louise's father, had his game face on. "You'll need to move completely off the grid until we can be sure that you're safe."

"It had better be somewhere more exotic than Arlington Heights, Illinois," Louise said.

"Well, then you're going to love this idea," Michael said. "In fact, I'd go if I could, but Big Steve here is the lucky one assigned to your security detail."

"Somewhere warm, I hope," Big Steve said.

"Definitely not the Midwest," Louise agreed. "I am willing to pay with my own money if necessary."

"After extensive research, we have found an ideal location for you. The area is secure enough that you'll be able to live without a constant sense of hiding. Big Steve will be your security detail, but undercover working as your *Guy Friday*. He'll have a new identity too, which we have already prepared. Since you have often asserted that you would be willing to use your own funds to improve your living situation, you *will* have to do that. This can't all be funded through the witness protection program.

"What's the catch?" Louise asked.

"It's geographically remote," George replied.

"What's the weather like?" Big Steve asked.

"It's paradise," Michael said.

"So much for paradise," Louise said, draining the last sip of wine in her glass. This place is for the birds! Literally!" She threw a half-eaten shrimp and it landed on the beach were a seagull promptly swooped down and gulped it up.

"Y'all need an attitude adjustment, Karen," Big Steve said, addressing her by her undercover name. He stood on the other side of the bar from her rinsing and drying glasses. The mention of her fake name got her blood boiling.

"Oh yeah, *Étienne*?" Louise mockingly emphasized his undercover name, Étienne, which was the French version of Steve.

"Don't be callin' me Étienne. It's too girlie. Y'all can call me Éti, like we agreed." He enunciated the shortened version, *ay-tee*. Louise rolled her eyes, picked up the bottle of wine and walked out of the Tiki bar. "Them dive boats be here soon. Y'all get back here and help a brotha' serve the customers."

Louise ignored him and walked down the path of the private island to the secluded beach. Her mind was spinning unnaturally through a feeling of helplessness, which had been building for the last six months. When she had arrived on the island, the transition had gone smoothly. The witness protection program – mostly her father – had found the remote island for her, and she managed to negotiate the purchase for one of the few businesses in the area, a Tiki-themed bar that served the tourist divers, who were the main visitors to the area. Her witness protection identity, Karen Baker, dovetailed with her background story: she had used an inheritance to escape from cold Arlington Heights, Illinois, to a warm island paradise in the Caribbean.

Big Steve had become her *Guy Friday* and for the first six months of paradise, "Éti and Karen" quickly became the mainstay of the curious natives and visiting divers, establishing a first-class party bar. The thrill of the new life began to soften around month seven of the adventure, as the bar owner started to become her own best customer. The main island distributors who stocked her inventory were always accommodating, leaving an extra case or two of her favorite wines and potables. Even Big Steve started to notice her indulgence.

The last week had been the most challenging. Her head was spinning, either from another hangover or the feeling of one even when she wasn't drinking. It felt like her body was trying leave her skin, and there had been a couple times when she looked longingly at a dive boat, yearning to stow away on it and get the hell out of this straitjacket of an existence.

She laid down on a lounge chair and started to read a mystery novel a customer had left behind. But the words danced on the page, and her focus seemed to be falling into a black hole. She didn't as much fall asleep as pass out, as if trying to escape consciousness of everything around her.

"Karen, the dive boat's all gone," Louise heard Big Steve say, but it was if his voice was underwater. "I didn't want to wake y'all so I handled everything myself." She managed to lift her head toward the direction of his watery voice, and as she did Big Steve immediately knew something was wrong. She was pale and drawn. "You okay Lulu?" he asked, dropping all pretense of her fake name. She just stared at him, so he bent down and put his hands on her shoulders. "Girl, you shakin' like a leaf."

Big Steve helped her up and led her to her bungalow. "Lulu, what's wrong with you?" Louise began to cry uncontrollably, and he put a giant arm around her and patted her head. She continued to shiver involuntarily. "You cold? It's hotter than hell out."

"I can't help it," Louise said. "I think I'm having a panic attack." It was then that Louise fainted dead away.

When she awoke, she was in her bed. The simple island décor of her bungalow had a color palette of blues, greens, and whites. A mosquito net hung from the ceiling and draped over her bed made with crisp cotton sheets and plump down pillows. As her eyes adjusted, she saw one of the divers from the night before consulting with Big Steve. They turned their attention toward her when they noticed she was awake.

"I'm Dr. Blake Jenkins, Ms. Baker. I don't think I added the 'doctor' when we met last night. Éti called me back in from a dive to take a look at you," he said using both their locally known names.

"I remember meeting you," Louise managed to say.

"Éti described what happened," the doctor said. "I took your vital signs, and everything was fine, except maybe a bit of a fast pulse. Have you been eating?"

"Sure," Louise lied. She found that often once she drank her supper, she didn't really need breakfast.

"There doesn't seem to be anything physically wrong with you, that maybe some hydration and good meal wouldn't cure. So, I was just saying to Éti…"

"Y'all got rock fever," Big Steve interrupted.

Louise couldn't help but laugh. "Rock fever?"

"Your daddy warned me to be on the look-out," Big Steve said. "I was lookin' for it and I see it. Rock fever. Feelin' trapped. You gotta stay busy and do something, go out on the boat or something."

"Most likely that diagnosis is the best explanation," Jenkins added. "You may just need a change of scenery for a while. Take some time away from here."

Her thoughts were of frustration knowing that leaving was impossible.

"I'm too tired now," she murmured to the two men. "Just let me sleep." Louise snuggled up with her pillow and fell back asleep. Big Steve and Dr. Jenkins left her to rest.

꒰

Louise opened her eyes and saw the silhouette of a man.

"What happened?" Louise asked.

"You've been asleep for 24 hours," Big Steve said, standing just outside her door. Louise kept her eyes on the silhouette.

"Sri Sri Ravi Shankar?" Louise muttered unconsciously.

"No, I don't have that honor," the man said. Louise realized she wasn't dreaming. The man looked of Indian descent, lanky but sturdy, with a head of unruly hair and a gray beard. "My name is Iqbal Singh."

"I called him up for a consultation," Big Steve said.

"Are you a doctor?" Louise asked.

"No," Iqbal replied. "I'm a spiritual healer of a sort."

"You told me this type of healing helped when you were going through the trial," Big Steve added. "Dr. Jenkins told me that Mr. Singh runs a retreat on a nearby island."

Louise was still in a drowsy daze. "What time is it?"

"Time to get up," Iqbal said. "Dress in something comfortable and come out to the beach."

They left her and she drank some water, brushed her teeth, and put on shorts and a tee shirt. She walked down to her private beach of chalk-white sand open to steady sea breezes but protected by mangroves and sea grape bushes, which sheltered it from occasional hurricanes. Iqbal was waiting for her there.

"I'm starving," Louise said.

"Perfect," Iqbal said. "The best time to do yoga is early morning on an empty stomach."

"Yoga?" Louise asked.

"Your efforts will be rewarded 10-fold," Iqbal said. "I'll teach you the basics to help clear your chakras and get you on the path to healing. Soon you will be prepared to handle anything."

Iqbal talked Louise through repetitions of a sun salutation, which was basically a continuous series of yoga poses. She started out wobbly, but soon found a rhythm and felt the positive effects of how each pose opened a different emotional focal point.

"Let's end with a headstand," Iqbal said.

Louise imitated him, crouching down on her knees, interlacing her fingers and nestling her head on the sand supported by her linked hands. It took a few attempts with Iqbal spotting her, but she was finally able to balance herself, raising her knees slowly, then straighten her legs.

"You have a new perspective on the world," Iqbal said. "This pose opens the crown chakra. The most important, connecting to your spiritual self."

"It really works!" she said, feeling the benefits of the yoga like an epiphany. She lowered out of the headstand and faced Iqbal. She imitated him placing her hands together in front of her heart.

"Namaste." Iqbal bowed his head and Louise did the same.

As if on cue, Big Steve brought out a tray of fruits, beverages and other breakfast items. "Bon appétit," Big Steve said.

Louise was sweaty and winded from exertion, but she smiled. "I've never been so hungry," Louise said. "Thank you, Iqbal and Éti," Louise said as tears flooding her eyes. "It feels like I'm waking from a trance."

"You are most welcome," Iqbal said. "Now, enjoy your breakfast and continue your practice. I will return next week. When you are ready, I recommend taking part in the intensive yoga retreat on my island."

"I'm looking forward to it!" Louise said. "Would you like to join me for breakfast?"

"No, thank you. I must get back." Iqbal and Louise exchanged a hug and Big Steve escorted Iqbal back to his boat.

Louise devoured the food. It was as if a whole new perspective about her situation had suddenly occurred to her. Perhaps this *was* paradise.

PART I
TROUBLE IN PARADISE

ONE

December 3, 1999

The 18th century building, a bastion of affluence and luxury, stood sentinel in the darkness. Its marble floored corridors festooned in tapestries and antiquities provided safe passage between sumptuous chambers where its residents slept in tranquility.

"Help! Someone, please!"

Nurse Theresa Leigh was startled awake. The clock glowed 4:40 a.m. and the light under the door alarmed her. She put on a robe and cracked open the bedroom door. Her fellow nurse, Todd Mayer, held his hand over what appeared to be his own blood staining his shirt. Her first instinct was to rush out and help him.

"Stay there!" Todd whispered, coming closer.

"You're bleeding!" Theresa whispered back.

"I've been stabbed! Someone has broken in!"

Theresa tried to remain calm. "Who? Where?"

"Two men, I don't know who they are. They were wearing masks." Todd handed her a mobile phone. "Call the police and get Mr. Almasi to his saferoom. I'm going to get help!"

Theresa retreated back into her room and locked the door. She opened the inner door that led to her employer's adjacent bedroom.

"What the devil is happening?" Her boss, the 67-year-old Israeli banker, Ekram M. Almasi, stood next to his bed looking panic stricken. He suffered from Parkinson's disease, and the terror in his eyes made him appear even more helpless.

In a calm but forceful tone Theresa said, "There are intruders. We must move to safety."

Theresa entered his bedroom and darted into the large dressing room. Almasi followed her, slammed the armored door and activated the deadbolt. The expansive chamber had been converted to a bunker-like fortified room that included ample supplies, a wet bar, and a full bathroom.

Theresa pushed buttons frantically on the mobile phone. "I'll call Sofia."

"Call the police!" Almasi shouted.

Theresa ignored his order and continued to call the head nurse Sofia Helm. "It's Theresa. There has been a break-in. Todd has been stabbed. Please call the police!"

"A break-in?" Almasi echoed. "That's not possible. This is a secured building!"

Theresa stared at the phone poised to answer. Finally, at 5:12 a.m. they heard the bleating of approaching sirens. "The police are here. We are safe." Theresa moved to open the door, but Almasi pulled her back.

"No!" Almasi shouted. "The intruders!"

Theresa waited, listening. Then they heard more sirens and Theresa called Sofia again. "What's happening? We hear sirens from the fire brigade."

"Tell her to call my security team!" Almasi shouted.

Theresa listened to Sofia, then hung up. "The police are in the lobby searching for the burglars."

"They are not burglars!" Almasi insisted. "They're assassins!"

"Assassins?" But Theresa was suddenly distracted by smoke. "There's a fire!" Almasi and Theresa coughed violently as smoke billowed in through the ceiling. "Please open the door, Monsieur Almasi! We won't survive this smoke more than ten minutes."

"Stand back!" He forced her into the corner. "Call my security team!"

"They are not here in Monte Carlo! We must get out now!"

"No! They'll kill me!" Terror fueled his panic as he scrambled to place wet towels along the bottom of the door in a futile effort as the conflagration engulfed the penthouse. Almasi groped for the pendant around his neck and held it up like a talisman warding off evil.

Theresa frantically made one final call to Sofia. "Please help us! We are dying!"

Flames burst through the ceiling, but Almasi kept Theresa pinned in the corner until she fell unconscious. Almasi inched toward the door, hearing shouts from the firefighters just on the other side. He made it to the armchair before collapsing. The yelling faded as the fire chief moved his team out of the doomed penthouse wing. The saferoom was now a furnace, the smoke searing Almasi's lungs, his eyes bulging with the realization of his self-fulfilling prophesy, being murdered by the devil himself.

The first rays of the sunrise shimmered on the serene Mediterranean Sea, waves lapping the shores beneath the soaring bluffs. Palatial structures adorned the cliff tops, as seagulls busy with their breakfast squawked overhead, oblivious to the singular devastation. A Maritime Police chopper hovered over the duplex penthouse, the pilot surveying the rooftop blaze, which was burning out of control. Vacationers crowded onto the terrace of the luxury Hôtel Hermitage across the street and gawked at the frantic activity.

Unsure if it had been a terrorist attack, the city was on high alert. Police, fire, and military personnel rushed to impose a sense of order. Emergency vehicles lined the cramped streets where buildings huddled at angles to fill every meter of real estate.

"Where is Almasi's chief of security?" shouted Patrick Roblot, Chief Superintendent of the Monte Carlo Urban Police Division. He was middle-aged tall and burly, with a buzz-cut that minimized his male-pattern baldness. Taking control of a situation was second nature for him. One of his officers approached for instructions. "The owner of this building, Ekram Almasi, has a private security team. The head of Almasi's security detail is Jordan Coen. Find him and bring him here, now!" Roblot barked. The officer nodded in affirmative and ran off to fulfill his mission.

Roblot was scribbling notes on a small pad when the Superintendent of the Criminal Police Division, Paul Dupont, approached with two of his own officers.

"I'll take over from here," Dupont said.

"What the hell is the CPD doing here?" Roblot protested. "This is an Urban Police Division matter."

"Correction," Dupont said. "I am responsible for coordinating with Interpol. If we don't get this situation under control, it will cause an international incident."

"Correction," Roblot countered. "You are responsible for protecting Monaco's image."

"CPD has been instructed to take over," Dupont said in rigid defiance.

"By whom?" Roblot asked.

This is now a crime scene, and we must take every precaution to collect and preserve the evidence. We will want this investigation to be airtight."

"That is acceptable," Dupont replied. "As long as it's done under my observation."

"As you wish," Roblot said.

Roblot and Dupont stood over the carcasses of the billionaire and his head nurse. The ghoulish sight of Ekram M. Almasi, his eyes popping out of his head, his remains blackened with soot, his skin incinerated, gave Roblot a sense of foreboding.

"Mon dieu," Dupont said.

"Such a respected public figure perishing in this way will create a shit-storm," Roblot said. "My forensics team will collect and log every crumb of evidence. I will leave nothing to chance." He scribbled notes and Dupont observed closely as the forensic team began the gruesome task of picking through debris to recover evidence. They placed the cell phone found near Almasi into an evidence bag, tagged and logged it, then repeated the process with the cell phone found near Theresa.

The medical examiner and his assistant arrived. "Bonjour, Inspector Roblot."

"Bonjour, Doctor," Roblot replied.

The ME shook hands with Dupont and introduced himself. "Doctor Gilles Masseron, médecin légiste, and my assistant, Jean Ambroise."

"Paul Dupont, Superintendent Criminal Police Division. I'll be oversee-ing the investigation, so you'll be reporting your findings to me."

Masseron put rubber gloves on and kneeled to examine the remains while his assistant prepared the body bag and trolley. "Based on the bulging of the eyes, the cause of death appears to be asphyxiation. But I will need to do a thorough examination back at the lab," Masseron said.

Roblot took notes. "You are welcome to observe as long as you don't interfere with my operation," Roblot told Dupont.

"It's a national security issue for CPD," Dupont insisted, testing Roblot's patience.

Oblivious to the ongoing power struggle, Dr. Masseron interrupted them. "This woman's neck has been crushed."

The superintendents shifted on their feet and turned to the medical examiner in a display of surprise.

"Possibly by Almasi himself," Roblot speculated. "To keep her from opening the door. Almasi was a known paranoiac."

"I'll know more after I question the suspects in custody," Dupont said.

"Excusez-moi," persisted Roblot. "But the UPD will be conducting the interrogations."

The medical examiner jotted notes on his clipboard. "There's not much else I can do here. I will confirm cause of death after I get the lab work."

"Continue to gather evidence here while I go speak with the minister of state," Roblot told his officers then walked out.

"I'll join you," Dupont said, following Roblot.

"With all due respect, Minister, why did you order Almasi's chief of security to be taken to military prison for questioning when he had the key to the safe house?" Roblot asked. "A key that may have saved the lives of monsieur Almasi and his nurse. That makes CPD partially responsible for Almasi's death and now they are interfering in my investigation."

Minister of State Lévêque listened to Roblot respectfully. His impressive career spanned over thirty years of consulate, embassy, and government posts for France, London, and the United Nations. His ability to pick up verbal cues as well as body language gave him an advantage when dealing with members of law enforcement.

"Superintendent Roblot," Lévêque replied. "You are a good man and a great cop. However, this is an international incident. I'm sorry, but this is no longer your jurisdiction. Anything you uncover in your investigation must be shared with the CPD."

"But, Minister!"

"Monsieur Roblot," Lévêque interrupted. "I am aware of your passion for justice. But this is not your cause célèbre."

Roblot was flustered by Lévêque's very personal admonishment. "Understood, sir," was all Roblot could muster.

"Thank you, Roblot. You are excused," the minister replied. "You too, Superintendent Dupont, sauvez-vous."

Dupont followed Roblot out of the minister's office. "No hard feelings, mon vieux," Dupont said, giving Roblot an overly chummy but firm slap on the back.

Roblot stopped and looked Dupont in the eye. "Make no mistake," Roblot said. "I'm not backing off this case."

"You are no longer in charge of investigating this case," said Dupont, stepping into Roblot's personal space.

"Try to stop me," Roblot said, breaking the staring contest by walking away. "And, I'm not your *old man*."

"You will have to share any evidence you uncover with the CPD!" Dupont yelled after Roblot, who kept walking.

December 14, 1999

"You must be very proud of your niece, Monsieur D'Atout. She is quite an accomplished young lady for a fourteen-year-old." The woman was in her forties and spoke English with a combined posh British and literary Central Russian accent. "She has been a wonderful student. I shall miss her."

"Your tutelage made all the difference, Madame Petrov," Arnaud D'Atout said. He looked expectantly around the room. "Where is Annabel?"

"She's saying good-bye to my daughter, Evelyne. They have become quite close over the time she has spent here." Like her name, Madame Petrov was stony-faced as she summoned the girls. "Evelyne, it's time to say good-bye." The two girls emerged from the adjacent room their arms interlocking and their foreheads touching. Evelyne was emotional, her wide blue eyes teary and her fleshy red lips quivering. Annabel was tall and svelte and carried herself with the grace of a dancer. They both had long blond hair, but Evelyne's natural platinum hair with her striking facial features threw Arnaud off. "Say hello to Monsieur D'Atout, Evelyne." Evelyne curtseyed politely.

"Come on, now, Annabel," Arnaud said. "It's getting late and Madame Petrov is very busy."

"Merci, Madame Petrov, au revoir," Annabel said, giving Madame Petrov two cheek kisses. Then she gave two cheek kisses to Evelyne and walked toward the door. Evelyne followed Annabel, revealing a slight limp, but carrying herself with grace and poise. Madame Petrov took Evelyne's hand to keep her from going further.

"Au revoir, Evelyne," Annabel said, hesitating to leave.

"Come now," Arnaud insisted. "You can visit your friend again some-time." His promise seemed to cheer up both girls' enough to get Annabel to leave.

TWO

December 10, 2001

Crystal blue Caribbean waters turned milky against the white sand, the rhythmic swishing was accompanied by heavy breathing and an occasional grunt. Louise pondered the view. The palm fronds casting symmetrical shadows over her paradise like prison bars.

"If you must force it, you're doing it wrong," Louise said.

Flip-flops littered the entrance to the high-ceilinged thatch-roofed structure. Bare toes spread on yoga mats and the heavy breathing continued. An athletic silver-haired woman gracefully held a plank pose, her sinewy arms in a push-up position, her strong legs and back rigid. In one motion, she bent at the elbows, lowered her body, glided forward, and lifted her head and chest up into a cobra pose. Next to her, wearing a matching wedding band on a pudgy ring finger was a man doing a shakier version of the pose and providing the grunts.

"Relax into it," Louise Moscow said. "Now, lower your head and raise your sit bones up to the sky, arms straight, head down, in downward dog." The pudgy man struggled with the inverted V-pose. Louise gently pressed her hand between his shoulder blades as he strove to straighten his legs. "Bent knees are fine. Relax your neck and let your head drop gently to make sure you're not holding any tension. Breathe." Her coaxing seemed to relieve his strain. "Now, walk your feet to your hands and come into a standing position, Tadasana, Mountain Pose. Hands together at your heart. Let's do one more sun salutation. Reach your arms up. Now bend forward at the hips. Let your arms fall toward your feet. Excellent. Your chakras are opening. Your efforts will be rewarded 10-fold, with an icy Gin Ginger Baker."

Whoops of excitement from the group sounded like birdcalls. Louise returned to the front of the class and sat on her mat. "Sit with legs crossed in Lotus Pose, hands resting on your knees. Breathe deeply. Exhale. OM." The group hummed *OM* in unison, reaching the *Shumann resonance* of 432 Hz,[2] the fundamental "beat" of everything in nature. "Remember, the last three syllables of *individuality* spell *duality*. Hands together at your heart." Louise bowed her head. "Namaste."

Louise rose and walked to the bar, the yogis following like imprinted goslings. They squatted on the teakwood barstools or at tables on the beachfront terrace. Equally in her element behind the bar as on the yoga mat, Louise poured fresh-squeezed grapefruit juice into the blender, added ice, fresh ginger root, gin, and a splash of ginger liqueur, then blended until smooth.

"That sound is like OM in another key," said the silver-haired woman who sat at the bar in front of Louise.

"Ha! I'm going to use that one," Louise laughed.

"Genius!" the husband said, reading a sign above the bar. "*Do three sun salutations and get a free Gin Ginger Baker.*" On cue, Louise slid the frothy libation in front of him. He sipped. "Mmmm, worth every drop of sweat."

His wife pointed a thumb at him and smirked. "I've been trying to get him to do yoga for thirty years. Cheers to you." She raised her glass in a toast and drank. She introduced her husband and herself. "Pat and Mike."

"Nice to meet you, Pat." Louise put her hand out to the woman. "I'm Karen."

"Actually, I'm Mike," the woman said, shaking Louise's hand. "He's Pat. My mom was a big John Wayne fan."

Louise looked perplexed for a moment. "Oh, that's right, Marion Michael."

"I didn't like Marion, so I took Michael, which became Mike."

"Michael is a great name," Louise filled glasses on a tray.

"This is a great place," Mike said. "Are you on SixDegrees.com?"

"No Internet," Big Steve said, carrying a bucket of ice out from the kitchen and pouring it into one of the bar sinks.

"This is Éti," Louise said, easily slipping into their undercover names.

"How do you get the news out here?" Mike asked.

"TV," Big Steve aka Éti said, pointing to a questionably dusty Sony Trinitron behind the bar. Being a huge black man, Big Steve always came off as intimidating at first, until he grinned. "Welcome to paradise!" Big Steve

---

[2] attunedvibrations.com/432hz-healing

went about his work, wiping glasses and serving customers. But his eyes were in perpetual motion. He took the tray of drinks and left the bar to distribute them.

"Quite an imposing man," Mike said.

"Éti? We go way back," Louise said, quickly changing the subject. "Can I top you folks off?" Without waiting for a reply, she emptied the remaining contents of the blender into their glasses.

"So, you're not on SixDegrees?" Mike asked again.

"We don't advertise. The only way to find this place is through a certified PADI dive master," Louise said.

"What did you do before this?"

"School teacher."

"A teacher!" Mike laughed. "That's why you're such a good yoga instructor."

"I'll take a yoga mat over a chalk board any day."

"Don't you miss civilization?" Mike asked.

"Let me see." Louise's pretended to think about it. "Nope. Not for a minute. If I want a bath, I walk a few yards and jump into the clearest waters in the world. The saltwater is better than any hair gel, and coconut oil is my moisturizer."

Louise had completed her adjustment to island life. After the precarious beginning, and her yoga breakthrough, she had gone native and was now quite convincing in her new role. After her mini-breakdown, she convinced the "protection program" – mostly her father – to allow her to get off the island every six months or so to attend Iqbal Singh's yoga retreats, and soon her modest initiation into that spirituality morphed into a new lifestyle as Singh's most ardent pupil. The master even allowed her to teach yoga techniques to others, and she became a certified instructor.

The combination of the yoga and the Tiki bar had become the talk of the islands, and even tourists who weren't divers found their way by boat and came to her shores. She was radiant in the adjustment, her soft skin effortlessly hydrated by the humidity and her blonde hair naturally highlighted by the sun. Her sparkling eyes the color of the green sea glass dangling from her hand-made mobiles were also in constant motion.

After a while, weary from spirits, sea and sunshine, the customers hopped back on the dive boat to the mainland for siesta.

"I'm gonna take a break," Louise said, wiping her hands with a bar towel.

"Go on. I got dis," Big Steve said.

"Call me when the afternoon dive boats arrive."

Louise slipped out the back down a pathway to her bungalow and changed out of her yoga pants and into a bikini. She wrapped a sarong around her hips and walked down the path to her private beach. She switched on jazz sitar music and opened to the bookmarked page of a first edition, *A Course in Miracles*, by Helen Shucman. But her neck was tight, and she couldn't focus.

She got up and removed her sarong. Then, as though on wires, she did gravity-defying yoga poses. She bent at her hips pressing her upper body down against her legs, then placed her hands on the ground and lifted her legs into a handstand. She held for a minute, taking in the full effect of the blood flowing to her brain and to see things from a different perspective.

The sound of a violin lilting over the sitar music set her thoughts to Jean-Philippe and Paris and how she had gotten to the island in the first place. She had been enlisted by the CIA and FBI for an inside job, a strategy that had exceeded expectations. But when the dust had settled, she had lost the job, the Paris apartment, and her fiancé, Jean-Philippe. The only consolation prize was a letter in the mail from Jean-Philippe, containing a check for a million dollars, proceeds from the sale of a Stradivarius violin sold through the offshore company she had helped him set up.[3] She would gladly have exchanged the money for the love of her life.

She blessed the yoga techniques for getting her through the last three months. Ever since September 11th, 2001, she felt the old isolation symptoms returning, especially being far from her friends and family during that tragic time. Adhering to the yoga therapy eased the pain of the loss and allowed her to gain perspective on it, while admitting to herself there was a lingering need to help out, to go somewhere and solve some aspect of the post-9/11 world. She was craving some different type of action.

She moved through punishing yoga poses, raising her heart rate and triggering profuse sweat. After that first lesson with Iqbal, yoga had become a self-medication. As her technique evolved, so did her ability to create inner calm from life's chaos. Louise finished and rested in child's pose.

---

[3] From the author's first novel in the Louise Moscow series, *Foliage: An International Banking Spy Thriller*

"Karen, the first dive boat just got here," Big Steve said, using her island name in case anyone could hear.

She remained in the fetal-like pose, letting her heart rate return to normal. "Is it already after 3 o'clock?"

"Yep, gotta bunch-a thirsty divers."

"No drinking while diving, so they will want booze."

"Hungry too. I got the conch salad ready."

"What would I do without you, Éti?" Louise sprang up to a handstand that continued into a walkover and back to her feet. She followed Big Steve up the path stopping at the outdoor shower. She pulled the chain and the rainwater rinsed away sand, sweat and sorrow. She tied the sarong around her hips and caught up with him.

"Feelin' better?" Big Steve asked.

"Paradise just isn't the same after 9/11," Louise admitted.

"You comin' down with rock fever again?"

"Maybe."

They entered the bar, which was now bustling with customers, all of whom turned to look at Louise. Unflustered by attention, Louise wore her beauty like secondhand clothes, humbly salvaged for a new life.

"Karen!" The dive master greeted Louise with a hug.

"Larry! How's the dive season looking this year?"

"The recession and 9/11 haven't helped."

"But divers will always find a way to get out there."

"We should get you back out there," Larry prodded. "You'd be the main attraction."

"I'll practice balancing a ball on my nose." Louise lined glasses up on the bar. "What can I get you folks?"

"Diver's Delight for everyone," Larry said. "I've been bragging about it all morning and expectations are high."

"Conch salad and Gin Ginger Bakers coming right up. There are live conchs out in the beds if anyone wants fresh conch penis," Louise said, turning heads.

"Who wants penis?" Larry yelled to the divers, which were a mix of couples and single men and women, all highly experienced divers and avid lovers of the sea. Only one hand went up for conch penis, a gregarious man in his late forties.

"Robert wants conch penis!" Larry said.

"Okay," Louise said. "Follow Éti!"

Half the group followed Big Steve out to harvest a live conch. The rest of the group hung out at the bar with Louise.

"Now for the sane people," Louise said, filling glasses with her special cocktail. The people on the beach cheered, Louise turned up the music and it was a party. She grabbed her Polaroid camera and went out to the beach. It took a steady hand to extract the conch penis without damaging it. Louise snapped photos as Big Steve performed the procedure and dangled the clear noodle-like penis over Robert's mouth. He slurped up briny delicacy and grinned.

"Aphrodisiac!" Big Steve said.

"Look out, everybody!" Robert exclaimed.

Louise continued to take photos as two more divers performed the ritual. Then they all headed back into the bar. Louise set out platters of salad, bread, and cheese, then mixed another batch of drinks.

Big Steve placed large bowls of fresh conch salad on the bar.

"Pièce de résistance," he said turning the music louder.

Robert approached Louise. "I heard there was a specialty drink being served?" His irresistible charm and dimples caught her off guard.

"Is this your first Gin Ginger Baker?" Louise asked.

"Yes, I was busy eating conch penis," Robert said.

Louise poured him a cocktail and one for herself. They clinked glasses.

"To paradise," Robert said.

"To conch penis," Louise said.

THREE

The sound of steady thrashing and a stifled moan reached a crescendo of agony in a final release, then silence. Sun rays refracting through the stained-glass window illuminated Jean-Philippe's glistening brow. Wisps of dark hair stuck to his jawline creating a wild frame for his face. His eyes were like black agates trained on the figure of the Virgin Mary gazing down on him.

"*We fly unto thy patronage, O Holy Mother of God. Despise not our petitions in our necessities, but deliver us from all dangers, O Ever Glorious and Blessed Virgin.*"

Jean-Philippe raised the cat o' nine tails again for the next sequence of lashings.

"Such sanctification is a dwindling practice."

Jean-Philippe ceased his ritual, recognizing the voice as though it were his own. He rose to his feet gathering the loose ends of the whip in his left hand and the rosary in his right, then folded both into his vestment sleeves.

"Father, what brings you here?"

Jérôme de Villeneuve stood face to face with Jean-Philippe. A mirror image except Jérôme's dark mane was streaked with gray.

"My only son has become a recluse. I am concerned."

Jean-Philippe waved his hand indicating the place of worship. "This is my home now, Father."

"Working undercover was one thing. But this abstinence and religious devotion is excessive."

"I made a commitment," Jean-Philippe said.

"You fulfilled your obligations."

"Would you have me relinquish my moral obligations just because I solved one case?"

"You saved our family from scandal and ruin," Jérôme said. "Criminals were trying to extort us and destroy our name."

"So, I saved the family name and now I should move on?"

"Do you intend to do this undercover work indefinitely?"

"Interpol has more important cases than my inheritance."

Jérôme's usual diplomacy skills were being tested. Exasperated, he went for the jugular. "Your mother needs you."

"*Mother* needs me?"

With clenched jaw, Jérôme conceded. "*I* need you. You are the sole heir…"

"A good name is more desirable than great riches. To be esteemed is better than silver or gold."

"Jean-Philippe…"

"Father."

"Yes, son?"

"No. *Father* Jean-Philippe."

Jérôme took a breath then continued. "We are praying for you to come home. Live your life."

"The life I knew is gone forever."

"You can pick up where you left off…"

Jean-Philippe cut him off, "As long as it's without Louise. Yes, so you have said."

"Our family name was already in peril. The international banking scandal Louise Moscow was involved in would have completely destroyed us. Then she conveniently disappeared…"

Jean-Philippe's grip tightened on the whip. He bowed his head to hide his anger. "This is my life for now, Father."

Jérôme made one final plea. "Your mother and I expect you to carry on the family legacy."

"An inheritance claimed too soon will not be blessed at the end," Jean-Philippe replied.

"You have a bible verse for everything, yet you abandon your own family."

Jean-Philippe locked eyes with his father's. "I promise you, when my work here is done, I will return. For now, this is where I belong."

Jérôme conceded the battle. He took a sealed envelope from inside his jacket. "This is why I came. To give you this."

"What is it?"

"I did not open it. But it looks official. Apparently, they didn't know how to contact you, so they delivered it to us."

"Please give Mother my love." Jean-Philippe took the envelope and embraced his father.

"We will be waiting for you when you are ready to come home." He turned to leave, his silhouette fading down the aisle and out of the cathedral.

Jean-Philippe unclenched his hand that held the whip and eyed the pattern of the woven leather embedded in his palm. Placing the whip under his arm he opened the envelope and read the notice. He returned to the statue of Mary, knelt down on the cold stone floor and resumed his penance, striking more forcefully than before.

After ten more blows, the mortification of the flesh was complete. He was grateful for the salvific practices he had learned while working undercover in the monastery. Not only had the cover served him in his Interpol investigations, but immersing himself and fully assimilating into the spiritualism had given him the strength to endure the emptiness of life without Louise. Jean-Philippe rose, the throbbing in his knees dissipating as he strode past the medieval fresco of Saint Dominic kneeling before the crucifix clutching an instrument of discipline. Jean-Philippe donned a wide-brimmed black hat that hung by the door, but it did little to counteract the blinding sun as he exited.

"Good morning, Father Jean-Philippe," a passing monk said.

"Good morning, Father Gregory." The two men continued up the path together.

"We missed you at breakfast. You should eat before working up a sweat." Father Gregory drew a pistol from inside his cassock.

"Heading to target practice?"

"You have your morning rituals, I have mine."

They separated at a fork in the path. "See you at the assembly, or has your papa summoned you back home?"

"I'll be there," Jean-Philippe said.

He continued to the dorter[4] and Father Gregory headed down the path that led into the Sonian Forest. Jean-Philippe opened the door to his dwelling just as Father Gregory's gunshots rang out in the distance. He closed the door of the cramped quarters furnished with a simple chest of drawers, a chair, a twin bed, a pillow, and a wool blanket. He set the envelop

---

[4] A monastic dormitory. Sometimes the monks slept in isolated rooms called cells.

down and removed his robes, revealing welts from self-flagellation on his muscular back. He grasped the horizontal bar above the doorframe and pumped out twenty repetitions each of pronated and supinated pull-ups then continued his workout on the stone floor, doing pushups and crunches.

After the alternate mortification of the flesh, he threw a towel over his shoulder and walked naked to the balneary. Another passing father nodded respectfully, unfazed by Jean-Philippe's lack of modesty. The cold water worked its magic on his aching muscles, and he lingered enjoying the one simple pleasure of the flesh that he would allow himself.

Jean-Philippe's steps echoed dully in the cloister of the 14th century monastery, the light of iron sconces casting intermittent shadows of his robed figure. The heavy wooden door creaked open, and he entered the chapterhouse lit by a circular medieval chandelier with more of the wrought iron sconces on the walls. A dozen monks milled about conversing in hushed tones around a long table lined with wooden chairs.

"Let's commence," Jean-Philippe said as he walked to the head of the table and took his seat.

"Father Gregory has not arrived yet," said a sheepish monk, Father Timothy, as he sat to Jean-Philippe's right.

"Father Gregory can read the minutes later."

"Father Gregory is the secretary," Father Timothy contritely reminded him. The monks settled into their seats. Jean-Philippe clasped his hands and they waited in silence.

Finally, the massive door creaked opened, and Father Gregory entered apace. He cradled a leather-bound tome in his left arm and a fountain pen in his right hand. The massive book came down with a thud on the table in front of the last empty chair to Jean-Philippe's left. Father Gregory sat and opened the book, searching the pages for the last writings. He held the pen expectantly over the next blank page, poised to take notes.

"This meeting of the Fathers of Mercy is now called to order at 15 hours and 13 minutes, December 11th, 2001," Jean-Philippe said. When the sound of Father Gregory's pen nib scratching the parchment stopped Jean-Philippe continued. "Old business, Father Gregory?"

Father Gregory read from the previous minutes. "Old business, the ordination of the Solemnity of the Immaculate Conception, our yearly novena to our Lady, a solemnity proper to our congregation, according to the original constitutions drawn up by Father Rauzan, affirming the belief that one goes surely to Jesus through Mary, on December 8th was completed by all here."

In sync, the monks crossed themselves. "Amen."

Father Gregory scanned his notes to the next item and continued. "New business: planning of our next ordination of the Solemnity of Mary, the Holy Mother of God on January 1st."

"Very well," Jean-Philippe said. "Father Timothy, will you form a committee and draft a budget for the next ordination to present at the next meeting?"

"You can count on me," Father Timothy said enthusiastically. Father Gregory forged it into the notes.

"Next order of business," Jean-Philippe said. "It has come to my attention that the Marian shrine at the Catholic retreat center near Genval has been compromised. It will require the unique skills of Father Gregory to remedy. Effective immediately, he is to be relocated to Genval until further notice."

The scratching of the pen nib slowed as Father Gregory wrote his own name. His eyes widened as he realized he had just been given a new assignment.

"Moi?" he asked, pointing to himself with the pen.

"Is there a problem?" Jean-Philippe asked.

"No problem," Father Gregory said. "Thank you for entrusting me with this mission. You will not regret it."

"You haven't heard it yet."

"You are correct," Father Gregory said, holding the pen above the page again. "Please, continue."

"There has been an infestation of gophers that has compromised the grounds," Jean-Philippe said. "You will literally have to take matters into your own hands."

Father Gregory shook his head vigorously in the affirmative as he wrote, then his pen slowed again in realization. He looked up from the page. "You mean..." He pointed the pen with his thumb raised like a gun.

Jean-Philippe nodded yes.

"Oh," Father Gregory said, resuming his writing. The other monks crossed themselves, and some began rosary prayers.

"Meeting adjourned," Jean-Philippe said. "Father Gregory, please stay so I can brief you on your assignment."

A collective whisper rose as the monks exited the chamber. Once the door closed, Jean-Philippe was able to speak freely to Father Gregory, who remained with his pen poised to take notes.

"This is off the record," Jean-Philippe said.

Father Gregory lowered the pen and closed the book with a thud. "I'll take mental notes," he said.

"After four years of infiltrating a crime ring here in Belgium, Interpol is close to having enough evidence for an arrest," Jean-Philippe began. "The Catholic retreat in Genval where I have assigned you is a château owned by a nobleman. The owner is in hospice, but his son, Arnaud D'Atout, resides there with his niece."

"His niece?"

"Yes, a young debutante, whom he is grooming to come out in society. Apparently, her parents died tragically, and as her uncle he was next of kin. But he is involved with some questionable characters. It could be a dangerous assignment."

"That's not a problem," Father Gregory said, patting his robe where his firearm was concealed.

"Let me have your gun."

"My gun?"

"Yes, it is too conspicuous for this assignment," Jean-Philippe said. Father Gregory reluctantly took his Beretta M9 from his robe and placed it on the table. Jean-Philippe took a pistol from inside his robe and handed it to Father Gregory. The .32 caliber pistol had a 6-inch octagonal metal barrel with a mottled gray patina and walnut grips. The side bore the heraldic emblem of the Swiss canton of Basel-Landschaft.

Father Gregory handled it with expertise. "This relic? You're kidding, right?"

"It shoots true and should be more than enough for little critters popping out of the ground."

"What about big critters popping out of the woodwork?"

They got up from the table and walked to the door. Jean-Philippe stopped and placed his hand on Father Gregory's shoulder. "This probably won't be a car-chase or shoot-out kind of mission. But it could be the pay-off we've been working toward all these years, old friend."

"Do you think you'll leave the monastery if we ever crack this case?" Father Gregory asked.

"I've made a promise to my father to do just that."

"Good, because I can't wait to get back to the real world. What will you do?"

Jean-Philippe thought for a moment. "Perhaps I'll take up the violin."

FOUR

December 11, 2001

The atonal tuning of violins evoked Henny Youngman scratching out scales on his fiddle. The cacophony of the instruments contrasted with the majestic ballroom overlooking the formal gardens of the Renaissance château and the Meuse River in Wallonia, Belgium. A string quartet of young women, one more beautiful than the next, tuned their instruments. The tallest of the four stood out, with long blonde hair, rosy cheeks, ruby lips, and wide-eyed anticipation. She wore a simple strapless blush satin gown, her naturally golden tresses cascading over bare shoulders.

The bloated middle-aged Arnaud D'Atout observed the girls haughtily, his comb-over threatened by droplets of sweat, his regard fixed on the blonde violinist. He became momentarily distracted by the tempting delicacies on display. Succumbing, he reached over the table, taking a napkin and helping himself to a canapé of caviar and crème fraîche. He gulped it down then used the napkin to blot the beads of sweat and returned his attention to the girl.

The clinking of a champagne glass drew everyone's attention to the hostess, Julia Almasi, the widow of the late banker Ekram M. Almasi.

"Dear friends, your presence at this very special event means the world to me." Julia was the definition of impeccable elegance wearing her signature beauty-salon blonde bouffant, black eyeliner, thick black mascara, and an understated black Chanel gown.

"As you know, I have devoted my life to philanthropic causes. The most important to me being, for obvious reasons, research on Parkinson's disease, which afflicted my husband. Your donations will help continue the vital search for a cure to end the heartbreak of Parkinson's disease." She composed herself and continued. "Now, please, enjoy the party!"

On cue, the quartet played Mozart's String Quartet No. 14 in G major with surprising virtuosity. The music seemed to lift the mood while the venust young blonde's passion captivated the audience. She played most of the piece with her eyes closed, rarely checking the sheet music, letting the spirit of Mozart guide her. Her porcelain skin, ruddy with emotion, enhanced her symmetrical features. During the crescendo, she gazed upward, her dark lashes intensifying her almond-shaped hazel eyes.

Arnaud studied the guests' reactions, then compulsively raised his right hand to his head, plucked a single hair, and rolled it between his fingertips. The recital ended with Mozart's string Quartet No. 23 in F major to a standing ovation. Faces were flushed with enthusiasm, and pockets were flush with cash. As the quartet disassembled, admirers approached eager to meet the violinists and donate to the cause. Arnaud cut ahead of a young man waiting to meet the beautiful blonde violinist.

"Annabel, bravo!" Arnaud said, holding his arms out to her.

"Uncle!" She hugged him excitedly then kissed him on the cheek. "Did you enjoy the performance?"

"It was perfection. I'm very proud of you, my dear."

"Is Evelyne here?" Annabel pronounced *Evelyne* in French with a long *e* for the *y*. "Evelyne!" she called out, craning her neck and searching the faces in the crowd.

"No, darling, Evelyne couldn't make it."

"But you promised!" Her bottom lip quivered in frustration.

"You will see your friend soon," Arnaud lied. "Come, gather your things. I'll take you home."

"But couldn't I just stay for a while? It's a lovely party."

"Next time. You need your rest. It's been a long day."

She retrieved her coat and violin case and they made their way toward the exit, stopping only to thank Mrs. Almasi.

"Julia, thank you for having us," Arnaud said.

"Thank you for attending, Arnaud." Julia turned to Annabel. "And thank you for performing, Annabel. You played beautifully."

"Thank you, Mrs. Almasi." The sixteen-year-old was still glowing from her first public appearance. "I'm looking forward to performing again. This is such a wonderful party."

"Will you stay and do a solo for us?" Julia asked.

Beads of sweat formed on Arnaud's brow again, jeopardizing his immovable hair. "Annabel needs her rest. She has been rehearsing so much."

"How is your father?" Julia whispered.

"Not well, I'm afraid."

"My prayers go out to you and your family," Julia said.

"Thank you again," Arnaud said. "Goodbye."

He rushed Annabel out to his sedan and sped off. They drove about thirty minutes to the town of Genval and arrived at a private château. Arnaud pulled into the parking area and got out to open Annabel's door. She held the cherished violin case in one hand and took his arm with the other. They walked down the pulverized gravel path and ran into Ferdinande, the manager-in-residence, carrying a wicker trug containing neatly stacked long thin votive candles.

"Bonjour mademoiselle Annabel et Monsieur Arnaud," Ferdinande said in twangy Belgian French. "How was your recital?"

"It was marvelous!" Annabel beamed proudly. "They gave us a standing ovation."

"It was a great success," Arnaud interjected. "But Annabel needs her rest now."

"Of course," Ferdinande said. "Will you be needing anything, Monsieur?"

"No, merci," Arnaud said, walking away. "Good day."

"Good day. Give your father my best."

They continued down the path to a private entrance in the back of the sprawling seventeenth-century château flanked by two Rapunzel towers. Arnaud took out a keychain to unlock the heavy wooden door of the rear tower. The frigid entryway had original stone floors and walls. A medieval chandelier and a narrow beam of daylight from a single window were the only sources of light.

They climbed a curved stone staircase to a landing with another solid wood door. Using a different skeleton key, Arnaud opened the door to Annabel's quarters. Inside, the décor contrasted sharply with the uninviting stairwell. It was a sumptuously furnished apartment with a comfortable lounging area in the center. In one corner there was an easel with paints, brushes and palettes set up near a window overlooking the Sambre River. A half-finished oil painting on the easel bore witness to more of Annabel's remarkable talents. In another corner was her rehearsal area with a chair and a sheet music stand. Annabel set her violin case down there as Arnaud lit a fire in the large stone hearth.

"Get some rest," he said, kissing her on the forehead.

"Did I make you proud, uncle?"

He gently brushed some loose hairs from her face. "I have never been so proud of anyone in my life."

"When will I see Evelyne?"

Arnaud tried to conceal his frustration. "I'm afraid it will be longer than expected." The emotions of the day's events welled up in Annabel's eyes. "Come, take a nap before dinner. You'll feel much better." He sat her down on the four-poster bed, then hurried out, locking the door behind him.

FIVE

"He's either a psychopath or a sycophant," Superintendent Paul Dupont said. "But there is no doubt, Todd Mayer acted alone in the murders of Ekram M. Almasi and Theresa Leigh. He is a trained Green Beret who knew what he was doing when he stabbed himself and started that fire."

Monaco's Attorney General, Daniel Graham, sat behind his desk listening to Dupont make his closing statement in favor of the case being ready to go to trial. Patrick Roblot fumed, knowing by the way the AG nodded that he had already lost his argument.

"With all due respect to the prosecution, Mr. Attorney General," Roblot interrupted. "I have been researching this case for over a year and have documented evidence indicating that Mayer could *not* have acted alone. Yes, Mayer served as a Green Beret, but as a *medical auxiliary*. He had no more experience in combat than he did of high style living. He was there to tend to his employer in a nursing capacity, not as a bodyguard. Almasi had a security team for that, still, he so feared for his life that he built a saferoom."

Dupont cut him off. "Which explains why his own security team was not at the Monte Carlo residence at the time of Almasi's death. His residence was reinforced, making him feel safe enough to keep the security team at his villa La Leopolda ten miles away."

"Then why did you arrest Almasi's chief of security?" Roblot asked.

"I only detained him for questioning," Dupont replied smugly.

Roblot was not ready to concede his case. "Sir, when I interrogated Mayer, he was very clear. He said that two hooded intruders had penetrated the apartment and stabbed him."

Dupont interrupted again. "Then several days later, he retracted and confessed that the stab wounds were self-inflicted. There were no holes from the stabbing through his clothing, only to his abdomen and leg. He slashed himself with his own switchblade to corroborate his story about the intruders. You said yourself that he was a trained medical auxiliary. Therefore, he would know how to inflict non-lethal wounds."

Roblot knew he had little time, so he got to the point. "Almasi's involvement with the FBI indicates this may have been a well-executed Russian mob hit, and Mayer is just a patsy."

"Well they must be Russian ninjas then. Monaco is the safest, most tightly controlled city in the world! There is one policeman for every one hundred inhabitants. You can barely take a step in Monte Carlo without being monitored by closed-circuit cameras, which are on the streets, in underpasses, in the halls of hotels, and in the casino."

"And you didn't find any other suspects on those surveillance tapes?" Roblot asked, knowing the answer.

"Unfortunately, much of that evidence has been lost," Dupont said.

"Which brings up my final plea, sir." Roblot took a document from his file and handed it to the Attorney General. "This case has clearly been compromised. Evidence has been destroyed in what appears to have been collusion between chief investigative Judge Christophe Herly and a member of Mayer's state-appointed defense team."

"The missing surveillance tapes had no bearing on this case!" Dupont interjected, losing patience. "Mayer confessed to setting the fire. He had staged it to win favor with Almasi. He said that he had started a fire in a wastebasket to create a situation where he could then save Almasi and be a hero. Case closed!"

"Oh, so, that's it? The case is all tied up with a neat bow, the guilty party is in custody, and the principality of Monaco is safe again," Roblot said oozing sarcasm. "No one believes that this story is as simple as that!" He shook his file folder in the air. "I have here enough evidence to subpoena at least three more plausible suspects!" He opened the folder and read from one of the pages. "In 1998 and 1999, Almasi collaborated with the FBI to expose the Russian mafia's international money-laundering operation. Almasi kept eleven bodyguards with machine guns, many of them veterans of the Mossad in Israel, who worked in shifts and were always with him. Witnesses saw Almasi at Cap d'Antibes with Boris Berezovsky, the Russian oligarch implicated in the 1999 Aeroflot scandal, in which tens of millions of dollars were diverted from the state-controlled airline. Witnesses also place Almasi at the restaurant of Hotel Martinez in Cannes quarreling with two other Russians."

"Nonsense! Almasi suffered from advanced Parkinson's disease," Dupont countered. "He was too ill and too medicated to have been at either place."

Roblot ignored him and read from his folder. "One year before his death, Almasi informed the FBI about Russian money-laundering activities at Bruce Rappaport's Bank of New York."

"Enough!" The Attorney General stared in astonishment at Roblot. He rose from his desk and walked over to Roblot. "Inspector Roblot, are you suggesting we subpoena the head of the Bank of New York to question him about Almasi's murder?"

"That would be a good start," Roblot said.

The attorney general took the file from Roblot and leafed through it. As he read the notes, his anger flared, and he brusquely closed the folder. "Roblot, you are the best investigator in Monte Carlo. But my patience is wearing thin. We have no time for wild conspiracy theories. You are dismissed from this case." He handed the file back to Roblot. "I have all the evidence I need."

"Sir!" Roblot protested.

"This case is going to trial with the evidence on record."

"I was afraid you would take this position," Roblot said. He removed a sealed envelope from inside his suit jacket. "Therefore, I have prepared my resignation."

The Attorney General took the envelope but didn't open it. He tapped it against his fingers. "Resignation not accepted." He went back to his desk and placed the sealed envelope in the top drawer. "…Yet. Think about what you're doing, Roblot. I will give you one week to rescind your resignation."

"I don't need one week or even one minute. Whether you accept my resignation or not, I am filing a request for Judge Hullin and the lead prosecuting attorney to recuse themselves from this case as they are clearly complicit in a cover-up."

"I *am* the lead prosecuting attorney on this case," the AG said, his voice no longer hiding his anger.

"See you in court," Roblot said, then turned and walked out.

"You quit your job?"

Patrick Roblot's wife Lisette was of a certain age, but her wholesome beauty was ageless. She shunned the high maintenance treatments that most Monégasque women ritualized. Clean living and the love of a good man were her beauty secrets. Roblot continued to pace the floor silently in his den, until she stepped in front of him stopping his stride. Seeing her concern, he kissed her on the cheek and walked to his desk.

"What about the trial?" Lisette asked.

"All my findings were brushed aside. There are at least three possible suspects in Almasi's murder, but the Attorney General refuses to accept any new evidence that doesn't support convicting Todd Mayer."

"But, didn't Mayer confess?"

"Under duress!" he barked in frustration. Then he realized she was just as ill-informed as the general public. He needed to explain to her just enough to understand his plan. "Here, I'll show you." Roblot rifled through his file and pulled out a document. "A year before his death, Almasi gave evidence to the FBI concerning the diversion of a $4.8 billion International Monetary Fund stabilization credit that never reached those for whom it was intended in Russia. The Geneva prosecutor, Benjamin Bartolo, maintained that Almasi was murdered for giving evidence to both the FBI and Swiss prosecutors concerning the diversion of the IMF credit, which went from the New York Federal Reserve Bank to Almasi's New York Republic Bank in Monaco and then to various banks in Switzerland and elsewhere, but *not* to Russia. A year before his death, Almasi's New York Republic Bank provided information to the FBI on those Russian money-laundering activities at Bruce Rappaport's Bank of New York. Rappaport used his base in Geneva to pursue investments in a wide range of places, including Belgium."

"So?" Lisette asked.

"So, I'm getting stonewalled here in Monaco. Meanwhile, investigators in Geneva and Belgium are making connections. So, I have no choice but to go to Belgium."

"Belgium!" Tears filled her eyes, no longer able to contain her exasperation.

"Don't worry," Roblot held her in his arms. "It will be a short trip. But it will go a long way in helping me solve this case."

Lisette pulled away. "Some mysteries can't be solved." Roblot's expression was heartbreaking, and she regretted the words.

"Thanks for reminding me, Lisette."

"We have survived the worst together. Isn't that enough? Why must you pursue causes that mean nothing to us?"

"There's more to it than that."

"When will it end?"

"This will be my final case."

"I don't understand. You just quit the police force."

"That's correct. There are powerful dark forces who want to cover this up. But there are also powerful people, good people, who want the truth to come out."

"Who?"

"Someone who has hired me as a private investigator. The less you know the better. Suffice it to say, the case is not closed and this time I'm working for the good guys." He kissed her and took his jacket. "I'll be back soon. Don't wait up."

Shadowy figures come in all varieties, and not all of them are the evil kind. Frédéric LaFontaine was not publicly known the way George Soros or other billionaire philanthropists were. He preferred staying out of the spotlight and disdained any recognition for his good deeds. He literally floated under the radar, helping where he saw the greatest need. Ever since he had made his wealth by developing a patented online interface software that was used by every bank in the world, he was able to go off the grid, living on his mega yacht, helping change the world for the better. To that end, he had gradually built a network of allies of all different skillsets whom he could enlist depending on necessity.

For LaFontaine, the death of such a revered personage as Ekram Almasi was too suspicious to be handled through the usual law enforcement channels. The only way to bring justice was with the help of highly trained individuals one degree removed from official roles. Despite LaFontaine's repeated attempts to recruit the inspector previously, Roblot had remained loyal to UPD. But the Almasi murder case was the final straw and Patrick Roblot didn't hesitate to hand in his resignation when he saw where Almasi's murder trial was headed.

"Welcome aboard!" LaFontaine greeted Roblot with a warm hug and jovial laughter. His buoyant presence had a way of making anyone feel relaxed.

"It's great to see you, Frédéric," Roblot said.

He boarded the yacht as he had done many times before, but it still never failed to impress him. He followed LaFontaine to the elegantly furnished saloon where they were served potations and hors d'oeuvres.

"Champagne?" LaFontaine offered, to which Roblot nodded yes. He poured two glasses and they clinked in a toast.

"To semi-retirement," Roblot said.

"You handed in your resignation?" LaFontaine laughed cheerily. "Congratulations! Now the real adventure begins."

"As long as my wife will put up with it," Roblot warned. "I told her this was important."

"There is not much more important than the truth."

"She's mostly concerned about me traveling," Roblot confided. "But, for this case, I'll go wherever I'm needed."

"Assure her that I will provide full comfort and safety. We have additional help on the ground in case of emergencies."

"That is reassuring," Roblot said, taking a relaxing sip of champagne. "I'm not afraid for myself, of course."

"Of course," LaFontaine said. "Your wife has been through enough. Your work so far has been invaluable, and we only ask your help to finish what we started. After that, you can truly retire."

"That is all I ask, as well," Roblot said taking another sip. "So, you need me in Belgium?"

"Actually, I need you a little further southwest."

SIX

Although it didn't happen as often as before since Louise had discovered yoga, the buzzing in her ears and the aching in her head were all too familiar and indicated that the fun party at the bar the night before had been a wee excessive. She stirred, because she wasn't alone, her body in a state somewhere between arousal and agony. Oddly, the hangover had brought on a super-relaxed state. Lying on her back naked under the cotton sheets, her knees up, legs slightly apart, she was open to temporary relief. A hand caressed her inner thigh and a mop of hair brushed her gently like a sex toy. The tongue lashing was spot on, his finger entered, moving side to side against the upper vaginal wall, intensifying the hangover remedy as she climaxed.

Deaf to her own cries of ecstasy, she opened her eyes and saw Robert's adorable dimples and irresistible smile. Ready for full penetration, she bent her right knee as he positioned himself, when her ears were suddenly ravaged by the sound of a blaring horn.

"Shit!" Robert said, checking his Rolex Submariner dive watch. He sprung off the bed, his erection waving goodbye as he hopped on one leg to put on his board shorts.

Louise's pupils contracted as she looked toward the morning sun diffused through the sheers that billowed in the sea breeze. An idling boat engine rumbled, and Robert gave her the same dimpled smile that had landed him there.

"My ride is here."

She lifted herself on one elbow. "Can't you stay for breakfast?"

Robert slipped on his Vans and leaned over to give her a kiss on the lips. "I just ate."

"Ha, ha. Do you really need to go on another dive trip? Those boats are for tourists."

He grinned. "It's my boat."

Louise kissed him back. "See ya' 'round."

Robert headed out to the beach while Louise put on her kimono and went to the bar where Big Steve poured her a cup of coffee.

"Y'all got crazy up in here last night." He slid a mug of hot coffee in front of her. She held it with both hands like a holy chalice and drank gratefully.

"Big Steve, what the fuck am I doing?"

"Livin' large, girl," he replied fiddling with his cell phone.

"Where'd you get that? Did someone lose it?"

"It's mine." Louise snapped her fingers and he reluctantly handed it to her.

"This is state of the art."

"Dat's right, Lulu. From the boss-man."

"Michael sent it you?"

"Yo' daddy."

"Wait. What?" Her head throbbed as she tried to clear her thoughts. "My father, George Moscow, is sending you state-of-the-art technology, but he won't even let me call my own mother?"

"Y'all could still be in danger, especially after 9/11, and your daddy and Michael want me to be ready for anything."

Louise hopped off the bar stool and Big Steve winced like she was going to hit him, but she just handed him the phone.

"That's fine, Éti," She said mocking his fake name. "I'm not mad at you for going behind my back. It's just that I really miss my parents." Louise walked behind the bar and poured herself more coffee. She took her cup and headed back to her bungalow.

"Ya'll want breakfast?"

"I'm not hungry."

"You gotta eat!"

"I gotta lie down."

The desperate feeling of frustration was washing over Louise, mixing with the hangover and the post coital buzz, as she continued past her bungalow down to the beach. This "paradise" had been the compromise she had made with her father. But the dark forces it protected her from still infiltrated her soul anyway, especially in the up-and-down anxiety since September 11th. The enforcers of the banking industry, the so-called Black

Network, were still out there possibly plotting to avenge her BCCI whistle-blowing, and perhaps even had a hand in the 9-11 attacks.

She missed her old life more profoundly now than she had during all the years living on the island. The physical buzz also reminded her of Jean-Philippe, and how distant he had become to her. Staring out at the horizon, she was surprised to taste her own tears of discontentment. But at the same time, her heartbreak seemed insignificant compared to the vast and briny sea. There was something deeper at play at that moment. She knew the time had come to dive back into her old life.

Although usually jovial and deferential around Louise's father, Michael Fuentes was almost unrecognizable in this enraged state. His dark eyes, powerful jaw, and high school varsity gymnast's shoulders made him appear menacing.

Michael had first met Louise when she was an undergrad at Princeton, before she went on to earn her Harvard MBA. Shortly thereafter, Michael had graduated from West Point and was recruited by the FBI, not only for his academic achievements but also for his language skills. He had grown up in Rome with a Chilean mother and Spanish father, so he spoke four languages from birth. His mother had been a Chilean ambassador in Spain and his father a foreign correspondent covering the Spanish Civil War.[5] His parents had instilled in him diplomatic instincts, which dovetailed nicely with his FBI work. But today Michael was less restrained.

"Goddamn it, George! We knew this was going to happen but did nothing to prevent it!"

George Moscow listened calmly from behind the desk of his home office in Westchester County, New Jersey. George was a Harvard Law School graduate, but he looked more like a button man for the mob than an intellectual. He was six feet tall, and over two hundred pounds, with hooded eyes and a nose that appeared to have been broken at least once. Street smart and tough, he talked out of the side of his mouth, but never said anything confidential or incriminating. He was the New York City detective in charge

---

[5] From the author's first novel in the Louise Moscow series, *Foliage: An International Banking Spy Thriller*

of white-collar fraud who had been instrumental in taking down BCCI with the help of his daughter, Louise Moscow. George got up to pour Michael a scotch on the rocks.

"Yes," George said, handing Michael the drink. "The intelligence community knew of an imminent attack by Al-Qaeda but could not get the attention of the Bush administration even with the director of the CIA, George Tenet, running around like his hair was on fire."

Michael barely sipped his scotch and went off again. "No shit! I was at the White House meeting in July with the FAA, the Coast Guard, the FBI, the Secret Service, and the INS when Richard Clarke stated in no uncertain terms," Michael made air quotes, "'Something really spectacular is going to happen here, and it's going to happen soon.' No one knew it would be this spectacular, or this soon!"

Michael's cell phone pinged. He looked at the screen, and his eyes showed yet another blow to his already frayed psyche.

"Great!" Michael waved his phone in the air. "Guess who?" Without waiting for a reply, he continued, "Jean-Philippe! Not a peep from him for years, then suddenly." He shrugged sarcastically. "I wonder what *he* could want!"

"He might want to check on Louise," George speculated. "I've alerted Big Steve to start working on Louise to come out of protection."

"You mean *Éti*? Man! Talk about a cushy gig. He's been living blissfully on a remote island in the Caribbean."

"Taking care of my only daughter."

"I didn't say it wasn't an important gig," Michael said.

"Well, his little dream job might soon be more than he bargained for," George said.

"Trouble in paradise?"

"Big Steve has been worried about Louise. Being away for so long had already been taking its toll on her. He said the distress from 9/11 is pushing her over the edge."

"I don't envy Big Steve handling Louise," Michael said.

"He said she's taking it well."

"That can't be good."

"Exactly."

"I assume you have a plan?" Michael asked.

George sat down at his desk and chose his words. "Perhaps Jean-

Philippe can be a part of this."

"We all need to work together now, officially or not," Michael admitted.

"You get on a military aircraft tonight and meet with Jean-Philippe to gather intelligence, see what he's working on," George said. "He might have some input on getting Louise involved in an investigation."

Michael leaned forward his attention piqued. "The last time we enlisted Louise's help in an investigation we set her world and the banking world on fire. Now you want to bring back the man who she feels burned her?"

"Interesting choice of words," George replied.

"Wait, are you opening an investigation into the banker accidentally killed in a fire last year?"

George sipped his scotch. "If anyone has the tenacity to pull this off, it's Louise Moscow. See if you can convince Jean-Philippe that we need to bring Louise out of protection."

SEVEN

December 12, 2001

"Can you convince George Moscow to bring Louise out of protection?" Jean-Philippe asked in a heavy French accent. Michael was sitting in the same chair that Father Gregory had been sitting in when Jean-Philippe assigned him to culling gophers at the Catholic retreat in Genval.

"Maybe, but I'll need more to work with," Michael bluffed.

"We have infiltrated a hub of suspicious activity involving the son of a local nobleman."

"Organized crime laundering drug money?" Michael asked.

"It definitely involves illicit trade," Jean-Philippe said.

"Where does Louise fit in?"

Jean-Philippe hesitated but then got to the point. "We believe there could be links to the death of a prominent banker."

Michael was quick on the uptake. "The Almasi case? You don't think they caught the right guy?"

"There are way too many suspects with money at stake."

"And lots of it," Michael added.

"*Whoever loves money never has enough* – Ecclesiastes 5:10," Jean-Philippe quoted.

"*Those in the sole pursuit of gold, money, and power will stop at nothing*. I think I read that in Newsweek," Michael retorted. "So, you're thinking the Banker's Grave?"

"A banker who knows too much…"

"It's not a conspiracy theory if it's true." Michael lean back and pondered. "I can think of three suspicious deaths of prominent bankers right off the bat. The chairman of Banco Ambrosiano, Roberto Calvi, hung by the neck beneath Blackfriar's Bridge in London in 1982. Then, there's the owner of Franklin National Bank, Michele Sindona, who died after drinking coffee laced with arsenic in an Italian prison in 1986…"

"And now the owner of New York Republic Bank, Ekram M. Almasi, who burned to death trapped in his heavily guarded penthouse in Monaco," Jean-Philippe said.

"Each of these dead bankers knew a lot of secrets. But, Calvi and Sindona were murdered *after* their banks collapsed."

"Exactly!" Jean-Philippe said. "Of those three, Almasi's death is the most curious. He died with his financial empire intact." Jean-Philippe spoke passionately, rising to his feet, pacing and emphasizing with his hands. In the setting of the dimly lit 14th century monastery anyone else would have thought Jean-Philippe had lost it. But Michael knew what it was like to have loved and then lost Louise Moscow. The heartbreak turned to wretchedness, which eventually evolved into tempered steel will.

Before Jean-Philippe had met Louise, he had been widely known as a somewhat eccentric national hero in France. He came from a very old lineage of the French aristocracy, including a long line of commandants with the French Royal Navy, dating back to Napoleon I. He had fought with the French troops against Gaddafi when Libya invaded Chad, earning him the title of Chevalier, which is the French equivalent of knighthood. Believing he should honor that title he devoted his life to his country, and it was not uncommon to see him riding his horse through Paris Tuileries Garden.[6] Now since his self-imposed exile – along with his horse – at this 14th Century Belgian Monastery, Jean-Philippe had made it his mission to stop a dangerous criminal organization he had helped uncover.

Michael's own patriotism was strong, but Jean-Philippe was the proverbial Hero, a modern-day Beowulf. That's why Michael could never be jealous of him. He was worthy of Louise's undying love. Michael listened patiently to Jean-Philippe's soliloquy.

"The commonly accepted explanation for Almasi's murder is convoluted, unconvincing, and highly improbable." Jean-Philippe raised his hands indicating a headline, "*Male nurse murders Ekram Almasi.* Ridiculous! The prosecution argues that Todd Mayer, a former Green Beret, started a fire in a wastebasket so he could then save Almasi and gain his respect. He did not intend to kill Almasi, he just wanted to get back in his favor by rescuing him. Nonsense! A far more plausible explanation for Almasi's fiery demise is his

---

[6] From the author's first novel in the Louise Moscow series, *Foliage: An International Banking Spy Thriller*

connection to shady banking dealings."

"Jean-Philippe, is it possible you have been cooped up in this monastery too long?"

"Not at all! Don't you see? This is an epic drama. Like an opera with a gigantic cast of characters you can never keep straight, all hiding something, and half of whom are in disguise most of the time. But in this case, the plot is hidden bank accounts, camouflaged ownerships, and dirty money. It is not so different from the endless deceptions that the characters in operas are perpetrating on each other and on the audience. Also, as with the opera, bizarre, unexpected connections keep turning up."[7]

"What connections have you made?" Michael asked, trying to keep Jean-Philippe on topic.

"These high-society people form secretive organizations, such as the 1001 Club and the Bilderberg Group, which tend to attract some questionable individuals."

"Isn't the purpose of the 1001 Club to raise funds in support of the World Wildlife Foundation?"

"Yes, of course. It is a noble cause. But there are some, shall we say, interesting delegates. People like Dr. Alfred Hartmann, a former director of Rothschild banking group who was also a high-ranking executive at BCCI."

"BCCI, Louise's old employer."

"Exactement. Dr. Albert Hartmann was director of Swiss Military Intelligence and a former general manager of Union Bank of Switzerland and later chairman of Hoffman-LaRoche. Hartmann resigned from LaRoche after a price-fixing scandal. He also resigned as board director of the Rothschild family bank holding companies after payments from Rothschild A.G. Zurich were traced to the assassins of Roberto Calvi."

"One of the murdered bankers!" Michael began to see the connections. "If I recall correctly, Hartmann was also chairman of BCCI's audit committee in Luxembourg, but the FBI never investigated him."

"Correct," Jean-Philippe said. "Hartmann also ran Banque de Commerce et de Placement in Geneva for many years. BCCI's gold dealings for Colombian drug cartels passed through BCP. Large sums of money earned by market rigging activities laundered through BCP were believed to have played a part in the Iran-Contra affair. But most interesting, Hartmann was

---

also vice president of the CIA-connected Inter-Maritime Bank and was also a CIA asset. His controller was Edwin Wilson."

"Remind me again who is Wilson?" Michael asked.

"Wilson was the CIA operative who specialized in gay and pedophile blackmail stings against political targets."

"Yes!" Michael recalled. "He also specialized in creating financial fronts for the CIA."

"Like I said, shady bank dealings," Jean-Philippe said.

"Any other connections to Almasi?" Michael asked.

"Yes. Hartmann has close links to Bruce Rappaport."

"The Bank of New York's Bruce Rappaport?"

"That is the one. It's all connected. Rappaport opened Inter-Maritime in Geneva in 1966. Through that bank, he helped provide the Bank of New York with important business contacts in Russia. They channeled millions of dollars through Bank of New York and Inter-Maritime. Payments linked to one of the biggest money-laundering schemes in the United States. After aggressively seeking business in Russia for years, Bank of New York is now under federal investigation for money-laundering. See what I mean by *opéra*?"

"That's where Almasi fits in," Michael realized aloud.

"Oui!" Jean-Philippe confirmed. "One year before his death, Almasi's Republic Bank had provided information to the FBI on Russian money-laundering activities at Bruce Rappaport's Bank of New York. The banking aspect is why I believe it would be beneficial to bring Louise in."

As an FBI agent Michael couldn't give specifics on his knowledge about the Bank of New York investigation, but he knew this connection was legitimate. "That should be good enough for George Moscow," Michael concluded. "I'll tell him we are bringing Louise out of protection with the help of our intermediary."

"You aren't in direct contact with Louise?" Jean-Philippe asked, stoically maintaining an air of impartiality.

"We felt it was better to keep our contact at arms-length while Louise is in witness protection. We have a guy, Charlie, who is a former Navy SEAL and has a private investigation agency in the Caribbean. We asked him to refer clients looking to set up offshore businesses to Louise, under the pretext that he doesn't do that kind of work. It had the added benefit of keeping tabs on potential elicit offshore banking activity. Anyway, exactly what kind of mission did you have in mind for Louise?"

"There is a former police superintendent from Monaco, Patrick Roblot, who has an interest in the Almasi murder. Perhaps this Charlie could refer Roblot to Louise?

"That sounds like a symbiotic relationship," Michael agreed.

"Yes, it does," Jean-Philippe said. "The more I think about it, the more I think Louise will be a great asset. We have the Belgium situation covered here, but we need someone in other areas where we believe there is related criminal activity. For example, we have Intel on substantial nefarious activity in France that needs to be fleshed out. Louise would be a perfect plant. Roblot cannot make known his involvement with the investigation since he left the Monte Carlo police on sour terms. But he has a man who can get her on the right track. Roblot was involved in the Almasi murder investigation and will be a crucial, albeit off-the-record, resource to this investigation."

"Okay I'll give you the coordinates and you have this guy Roblot contact Charlie."

"Understood," Jean-Philippe confirmed. They both got up to say good-bye. "One last thing," Jean-Philippe said. "There is some Intel floating around that we think is a code word you might want to look into."

"Sure, what is it?"

"*Maltese Falcon,*" Jean-Philippe replied.

Michael laughed, not sure if it was a joke. "Maltese Falcon? A little cloak-and-dagger, don't you think?"

Jean-Philippe remained impassively good-natured. "Yes, it could be nothing," He walked with Michael to the door. "But there have been several mentions of it in our surveillance."

"What do you think it could be?"

"It could be a delivery, maybe an arms shipment. We have been on high alert here for any chatter alluding to it."

Michael began to see the potential importance of the clue. "Okay, I'll check with the FBI for any COMINT on *Maltese Falcon*. And I'll let Charlie know Roblot will be in touch." Michael shook Jean-Philippe's hand.

"Will you be in town long?" Jean-Philippe asked.

"Nope," Michael replied. "I'm getting right back on the military aircraft to New York."

Jean-Philippe gave Michael a warm priestly hug. "Thank you, my friend. Safe travels."

At 1400 hours Charlie Nielson maneuvered *Sealed Fate*, his brand new 60-foot Marlow yacht, away from his dock like a man on a mission. The former Navy SEAL had a top-paying client with an emergency: His daughter had dropped a beloved toy overboard and needed Charlie to dive for it. Although his client was an experienced diver, the object was below 150 feet and didn't want to chance it.

Charlie wished all his gigs could be this cushy. This particular client paid him a generous monthly retainer plus expenses, literally for child's play. His last commissioned job entailed extricating 50 kilos of cocaine and three cadavers from a drug lord's sunken cruiser. For this client he was basically being paid to take his new Marlow out on a test drive. It handled like a dream and within a half hour he was less than a mile from the nautical coordinates of the toy emergency. As he followed the coordinates to his client's mooring place, a voice came over channel 16 of his VHF radio.

"Sealed Fate, Sealed Fate, Jenny, over."

"This is Sealed Fate, over," Charlie replied to his client.

"Six eight?" his client said, offering an open channel.

Charlie switched the channel to 68 and keyed the mike. "Sealed Fate, Jenny, over."

"ETA, Sealed Fate. We're going to DEFCON 5 here. Major Bratz anxiety, over."

"ETA 15 minutes, over," Charlie replied.

"We'll hang tight, see you in 15. Over and out."

Charlie signed off just as channel 16 pinged again.

"Sealed Fate, Sealed Fate, Coast Guard, over."

Charlie had a sinking feeling as he replied, "Sealed Fate, Coast Guard, over."

"Six eight, over," came the command.

Charlie switched back to channel 68 and keyed the mike. "Sealed Fate, Coast Guard, over." But an unexpectedly friendly and familiar voice replied.

"Be careful what you wish for, Sealed Fate, over."

"Well, I'll be, Michael Fuentes," Charlie said. "What are your coordinates? Over."

"Sadly, I'm calling from the Staten Island Coast Guard," Michael said. "Maybe I can get out to your neck of paradise next time, over."

"This day just gets better and better. Which of my wishes came true now? Over."

"Well, the time has finally come for you to actually meet Ruby Red, over," Michael said, using Louise's code name. There was a moment of silence, so Michael checked the mike. "Sealed Fate, did I lose ya? Over."

"I'm here. Happy to help. What's the mission? Over."

"As soon as you get on land call my encrypted phone line, over." Michael replied.

"Roger that, I'd do it right away, but I'm in the middle of…" Charlie hesitated to tell Michael the nature of the job. "Let's just call it a family emergency. Can I call you in a couple hours? Over."

"Copy that, over."

"Over and out." Charlie loved that it was okay to be blunt on VHF radio.

He arrived at his client's mooring and suited up for the dive. The client showed him a photo of the object and about where it had gone overboard. Charlie gave a salute and flipped backwards into the clear waters. His underwater vision was exceptional. Between working as an open water divemaster and scavenging crime scenes, he was trained to quickly spot anything from the most stealthily camouflaged creature to an out-of-place object.

In less than half an hour he had recovered the toy, made a safety stop and broke the surface with the toy raised above his head to cheers. He climbed aboard the client's boat and took something out of his buoyancy vest before handing the doll to the little girl.

"This is a tether." Charlie slid her hand through a slip knot on the end of a nylon strand and clipped the other end to the soggy toy. "Now your doll will stay with you even if you drop her."

"What do you say, Isabella?" Charlie's client said.

"Thank you," Isabella said.

"You're welcome. What's her name?"

"Cloe," Isabella replied, hugging her Bratz doll.

"Nice to meet you, Cloe and Isabella," Charlie said, getting back on his boat and waving good-bye as he sped off.

Once dockside, Charlie input Michael's encrypted phone number into his mobile. The conversation was short and to the point.

"So, Ruby Red, eh? Karen Baker AKA Louise Moscow. I haven't seen her since I took her yoga class about a month ago, under-cover operation to check in on her, of course."

"Well, now it's time for your big reveal," Michael replied, "We need you as our liaison to a private investigator from Monaco, Patrick Roblot."

Michael detailed Roblot's background, the timing of his arrival, and some additional instructions for Louise once Roblot outlined the operation for her.

"Am I privy to the reason I'm picking up a retired cop from Monaco and introducing him to Louise?"

"You'll find out soon enough when Roblot briefs Louise." Michael then paused, almost dramatically. "Let's just say that Karen Baker will be leaving your neck of the ocean very soon."

EIGHT

December 13, 2001

Louise and Big Steve descended a skyscraper in a glass elevator the size of an office. Outside the elevator, they could see a vast metropolis of gleaming metallic towers and soaring motorways clover twisting to unite roads to nowhere. Big Steve nattered indistinctly as Louise reassured him.

"Don't worry." Just as Louise spoke, the elevator began to jostle them. "This is normal. Elevators are built to withstand extreme tremors." Then the elevator began to swivel and screech under the pressure.

In the near distance, a large plume of smoke rose from a commercial high rise beneath them. Louise tried to avert Big Steve's attention by pointing in the opposite direction. But she saw more disturbances in each direction. Fires blazed in patches below, making it clear the city was under attack. Streams of artillery fire and rockets traversed the skyline, some coming close to the elevator, until one finally made contact. Big Steve continued to chitchat seemingly oblivious to the onslaught.

Louise crouched down to the floor and shouted, "Get down!" But Big Steve ignored her and suddenly appeared to be sitting behind a desk, with total disregard for the dangers outside.

Louise could see uniformed soldiers lined up in formation on rooftops, wearing imperial-shaped helmets that sloped down to their shoulders. It was an invasion, and the country was under attack from a great military led by corrupt forces.

"If we survive this elevator ride, we should commit suicide instead of being taken prisoner," Louise said. "Some evil force has hacked into our system. The FBI is in league with a corrupt government. Only the CIA can help us now…"

Startled awake, Louise checked the clock, 7:30 a.m. Hunger pangs coupled with lingering dread from the bizarre nightmare forced her out of bed. Ever since the events of 9/11 she had been having recurring anxiety dreams.

She shook it off and went out to the bar where she found Big Steve at the computer.

"Mornin', sunshine."

"Wow, this place is immaculate."

Big Steve peered at her over the reading glasses halfway down his nose. "Got the bookkeeping done too."

"Okay, what's going on, *Éti*?"

He got up and poured her a cup of coffee. "Can I make you some eggs and toast, Karen? Y'all must be starving."

"I'm famished." Louise drank the coffee like an elixir. She stared at the television that was locked on CNN with the sound muted and jazz playing soothingly over the stereo speakers. Big Steve brought a plate of hot food. "Wow, breakfast, coffee, the bookkeeping done, and spring cleaning in December. What gives?"

He shrugged. Louise picked at the food and ate a forkful of eggs. Her stomach growled its appreciation, but her heart sank from the CNN news ticker. She put her fork down.

"Any word from Charlie?"

"If y'all don't eat my cookin', I goin' on strike."

Louise bit off a corner of the toast and chewed joylessly.

"By the way," Big Steve said. "Charlie contacted me this morning and said he'd be passin' by soon."

"Why didn't you say so? I better get ready." Her mood lifted and Louise ravenously forked eggs and toast into her mouth then ran to her bungalow.

Big Steve shook his head. "Girl sho' can eat."

All dressed up with nowhere to go, Louise glared at the group of divers disembarking on her beach. She could always tell what kind of customers they would be at first glance. Usually, it was a mix of affable older married couples, newlyweds, and a few singles out to discover the underwater wonders of nature. But occasionally they were spoiled assholes literally in over their heads. The arriving group appeared to be the latter, twenty-something guys on a bachelor party excursion. They invaded the island and thought it was funny to sound like the Pirates of the Caribbean.

"Yo ho, yo ho, a pirate's life for me! We pillage, we plunder, we rifle and loot! Drink up me 'earties, yo ho! We kidnap and ravage and don't give a hoot! Drink up me 'earties, yo ho!" sang one diver with a slight Texas twang.

"And a bottle of rum!" shouted the guy who appeared to be the organizer. He raised his arm holding an invisible sword. "To the Tiki bar! Argh!" He ran toward the bar and the others followed making pirate sounds.

"Éti, can you deal with these guys?" Louise asked using his undercover moniker.

"Sho' 'nough," Big Steve said. They swarmed in, and Big Steve seated them all together near the terrace, away from the bar where Louise started to prepare drinks.

"A bottle of rum, arghh, matey!" the leader said.

"Y'all settle in and we'll take care of everything," Big Steve said calmly and professionally.

The dive master shook Big Steve's hand. "How's it goin' there, Éti? Just give everyone the usual."

"Ten Diver's Delights, comin' right up," Big Steve said.

The conversations overlapped as the young men excitedly recounted their dive of the Bloody Bay Marine Park, so named after a naval battle.

"That wall dropping off a sheer 3,000 feet into the blue was amazing! Did you see that shark, y'all? I almost shit my wet suit!" said the twangy Texan.

"It was just a reef shark," the group leader said. "They have no interest in you." He turned and tipped an invisible hat toward Louise behind the bar. "Excuse my buddies, ma'am. They're a little excited about the dive."

"It's quite all right." Louise replied. "I've done that dive many times, and it's always amazing." Big Steve came over to help Louise with the drinks and food. "I thought Charlie was coming today," she muttered.

"Maybe he already here," Big Steve said, subtly nodding to a single man at one of the tables.

"You might be right. We don't know what he looks like."

As the divers' conversations rose to a din, Louise eyed the man sitting quietly alone staring into his drink. He was tall and muscular, his face framed by a carved jawline and distinguishing gray temples. He had the air of a former marine or perhaps a Navy SEAL. He felt Louise watching but avoided eye contact. Oddly, his ominous presence was reassuring.

"I served him a rum shot with a beer chaser," Big Steve said, reading her mind.

"He sure is taking his time drinking it," Louise said.

"Maybe he's lonely."

Louise went to his table. "Anything wrong with the rum?"

"Sorry?" he said, looking up from his glass.

"Are you just going to stare at it or drink it?"

"It's funny you should ask," he said. "Recently, I find that looking at it is just as satisfying as drinking it, and therefore I don't drink as much."

"Yeah, I do the same thing with French pastries."

"Cheers." He raised the shot glass and drank it down, then swallowed the beer in one gulp. His face brightened into a gluttonous grin. "Even better than French pastry."

"To each his own. Can I get you another?"

"Depends. Will you join me?"

"I'm a little busy right now," Louise said, indicating the noisy group.

"Come 'on. Let me buy you a drink. It won't kill you."

Loaded words, Louise thought. "But will it change my life?"

"Tough terms."

"It's all about the negotiation," Louise said.

"Are we still talking about rum shots?"

"I don't know, are we?"

"You seem to live a sheltered life here." As he said it, the bachelor party, which was on the third round of drinks, started getting ugly. Big Steve moved closer to triangulate with the dive master, both of whom had seen it all before.

"I keep up-to-date where it counts. Banking and finance regulations, global warming, rising sea levels," Louise said. "Is there something I missed?" But the man wasn't listening to Louise and focused on one of the divers who now approached Big Steve.

"Hey, brotha', you gotta mighty fine woman there. Y'all couldn't get away with that where I come from." The man with the Texas twang said. Then he swigged the rest of his drink and slammed it down on the table. Big Steve took the stance of security guard, feet wide, arms crossed, composed, neutral expression.

Charlie got up and placed a generous tip and a folded pieced of paper on the table. "I have a new client for you," he muttered to Louise. Then he walked toward the exit past the divers.

"Thanks." Louise cleaned his table, pocketing the tip and picking up the note. It contained simple directions, longitude, latitude, time, date. Signed, *Charlie.*

Big Steve eyed Charlie and said, "How's it going?"

"All in, all the time," Charlie replied. The Navy SEAL reference was not lost on Big Steve, the dive captain or the leader of the bachelor party, who placed his hand on his buddy's shoulder.

"Come on, bro. Don't run to your death. Your wedding is soon enough for that."

After a moment of strained silence, the tension broke and everyone laughed. The Texan approached Big Steve still puffed up. But he suddenly relaxed, grinned and held out his hand, which Big Steve shook. The Texan sat back down and Big Steve went to the bar to turn up the stereo and the party resumed.

Louise looked for Charlie, but he was already gone. She wiped her hands on the bar towel and handed it to Big Steve.

"Hold down the fort." She went to her bungalow to change.

With the wind in her hair and 600 horsepower twin engines under the hull, Louise sliced through cobalt waters. There was no better way to travel. Her 36-foot Spectre Power Cat got her quickly off her little island with two electronic fuel injection engines in case one engine broke down or if she needed swift evasive tactics. She neared top speeds almost blowing her favorite hat off. It was a cotton pinstriped men's bucket hat that she had stolen from Jean-Philippe on a trip to the Caymans, which had become perfectly broken-in over the years.

She checked her GPS headings for the coordinates on the handwritten note Charlie had given her. Careening through the wakes from crafts of all sizes, she passed yachts coexisting with fishing boats, all taking varying degrees of care to avoid dive boat mooring buoys. September 11th had impacted travel, so the traffic was lighter than normal at this time of year. That, along with her GPS, made it easier to track down Charlie's location. Before May 2000, GPS signals had been subject to Selective Availability, or SA, which meant that for ordinary users, the signals were only accurate to approximately 50 meters. Since then, SA had been removed and GPS signals were generally accurate to a few meters. Louise spotted a boat at the exact coordinates and made a beeline for it.

"Right on time!" The former Navy SEAL shouted to Louise as she expertly maneuvered the unwieldy high-powered engines alongside his 60-foot Marlow Explorer and tossed Charlie a line.

"Yes, old banking habits die hard."

"Climb aboard," Charlie said as he tied up. She deftly stepped over the gunwale and onto his deck. "Nice hat."

"Nice boat," Louise said, running her fingers along the gleaming hardwood finish. "This teak wood is stunning."

"Thanks," Charlie replied. "She's a dream come true. Every Marlow Explorer is crafted from a single teak log, handpicked in Thailand to ensure that the wood is consistent throughout the boat."

They entered from starboard into an enclosed fly bridge. The pilothouse featured a fully equipped gourmet galley, a dining settee, and a very spacious helm area. The natural marble and granite countertops in the galley enhanced the luxury. There was even a Sub-Zero refrigerator and Fisher-Paykel dishwasher.

"I could definitely live aboard," Louise said.

"While I'm working, I do," Charlie replied.

Two steps down they entered the large saloon with horseshoe seating, a teak dining table for ten, and a large-screen television. There was also a custom bar with built-in barstools where a bottle of Veuve Cliquot chilled in an ice bucket. A man seated at the bar rose to greet her.

"Mademoiselle Moscow." He shook her hand. "Thank you for meeting with me."

Louise was taken aback. All of the other clients that Charlie had sent her had accepted the Karen Baker moniker, no questions asked.

"You're welcome," Louise replied. "You know my name, but I don't know yours."

Charlie made introductions. "This is Patrick Roblot, from Monte Carlo."

"It's nice to meet you," Louise said. "But I get the feeling this isn't a pleasure cruise."

"Please, have a seat," Roblot said, offering her the barstool. "Champagne, Mademoiselle Moscow?"

Louise took the glass and they clinked. "To family."

"You two have known each other long?" Roblot asked.

"I just met Charlie today," Louise said. "But he seems like family. Right,

Charlie?"

"Since Louise moved to her island paradise, she has become a highly sought-after consultant for her knowledge of offshore business. I have referred several satisfied clients to her."

"But I only work with legitimate businesses." Louise felt there was no time like the present to preface her working terms. "Certain international companies are inherently logical candidates. In such circumstances, it makes perfect sense for a company to be based in a tax-free territory if most or all revenues are of foreign origin. However, I won't take a client who appears to be funneling illegitimate money into a legitimate business for the purposes of laundering it. I can tell the difference. Which category do you fall into?" She asked Roblot.

Charlie cut in. "Inspector Roblot is not my typical referral,".

"*Inspector* Roblot?" Louise echoed.

"Charlie said you could help me with a case that has gone cold," Roblot continued. "At least as far as I'm concerned."

"Oh, Charlie said that, did he?" Louise was catching on quickly that her father was behind the mysterious rendezvous.

"Patrick was superintendent of Urban Police Division of Monte Carlo during the time a high-profile murder took place," Charlie added.

Louise took a sip of champagne. "I'm listening"

"It happened almost exactly two years ago, and it has been one year since the case was solved." Roblot said with a hint of sarcasm in his voice.

"Let me guess. The murder of the banking mogul, Ekram Almasi," Louise said. "Didn't the trial already end with a conviction of their prime suspect, the male nurse?"

"I see you aren't completely shut off from the rest of the world," Charlie remarked.

"My news sources are mostly the Tiki bar grapevine and occasional perusal of Usenet. CNN used to be reliable but…"

"Calling *Crossfire* a debate show is like calling WWE an Olympic sport," Charlie said, finishing her thought.

"Usenet is the only news source I can even tolerate."

"The first rule of Usenet is that you do not talk about Usenet," Charlie said.

"Say no more," Louise said, punctuated by the pop of a cork from a bottle that Roblot took the liberty of opening.

"You both lost me at grapevine," interjected Roblot. "More champagne?" Louise didn't refuse.

"So, Patrick, how are you involved with this cold case?"

"Let's just say that I retired from the UPD. But I am not completely retired," Roblot explained. "I've been hired by an interested third party for my special skills, who put me with Charlie for his special skills,"

"You strike me as Navy SEAL," Louise said, eying Charlie.

"Correct. My dad was my hero, so I followed in his footsteps and joined the Navy, became a SEAL and helped fight the Hong Kong triads, among other missions. I'm also an advanced certified pilot, skydiver, and open water scuba diver. But now I work as a private detective specializing in maritime crimes, mostly in the Atlantic. This case is related to international banking, the kind of work, as you know, I have been referring to you."

"It's nice to finally thank you in person," Louise said.

"You're quite welcome. As I said, this is your domain."

"So, you're thinking follow the money?" Louise surmised.

"Exactly," Roblot replied, "You were right, Charlie. Ms. Moscow is very astute."

"Why do you think the case is unsolved, Patrick?" Louise asked, staying on topic.

"Monaco wanted it all hushed up," Roblot said. "But my investigation pointed to any number of other entities such as the Russian Mafia or Middle Eastern terrorists, with stronger motives to do away with Almasi."

"Almasi wasn't really known to the public at large," Louise said. "But he was very prominent in the worlds of international banking and high society and also for his philanthropy. I even had dealings with him at BCCI. He was highly respected and even considered the most brilliant banker of his time."

"Precisely," Roblot agreed. "And yet, the only suspect in his murder was his nurse, Todd Mayer."

"Wasn't he Green Beret?" Louise tried to remember aloud.

"Yes, but Mayer trained as a medical auxiliary in the Green Berets. He had no experience in combat. He was there to tend to his employer in a nursing capacity, not to protect him. For that, Almasi had Mossad bodyguards. But he didn't house them in the Monte Carlo residence, because he felt safe enough to keep his security detail 10 miles away at his villa La Leopolda."

"Was there any evidence of other suspects at the crime scene?" Louise asked.

"Mayer's own testimony for starters," Roblot replied. "In Mayer's early statements, he claimed that two hooded intruders penetrated the apartment, stabbed him, and started the fire that killed Almasi. However, after three days of interrogation, Mayer changed his testimony and confessed to having started a fire in a wastebasket so he could come off as a hero by saving Almasi."

"What about the stabbing?" Louise asked.

"Mayer also claimed that the stab wounds were self-inflicted," Roblot explained. "Which would have been consistent with the official evidence showing no holes from the stabbing through his clothing, only directly to his abdomen and leg."

"Would have been?" Louise repeated.

"His clothing was lost in evidence too."

"Interesting," Louise said.

"Also, at any moment during the fire, Almasi could have saved himself by opening the door to the saferoom. But he was so afraid of being murdered by the intruders that he refused to unlock the door, even for the fire brigade. When we finally got into the saferoom two hours later, he and his other nurse, Theresa Leigh, were dead. She had a cell phone on which we noted several outgoing calls. Todd Mayer admitted to giving her the cell phone to call for help."

"That sounds premeditated," Louise conjectured.

"Another thing," Roblot continued. "According to the medical examiner's report, Leigh's neck had been crushed."

"Did the report say how?" Louise asked.

"That information was not made public on the premise that Almasi could have done that to keep her from trying to escape. He was known to be paranoid, and rightly so. His specialty was private banking for wealthy clients, something you can relate to," he added, to which Louise nodded in agreement. "He would have known all the secrets of the financial planet."

"Meaning, he had enemies," Louise concluded.

"Almasi insisted on keeping eleven bodyguards, outfitted with machine guns, working in shifts to always be with him, often to the consternation of friends who disliked being surrounded by armed men every time they arrived for a visit."

"I would be too," Louise said. "Wouldn't it be ironic if the death was in fact caused by a clumsy attempt by a sycophant?"

Roblot shook his head. "It's just too convenient. One year before his death, Almasi provided information to the FBI on Russian money-laundering activities at Bruce Rappaport's Bank of New York. Almasi collaborated with the FBI to expose the Russian Mafia's international money-laundering operation. Ten months later, he had been seen with Boris Berezovsky, the Russian oligarch implicated in the 1999 Aeroflot scandal, in which tens of millions of dollars were diverted from the state-controlled airline. Then in the restaurant of Hotel Martinez in Cannes the two men had a three-hour conversation in raised voices, after which Almasi fled in a panic to his heavily fortified Monte Carlo residence. Two months later he was burned to death in that penthouse."

"It does sound like KGB tactics," Louise said, thinking of Vladimir. "Also, correct me if I'm off base, but so much of the story reminds me of the BCCI scandal,"

"Which is why we have come to you," Roblot said. "I am just a humble police officer. These international banking scenarios are beyond my area of expertise."

"That's what these kinds of criminals count on," Louise said. "They intentionally take what should be straightforward, traceable transactions and send them through a maze of companies and banks, thinking no one will take the time to sort them out. So, do you have any evidence that suggests Mayer was just a fall guy?"

"After Mayer was arrested, I personally questioned his wife who said three men dressed in black grabbed her off the street, threw her into a car, and took her to her hotel room, which they ransacked and took her passport. They then took her to the police station and cancelled her return plane ticket to the United States."

"And you believed her?" Louise asked.

"Why would she make that up?" Roblot said. "Whoever took her to police headquarters was not ordered to do so by me." Roblot continued to paint a picture. "Another officer, Paul Dupont from the Criminal Police Division became involved in the investigation. The CPD has three departments. Dupont was superintendent of criminal investigations. There are also the Criminal Identity and Resources departments. The Criminal Identity department coordinates with Interpol."

Louise's eyes widened. The first time she had been introduced to Interpol, the love of her life, Jean-Philippe de Villeneuve, was recruiting her to become an informant. "And you think the Criminal Identity department and officer Dupont were working autonomously?"

"That seems obvious to me if I believe Mrs. Mayer, who seemed to be telling the truth." Roblot finished his champagne with one gulp then took the champagne bottle from the ice bucket and refilled Louise's glass.

He started to refill Charlie's glass, but he waved him off. "I think I'll switch to something a little stronger," Charlie said.

Roblot poured the rest of the champagne into his glass and plunged the empty bottle upside down into the ice bucket. Charlie took this as a signal to retrieve another bottle. Roblot shook his head in self-reflection and continued. "There are also the Division of Administrative Police responsible for the movement of foreign nationals through Monaco's borders, as well as the Maritime and Airport Police Divisions that police the seas and skies of Monaco."

"Sounds like there are a lot of moving parts to this story," Louise surmised.

"A multi-dimensional chess game," Charlie rejoined.

"Monaco intentionally built separation of powers into its system of controls," Roblot explained. "For example, the medical examiner is part of the justice department, not the police department. The ME's report becomes part of the attorney general's case for prosecution. My department has no control over that report. The Monaco prosecutor claimed Todd Mayer tested positive for drugs and alcohol. But records from Princess Grace Hospital proved that, contrary to the Monaco prosecutor's claim, Todd Mayer had no alcohol or drugs in his system."

"So, you think someone influenced the prosecutor?"

"That's one possibility. Also, Mayer's wife claimed that her husband's actual statement was different than what was officially reported as his confession. She claimed he confessed only to lighting the fire in a wastebasket to set off the fire alarm. But, during the interrogation, officers showed Mayer his wife's passport and told him she was being detained for questioning too."

"Intimidation tactics," Charlie said.

"It gets worse," Roblot said. "They then proceeded to constrain Mayer, catheterize, and keep him awake for three days to interrogate him, after which, he confessed to stabbing himself and that there were no intruders.

They forced him to sign the confession written in French with no English translation.

Louise shook her head. "Let me guess. He doesn't speak French."

"Correct. Mayer doesn't speak a word of French."

"Weren't there surveillance videotapes?" Louise asked.

Roblot tapped his temple. "Excellent question, Ms. Moscow," he said. "The tapes have also vanished. The judge received a blank tape and an old tape showing guests arriving at a party. Subsequently, someone discovered one of the original tapes, but the authorities won't publicly reveal what is on it. I'm no longer with the police department so I have no way of viewing it."

"So, the Monégasque authorities have no idea you are working this case?" Louise asked.

"Correct. And they must never find out that I am working on behalf of a third party who is only interested in the truth."

"Your integrity is refreshing," Louise said.

"Louise," Charlie pressed. "Not only is this your exit strategy off the island. This could be an opportunity to bring down the very people who forced you into protection in the first place."

"You don't have to do the hard sell, Charlie," Louise assured him. "After 9/11, I can no longer sit safely on my island and do nothing. But what exactly can I do to help?"

"We have some leads for you to pursue," Roblot said. "It will be necessary for you to infiltrate certain regions of France."

"When would you like me to start?" Louise asked.

Charlie intervened on her question. "According to my source, not until you get the proper tools."

"Tools?"

"Since you're eager to accept this assignment," Charlie said, "you'll be outfitted with the latest 'tricks of the trade.' Technology has changed since you've been here. Is there a time when no customers are at your bar?"

"No divers on Wednesdays," Louise said.

"I should have received everything you'll need and will be in touch next week," Charlie said.

"In the meantime," Roblot added, "we will wire $50,000 to an offshore account that you will have access to."

"Who's funding all this?" Louise asked.

"Not all wealthy people are corrupt," Roblot said. "Some use their wealth to get into heaven."

NINE

Stingrays formed a constellation above Louise. Suspended in the blue abyss, Louise breathed calmly through her regulator and checked her tank, 1,000 PSI. She had ventured only 30 feet down the reef wall for a quick morning dive. It had been months since she had been underwater, and the Caribbean was calling her. She wore a neoprene bikini with no wetsuit, so she ascended to fifteen feet to avoid lowering her body temperature too much. After a five-minute safety stop, she swam back toward the shore but spotted an easy catch and dove for it.

Big Steve had waded out from the shore and was looking for Louise, when suddenly a gloved hand holding a lobster broke the surface, pinchers waving in the air. Louise's arm appeared, then her head and torso as she walked up the sandy bottom like a Bond Girl.

She pulled the regulator from her mouth. "Breakfast!"

"Damn, woman, y'all gave me a fright!"

"I was just checking out the reef." She handed Big Steve the lobster and her flippers then removed her facemask.

"I was looking everywhere for you when I saw bubbles on the surface. Y'all need to let a brother know before y'all disappear."

Louise rested the tank against the dock and removed the buoyancy vest. Big Steve picked up the equipment and handed Louise the lobster just as the Marlow yacht pulled up to the dock.

"Good morning!" Charlie shouted.

Louise waved the lobster and shouted, "Welcome ashore!"

Charlie and Roblot docked and followed Louise and Big Steve into the Tiki bar. Still in her two-piece bathing suit, Louise towel-dried her hair, then went behind the bar.

"Coffee?" The men nodded yes, and she poured three cups. "Big Steve is making fresh lobster omelets. Have a seat."

"If I had known you were diving for lobster this morning, I would have come earlier and joined you," Charlie said.

"It was a whim," Louise said. "I had the feeling it would be a while before I got back into the water again."

Charlie placed a duffle bag on one of the tables. "We come bearing gifts."

Louise put the coffee on the next table over. "Let's have breakfast and then you can show me what you got."

They sat, and Big Steve brought plates of perfectly cooked omelets filled with fresh lobster.

"I won't report you for the lobster," Charlie said. "It looks too good to pass up."

"Eating lobster is illegal?" Roblot asked, stressing the last syllable of ille-GAL in his French accent.

"It must be caught free diving, and I was wearing a tank, so technically, I caught the lobster illegally," Louise said. "But, considering all the times I snorkeled and didn't take any, it all evens out. Bon appétit!"

After they cleaned their plates, Charlie took the items out of the duffle bag and spread them on the bar as though presenting them at the latest tech convention.

"You're going to love this," Charlie said, picking up the first item. "This is a government issued GlobalCom handheld satellite phone. It provides voice and data service in remote areas. They are primarily used on cruises and hunting trips."

"Sounds expensive. My Nokia works fine."

"You can't even see your screen half the time," Big Steve said.

"Well, excuse me, I didn't get a secret spy phone from my dad like you did."

"All costs are covered," Charlie said.

Louise took the sleek GlobalCom satellite phone and used the up and down arrows to scroll the contacts. "There are already a bunch of numbers programmed in. My dad, Michael…"

"Check this out," Charlie said, taking out a silver slab with an Apple logo on it. "A Mac Titanium PowerBook G4. It's a mind-blowing product, just one inch thick." He booted it up and walked her through the basic functions. "It's a laptop computer that allows you to write documents, even surf the Internet and upload photos. Speaking of photos," Charlie said, taking what appeared to be a normal pen and handed it to Louise. She clicked it a couple times.

"You might want to use it sparingly, so you don't run out of memory," Charlie said.

"Memory?"

"May I?" Charlie took the pen, and he pointed to the tiny lens at the top. "It looks and works just like an ordinary pen, except that it has a hidden camera. It operates with a simple click of the pen to start recording and click to stop recording. There are three modes: audio, photo, and video. The resolution is quite decent."

"Whatch ya'll need these fo?" Big Steve asked. Louise could tell he was getting protective by his pursed lips and flared nostrils.

"They have asked me to work on an investigation, Big Steve. You can hold down the fort here." Big Steve put his fists together in front of his body and puffed up his chest, which Louise knew was his way of protesting.

"Most importantly," Roblot added, handing Louise a packet. "This is a photocopy of all my notes on the investigation. This is top secret so please be very discrete."

"I'll keep it very close," Louise said, placing the packet inside the computer bag.

"Well, thank you for breakfast," Charlie said, getting up from the table.

"One more thing," Charlie said. "You will be traveling in France so you might want to change your look."

"I'll figure something out," Louise said, accepting the challenge.

"We already have," Charlie said. "There are more things in the duffle for you." He handed Louise an envelope. "Here are your plane tickets, identification, and bank card. I'll text you the PIN."

Louise looked inside the envelope to find a one-way ticket to New York City, leaving the next day, the bank card and her new passport, all in the name of Karen Baker. The passport picture was her, but the hair was much darker. Charlie caught her surprised expression as it sunk in.

"Yep, I even included a way to help you match the photo," he said, pointing to the duffle bag. "Please stay in close contact."

"I'll call you with any updates," Louise said, pointing to new phone. They shook their hands and left. She turned to Big Steve who remained silent. "Come on Éti, Karen Baker needs to get ready."

❦

Big Steve paced back and forth outside the open door of Louise's bungalow. "You can't leave me here to tend the Tiki bar all by myself, Lulu! What if the books don't add up?" Louise came out of the bathroom, wearing a kimono with her hair wrapped in a towel.

"Big Steve, you do the bookkeeping better than I do. Remember the time you solved that error? It was driving me nuts and you went right in and found it."

He dismissed her argument with a wave of his hand. "You can't be travelin' 'round all by yo' self."

Louise packed toiletries into her carry-on bag and looked in the closet. "None of my island wardrobe will work for this trip, except for maybe one thing." She flipped through pieces that hung in the back from her treasured collection of Myrna Loy outfits worn in "The Thin Man" movies.[8] Louise's great aunt had been the costumer at MGM during the 1930s and 40s and took possession of the Loy collection after the series ended. Louise had fallen in love with the stylish garb as a child, and after her aunt died, she inherited the whole collection. She selected one item. It was a burgundy pencil dress with short puffy sleeves, a notched neckline, and a small rounded collar. "I'll have to go shopping in New York."

She went to her bed and picked up a well-loved stuffed pig, squeezed it and kissed its snout. "Sorry, Squeaky. You have to stay home this time." She placed the pig back on her pillow and unwrapped the towel from her head, revealing her new hair style cut into a bob and dyed dark brown with the supplies Charlie provided.

Big Steve's eyes opened almost as wide as his mouth. "Whatch' y'all done to yo' hair?"

"You don't like it?" Louise looked in the mirror and puckered her lips in satisfaction. "*Pas mal.*"

"Not bad?" Big Steve said. "I don't even recognize y'all!"

"That's the point."

"At least lemme' call my buddy who I used to bodyguard Michael Jackson with to meet y'all in New York."

---

[8] From the author's first novel in the Louise Moscow series, *Foliage: An International Banking Spy Thriller*

Louise walked over and gave Big Steve a kiss on the cheek. "Stop worry-ing," she said, closing the bungalow door on him. He remained outside the door speechless for a moment, then went back to his work at the bar, leaving Louise to finish preparing for her trip.

T E N

December 22, 2001

It was a perfect winter morning in paradise. Palm fronds rustled in the breeze, waves lapped the shoreline, and boat fenders banged gently against the dock keeping a syncopated beat.

But the serenity was lost on Big Steve, who came out to the bar sleepily mumbling his protest.

"Undercover espionage bullshit."

He flipped the switch turning off the Christmas lights on the palm tree and started a pot of coffee.

Louise walked in wearing fitted black jeans, leather biker boots, and black leather jacket, contrasting starkly with the tropical setting. Big Steve handed her a coffee, which she drank gratefully.

"Allez, on y va," Louise said, picking up her small suitcase and a computer bag containing the new gadgets and walking out to the dock.

Big Steve followed her. "You ain't gonna blend in anywhere lookin' like dat, Karen!" he said, getting one more dig on her name.

Louise ignored him. "Come on. You need to drop me at the airport and get back here before any customers arrive. If anybody asks, I'm off on an extended yoga retreat."

Big Steve loaded her bags and climbed aboard. Louise took the helm and after an hour at cruising speed, they arrived at Blossom Village located at the southwest tip of Little Cayman. Louise pulled up to the public dock, and Big Steve took the helm.

"Merci, mon ami." Louise gave Big Steve a kiss on each cheek and hopped out. "Don't forget to fill up the tank before you head back." She walked up the dock pulling the rolling suitcase and carrying the computer bag.

"Lemme know when y'all get there!" Big Steve shouted.

Louise gave a backhanded wave and continued walking another 200 yards to the airport terminal. The towering palm trees waving in the warm breeze seemed to beckon her to stay. She ignored them and arrived at the 600-square-foot structure. A tattered wooden sign nailed over the porch read Edward Bodden Airport. Louise entered the screen door and checked in for her flight, then went back out to wait with the other passengers under the small hanging wood sign indicating Terminal A Gate #1.

Two pilots and nine passengers boarded the Short Takeoff and Landing Turboprop De Havilland DHC-6-300 Twin Otter aircraft. Louise took a seat just behind the cockpit to observe the pilots flying the craft that had about the same horsepower as her speedboat. She pondered getting through security and customs at the main airport with heightened security since 9/11. This was her first time heading back to a whole different world, with a whole different appearance since the trial.

The plane took off, fishtailing gently toward her new life. After less than half an hour they landed in Grand Cayman. She disembarked and went to the terminal to withdraw cash from an ATM using the new bank account debit card. Then she hopped on a direct flight to New York City JFK International Airport, arriving at 8:04 p.m. in the same time zone she had left.

Louise would need a car to visit her parents so she figured she might as well rent one at the airport. She chose one of the National Emerald Club cars available in the parking lot and threw her things in the trunk. As she drove into Manhattan, she was expecting a gloomy post-September 11th atmosphere. But instead she was greeted by surprisingly busy streets, Christmas shoppers and tree merchants doing a brisk business. It was as though people were more determined than ever to celebrate holiday traditions. She also noted the yuletide shrines of roses and American flags for those lost on that day, as well as the open doors of the fire stations inviting conversations with the first responder heroes. Yet, it was the altered skyline that was the most jarring sight, the Twin Towers missing like a phantom limb.

Louise checked into the room she had booked at The Surrey, which was the most discreet of all Manhattan hotels. From there, she could fly under the radar and test out her Karen Baker identity, in preparation for traveling incognito. The hotel was built in 1926 and had served as a residence to many of New York's most eccentric celebrities including John F. Kennedy, Bette Davis, and Claudette Colbert, all of whom had taken advantage of its exceptional, discreet service. The name resonated with the feeling she had being back in Manhattan: surreal. She ordered room service and went to bed.

December 23, 2001

Louise woke up late having slept until 9:00 a.m. feeling disoriented and panicked. She sent Michael a text on her new satellite phone: FOLIAGE

He replied almost immediately: R U KIDDING ME?

She smiled and texted back: YES

WHERE ARE U?

She replied: CHOWDER IN ONE HOUR?

By the time Louise had arrived at the Grand Central Oyster Bar, Michael was already seated in their usual spot at the counter.

"Is this seat taken?" Louise expected Michael to welcome her with open arms. But instead, he did a triple take.

"Holy shit, I didn't recognize you."

"Hello, to you too."

Michael hugged her then felt her taut biceps. "Wow you're so buff." He stepped back to look. "And your hair…"

"You don't like it? I was instructed to match my passport photo." She presented it to him as if she was identifying herself.

"I like it fine," he said, peering at her eyes. "It's the makeup with the dark hair that make your eyes insanely green."

"Thanks?"

The soup chef behind the bar placed two steaming bowls in front of them.

"I took the liberty of ordering for you." Michael picked up the bowls and Louise followed him to a more private table of the bustling restaurant. They sat facing each other. "Well, this is a surprise," Michael said tasting the soup.

Louise tasted hers, and they took a moment to enjoy the comforting sense memory.

"A pleasant surprise, I hope?" Louise replied.

"Of course," Michael said.

"Weren't you expecting me? I mean, you are the one who sent Charlie, right?"

"Yes, but you really threw me." He couldn't take his eyes off her. "It's surreal to see you. How long has it been?"

"Surreal is the right word," Louise agreed. "Going on six years since being exiled to my little island."

"Right," Michael said, his telltale dimple forewarning her of impending sarcasm. "Poor you, having to move to paradise instead of witness protection."

"You never bothered to visit."

"I couldn't risk your cover," Michael said.

"You mean you couldn't risk my wrath."

"Here we go," Michael said, flagging a waiter.

"What the hell? You force me to cooperate with the FBI. Then help disappear my fiancé and send me into exile, and I'm overreacting?"

"It was for your own safety." The waiter arrived. "Two dry vodka martinis, up, olive."

"Coming right up," the waiter said, buzzing away like a bee to the next flower.

"Hiding on a remote island was perfect for you," Michael continued. "You fit right in there."

"Did I have a choice?" Louise asked.

"Yes, witness protection or The Banker's Grave. You saw those thugs after the hearings. You still know too much."

"Where's that drink?" Louise asked. On cue, the waiter placed two ice-cold martinis in front of them. They clinked glasses and sipped.

"So, you're staying for Christmas with your family?" Michael asked changing the subject.

"That's the plan," Louise said, taking another sip. "We have a lot of catching up to do. Some of which won't be pretty."

"It's not like you to hold a grudge."

"I'm not holding a grudge," Louise said. "I just don't like being treated like a leper."

"Look, it's Christmas and you're leaving soon. That doesn't give us much time to prepare you for this mission."

"As an undercover agent?" Louise pressed her hand under her bobbed hair in that retro-60s way.

"This isn't a game," he paused as if to emphasize the point, "Karen Baker."

"Humor is my defense mechanism, but I don't find you funny at all." Her emotions bubbled uncontrollably to the surface and she took another sip of courage. "There is something about this case that seems very close to home. Maybe it will help me move on…" Her lower lip quivered, and she looked down at her martini as a tear fell, making a splash. She held up her glass, clinked Michael's and drank. "Cheers to tears."

Michael had expected Louise to have a culture shock moment of release. He wished he could ease her heartbreak by telling her that Jean-Philippe wasn't in any better shape. Instead he stuck to the subject at hand.

"So, where do you want to start?" Michael asked.

"Can you tell me where to find Vladimir?"

"That I do not know. But I'm sure you won't have any trouble. My suggestion is to start in Paris. I'll book your flight."

"Speaking of Paris." Louise looked at her watch. "Time to shop." She got up and kissed him on the cheek. "See you for dinner tonight at the hotel."

"Where are you staying?"

"The Surrey, of course."

Her goal shopping for under-cover attire was to keep it simple. Versatile and interchangeable pieces that were easy to pack, all in black, from outerwear to underwear were best. Her new darker persona was a natural, finally matching her feelings about being Karen Baker, and somehow creating her. Some women couldn't pull off going from blonde to dark hair. However, something about the brunette against her fair skin and green eyes was very striking.

Soho was the obvious shopping district of choice. At the Dr. Martens boutique, she bought a pair of lace-up leather boots. Then at another shop she bought two each of jeans, skirts, and tops, and a cashmere sweater, all in black. Her classic black leather bomber jacket was irreplaceable. The thick, rugged-grained leather was indestructible, and it hugged her shape perfectly. The best clothes were the ones that one could put away for ten years to bring back when no one else was wearing it.

After shopping, Louise went to her room, freshened up and changed into some of her new clothes then went down to meet Michael in the Bar Pleiades. The décor, inspired by fashion icon Coco Chanel in the elegant lines of 1930s Art Deco, featured black and white lacquer finishes, French doors, and quilted walls. Louise looked striking in her sleek dark hair and outfit and Michael eyed her as she approached him already seated at a secluded booth.

"It really is a transformation," Michael said.

"You think I'm fooling anyone?" Louise asked.

"You already fooled me twice." The server arrived and they ordered. "Are you going to try to fool the parents, or is that a naughty thing to do before Christmas?"

Louise pondered Michael's suggestion. "That's a great idea. It would be the perfect trial run."

"Yes, it would be good practice and I happen to know where your mother will be tomorrow."

Louise's heart raced at the mention of her mother, to whom she had barely spoken in six years, much less seen. "You know where my mother will be?" she asked.

"Yes, she and my mother started meeting for lunch every Christmas Eve at the same place right here in the city." Louise found it odd that their mothers had become friends when she and Michael were a couple long ago, even though Michael was from Stanford, Connecticut, and she was from Edison Park, New Jersey. She remembered that their mothers would meet for lunch occasionally in New York City, the halfway point between the two towns, but the Christmas tradition must have been new.

"It's unlikely I'll fool my mom, but I'll give it a try. Where do they meet?"

ELEVEN

December 24, 2001

The next day, Louise sat at a corner table in Serendipity 3 restaurant, with a clear view of the entrance. Finally, the two moms, Mary and Judy, entered and the hostess seated them on the other side of the restaurant. Louise patiently spooned butterscotch sundae into her mouth and waited for the right moment. After their meal, Mary rummaged through her purse to pay the bill and dropped her car keys. Louise calmly rose and walked to their table, bent down, and picked up the keys. She handed them to Mary who looked up at her and smiled.

"Thank you, my dear."

"You're welcome." Louise realized she was wearing her new oversized black frame sunglasses. So, in fairness, she flipped them up on top of her head and gave her mother a polite close-lipped smile. Louise turned and started to walk away.

"Excuse me," Mary said. Louise stopped and turned back to the two women now both staring at her. "I'm sorry, you look like someone I know."

Judy was in equal wonderment. "She's the spitting image."

"Well," Louise said. "I hope that's a good thing."

"She sounds just like her too," Judy said.

Louise shrugged. "See you at home, Mom." Louise turned to walk away.

"Young lady, you get back here," Mary said in her Midwest accent, not loud enough to draw attention, but a dog whistle for Louise. She came back and gave them each a hug then took the seat between them. "If I wasn't so happy to see you, I'd be mad at you." Mary took out a handkerchief and dabbed her eyes. Her face turned red and her bottom lip quivered.

"I'm sorry, Mom."

"Don't try that on your father," Mary said. "You'll give him a heart attack."

"I don't think I could fool him."

"You're probably right," Mary agreed. "But, just in case, don't risk it."

"It's great to see you, Karen," Judy said, winking knowingly. Louise looked at Mary, who shrugged guiltily for telling Judy her undercover name. "What happened to your hair?" Judy asked.

Louise fiddled with the ends. "You don't like it?"

"It's lovely, but does Michael like it?" Judy was cut from the same Midwest cloth as Mary. They put up no pretense and cut through the crap.

"I wouldn't know," Louise lied.

"Then how did you find us?" Mary asked.

"Okay, you got me. Michael liked it fine." Louise checked her watch. "Oh, look at the time. Shouldn't we be getting home?" Louise got up and grabbed the check. "Let me get this." She gave Judy a kiss on the cheek. "It was great to see you, Mrs. Fuentes."

"Please don't get home before me," Mary said.

"I have a few errands to run first. See you at home."

After stopping at a drugstore for some hair coloring and checking out of the hotel, Louise wound the four-wheel drive down the snowy backroads to her family home. Except for an occasional new house and taller trees, the scenery had not changed since her childhood. Snow frosted the forest and fields like a birthday cake. The tires moaned as they forged through the snowbank then crackled on the salt in the driveway that her father had shoveled. From the other tire tracks, she could tell her mother had returned and both cars were in the garage.

She had not seen her father for almost six years, since the end of the BCCI scandal. Nervous knots contracted in her stomach, but she toughened her resolve and got out of the car. The familiar surroundings and the invigorating cold conjured fond memories as she gingerly hurried down the walkway to the back door. Having left these intemperate climes to move to Paris, vowing never to buy winter clothing again, her leather bomber jacket and boots would have to suffice. But given that she'd spent six years in temperatures that rarely got below 70 degrees, she could have been dressed like Nanook of the North and still not have been warm. Through a slightly open kitchen window, she heard the clanging of pots and pans and smelled familiar aromas. Louise kicked the doorstep, loosening the snow off her boots.

"Louise is home!" She heard Mary shout to everyone and no one. Louise opened the door, and the sudden warmth and emotions brightened her already ruddy complexion.

"Hi, Mom."

Mary hugged her. "Welcome home, Lulu."

"It's great to be back." Louise hugged her more tightly now that they were in the privacy of home. "I missed you."

"Did you miss your dear old dad or is this just a girl thing?" George Moscow entered and rubbed Louise's head, mussing up her hair with his big hand. She enveloped herself in his arms silently trying to hold back tears. George sensed her emotion and broke the tension. "How about some champagne while you tell us what happened to your hair?"

"I love it," said Mary, licking her fingers and patting down some of Louise's static fly-away wisps caused by the lack of humidity. "It reminds me of a boy I had a crush on in school."

"What's his name?" George asked. "So, I can track him down and disappear him." The pop of the cork provided a compelling yet comical sound effect.

"That's great, Mom. I remind you of a sixteen-year-old boy from the 1950s." George handed them flutes of champagne and they clinked glasses.

"Cheers, big ears," George said, rubbing her earlobe.

"Well, Lulu, I'm happy you made it home for our annual Christmas Eve dinner, but I have a lot to do." Mary put her champagne glass down and hustled to finish her cooking. "Go to your room and relax. I'll call you when the guests arrive."

"Yes, ma'am," Louise said, heading to the back door to go to her car.

"You go on up and get settled," George said. "I'll get your bags from the car."

"Thanks, George." For Louise to call him by his given name was her way of warning him things weren't back to normal yet. Louise went up to her old bedroom and splashed water on her face. She dried off with a hand towel and looked in the mirror. She would never be able to un-see the image of a teenager in a Beatnik hairstyle that her mother had evoked.

"Here's your bag." George placed her carry-on and computer bag on the chest at the foot of her bed.

"Thanks." Feeling cornered, Louise made a show of unpacking her things.

"The hair is a nice touch."

"Yes, I even fooled Mom." Louise put her reading glasses on, sat on the bed and fidgeted with some of her childhood souvenirs on the nightstand.

George sat next to her. "Thank you for trusting me enough to come out of protection and work on this investigation," he said.

Louise looked at George. "Do you trust me?"

"Not only do I trust you. I'm your biggest fan." He rubbed her earlobe between his index finger and thumb, like a worry stone, relaxing her. Then he stuck his finger in her ear pissing her off. She squirmed away and stood over him.

"After going through the trial, and then living so far away all these years, I was able to get over how you manipulated me. But now, after 9/11, everything is coming back and I'm just so angry."

He stood, now towering over her. "Good. Stay angry." He held her shoulders. "That's your superpower."

"I'm just tired," Louise said, pulling away. "Tired of worrying, tired of being angry."

George paused, not wanting to spoil the reunion with the daughter he adored. But he knew he had to be frank and to-the-point, as time was of the essence.

"This is beyond you and me," George said. "It's about national security. The dark money and the so-called black network are still out there. More than ever now as we saw with 9/11. You are the best person to see what is going on in the underworld of finance. And, dare I say, to see if they are still looking for you."

The goal of this investigation finally hit home for Louise, and she was stunned by the realization. "I'm all for helping expose those behind 9/11. But, do I understand you correctly, that I'm serving as my own bait."

"You could say that. But with a new identity and protection."

"You mean, Charlie and inspector Roblot," Louise said.

"And Michael, and me." He paused and Louise half hoped he would say Jean-Philippe, but he didn't. "You're the best we have for this," George continued. "You know the terrain. You can get in close, turn over some big rocks."

"I hate those little squirmy things under rocks."

George tried a different tactic, "Those reading glasses remind me of when you were little and used to take your magnifying glass and study all those little squirmy things. Your hair was all crazy like Albert Einstein's…"

"Stop joking, George," Louise said.

"Don't call me George," her father said.

"George! Louise!" Mary called from downstairs.

"It's not funny, George!" Louise ran down the stairs.

"What did Daddy do now?" Mary asked.

"Nothing."

"Did you take a nap, sweetheart?" Mary asked.

"I'd rather stay awake and sleep on the plane."

"Are you going somewhere fun for New Year's Eve in your new costume?" Mary asked.

"Mom, this is not a costume!"

"Why don't you go back to your crazy Einstein hair?" George said, messing up her hair.

"Yes, you have the reading glasses now too!" Mary added.

"This is the *new* me." Louise pouted, straightening her hair and taking off her glasses.

"Old or new, I love all of yous. Or should I say *vous*?" They heard the familiar sound of boots kicking the doorstep outside, followed by a knock. "Come on in!" Mary shouted.

The door protested against the cold in E flat and Michael popped his head in. "I come bearing gifts."

"Wise man," George said.

"Michael!" Mary ran over and let him in. She kissed him on the cheek and closed the door.

Michael held a bottle of wine. "1938 Côte d'Or Burgundy wine for you, Mary." Then he handed another bottle to George. "Macallan 18-Year-Old Sherry Oak Single Malt Scotch Whisky."

"That's very generous," George said. "But…"

"Before you say anything, I inherited quite a collection, and I'd love for you to have these."

"We were very sorry to hear of your father's passing," Mary said.

"He lived a long and fulfilling life. My mom doesn't really drink so she gave his whole collection to me."

"Well, cheers to your dad." George started to put the bottle away.

"But maybe we can crack that open a little later?" Michael proposed.

"No better time than the present." George took out two rock glasses and broke the seal.

Louise noticed Mary staring at the bottle of burgundy. "Mom, are you okay?"

Mary jolted. "Oh, yes. This just brings back memories."

"What memories?" George asked.

"Oh, nothing really. I'm not sure exactly, but this label seems so familiar to me."

"Do tell," Louise insisted.

Mary realized she had gotten lost in a memory that she couldn't share in this setting. She recovered. "Probably something I saw on the Rick Steve's show." Mary set the bottle down and resumed working in the kitchen.

Michael handed a Christmas card to Louise. "Here's something for you to open later."

"I don't have anything for you," Louise joked, knowing it was her plane ticket to Paris.

"Your being here is the best gift." Michael raised his glass of scotch. "Here's to Louise coming home." George and Michael clinked their glasses and sipped.

"Shall we?" George said to Michael.

"After you," Michael replied, and they disappeared into George's office.

"There they go," Mary said. "Leaving the women to toil in the kitchen without offering us anything to drink."

"Well, let's take matters into our own hands, shall we?" Louise picked up the burgundy, but Mary stopped her.

"Let's finish off the champagne and save this for a special occasion." Mary took the burgundy and placed it in the wine rack below the stairs.

"Since when are you such a wine connoisseuse?" Louise asked. "This is a side of you I've never seen."

"It was before your father and I met." Mary raised a finger to her lips shushing her.

"Enough said," Louise replied. "But I'm very intrigued."

Mary took the champagne out of the fridge and handed it to Louise. "Pour, please."

"I'll ply you with champagne until you talk." Louise refilled their glasses and they clinked. "Tchin-tchin." Louise noticed that Mary suddenly lacked the usual sparkle in her eyes. She was almost unrecognizable. "What is it,

Mom?"

"It wasn't a lost love or anything like that." Mary took a sip and closed her eyes, disturbed by the intensity of her memories and where they were flowing.

Louise noticed and steered the conversation. "Okay, never mind, Merry Christmas," Louise said, trying to bring back her smile. "Now that I have returned to civilization, I can come back to visit you any time."

Mary looked Louise squarely in the eyes. "I've been with your father long enough to know when not to ask questions. But, if you ever need anything, please know you can always come to me or your father."

"Thanks, Mom. But everything is fine." Louise shivered from a slight temperature drop and went to the living room to put another log on the fire. She noticed gifts under the Christmas tree. "What are all these presents for me doing here?"

"Those are for each year you didn't come home. I have been putting them out every Christmas, so this year you hit the jackpot."

"I still have my stuffed pig," Louise said.

"What a soft, sweet piggy that was," Mary said.

"I've taken it with me everywhere," Louise said. "But I didn't bring Squeaky this time."

"There might be a few things you'll want to take with you under the tree as well. As you can see, everything is small."

Michael and George emerged from the office.

"That smells wonderful," Michael said.

"You have a standing invitation to Christmas dinner, Michael, so you don't need to hint." Mary said.

He rolled up his sleeves. "Well then, how can I help?"

Mary took out a respectable pinot noir from the wine rack and handed it to Michael. "Open, please."

Michael pulled the cork while Louise set out four large wineglasses. Michael splashed half an ounce into one of the glasses, Louise swirled it, stuck her nose in, and inhaled deeply. She sipped, chewed, and aerated by sucking her lips into a slightly open pucker.

"It's fine," Louise said.

Every year, the Moscows hosted a Christmas Eve dinner with a traditional gathering of friends, work colleagues and any "Christmas orphans" they came across. As Michael filled the glasses, the first guests rang the doorbell and they continued the festivities. After dinner was served, and Louise had entertained the table with island stories – careful to give it a different contextual spin – everyone gathered around the tree to watch Louise open six years of presents. The slightly tipsy crowd cheered each unwrapping, as she pulled out a Hermès scarf, fleece-lined gloves with matching fleece hat, and a travel corkscrew. After everything was un-wrapped, George handed her a small box.

"I've been saving this for you."

Louise stood up and opened it. Seeing the contents sent a shock to the back of her knees like when she was a child feeding a cow and rested a handful of grass on an electric fence. She stared at the same ancient Egyptian scarab her father had given her over ten years ago.[9] The last time she had seen it was when she had entrusted it to Jean-Philippe. It had disappeared along with him.

December 26, 2001

The years had flown by, only for Louise to come full circle, once again on a flight to Paris, her scarab on the chain around her neck. *How had her father gotten the scarab back? Where had Jean-Philippe been all these years?* She had speculated many times. He must have taken on a new identity and gone deep undercover. She was sure there was some important and perilous mission that required a complete break from his past. She had never met a more courageous and compassionate man, but his air of mystery had also frustrated her. His was a chapter of her life that would continue to haunt her, the proverbial *one that got away.*

"Something to drink before takeoff?" the flight attendant asked.

"Champagne, please." The flight attendant noted her request and moved to the next row.

Louise closed her eyes and took a deep breath to start meditating, when a voice said, "Everything is connected." She opened her eyes and there was no one in the aisle seat next to her. In the row behind her a man in the aisle seat was leaning forward checking the cable of his headset. He sat back,

---

[9] From the author's first novel in the Louise Moscow series, *Foliage: An International Banking Spy Thriller*

looked at the flight attendant, and pointed to his headset. "Nothing," he said. The flight attendant gently pushed the button to increase the volume, and the man smiled, shaking his head in the affirmative.

Louise closed her eyes and slipped into a meditative state, repeating her mantra, *shiama*. But the words, *everything is connected,* echoed in her mind.

"Please fasten your seat belts." The captain's voice over the intercom broke her trance. She opened her eyes and looked at her watch. Thirty minutes had passed. "Flight attendants, prepare the cabin for takeoff."

A glass of champagne sat untouched on the small retractable tray that stuck out from her armrest. She sipped as the 5:30 p.m. flight took off, heading westward into the wind then turning back east toward Europe. In the wintery darkness she could sense the empty space where the Twin Towers used to be. The terror of seeing them toppling on television brought up old emotions. Especially the second tower, which in her mind she had anthropomorphized into it not wanting to exist alone, a projection of herself not wanting to exist alone without Jean-Philippe. But she had somehow managed to survive and was even stronger than ever.

At seven in the morning, she would arrive in Paris, on a new day in a familiar place that was full of old memories. It would be the starting point to retrace her footsteps, connect the dots, and perhaps find more meaning behind the "old haunts."

PART II
SECRETS TRAVEL FAST IN PARIS

TWELVE

December 27, 2001

With only carry-on bags, a taxi ride from Charles de Gaulle Airport had Louise in Paris by 9:00 a.m. She had booked a room at her favorite Hôtel Le Littré. It was risky going back there, but she loved it and also wanted to test her new identity with any old personnel. The hotel was four-star with elegant traditional French décor. The neighborhood was five-star, right in the middle of the Latin Quarter, and rooms with direct views of the Eiffel Tower.

"Bonjour, Madame."

"Bonjour." Louise handed her passport and a credit card to the twenty-something front-desk clerk. "I have a reservation and was hoping to check in early," she said, dusting off her French skills.

"Let me look."

"Bonjour, Madame," the hotel owner interrupted. "It will be my pleasure to check you in early." He looked discretely at her passport and back at her more than once. Even after ten years, they remembered each other but neither let on. This man's sense of discretion was on par with that of Louise's father. His masked confusion about her identity only corroborated his aptitude for placing faces with names. He had had enough experience with celebrities, diplomats, and spies to know when to stroke a guest's ego by showing recognition and when to just let the ambiguity lie.

"Voila," he said, handing her the passport, credit card, and room key. "Bon séjour, madame Baker."

"Merci. Could you send up a continental breakfast?"

"Avec plaisir," the owner said.

Louise entered her room and put her bags down. Her one indulgence in life had always been traveling well. Paying extra for comfort was worth it if one could afford it. But she offset it by self-denial in other things. On the island she lived simply and did her part to preserve nature. The island was completely off the grid, a veritable biosphere, with cistern, compost, and renewable energy sources. Her cover as a French teacher warranted a simpler lifestyle and more inconspicuous appearance too. But the hotel staff didn't know her new background story, so for now, her mysterious dark persona would serve her well.

Someone knocked, and she opened the door to let room service bring in a cart of coffee, steamed milk, orange juice, freshly baked croissants, butter, and apricot preserves. He set up the breakfast and wheeled the cart out of the room.

"Can I get you anything else?"

"No, merci." Louise tipped him and he left. She poured herself a café au lait and looked out the window at the Eiffel Tower. "Hello, old friend."

As soon as she sat down to eat, she received a call from Big Steve on her satellite phone. She could hear the heavy bass of the rap music in the background.

"It sounds like a party at 3:00 a.m. over there."

"We havin' a good time up in here."

"Don't let anyone in my bungalow, okay?" Louise said.

"Naw, they got a yacht! Just checkin' on y'all."

"I'm in Paris, safe and sound. Take care of the Tiki bar. *Je compte sur toi.*"

"You can always count on me, Lulu."

"Ciao bello."

It was just after 9:00 a.m. in Paris, but she felt the 3:00 a.m. grogginess. Still, the well-founded rule of thumb was to stay awake until local bedtime. She finished the coffee and went to shower off the layer of travel grunge. As the steady stream of water massaged her neck, the same mantra played in her mind. *Everything is connected. Just turn up the volume.* She did her hair and make-up, dressed in black and went out to explore Paris.

The doorman offered to hail her a cab, but she waived him off. It was only a 15-minute walk through Luxembourg Gardens to her destination, and she had all day. She took the scenic route, turning right off Rue de Vaugirard onto Rue d'Assas, then left on Rue de Fleurus, which led to the western gate of Luxembourg Gardens. The decomposed granite path crunched under her boots. She passed a large population of statues installed throughout the 1800s, along with a newly constructed small-scale bronze replica of Bartholdi's Statue of Liberty.

The beautiful garden hidden behind the Latin Quarter had a special serenity about it. A large octagonal pond in front of Luxembourg Palace was the centerpiece of the gardens. Miniature boats floated across the Grand Basin, tiny reminders of turbulent times of yore. Children used batons to push the toy boats hoping the breeze would get them from one bank to the other. Louise wished she could play too but she walked on until she arrived at Millésimes Wine Bar in time for lunch.

The dimly lit bar with smoke-stained walls used to be a second home to her. It now felt worlds apart from her Tiki bar, evoking a feeling of déjà vu seeing Max cooking on a hot plate, cigarette in his mouth, red wine close at hand. Louise inconspicuously took her usual seat as though nothing had changed since her last appearance. Max's nonchalant double take turned into twinkling eyes of welcome. He poured another glass of Chinon and walked over to Louise's table.

"Lulu! Ça va?" Always a man of few words, Max placed the glasses down, kissed her cheeks, and sat across from her.

"Ça va bien. Et toi?" They clinked glasses and drank.

"Ça va bien. It has been a long time," Max said in fluent English laced with a heavy Parisian dialect.

"Oh, you're speaking English now."

"Zee toureesme demands it. Plus, it can be secret language, n'est-ce pas?"

"Oui, c'est pratique," Louise agreed. Over the years, she had taught Big Steve to speak French, which was practical when they didn't want customers to understand what they were saying.

"So, Miss Lulu, eet eez nice to see you. But what happened to your hairs?"

"Tu n'aimes pas?"

"Yes, I like it. It suits you. But, why the déguisement?"

"It's not really a disguise, just a new identity."

"C'est la même chose, non?"

"Yes, it's the same thing, I guess. I'm working undercover. Je m'appelle Karen Baker."

"Enchanté, Mademoiselle Baker."

"I need your help finding Vladimir."

"Hélas, désolé, I haven't seen Vladimir since the last time I saw you."

"Merde alors."

"But I did see Greg once or twice at one of the places where I sometimes go."

"Can you tell me where?"

"It eez a very excluseeeve place. *Très difficile* to find and even more difficult to gain entry, called *Silencio*."

"Silencio," Louise repeated.

"Oui, private club owned by a famous movie director."

"Are you a member?"

"No, but zee owner loves my work," Max said with a wave of his hand indicating some of his artwork hanging on the walls. "So, he asks me to make special appearance sometimes."

"Can you take me there?"

Max indicated the wine bar with a whirl of his cigarette. "I am zee only employee here. No one goes to Silencio until at least 11:00 p.m., and I am working or home asleep by zat time. But I will make a call for you to entrée."

"No, that's okay. I'll manage," Louise said. "If you had to make a guess, what night of the week would they be at Silencio?"

"C'est tout bête," Max said. "Saturday night."

Louise gazed at the art on the walls. "Bravo, Max. Your work is beautiful. But, don't you worry about leaving it on the walls with the smoke from cooking and cigarettes?"

"Ha! That is part of my processus! Zee smoke and dust discolor my works to zee perfect patina."

Louise smiled at his endless creativity. "These are newer," she said, pointing to a few pieces that hung directly across from Max's cooking area. "They look different."

Max pointed upward. "A voice from *le ciel*."

"An angel speaking to you from heaven," Louise said, referring to her close friend and Max's wife, Diana, whom Louise believed was killed by BCCI's Black Network.[10] "Well, if you can part with any of your paintings, I'd love to buy one."

"I will give you one, *en cadeau*."

"That would be a wonderful gift. I'll be back before I leave Paris." Louise stood up to leave.

---

[10] From the author's first novel in the Louise Moscow series, *Foliage: An International Banking Spy Thriller*

Max stood up too. "D'accord, ma belle." Max gave her two cheek kisses. "À très bientôt."

"Au revoir." Louise headed back to the hotel.

Having a whole day to kill before Saturday night when she would stake out Silencio, she approached the concierge desk.

"Bonjour," Louise said.

"Bonjour, Madame. How may I help you?" The concierge was the quintessential French hospitality professional. He wore a well-tailored grey suit, pink Hermès tie, and a crisp blue Façonnable shirt. He was impeccably coiffed with short dusty brown hair just mussed up enough to give the impression that he would know the finest restaurants as well as the trendiest clubs.

"Where is the library?" Louise smiled to herself for asking, *Où est la bibliothèque?* in Freshman year high school French.

"What are you looking for?" He replied in French.

"Periodicals, reference books. It's research for my novel."

"There is an excellent library nearby. La Bibliothèque André Malraux on rue de Rennes, not far from here."

"Merci."

After a short walk, Louise entered the library and put on her reading glasses. At the entrance was a display about André Malraux. As France's Ministère of Culture in 1945, Malraux launched the innovative program to clean the blackened façades of notable French buildings, revealing the natural stone underneath.

Also interesting was that Malraux had been an outspoken supporter of the Bangladesh liberation movement during the 1971 Pakistani Civil War. Louise's former boss and founder of BCCI, Agha Hasan Abedi, had been a survivor of that war, too, but on the losing side. Abedi ended up one of millions of Mohajirs forced to immigrate to the newly formed state of Pakistan.

She searched through periodicals and books for anything she could find on Almasi, cross checking the notes from Roblot's investigation. After two hours she had a good sense of navigating the library but could no longer fight the time difference. She went back to the hotel for an early dinner and sleep.

The following day she woke up early, had breakfast and walked around Paris until the library opened. She continued her research reading and transcribing newspaper and magazine articles to her laptop, again cross checking Roblot's notes. She felt she had a solid grasp of Ekram M. Almasi's life. The photos of him reminded her of his appearance, dignified, bald, of medium height and stocky build, as well as his life. But she had found very little about his death. The man convicted of Almasi's murder was his male nurse, Todd Mayer. News reports had confirmed that the security guards never stayed at the Monte Carlo residence because of how safe the neighborhood was. There was a lot of editorial speculation that either Mayer let the killers in, or he committed the murder himself, either accidentally or intentionally.

Louise would need to make close contact with reliable sources to find out any real information.

THIRTEEN

December 29, 2001

After a day at the library, it was finally Saturday night. Louise dressed for the nightclub scene and hailed a cab.

"Please take me to the 3rd arrondissement near the Paris Bourse Stock Exchange," she said in French.

"D'accord," the cab driver agreed. "But the Bourse is now called Paris Euronext after merging with the Amsterdam, Lisbon, and Brussels exchanges in September 2000," he informed her.

"Oh, wow, I didn't know that," Louise said. She had to acknowledge to herself that the years on the island had kept her out of the loop. "Is there a café near there?"

"Yes, La Petite Bourse," he said. Louise recognized the reference of the café's name to the 1800s underground stock exchange in the novel *L'Argent* by Émile Zola. The taxi dropped her at the café on rue Montmartre just across the street from Silencio, perfect for her stakeout.

"Thank you, bonne soirée." She paid and got out.

Louise drew a few stares as she entered the bistro dressed in all black mini skirt, fishnet stockings and boots, slicked-back hair, and heavy eye make-up. The only thing missing from her goth-chic style was a cigarette, but that was something she could never quite pull off. She sat by the window and ordered a house burgundy and coq au vin. She lingered after her meal watching the non-descript entrance of Silencio, which looked more like a back-alley service door. She read the gothic novel she had in her purse, Ann Radcliffe's *The Italian*. It was hard to remember to look up from the pages every few minutes as the mysticism of the novel kept her riveted.

> *He instantly observed the agitation of her spirits, and that her purpose was not yet determined, according to his hope. But, though his mind became clouded, his countenance remained unaltered; it was*

grave and thoughtful. The sternness of his vulture-eye was, however, somewhat softened, and its lids were contracted by subtlety...

The passage was foreboding, as something caught Louise's eye, and she looked up to see Greg, her old friend and sometimes lover. He seemed to be looking right at her from across the street. His steel-blue eyes pierced through the darkness, leaving her feeling exposed under the artificial lights. Louise held the book up to obscure her face then peeked out at Greg still looking in her direction. A tap on his shoulder turned his attention to Vladimir. Bingo! Louise had struck gold. Greg took a backward glance toward her before disappearing into Silencio with the Russian that Louise wanted to reconnect with.

"L'addition, s'il vous plaît," Louise said. The waiter promptly placed a cash register tape on the table. Louise paid in Euros and gathered her things not waiting for change.

As she crossed the street, Louise observed a few people loitering hopefully in front of the club, barred by two unsympathetic bouncers. She shut down her cell phone and got into the character of a frazzled American, smiling meekly as she approached.

"Bonsoir," she said in an American accent. "S'il vous plaît, did two American gentlemen just go in by any chance?" The bouncer responded with a blank stare. "Do you speak English?"

Looking her up and down, he softened. "Who are you looking for, mademoiselle?" Even approaching forty years old she still barely looked thirty.

"Two American guys, one with silver hair. I was supposed to meet them out front at this address, but I'm late and my cell phone died." She showed him the blank cell phone screen and gave it a shake for added effect.

"Sorry, we cannot let you in if you are not a member or a guest of a member."

Louise played forlorn quiet desperation, staring down the street, shifting on her feet in the chilled late December temperatures. The bouncer was unmoved on the surface, but he spoke into his walkie-talkie to someone inside. She displayed no understanding of French, while listening to the bouncer ask if he should let a *nana* inside. He received the okay then silently opened the door and stepped aside for her to enter.

"Merci," Louise said demurely. "Bonne soirée."

The interior décor contrasted sharply from the exterior. In complete silence, she walked down the stone steps into the sixteenth century structure. It reminded Louise of the last time she had seen Jean-Philippe before descending into the Paris catacombs. The arched stone caverns and dark walls were hued by soft red and golden lighting. Silencio was a sort of successor to the Parisian salons of the seventeenth century literary circles, a famous one called Tabou for the Existentialists in Paris, another called Cabaret Voltaire for the Dadaists in Zurich.

Louise gave a faint smile to the coat check girl as she made her way down the hall to the belly of the establishment. She passed several rooms including a photo gallery, a twenty-four-seat cinema, a library, and two bar lounges...but no sign of Greg and Vladimir. She reached a lounge where a jazz trio played. Standing tall, she cat-walked in, which made her better than invisible. It made her unapproachable. All eyes were on her, but no one could see *her*. She glanced nonchalantly at the intriguing clientele but did not see her friends. She disappeared into the shadows of a darkened hallway that led to the next chamber.

Leaning against a wall she regained her composure, then redoubled her courage and resumed her search. The faint whiff of cigar and cigarette smoke indicated she was entering the *fumoir*. Knowing the smoking room was a likely place to find Greg and Vladimir, she stopped to think of a strong *moment before* and imagined herself going into a meeting with high-net-worth clients. Wearing the goth style attire heightened her sense of empowerment as she entered making no eye contact.

She walked straight to the bar and ordered. "Un cognac et un Cohiba, s'il vous plaît." She sat on a leather stool while the barman placed a snifter of cognac in front of her. She cupped the glass in her hands to warm the golden liquid, then sipped. The barman placed a heavy amber glass ashtray in front of her, snipped the end of the Cohiba, and handed it to her. She puffed as he lit it. Then she leaned back and sipped brandy, taking short puffs off the cigar and attempting smoke rings.

Feeling them watching her, Louise put the cigar down, took a satisfying sip from the glass, and turned to look directly at Greg. Just like earlier, his steel blue eyes saw straight through her disguise and he recognized her. Louise picked up her drink but left the cigar and walked over to their table in the dark corner.

"Greg. Vladimir." They stared up at her, nonplussed.

"Louise Moscow, well I'll be," Greg finally said, making Vladimir do a double take.

"Louise Moscow?" the Russian American repeated.

Louise smiled. "What? No bisous?"

Greg stood and gave Louise two cheek kisses then touched the ends of her hair. "This is a great look for you."

"Finally, someone who knows how to give a compliment." Louise turned to Vladimir whose mouth was still agape. "What do you think, Vlad?"

"Your eyes...look different..." He rose and gave her the obligatory cheek kisses.

"Nice to see you too." Louise sat.

"How long has it been?" Greg asked.

"Almost ten years since I left Paris. I'm back on business."

"Business? Is there a new Tiki bar opening in Paris?" Vladimir dead-panned.

"How comforting that you have been keeping tabs on me."

"Apparently neither of you is very difficult to find," Greg quipped.

"You must stand out like a sore thumb in the Caribbean," Vladimir said.

"Yeah, that bartender almost dropped his towel when you walked in," Greg added.

"I was just minding my own business."

"And what kind of *business* is that?" Greg asked.

"Well, I'd tell you," Louise began. "But then I'd have to kill you."

Vladimir gave a crooked smile, the kind that either looks sinister or devilishly handsome. In his case, it was somewhere in between. "What brings you here, Louise?"

"Since you asked, I'd like to talk to you, but not here. Can we meet to-morrow?"

"I'm available anytime," Greg volunteered.

"I have a flight first thing in the morning," Vladimir said.

In fluent Russian Louise said, "Я расследую убийство израильского банкира," explaining that she was investigating the murder of the 'Israeli banker' to avoid revealing the name 'Almasi' to Greg.

"Since when do you speak Russian?" asked Greg.

"What else is there to do on a private island in the middle of the Carib-bean?"

"Let's meet tomorrow morning," Vladimir interrupted. "Where are you staying?"

"Hôtel Le Littré."

"Okay, I'll meet you in the hotel café at 7:00 a.m. before my flight." She nodded yes and left it at that.

"Thanks for the offer," Greg said. "But I'll be in my bed asleep at 7:00 a.m."

"Let me buy a round of drinks and Cohibas," Louise said.

"You left your cigar at the bar," Greg pointed out.

"Yes," Louise said. "After a few puffs, I get dizzy."

"Bring it over here," Greg said. "I'll finish it."

Louise went back to the bar and ordered two more Cohibas and a round of drinks, then closed out her tab. She grabbed her partially smoked cigar from the amber glass ashtray and returned to their table.

"Here you go." Louise handed the cigar to Greg.

"Thank you, ma chère." Greg relit the cigar and took a puff. "One of the perks of living abroad, Cuban cigars are legal."

The barman brought the drinks and two more cigars. Greg purloined one of the new cigars and placed it in the breast pocket of his Edward Sexton Savile Row blazer. Vlad picked up the other cigar, rolled it between his thumb and forefinger next to his ear to listen for relative firmness and humidity, not too much, not too little crunch. He nodded his approval and handed it back to the barman who took a guillotine cutter from his vest pocket and expertly snipped off the tiny round bit of tobacco leaf that capped the end. He handed it back to Vlad, pulled a lighter from his vest pocket and held the flame as Vlad puffed until the tip glowed and retreated.

"To Max and Diana," Louise said, and they clinked glasses.

"So, we have Max to thank for this reunion?" Greg asked.

"Maybe it was sheer chance that I happened to be sitting at that café across the street when you two showed up."

Vladimir resumed the conversation with Louise in Russian. "Is it awkward, sitting with two men you have slept with?"

"Greg doesn't know that," Louise replied in Russian. "Unless you told him."

"No, I did not."

"Then, it's not awkward for me. Is it awkward for you?"

"It is impolite to speak a foreign language in mixed company," Greg cut in.

"Well," Louise said, standing. "I'm jetlagged, and it is way past my bedtime." She kissed Greg on both cheeks. Then she moved over to give Vlad two cheek kisses. "See you tomorrow."

December 30, 2001

"The new look is a nice touch." Vlad sat across from Louise. They were the only diners in the rooftop restaurant overlooking the Eiffel Tower. The waiter served them café au lait.

"It gives me a sense of anonymity." Louise added sweetener to the café au lait and drank. "Kind of like a hijab."

"So, why are you investigating the Almasi case?" Vladimir asked. "It has been resolved as far as local law enforcement are concerned."

"Some people don't like loose ends. Especially in international banking."

"Your specialty."

"I still dabble."

"Do you have a new name to go with your new look?"

"So, you know where I've been, but you don't know who I've been?"

Vladimir gave her his crooked smile. "Well, Karen Baker from Chicago, perhaps you shouldn't pull those loose ends."

"Sometimes one must unravel the knitting to get the sweater right."

"I'm afraid I can't help you with your knitting."

"What *can* you help me with?" Louise insisted.

"You like mysteries. So, I'll give you three clues."

"Three is better than none."

"Your math skills are still sharp, I see," Vladimir said in a rare display of levity. He leaned closer and held up his thumb, in the European manner of counting on fingers. "One: follow the money." He put up his index finger like a gun. "Two: speaking Russian could come in handy." He leaned back and sipped the last of his coffee. "Very impressive, by the way."

"Thanks. Studying it helped me to keep my sanity in exile. Having the occasional Russian tourists at the Tiki allowed me to practice. But mostly reading and listening to Russian radio."

Vladimir leaned forward and got in her face, almost close enough to kiss. "You are an impudent woman." He got up and placed enough Euros on the table for their coffee. He leaned over and kissed her gently on the lips reminding her of their singular sexual encounter for a steamy moment. "I've always liked that about you."

"And the third clue?"

Still looming over her, Vladimir took the drink menu and handed it to her. He pointed to one of the wines, *Pinot Noir*.

She stared at the words. "Wait, what does that mean?" But like a puff of smoke, Vladimir was gone. Irritated, she muttered to herself, "I prefer Côtes du Rhône Grenache grapes, personally."

After breakfast Louise approached the concierge desk.

"Bonjour, Madame. What are you researching today?"

"Can you tell me about pinot noir wines? Is there a particular region known for pinot noir grapes?"

"Oui, bien sûr," he said politely, although this was common knowledge to the French. "Pinot noir grapes are grown all over the world. However, the Burgundy region of France is famous for pinot noir. Specifically, in Côte-d'Or."

"That's not far from Paris, right?"

"Not far at all. It's just a couple hours south by car. It's a lovely drive through some historic French countryside too."

"Good idea." Louise handed him a twenty Euro note. "Could you find me some lodging in Côte-d'Or?"

"Avec plaisir," he said, taking the money. "What dates?"

"Arriving in Côte-d'Or in three days and staying for at least one month. Also, I would prefer a residence, not a hotel. Is that possible?"

"That is the custom in Burgundy," the concierge explained. "They have what they call *gîtes*. The residents rent out their homes, which encourages tourists to get an authentic experience."

"How charming."

"I'll put together a few options," he said. "Give me an hour?"

"Impeccable," Louise said. "Thank you."

As she returned to her room, something relating to Vladimir's third clue nagged at Louise. In her research she had read that Almasi sent his male nurse, Todd Mayer, to the town of Les Fontaines Salées in Burgundy, France, to find alternative cures for Parkinson's disease. This sounded like a connection, so Louise went back to the library.

After arriving there, she did a quick inquiry and learned that Les Fontaines Salées, meaning *salt fountains,* was an important Roman town in

Burgundy during the first century. As the name suggested, it was at the source of healing mineral springs. Before the Romans and the Celts, going back to Neolithic times, the springs were also an ancient place of worship and thought to be one of the most important healing sanctuaries in Gaul. Louise made copies of these passages and headed back to the hotel.

En route, Louise glimpsed her own reflection in a shop window and realized her all black attire might look out of place in agrarian Burgundy. She made the detour down Rue de Fleurus to the Sonia Rykiel boutique, whose retro-chic style suited Louise's teacher-turned-novelist persona. Her warm-weather blood was adjusting to the colder temperatures, but the weather would be slightly cooler in Burgundy. Louise purchased several winter items in the color palette of burgundy, ecru, and charcoal topping off the look with a black cashmere beret. Back at the hotel, Louise stopped at the concierge's desk.

"I found several gîtes for you," the concierge said showing her the lodging options.

"Which do you recommend?"

He pointed to a modern-looking apartment. "This is in the picturesque town of Beaune. You would have easy access to the region's wineries while also being central to cafés and attractions."

"Perfect. Please book it for me arriving Friday, January 4, and staying for one month."

"Avec plaisir."

Louise went to her room and plugged the laptop into the Ethernet to do more research on the Internet. After a couple hours of surfing Usenet, she freshened up and took a taxi to spend New Year's Eve with Max at Millésimes.

She arrived just in time to help Max serve customers, creating a private party atmosphere, like she did at her Tiki bar. Just before midnight, Greg walked through the door.

"I thought I'd find you here," Greg said.

"Perfect timing." Louise handed him a glass of champagne and a party hat.

Greg remarked on her modified Karen Baker look, accomplished at the boutique. "I see you're ringing in the new year with a sunnier look." His blue eyes were twinkling.

"I'll take the compliment," Louise said, clinking his glass.

Then they counted down to midnight and sang Auld Lang Syne in French, purging the crushing sense of loss as they bid good riddance to 2001.

After most of the customers had left, Louise helped clean up, then sat with Greg and drank champagne. Max brought a large black leather portfolio from behind the bar and gave it to Louise.

"Ne l'ouvre qu'au retours chez-toi."

"Okay, I won't open it until I get home. Thank you, Max."

Ever the man of few words, Max simply raised his glass toward heaven. "To Diana." They all toasted.

"May I accompany you back to your hotel?" Greg proposed, lighting his cigar and offering it to her.

"As tempting as that sounds, I have to get up early and catch a flight."

Greg resignedly raised his glass. "To the one that got away."

"To the one that got away." Louise clinked his glass. In essence, they also meant 2001.

FOURTEEN

"*We fly unto thy patronage, O Holy Mother of God. Despise not our petitions in our necessities, but deliver us from all dangers, O Ever Glorious and Blessed Virgin*," Jean-Philippe said, completing the opening prayers of the Fathers of Mercy for the ordination to the Blessed Virgin Mary on the Solemnity of Mary, Mother of God.

He had gone deeper into his undercover role as monk than even he expected. He found that he was starting to love the ritual, the self-flagellation, the sacrifice and the holy words he intoned on a daily basis. His old life was in the rearview mirror, appearing more distant with every alternative day. He knew it was still an undercover assignment, but unpredictably he felt a tiny pinpoint of light had brightened inside him, blazing stronger each day.

His sentiment was validated as a small crowd had gathered, intrigued by the group of robed monks. This spontaneous gathering of pilgrims alongside the monks, and his solemn prayer, were the quintessence of what his life had become.

"The year 2001 was a tumultuous one," Jean-Philippe continued. "Many suffered and now more than ever are reaching out to Mary Magdalene for comfort. Father Timothy has brought us to this location in Burgundy, for a very important purpose. Here at the Basilica of Saint Mary Magdalene of Vézelay we stand at the convergence of two symbolic roads, the Via Agrippa and Camino de Santiago. This Christian pilgrimage route, also known as Saint James's Way, has been a popular destination for centuries." Jean-Philippe turned to indicate the magnificent basilica with its Romanesque tower tending over the gathering.

"The word *Santiago* came from the Latin *Sancti Iacobi*, or Saint James Way." Jean-Philippe held up a scallop shell. "The scallop shell is the symbol of Saint James, who became a martyr by beheading in Jerusalem in 44 AD.

Legend holds that Saint James' disciples took his body by boat from Jerusalem to northern Spain, to be buried in what is now the city of Santiago de Compostela. A heavy storm hit the ship off the coast of Spain, and the body was lost to the ocean. Miraculously, his body washed ashore undamaged, covered in scallop shells."

Jean-Philippe pointed to the shell. "The scallop shell serves as a metaphor. The grooves in the shell, which converge at a single point, represent the various routes that pilgrims have traveled, eventually arriving at a single destination: the tomb of James in Santiago de Compostela. The shell is also a metaphor for the pilgrim. Just as the waves of the ocean wash scallop shells onto the shores of Galicia, God's hand also guides the pilgrims to Santiago." He waved a hand indicating the road. "The scallop shell can be seen frequently along the trails of Saint James Way if you look for it."

He put the crude leather twine attached to the scallop shell around his neck. The other Fathers ritualistically did the same with theirs. "Wearing a scallop shell thusly denotes that one is a traveler on the Camino de Santiago. The scallop shell also serves practical purposes for the pilgrims. The shell is the perfect size for gathering water to drink or for using as a spoon to eat." Father Timothy handed a simple stone bowl containing water to Jean-Philippe.

"Let us pray," Jean-Philippe said. Many of the gatherers bowed their heads along with the Fathers.

"*O God, who for the salvation of mankind has appointed water to be the foundation of Thy greatest sacraments, graciously hear our prayers and fill this element, which has in manifold ways been purified with Thy power and blessing so that this creature of Thine, for use in Thy mysteries, may be endowed with divine grace to drive away devils and to cast out diseases.*"

Jean-Philippe used the scallop shell to sip some of the holy water and passed it to Father Timothy who repeated the ritual and passed the bowl to the next monk.

Jean-Philippe held out his arms. "The priority of the Fathers of Mercy is to protect the Marian Shrines throughout the world. When Father Timothy chose this location before the Basilica for our annual consecration, it was not only a great symbolic gesture. It was also personally very special to me. You see, I was born right here in Vézelay. This is my hometown. As Fathers of Mercy, we must follow Mary's lead and welcome all those who have strayed. We are, all of us, whether we realize it or not, on a journey, and we choose the path. However, sometimes things can send us on another path. We must be of two minds, both vigilant and focused on our journey, but also open to the path of enlightenment. The next Jubilee Year will be Saint James' Feast Day, Sunday, July 25, 2004, and we look forward to returning to this very location on that date. Now, as we hold this sunset vigil, we look upward to the heavens."

Jean-Philippe looked skyward and the Fathers and gatherers did the same. The last of the sun's rays cast gold and magenta on the horizon, as the sky grew darker, revealing the constellations with the half-moon in a magical display.

"The Spanish name for the Milky Way is *El Camino de Santiago*. We are all stars on the pathway to enlightenment." Jean-Philippe turned to indicate the basilica. "We invite you to continue this moonlight vigil inside before the shrine and relics of Mary Magdalene." He walked to the Basilica, followed by the Fathers of Mercy and many of the crowd that had gathered. Jean-Philippe and Father Timothy stood outside the open doors to greet the gatherers.

"Father?"

Jean-Philippe recognized the voice and turned to the woman standing by him.

"Mother." He held her hands in his and she kissed them. "It's good to see you."

She was svelte, dressed all in black with wavy salt-and-pepper hair cut in a shoulder length bob. "I wanted to apologize for your father. We are proud of you and support what you are doing."

"Thank you, mother. I made a promise. Although I don't know when, as soon as my mission ends, I'll return home." He kissed her cheeks and she walked away down the cobblestone street. He looked up at the night sky just as a shooting star blazed a trail.

Louise was dressed and packed by 7:00 a.m. to catch a 9:00 a.m. flight to Monte Carlo. Before checking out of the hotel, she called Charlie Larsson back on the island with a progress report.

"Sorry to call you so late," Louise said.

"No problem, it's not even midnight here," Charlie replied.

"Tell Louise that my wife and I are staying here during the investigation for our safety," she heard Roblot say, not realizing he was on speakerphone.

"Did you hear Patrick?" Charlie asked. "We're still awake, but his wife is asleep, so you can speak freely."

"Oh, I'm glad you're there Patrick," Louise said. "I have a lead that is taking me to Burgundy, France. But first, I'm flying to Monte Carlo to do some sleuthing and have some questions about your notes from the investigation."

"Oui, j'écoute," Roblot said.

"You're notes say there were two bullets found in Ekram Almasi's body," Louise asked. "But I thought he died of smoke inhalation."

"That was the official cause of death," Roblot said. "But there was much more evidence that wasn't made public."

"To wrap the case up quickly," Louise concluded.

"Exactly," Roblot confirmed.

"That's a good place for me to start," Louise said.

"Yes," Roblot said, rifling through his copy of the notes. "There are so many inconsistencies it's hard to keep track. You should start by looking into the Criminal Police Division officer who arrived on the scene and interfered with my investigation."

"Interfered how?" Louise asked.

"Almasi's chief of security tried to give us the key to the saferoom that could have helped us save Almasi. But the CPD officer refused to take the key and instead took Almasi's chief of security into custody for questioning."

"What is that officer's name?" Louise asked, looking through the notes.

"Dupont," replied Roblot. "Paul Dupont. But I suggest you avoid speaking to him directly and raise suspicions."

"Maybe I can find someone within the local Monte Carlo police who might be willing to talk to me off the record."

"I can do better," Roblot said. "The person who hired me can give you more information. He has others like me on the inside and may have more information since the last time we spoke."

"And the man who hired you is?"

"Frédéric LaFontaine," Roblot said.

"How will I find him?"

"You do not find him. He will find you."

Louise hung up and checked out of the hotel. Before leaving, she stopped at the concierge and handed him Max's portfolio case containing the painting and a slip of paper.

"Could you ship this package to this address?"

"Avec plaisir, Madame."

"It is fragile so please send it special delivery. Just add it to my room charge."

"Express shipping?"

"No rush." She slipped him another 20 Euro note. "Merci."

Like a reimagined Grace Kelly, Louise wore the silk Hermès headscarf – one of the gifts from under the Christmas tree – as she sped along the coastal route Basse Corniche from Nice to Monte Carlo in a rented Mercedes. The seaside resorts of Saint-John Cap Ferrat and Eze-Bord-de-Mer with their elegant villas invited exploration. But Louise was on a mission, so she opened the sunroof, blasted the heat and drove on.

By noon, she had arrived at Hôtel Hermitage, parked the car with the valet and entered the lobby of the Belle Époque palace overlooking the French Riviera. Louise stopped to admire the stunning architecture. A placard informed her that Alexandre-Gustave Eiffel was the designer of the cupola in the Hôtel Hermitage's Winter Garden. Taking a detour, Louise entered the soaring stained-glass dome that delicately filtered daylight like a Tiffany lampshade. She was overwhelmed by the beauty and stood motionless staring upwards.

"A masterpiece, n'est-ce pas?"

Louise drew her eyes away from the ceiling to see an impeccably dressed Frenchman. His crystal blue eyes and alabaster skin contrasted strikingly with his dark hair. His age was anywhere from a couple years younger, to ten years older than her.

"His architecture is truly amazing," Louise said.

"Eiffel was a visionary magician of iron."

"The Eiffel Tower is my favorite place in Paris." Louise started to roll her suitcase back towards the lobby.

"Allow me." He took her bag. "Are you a guest of the hotel?"

"I hope so. Do you know where the front desk is?"

He laughed in a surprisingly jovial manner. "Certainly. Let me show you."

He escorted Louise across the lobby. "Did you know that Alexandre-Gustave Eiffel also designed the Statue of Liberty?"

"No, I didn't know that." Louise followed him through the large atrium imagining its original occupants in full attire of the era.

The man read her mind. "La Belle Époque of Western Europe from 1871 to the outbreak of World War I in 1914 coincided with the late Victorian and Edwardian eras in England and the Gilded Age in the United States. It was named La Belle Époque retroactively, in fond memory of the Golden Age before the horrors of the war. The arts flourished, especially in Paris when many masterpieces of art, literature, music, and theater gained recognition."

"Are you a historian?" Louise asked.

The man laughed giddily again as they arrived at check-in. He discretely instructed a young woman in French, then turned to Louise. "Mademoiselle Béatrice will be happy to assist you with anything you need." He handed Louise his business card.

"You are very kind." Louise read the card. It had only his name and a phone number. "Thank you, Monsieur LaFontaine." She shook his hand, and he disappeared as quickly as he had appeared. Just as Roblot had predicted, Frédéric LaFontaine had found her.

"Bonjour, Madame," Béatrice said with a friendly smile. "We have a deluxe room or a suite available. Both overlook the Monaco Harbor and the Mediterranean Sea."

"The deluxe room is fine," Louise said. "The view is the most important thing, and I won't be spending much time in the room anyway."

"May I have a passport and credit card?" Louise handed her the items and within a few minutes, Béatrice handed them back to her along with the room key. "Thank you, Madamoiselle Baker."

"Merci," Louise said with a singsong French accent.

"Merci, bon séjour!"

Louise entered her room and unpacked, then walked out onto the south-facing terrace. There was a winter chill in the air, but the Mediterranean Sea sparkled in the afternoon sun. She looked up to the right at the adjacent building where workmen on ladders were finishing the bright new mansard roof, characterized by two slopes, the upper slope almost flat and the lower slope at a very steep angle, punctured by dormer windows creating an additional floor of habitable space. This had been Almasi's penthouse home where he died in the blaze. It was also the former Republic New York Bank building, recently renamed Hong Kong and Shanghai Banking Corporation, commonly known as HSBC.

Louise cast her gaze downward and saw the terrace of the hotel's Vistamar Restaurant. The journey had made her hungry, so she headed downstairs.

"Will you be joining us for lunch?" the stunning hostess asked in French.

"Oui, merci," Louise said. "Is the terrace open?"

"Yes, of course." Louise followed the hostess who seated her on the heated terrace with panoramic views.

"Merci." Louise was immersed in the Michelin-starred Vistamar Restaurant's menu when LaFontaine set a flute of champagne down in front of her.

"Oh, merci!" Louise said. She indicated the seat next to her. "Please, join me."

LaFontaine took the seat and raised his glass of champagne. "À Votre Santé."

"À la votre," Louise said.

"You speak French very well."

"Thank you. But let's speak English in case anyone is listening," Louise said.

LaFontaine laughed loudly in an almost playful way that both startled and relaxed her. His blue eyes, although intense, also seemed innocent and unaware of their effect. "Your eye color with your hair is very *saisissante*," he said, reading her mind again.

"I was just thinking the same thing. Your eyes are striking."

LaFontaine gave another guffaw and gulped the champagne. "Shall we order? The food is fantastique." His French accent emphasized the last syllable of *fantas-TIC*.

The server came to the table and LaFontaine ordered a gourmet meal and a bottle of rosé wine from Provence.

"What brings you to Monte Carlo?" LaFontaine asked. "New Year's resolution?"

"Sort of. I am a French teacher on hiatus doing research for my first novel."

"What's your novel about?"

"I think it will be a mystery," Louise spit-balled, going along with the charade. If LaFontaine wanted to maintain an appearance of being random strangers she was ready to play the part.

"You think? You don't have the plot yet?"

"Not yet. I have been taking copious notes, but I'm waiting for inspiration." Her gaze hung over the Mediterranean Sea churning beneath manicured cliff-top gardens. It reminded Louise of the manuscript she had discovered in the hidden closet of her Paris apartment ten years ago that read like a first-hand account of the destruction of Atlantis. She vividly recalled the first passage. *Perched safely on the cliffs of Thera, high over the southern Aegean Sea, her screams of anguish were heard by no one as she witnessed the massive wave wash away an entire civilization.*[11]

LaFontaine waved a hand toward the sea. "Voilà, your inspiration!"

"Yes, this view is inspiring. But Monaco has no intrigue. No crime, no drama…"

LaFontaine let out another hilarious chortle then cozied up close to her. "Monte Carlo is a sunny place for shady people." He leaned back and elaborated. "True, Monaco is considered one of the safest cities in the world. However, there is much going on beneath the surface. In fact, we recently had a major scandal," his French accent emphasized the last syllable of *scan-DAL*.

"What happened?"

"The murder of the very prominent owner of that bank right there." LaFontaine nodded discretely toward the HSBC building.

"Murder?" Louise whispered.

"Second degree murder," LaFontaine clarified. "See the workers on that roof? A fire destroyed that entire penthouse with the owner Ekram Almasi trapped inside. The official records name Almasi's male nurse, Todd Mayer, as the sole perpetrator. He confessed to staging a break-in by stabbing himself and setting the fire in a trash bin, and then the fire burned out of control."

"Why would he do such a thing?"

"He wanted his boss to think he was a hero saving his life."

Louise surmised that LaFontaine's version of the events was consistent

---

[11] From the author's first novel in the Louise Moscow series, *Foliage: An International Banking Spy Thriller*

with that of Roblot so far.

"So, it was accidental?" Louise pressed.

"Officially, yes," LaFontaine said.

"Officially? You don't accept that explanation?"

"There are many who don't,"

"Why?" Louise asked.

"Almasi was a known paranoiac. He had converted his dressing room into a saferoom that was impenetrable. Many consider it ironic at best that Almasi and one of his other nurses would take refuge in that saferoom, that no one can get into, and a fire just happens to burn out of control."

"What a horrible way to die."

"Tragique. I watched the fire in shock from this terrace along with many other hotel guests." He motioned around where they were sitting. "Fire hoses had to be dragged through the lobby of the hotel and out to this terrace to combat the flames. It took three hours to put the fire out. The lobby was full of Monaco police dressed in riot gear and masks and carrying machine guns because they believed it was a terrorist attack. It was utter confusion." The waiter brought dessert, and LaFontaine abruptly changed the subject. "So, what are your plans in Monaco?" LaFontaine winked.

After the waiter left Louise whispered, "You're not supposed to talk about it?"

"No one talks about the case for fear of litigation. It was a top-secret investigation. Members of Almasi's nursing staff, butlers, and assistants were required to sign confidentiality agreements. Some received as much as $100,000 to refrain from speaking to journalists."

That was an interesting tidbit that Louise had read in Roblot's notes. She was happy LaFontaine had brought it up so she could get clarification.

"I suppose it's normal not to discuss an ongoing case."

"It was more than that. Almasi's death came at a particularly bad time for the principality. France had accused Monaco of being a major center for money laundering. Prince Rainier was seventy-seven years old and in poor health at the time of the murder. His son, Prince Albert, is in no hurry to get married and carry on the seven-hundred-year-old Grimaldi legacy. Princess Stephanie has had many unfortunate romantic alliances and an inappropriate marriage, making her an embarrassment. Even the beloved Princess Caroline's third husband, Prince Ernst of Hanover, is proving unpopular for his drunken behavior."

"So, Prince Rainier wanted to get the Almasi murder solved and out of the press as quickly as possible."

"Yes. Mayer is currently in the Monte Carlo prison. His lawyers are George Blot, who is a citizen of Monaco, and Donald Manasse, an American employed by the monarchy. Todd Mayer needs an Alan Dershowitz to come to his rescue."

"You mean someone capable of getting a person off on murder charges." Louise was impressed with LaFontaine's breadth of knowledge. Dershowitz was a famous American attorney whose most notable cases included getting the 1984 conviction of Claus von Bülow for the attempted murder of his wife, Sunny, overturned. He was also appellate adviser for the defense in the O. J. Simpson murder trial in 1995.

"A famous American attorney Michael Griffith has volunteered to assist with Mayer's defense. He is the attorney who represented Billy Hayes."

Billy Hayes, the name sounded familiar to Louise. "The American whose escape from a Turkish jail inspired the movie *Midnight Express*?" Louise asked.

"Bravo. Intriguing, non?" LaFontaine saw the server returning to their table. "So, what *are* your plans?"

"I was thinking of renting a boat to explore the coast."

"You know how to skipper a boat?" LaFontaine asked.

"I mean charter a boat with a captain. It seems like a great way to see the area."

LaFontaine sat up straight and gave her a military salute. "At your service."

"You have a boat?"

LaFontaine guffawed again. "Not only do I have a boat. I have *the* boat. May I take you on a sunset cruise?"

"Yes, I'd love that!" Louise said. Taking his cue to move on, they got up and gave each other double cheek kisses.

"Rendez-vous at fifteen hundred hours in the lobby."

Louise saluted him. "Aye, aye, Capitaine!"

FIFTEEN

January 1, 2002

Frédéric LaFontaine stood on the deck of the only home he'd known for the past four years. The boat was free to roam in the international waters of the world, one of the privileges of his considerable wealth. He owned the formula to a software program that had revolutionized banking, and the profit he had accumulated could take care of several generations of LaFontaines, if he would ever get around to fathering an heir.

He knew that the wealthy elite called him "Bruce Wayne" behind his back. Although it was true that he was orphaned as a child, his parents weren't killed in a dramatic robbery, just an old-fashioned automobile accident. His mission of altruism, especially exposing the corruption of oligarchs, was the other reason for his nickname. They despised him but couldn't touch him, given the nature of his financial knowledge – and most likely a backdoor access to all secrets in the electronic vaults – plus he was nimbly able to avoid having a fixed address living at sea.

Louise Moscow intrigued him, not only because she was a rare jewel of intellect and allure, but she seemed to have the same idealistic goals in regard to capitalism and wealth that he had, to even the playing field and let the best person or collective come out on top. The banking shenanigans she had exposed were part of the cheating and disruption that had collapsed the worldwide markets in the past, and both LaFontaine and Moscow instinctively fought against those who did evil in that realm.

LaFontaine had some secrets and he knew that Moscow was the person with whom he should share them, for she knew how to fit the pieces together. He made one more call to the ship's First Officer to make sure all was at the ready.

After a half hour power nap, Louise checked her hair in the mirror noticing the sprouting of blonde roots, but her fatigued eyes and wan complexion were more startling. She was making progress in the case, but at what price? She drank a whole liter of water, showered, and brushed her teeth. In front of the closet, she contemplated her options. It was safe to assume the *boat* would be more like a yacht, the kind chartered for Cannes Film Festival galas. Not to be overdressed, nor underdressed, she chose black jeans and a chunky cream cowl-necked cashmere sweater over an untucked white blouse with black wedge espadrilles. She topped off the look with a black knit watchcap, another of the small gifts from under the Christmas tree. She headed to the lobby where LaFontaine was waiting for her.

"Your ship awaits," LaFontaine said, taking Louise's arm and leading her out to the marina. They boarded a boat the likes of which Louise had never seen. It was an 85-foot motor yacht that looked like something out of a James Bond film. It had a powerful military-like exterior, suggesting superior mechanical capabilities. But the lavish interior décor was fit for the affluent locals' lifestyle. LaFontaine gave her a tour of the opulent cabins, ending in the expansive upper deck. It was well designed and tasteful with comfortable sofas, a saloon with full bar, and large windows, making it bright and spacious.

"The wide beam must make for smooth cruising," Louise said.

"You know boats," LaFontaine said.

"I read a lot."

"Then you will appreciate this." He took her to the engine room.

"Caterpillar C18 engines. What's the top speed?"

"Sixteen knots," LaFontaine said, now fully aware that she was more than a pretty face who read a lot. They went to the helm, and he maneuvered out of the harbor. As they cruised past the coastguard, several men stood at attention.

"Are they saluting you?"

A high-pitched laugh and a dismissive wave of his hand was all LaFontaine offered by way of explanation. He handed over the helm to the First Officer and they moved to the saloon where his crew worked quietly, opening champagne and putting out a platter of delicious cheeses, caviar and foie gras. They noshed and enjoyed the view of the Mediterranean coastline.

"La voila!" LaFontaine pointed to a sprawling estate. "Villa La Leopolda, Almasi's other home. That's where they filmed Grace Kelly and Cary Grant in *To Catch a Thief.*" LaFontaine poured two glasses of champagne and handed one to Louise.

"I love that movie!" They clinked glasses. "Most people assume that Alfred Hitchcock created the story. It was actually based on a 1952 novel by David Dodge."

"Speaking of writers, La Leopolda was built by American architect Ogden Codman Jr., who was close friends of Edith Wharton. They even collaborated on a book about interior design."

"You read a lot too, I see."

"I take pleasure in connecting the dots."

"Who owns the villa now?"

"Mr. Almasi's Brazilian wife, Julia Almasi. However, she has been living mostly in New York, working on her philanthropic causes. It is important to her to be well regarded at this point in her life. She had been treated quite unfairly in the French press."

"Was she a suspect?"

"Never officially. But the French were suspicious of her. She has led a fascinating and tragic life."

"Tragic? I mean, besides the murder of her husband, were there other tragedies?"

"She was wealthy before marrying Almasi. Her first husband, Mario Cohen, was an Argentinian multimillionaire. She divorced him and married a Brazilian named Alfredo Greenberg who changed his name to Freddy Monteverde. Freddy was a very rich owner of a chain of electronics stores and madly in love with Julia. After Freddy's shocking suicide, Julia inherited $230 million, which she put into the hands of Ekram Almasi."

"She must enjoy the high society lifestyle." Louise had read quite a bit about Julia Almasi's lifestyle in her research. But not much about her background, so she was interested in hearing more.

"Oui, Julia is an attention grabber with her haute-couture style and precious jewels. A diva." He emphasized the last syllable di-VA. "Ekram was the opposite, avoided the spotlight, preferred to quietly discuss financial matters with world leaders. Julia came into $3 billion after Ekram's death. Now her charitable causes are all that matter to her. She recently auctioned off $38 million in jewels for charity. In August, she donated a spectacular fountain to the restoration of Somerset House in London, with fifty-five jets of water shooting into the air, five being Ekram's lucky number."

"Five symbolizes protection in the talismanic hand." Louise blurted it out, having just run across that bit of trivia in her research.

"Ah, yes, I never made that connection before."

"So, if Almasi was so paranoid that he built himself a saferoom, why didn't he also hire security guards?"

LaFontaine's laughter rang out like a birdcall. "Almasi had a whole security team of former Mossad agents. But he didn't house them in Monte Carlo."

"Why not?"

"As a courtesy to the Monte Carlo police department, to maintain the perception that Monte Carlo was safe, the security team was housed right there, at Villa La Leopolda."

"Not a bad gig." Louise looked wistfully at the sprawling estate, its façade a blazing amber in the sunset. "So, case closed?"

"You ask the important questions." LaFontaine refilled their champagne glasses then settled into the sofa. "The short answer is yes, as far as the chief prosecutor, Daniel Graham, is concerned. Judge Patricia Rueff is serving essentially as a one-person grand jury to decide which charges Todd Mayer will face. Rueff is expected to finish her investigation and issue a report later this summer or early fall to a three-judge panel who, along with three civilian advisers, will try Todd Mayer next winter. If he is tried and convicted of arson causing death, he would face life imprisonment."

"That's the official story." The champagne was making Louise cheeky. "What couldn't you talk about at the restaurant?"

LaFontaine gave another chortle, but this time his blue eyes pierced hers as though to say, *I like your spunk*. "Yes, that's the official story. But there was speculation of a contract killing and cover-up. Mayer initially reported two masked men entered the penthouse and Almasi locked himself in the saferoom. The intruders were unable to break down the door, so they started a fire on the balcony, which spread to the roof causing Almasi and his nurse to die from smoke inhalation. There was no sign of anything having been stolen, which could indicate a contract killing."

"But could also indicate that Mayer started the fire."

"True. And, if there were attackers, according to Mayer they were armed only with knives, which should also rule out a professional contract killing."

"A contract killer would use a gun," Louise concluded. "Unless, of course, they're trying to make it look like an accident."

"You are very good at connecting the dots."

"I hate when things don't add up," Louise said.

"Well it gets stranger," LaFontaine continued. "Mayer later retracted and confessed to stabbing himself. Authorities believe that Mayer's nursing and military training made him capable of self-inflicting the non-life-threatening knife wounds, which he vehemently denied, initially. The problem with Mayer's revised testimony is that one of the knife wounds took one hundred staples to close, so it is difficult to argue they were self-inflicted."

"So, there could have been intruders armed with both knives and gun?" Louise tried to steer the conversation back to guns to try to learn more about the unreleased report of two bullet wounds found in Almasi.

"It's possible. There were many rumors of two bullets in Ekram Almasi's body. But no such information appeared in the official autopsy report that was released. A very high-level person was the source of the rumors about the bullets, but the coroner's reports were misplaced."

"*Misplaced*? As in, covered up?"

"Possibly. Apparently, the entire crime scene and investigation were irregular. For example, when Almasi's chief of security arrived on the scene, the head of the Criminal Police Division immediately took him into custody and brought him to a military prison."

LaFontaine was finally bringing up the CPD officer that Roblot had asked her look into, so she pressed him. "And that was irregular? Was he a suspect?"

"It was irregular considering that Julia Almasi told the head of the Urban Police Division that the chief of security had the only key to the saferoom. A key that could have saved Almasi."

This information was already in Roblot's notes, so Louise tried another tack. "What else was irregular?"

"The initial UPD law enforcement arrived before 5:30 a.m. But the CPD officer, believing that intruders might still be inside, insisted that the residence be searched thoroughly before permitting firefighters to enter. Firefighting efforts were impeded until 6:15 a.m. By that time the fire was raging."

That information was not in Roblot's notes. Was that something that had gone on behind his back? She decided to put a pin in it and ask Roblot about it later.

"Did anyone else see intruders?" Louise asked.

"Only Todd Mayer reported seeing them, but coincidentally the elaborate security surveillance system in the residence was inoperable on that night. Any surveillance videos that were recovered were subsequently destroyed."

"That is very suspicious, don't you think?"

"I don't think," he said ominously. "I know."

"What would the motive be for a contract killing?"

"Have you heard of the *banker's grave*?"

LaFontaine's words chilled Louise. "Something about people who know too much get killed?" she choked out.

"Precisely. The prosecution's conclusions were too simple. This was an illustrious Lebanese Jewish family. The name Almasi means diamond in Arabic. The Almasi dynasty began well over a century ago becoming the most trusted bankers of the Ottoman Empire for diamond trade between Alexandria, Aleppo, and Istanbul. When the Ottoman Empire began to unravel at the beginning of the twentieth century, Ekram's father, Joseph Almasi, opened the Joseph M. Almasi Bank in Beirut. Ekram joined the business at the age of sixteen and quickly took over the precious-gems division. In 1952 Joseph moved his base of operation to São Paulo, Brazil, opening the Banco Almasi de Investimento in 1955. Ekram was fluent in French, English, Italian, Portuguese, Arabic, and Hebrew. In Sephardic tradition, the family business should pass to the oldest son. But Ekram leapfrogged his elder brother, Elie, as the prime heir.

"By twenty-four years old, Ekram founded the Commerce Development Bank in Geneva, Switzerland, beginning with only $1 million and grew the bank to $5 billion. Almasi returned to the Americas in 1966 and founded the New York Republic Bank. In contrast to most banks, Almasi's was built on deposits rather than loans. This strategy led some to view Almasi's banks as attractive propositions for money launderers."

Louise was shocked by this last detail. "Just like the BCCI banking scandal ten years ago! Agha Hasan Abedi built his bank on deposits, rather than loans. How did Almasi track all the deposits?"

LaFontaine's laughter went up a whole octave. "The Almasis, well known for their discretion, keep all formal records in an ancient Arabic script known only to the Middle East's well-educated Sephardic communities."

"BCCI did the same thing. Only a few high-level officers kept records in Urdu," Louise said. "I'm shocked at the similarities in business practices with BCCI. But New York Republic Bank was not a third-world bank."

"On the contrary. By the mid-1980s, the New York Republic Bank was the third largest in the New York City, behind Citigroup and Chase Manhattan. Amazingly, the Almasi family had avoided scandal for centuries. But NYNB quickly became known for sending an armored car to pick up large sums of cash from its more secretive customers. At the time of Almasi's death, American customs officers were investigating Almasi's banks for laundering Colombian drug funds. Nonetheless, the prime suspects were *not* Colombian drug lords. It was the Russian *mafiya*."

"*Russian* mafiya?" Vladimir's words echoed in her ears.

"Three factors pointed to Russian mafia." LaFontaine started counting on his thumb. "First, New York Republic Bank's dealings with Russia were well documented. Under license from the U.S. government, New York Republic shipped around $10 billion of U.S. currency a year to Russian banks. Although perfectly legal, the shipments alarmed some U.S. state agencies. The problem was that about fifty Russian banks that New York Republic Bank was trading currency with were suspected of being fronts for the mafiya."

He held up his index finger making a gun. "Second, at the time of his death, Almasi was negotiating the sale of New York Republic Bank to HSBC. But the sale was stalled because the Russian accounts were frozen due to a U.S. Federal investigation into money laundering, which New York Republic Bank itself prompted by alerting the authorities to its concerns. The Russian mafia is ruthless. More than ninety bankers have been killed in Russia since the collapse of the Soviet Union in 1991. Since 1989, most of the two thousand Russian banks that were set up have collapsed. Many of the people behind them were from the black market with criminal backgrounds. So, when a Russian banker is killed, he was likely *mafiya*. Many believe a short-changed mafia chief sought revenge on Almasi."

He put up his middle finger, making a double-barreled gun. "And third, since the collapse of the Soviet Union, the French Riviera saw a sudden influx of newly wealthy Russians. The stories of Russian businessmen buying yachts and property became the gossip among salespeople up and down the coast. In the past three years, Monaco has expelled fifteen Russians suspected of illegal business practices, including a former KGB colonel.

Some lawyers have said that Monaco has adopted an unofficial policy of refusing entry to all Russians. A French investigation has shown that the *mafiya* has been laundering money through real estate, trusts, and the casino." LaFontaine paused and took a long sip of champagne.

"So, you believe it could have been Russian mafia?"

"Why do you think Almasi was so paranoid and superstitious? He was obsessed with the number five and always carried blue gemstones that ward off the evil eye because he was terrified of being kidnapped. In Mayer's initial testimony about the morning of the fire, he told Almasi's nurse that there were intruders and gave her a cell phone to call the police. When the nurse told Almasi about the intruders he locked himself and the nurse in the saferoom. When Mayer came down from the sixth-floor penthouse with knife wounds, the building receptionist called the police."

"Where was his wife Julia at that time?" Louise asked.

"Asleep."

Louise was taken aback. "In the same penthouse?"

"It is difficult to convey just how big the Almasi's flat was. But his wife's apartment was a good distance from his, and each door in between was reinforced. The whole time, the drama didn't even wake Julia. By the time the firemen had contained the fire, smoke was only beginning to affect her wing. That's when she came down and told the UPD officer, Patrick Rublot, that the head of security had the key to the saferoom. But by then it was too late."

Suddenly Louise interrupted. "What if..." Louise snapped her fingers as if trying to remember. "What was the CPD officer's name again?"

"Paul Dupont," LaFontaine replied.

"Right. What if Dupont had been preventing the firefighters from entering for two reasons? First, to give the intruders time to escape, and second, to let the fire finish off Almasi."

LaFontaine was visibly impressed with this theory. "Very interesting. The assumption has been that, there were no attackers, because no one knows how they got into the flat, or how they escaped. That's what convinced the police that it was an inside job and within two days of Almasi's death, Mayer was arrested. Shortly afterward, he confessed that he had stabbed himself, started a fire and there were no intruders. He said he was attempting to gain his boss's respect because the head nurse didn't like him, and he wanted to show his loyalty to Almasi. It was a very credible suspension of disbelief because it portrayed Mayer as trying to recreate his past."

"His past?"

"The reason Almasi hired Mayer in the first place was because Mayer found a lost camera in New York and was determined to return it to his rightful owner. That owner was Almasi. When Mayer returned the camera, Almasi was so impressed with his honesty that he hired him as a staff nurse."

"That story is damaging to Mayer. But that's exactly how the KGB functions. Creating credible lies to obfuscate the truth."

"Exactly. It corroborates the extraordinary turnaround from a story of high-financial corruption and international mafia, to a misguided attempt at a job promotion."

"It seems impossible that law enforcement would throw out so much other evidence of other suspects," Louise said.

"The judge handling the case even order a staged re-enactment. It was held in Almasi's penthouse from 10:30 at night until 5:00 in the morning. Everything exactly as it was on the night of the fire. Everyone who had been present during the hours of the fire was ordered to be at the reenactment, including Julia Almasi."

"That must have been awkward."

"Indeed. It was the first time that Julia was in the presence of Todd Mayer since Ekram's death. She had three lawyers, while Mayer was in handcuffs and a bulletproof vest. Mayer demonstrated everything including how he used a scented Howard Slatkin candle to set toilet-paper on fire in a wastebasket."

"Did the reenactment include intruders?" Louise asked.

"No, Mayer took full responsibility."

"Occam's Razor, the simplest answer is usually right."

"Except that nothing is simple. There was overwhelming evidence of other suspects. For example, Ekram and Julia Almasi had just received their Monegasque citizenship papers the day before he died. And, just days before that, shareholders had approved the sale of New York Republic Bank. Ekram had been so eager for the approval of the sale to go through that at the last minute, he lowered the price by $450 million, a totally uncharacteristic action for him to take. It broke Almasi's heart to sell his bank. He had wanted it to last forever, but he was ill, and his brother Alberto had his own bank in Brazil. Almasi's greatest disappointment was that he had never had children of his own to whom he could hand over the reins. On the day of

Almasi's funeral, the U.S. Federal Reserve approved the sale of New York Republic Bank to HSBC. Four weeks to the day after Almasi's death, the $10 billion deal was completed, netting Almasi's heirs $3 billion."

"That gives Julia motive," Louise interjected.

"That's where there are more irregularities in the case. The prosecution's official statement was that Julia Almasi was asleep and did not speak to her husband while he was in the saferoom. But, Julia's attorney, Marc Bronson, said that Ekram Almasi telephoned and spoke to Julia twice that night. Then he also spoke to his bodyguard, and to the police by phone."

"Then why didn't Almasi come out of the saferoom?" Louise asked.

"Bonnant said that everyone was still under the impression that two armed intruders were in the building, which is also why the fire brigade wasn't allowed to enter. Even stranger is that Julia said there were two fires. That corroborated witnesses who said that an incendiary device had been thrown into the penthouse."

"The intruders on the balcony in Mayer's initial testimony?" Louise took many mental notes. LaFontaine was clearly someone close to the facts of the case, but he would give them away only on his own terms.

"It would explain how the fire burned out of control," LaFontaine said. "Is that enough drama for your book?"

"More than enough." Louise played along. "But there are too many loose ends. I'd love to interview Todd Mayer."

"Hélas. The problem with that is, Mayer is not motivated to change his story again. He has been in prison now for eleven months. The prison in Monaco has forty-one cells for only twenty-two prisoners." LaFontaine swept his hand over the horizon. "He has a nice view of the Mediterranean and well-tended gardens below. On clear nights, the reflection of the moon ripples on the water. He can talk to his wife for twenty minutes once a week. Plus, he's an international hero. The Internet has been hot with indignation because of Mayer's imprisonment awaiting trial as a scapegoat for Russian money-launderers. He is referred to as a prisoner of war. But his own defense team does not see him as the victim. His priority is likely to do his time and stay alive."

Louise was overwhelmed with the information, but still needed to understand the link to Burgundy. She recalled the Fontaines Salées from her research. "What about Almasi's superstitions," she asked, hoping to keep LaFontaine talking. "What about alternative medicines?"

LaFontaine opened his eyes wide in realization. "Very astute," he said, pouring the last of the champagne into their glasses. "Almasi had progressive Parkinson's disease and wished to do everything necessary to keep himself mentally sharp. He even experimented with holistic medicines and sent Mayer all over to research cures. Mayer returned with news of a cure involving rituals performed using a lost relic."

"A relic?"

"It was said to be an ex votos of some kind."

"Ex votos?"

"A symbolic offering, usually small carvings of body parts, feet, hands, head. Mayer reportedly told Almasi of a very elusive ex votos, like a holy grail. In desperation Almasi went with Mayer to Burgundy, France on a quest for the object. But they quickly returned because Almasi became frightened."

"Burgundy, France." Louise was getting that queasy feeling in her stomach. This detail was too coincidental to ignore. "Isn't that where the pinot noir grape is grown?"

"That's correct."

"I'm not very familiar with pinot noir wine."

"You're in for a treat!" LaFontaine said. "I have been saving a wonderful Grand Cru for a special occasion."

He waved over one of his crew. "Open that bottle of the 1987 Domaine de la Romanée-Conti, s'il te plaît." The crewmember decanted the wine as LaFontaine explained. "This wine comes from the grand cru zone, that has a perfect eco-system for fine wine production known as the *miracle of Burgundy*. This is a prized pinot noir made with grapes that have been cultivated since 1241."

"Is it rare?" Louise asked nervously.

"Only 1.4 percent of Burgundy wines bear Grand Cru appellations. The second-highest classification level is Premier Cru making up 10.1 percent of total wine production. This 1987 bottle that we are decanting is worth over $10,000."

Louise's eyes opened wide as the crewmember poured the wine into large glasses. Louise and LaFontaine piously went about the tasting ritual, swirling, looking, smelling, toasting, tasting, and only then swallowing.

"I'm going to Burgundy," Louise said.

"When?"

"Tomorrow." They clinked glasses and sipped. The light claret color and the aromas of dark cherries, licorice, and exotic spices made the wine incredibly palatable.

"You can taste the explosive flavors, dry on the tongue from the acidity of the limestone soils," LaFontaine said. "It demands slow drinking." But LaFontaine seemed lost in thought.

"Are you disappointed in the wine?" Louise asked.

LaFontaine pensively took another sip. "Not disappointed at all. It's superb." He looked at Louise with his blue eyes. "Where are you staying in Burgundy?"

"I booked a gîte. It's an apartment in the center of Beaune."

"That's an excellent choice. However, may I suggest another gîte? It is a cottage on a very well-known vineyard. They grow pinot noir grapes and make a wonderful grand cru."

"That sounds ideal."

"I'll have the concierge at l'Hermitage arrange it for you," LaFontaine said. "Give me the name of your gîte, and the concierge will cancel it and book the other cottage."

"How kind of you." Louise took the paper with the gîte reservation from her bag and handed it to LaFontaine. They took another sip, and Louise closed her eyes, wishing this were the only thing she had to do.

When they headed back to the dock, the setting sun cast a glow in the evening sky. "Thank you for the tour. Are you staying at the hotel too?"

LaFontaine laughed then indicated the boat proudly. "I live aboard. A man without a country."

"Like living on a private island," Louise said.

LaFontaine gave her cheek kisses, then whispered, "Bon voyage, mademoiselle Moscow." Louise gave him a look of acknowledgement.

"I will have the concierge make the arrangements for your gîte in Burgundy. You have my coordinates."

"Thank you," Louise said. "I'll be in touch."

She went back to her hotel room, her head spinning from wine and wonder. It was impressive how LaFontaine had privileged information, including her own true identity. She entered his contact information into her phone, then texted Michael.

"FOLIAGE"

"REALLY?" Michael responded.

"YES.SEEYOUTOMORROW"

SIXTEEN

January 2, 2002

Louise woke up early and packed. She put on blue jeans and the white blouse with the cashmere sweater around her shoulders. Then she fished in her suitcase for her favorite bucket hat that she had stolen from Jean-Philippe and put it in her purse.

At check-out, Beatrice gave Louise the directions to the gîte in Burgundy that LaFontaine had arranged. Then Louise left her suitcase with the valet, handing him five Euros to watch her car for a few minutes. She grabbed the road map from the glove compartment and walked over to the newly minted HSBC building where Almasi's penthouse had been. She ducked into a cobblestone lane and rolled her jeans up to the ankles, put the bucket hat on and unfolded the road map. As she approached the HSBC building's residential entrance, an armed security guard eyed her but then resumed his patrol. He turned away and Louise wandered nonchalantly through the door and approached the receptionist.

"Well, these are some fancy digs," Louise said, gazing from floor to ceiling. "Is this the HSBC bank?"

The receptionist of a certain age was used to greeting confused tourists entering into the wrong door. "The banque is next door, mademoiselle. This is a résidence," she said politely in English with a French accent.

"Oh, the residence!" Louise moved closer to whisper. "You mean the place where that young man started that horrible fire? You would never know it. It's just gleaming! I could not believe that young man would do such a thing. An American no less! So tragic. Seems a little extreme to me. If you want to get a promotion, do a good job. Don't go stabbin' yourself and start the place ablaze!" Louise took out the camera pen Charlie had given her and began to write on the map.

The receptionist became flustered. "Mais…"

"What was that poor man's name again? Agassi?" She clicked the pen taking a photo of the foyer careful to capture the security cameras. Then she clicked an image of the distraught receptionist. "Oh, I am sorry my dear, bringing up such a subject." The receptionist blushed and her lip quivered. "Are you all right?" Louise clicked the pen twice to initiate video recording.

The receptionist began babbling in French. "They made a liar of me! I almost lost my job of twenty years. I am trained in emergency medicine. That knife wound could *not* have been self-inflicted. It's not possible that Monsieur Mayer stabbed himself." Not only did Louise understand what she said, she got it on video.

"Well, I'm sorry to have upset you. Have a nice day." Louise clicked the pen again stopping the recording just as the security guard walked in. Louise folded the map and hurried toward the exit, nodding to the security guard while snapping another photo. "Bye bye, now."

Louise drove back to Nice and caught the first flight to New York. With the time change she landed at almost the same time she took off. In a rented four-wheel drive SUV, Louise made her way up the Hudson River toward the Catskill Mountains. She got out and walked down the snowy path to the reservoir where Michael waited, arms folded, toe tapping, next to a snowbound rowboat.

"Aren't we a little old for this?"

"Speak for yourself." Louise pointed to his temple. "The gray looks good on you."

The compliment activated his dimples. "You like that?"

"It's too cold out here." Louise shivered. "Let's go back to my car." They crunched back up the path, reminding her of their college days together.

Michael read her mind. "Remember that time we drove all the way up to Niagara Falls, then all the way down to Pennsylvania to see the Liberty Bell?"

"You forgot, *in the pouring rain*. Taking a road trip in the middle of a deluge? No plan, just drive."

"That was the point. We didn't plan it. We just did it."

"You mean like today?" Louise unlocked the car and they got in. She revved the engine, encouraging it to warm up.

"Payback is a bitch," Michael said.

"Speaking of payback, I need to pick your brain."

"Nothing classified."

"You owe me."

"Like I said, payback is a bitch."

"You got that right," Louise said. "What do you know about the Almasi murder? Was there a cover-up?"

"That's a question for your friend Vladimir."

"Believe me I've already dipped into that well."

"Any buckets of wisdom?"

"Barely a drop. He gave me some vague but potentially important leads. I'm going to spend some time in Burgundy and do a little digging around."

Michael interrupted her. "Burgundy? The Burgundy in France?" Louise replied with an eye roll. He continued, ignoring her. "Okay, what does Burgundy – in France – have to do with the death of a banker in Monte Carlo?"

"You tell me."

"Look," Michael said. "You know the FBI doesn't have the same access to international Intel the CIA does. But we are very interested in this case, if for no other reason than how it ties to Almasi's banks in the U.S. I am not sure what your dad expects you to uncover in this investigation. But I imagine it's banking related."

"So, if you could tell me one thing on a need-to-know basis, what would it be?"

"All I can tell you is what you *don't* need to know. We have looked extensively into Almasi's banks in the U.S. and found nothing nefarious. Also, Almasi's wife Julia, her attorney Marc Bronson, Almasi's chief of security Jordan Coen, and Almasi's brothers are all clean and cleared of the murder. The Monte Carlo police are another issue. Coen made efforts to give the police the key to the saferoom. Not only did the police refuse to use the key, they arrested Coen."

"So, it's possible that someone with the Monégasque police were involved in a cover-up?"

"Let's just say that the Prince of Monaco wanted this resolved immediately and any loose ends were tidied up."

"So, Mayer was the perfect scapegoat, who 'acted alone.'"

"Correct. Any attempt to expand the case beyond involuntary manslaughter by Mayer was thwarted by the authorities. His best chance now is to serve out whatever sentence they hand to him and stay alive."

"Okay, that corroborates my initial investigation in Monaco. For the next month or so, I'll be working undercover in Burgundy." Louise stopped and took a breath.

"Is there something else?" Michael asked, sensing that this meeting was not the only reason she had made the trip.

"You can't tell my father I asked."

"Asked what?"

"Is there anything I should know about my mother's past?"

"Mary? Not that I know of. Why do you ask?"

"Never mind."

Louise watched her mom move around the kitchen with a master chef's ease.

"How long will you be here, Lulu?" Mary asked.

"I head back tomorrow."

"Back to where?"

"Burgundy, France."

George Moscow interrupted the conversation. "My two favorite girls, together again." He tried to give Louise a hug, but she turned away. The unconditional love from the first man in her life had instilled in her a remarkable self-confidence. He had been a tough man to live up to, but he had always played fair, up until he broke her trust with the BCCI case. Now that she was getting a sense of how dangerous the Almasi case could become, she was becoming guarded. "Louise, may I speak to you in my office?"

She followed George into his den. But, like a kid in the principal's office, she sat in front of his desk with her arms folded head down. George remained standing in a position of dominance behind the desk.

"Louise, I'm not letting you leave until we hash this out."

"You can't keep me here." Louise got up and took a step toward the door. George moved quickly and caught her by the arm. She turned reluctantly and faced him.

He lifted her chin with a finger. "I'll never understand where you got your temper."

"It's not in my nature to stand by quietly in the face of obvious corruption and injustice, the way you can."

"You believe I'm corrupt and unjust?" His voice rose a bit above normal conversation volume.

Sensing his uncharacteristic change in tone, Louise backed down. "No, of course not. I'm just not like you. If I see something wrong, I have to speak out. You are able to keep secrets. Where did that come from? Your father? Because he wrote about politics for *The New York Times*?" Tears of frustration began to flood her eyes.

"No, because I became a New York detective." Softening the situation, George wrapped her in his familiar bear hug that she didn't resist." We are not that different. Your determination is what got you where you are. My determination is very similar. I have goals and dreams just like you do. Mine require a different set of skills than yours do. Like I said before, your anger is your superpower. You work better under pressure. I work better in a pressure cooker."

"Your lid is squeezed on so tight, but you never explode."

"Your mother is my release valve." Louise laughed then cried and hugged her dad. "I'm sorry about putting you in that position with BCCI," George said. "But I'm so proud of how well you handled it."

This simple statement is what Louise had craved to hear, without knowing it. All through the trial and her exile to paradise, her father had kept the face of a by-the-book, world-weary detective. She realized at that moment that his attitude was designed to ultimately protect her and allow her to understand how to survive it on her own. There were a million things to say but she could only manage, "You've never spoken to me this way before. Thank you."

George tenderly kissed her on the top of the head and playfully squeezed her taut biceps. "You're so buff. Have you been working out?"

Louise giggled. "That tickles!"

"Louise! George!"

They walked out to find Mary setting the table. "What are you two conniving?"

"Just business."

"Business in Burgundy, France?" Mary pouted, strangely emphasizing the words Burgundy and France. Unlike George, Mary couldn't hide her feelings. The harder she tried, the more transparent she became.

Louise was becoming an expert on adjusting conversations. "Aren't you happy I'm back so soon, Mom?" she chirped.

"No. I mean yes." Mary was stumbling as if gathering her thoughts. "Maybe. I mean, of course. It's just that, maybe you shouldn't go to Burgundy. Stay here with me." Mary took a bottle of red wine from the rack under the stairs. "I have plenty of pinot noir here."

George took the bottle from Mary and uncorked it. He looked at the label, raising an eyebrow at the vintage. "Let's allow this beauty to breathe for a moment, shall we?" George poured the wine into a decanter.

"Mom, that's the expensive bottle that Michael gave you."

"Oops. We better invite him over to share it with us," Mary said.

"I'll give him a call." George went to his office leaving the two women alone.

Mary followed her husband to the hallway and waited until she heard his office door close. She turned and looked Louise straight in the eyes. "I do not want you going to Burgundy, France."

Those two words again, practically spit at her. Louise detected a change in her mother, as if she had become an instant stranger. She decided to press the issue.

"Mother, this is exactly why I came back so soon. You mentioned Burgundy, and now I'm going there. What aren't you telling me?"

Mary's reply chilled her. "There are some mysteries even you can't solve."

"Like what?" Louise countered. "Does Dad know?"

Mary gave her a look of defiance that Louise had never seen before. "There is nothing *to* know," she said in a tone of resignation. Louise was reeling. In her whole life, she'd never known her mother to capitulate to any anger or pettiness. She was Louise's mainstay and like the yarest ship on the sea. She had always been agile, responsive, and true to her course.

"Mom, if this is upsetting you so much, you have to tell me what it is all about."

"Michael is on his way," George announced, returning to the kitchen. He immediately realized he had walked in on something. "What's wrong?"

Mary's look silenced Louise. "Just girl stuff," Louise lied.

"Say no more." George turned on his heel and walked out. "Just be ready for guy stuff when Michael gets here." Both women waited until they knew he was out of earshot.

"Mom, you have to talk to me," Louise insisted.

Mary busied herself in the kitchen. "Just forget it."

"You can't keep this to yourself." Louise shocked Mary by grabbing her by the shoulders. "How long have you been hiding whatever this is?" Mary broke her daughter's grip and would not be swayed. Louise shot back, "Mother, if there's something you need to tell me, I expect you to do so before I go back to France."

Mary's eyes widened seeing the look on Louise's face, knowing all too well what it meant. She had dealt with it since her daughter was two years old. Then, in the midst of the standoff, there was a knock at the door.

"It's open!" Mary shouted, a bit too eagerly.

Michael delivered himself inside like a customized teddy bear. He was dancing, half from the cold, and half from greeting them with a magician's hands, as if to say, *Ta dah, I'm here*! But his charm was lost on the two women.

"Did I come at a bad time?" he asked, reversing the mood.

"Perfect timing!" Mary said, overemphatically. "Come in, give me your coat. We decanted your wonderful pinot noir."

George joined in, remarking on how quickly their guest had arrived. "That was fast," he said shaking Michael's hand.

"I was on the road when you called," Michael offered. "You forget that we live in an age where mobile phones mean mobility." He was trying to lighten the heavy mood he had walked in on.

In the meantime, Mary had put four red wineglasses on the counter and George poured. The four of them raised their glasses.

"What's the occasion?" Michael asked.

"Louise is home," Mary said airily. "May she never leave." They all clinked and drank.

"Delicious wine," Louise said. "Thank you, Michael."

"Pinot noir," Mary said.

"From Burgundy," Louise said.

"In France," Mary countered.

Michael and George watched in silence the tense back-and-forth between Louise and Mary.

Then Michael took it upon himself to break the tension. "Louise and I were just talking about Burgun…"

George put a hand on Michael's shoulder. "Girl stuff," he said shutting it down.

Suddenly the niceties of the visit were steered back by Mary. "Will you join us for dinner, Michael?"

"I wouldn't miss it for the world."

Louise said the first thing that came to her mind, like an eager child. "I'll set the table."

"I'll help," Michael added, his voice cracking like a teenager.

Mary took a big gulp of the pinot noir. "We might need to open another bottle."

George eyed her warily, but dutifully went to the wine rack. "Why not?" He added hopefully, "It's a special occasion."

They sat down to dinner, and fifteen minutes into the meal, Mary was on her third glass of wine. The mood became awkward. Mary was definitely over-serving herself and, combined with her earlier uncharacteristic tone, was increasingly unrecognizable. A sudden memory came to Louise of seeing her mother in a similar state only one other time. When she was sixteen and buying her first car, Mary had accompanied her to the dealership where a salesman tried to sucker Louise into a bad deal. Mary knew from experience what the salesman was up to and Louise sat wide-eyed as Mary berated the man.

"You should be ashamed. Let's go, Louise." Then Mary rose and walked straight out the door followed by Louise, with the manager, talking fast in a futile effort to work something out. Louise recalled the shock of seeing her mother in a different light, and how she had learned her greatest lesson in business that day: Walk away. Was Mary trying to tell her to do the same in regard to Burgundy?

"Delicious dinner," Michael said.

"Thanks," Mary replied. "Again."

"So, Louise," Michael said, trying to get the conversation going. "You leave tomorrow for France?"

"Yes," Mary said, draining the rest of her wineglass, then tipsily mumbling, "To Burgundy, France."

Michael tried to normalize the odd statement. "Oh, right, you mentioned that. How's the weather there this time of year?"

Louise's reply was even more mundane. "It shouldn't be too cold. Even though it's winter, Europe benefits from the warm air off the Atlantic."

"Right," Michael agreed. "The North Atlantic drift."

Something about the phrase "North Atlantic Drift" revived Mary back into the conversation. "Michael, why don't you join Louise on her trip to Burgundy? She could use male protection."

"Mom! Male protection? What is this, the 1950s?"

"I would love to be Louise's bodyguard, Mary," Michael said. "But who would protect me from Louise?"

After a moment, Mary suddenly started laughing and went into an uncontrollable and wine-fueled fit of the giggles. The rest of the table joined in, instantly breaking the latest strange interlude.

"Oh, Michael, you are the dearest thing." As Mary's laughter waned, her face reddened, and tears welled in her eyes. "Who wants dessert?" Mary got up from the table and took her dish to the sink. The three sitting at table looked at each other with relief. No one pushed Mary any further and they enjoyed dessert over pleasant conversation.

After Michael said goodbye and George had gone to bed, Louise filled a glass of water and went to join her mom in front of the fire. After her earlier state, Louise was ready to back down from insisting that Mary tell her what had happened in Burgundy.

"Aren't you going to bed, Mom?"

Mary sat on the sofa glowering in front of the fireplace, the light from which seemed to animate her features. She was sixty years old, but with her short, wavy, dishwater brown hair framing her face she could have been sixteen.

"You go on ahead," Mary said. "I'll just be a minute."

Louise remained standing, the only sound was a clock, ticking as if time and memory were moving backward. Mary looked up at her daughter and sensed that now was the right moment for some truth-telling.

"Your father doesn't know," Mary began. "I was a freshman in college."

Louise steadied her breathing and sat on the sofa next to Mary. She had to relax her eyes consciously, so they would not bulge while she listened.

"I had big plans," Mary continued. "I was going to school to be a simultaneous translator for UNESCO. Remember Louise? Just like Audrey Hepburn in the movie *Charade* with Cary Grant." She laughed. "I guess I also wanted to meet my Cary Grant." Mary looked directly at Louise and her momentary lightness turned back to a dark glare. "If I hadn't had such big ambitions, it never would have happened."

Louise held her breath, *what the hell was she talking about?* But she remained silent, afraid that if she spoke Mary would stop talking. Mary's face was suddenly ashen like granite, the fire reflecting off her now stony features.

"It all went terribly wrong!" her mother managed to finally say. "I was so smug, with my French major and translator internship in Dijon." She paused to take a breath. "But those people were monsters!"

"Who were monsters, mom, who?" Louise managed to say.

Now Mary was babbling almost incoherently. "What they did to those girls! It was a miracle I escaped. I tried to tell someone, anyone, but I also thought no one would believe me..." Suddenly the memories were crushing her, and she brought her fists to her eyes as if to smother her thoughts. She shook from inaudible sobs that squeaked out in chirps.

Louise held her mom, reversing roles in applying soothing embrace and security. "Everything is going to be okay."

Mary's tears flowed freely now. Her anguish had been released. She took comfort in her daughter's arms and rocked like a child who felt warm and safe. Allowing herself a purging sigh, Mary started speaking softly and told Louise the whole story of that long-ago summer. The daughter finally understood why her mother associated the region with danger and dread, adding yet another layer to an increasingly complex – and now personal – series of investigations. And it all seemed to be waiting for Louise in Burgundy. In France.

SEVENTEEN

January 4, 2002

The overnight flight had Louise in Paris and resuming her adventure by 7 a.m., albeit with the time change, on the following day. She sped off in a rental car from Charles de Gaulle Airport – she'd driven so much in the last month she was feeling her inner Parisian driver return – and headed toward Burgundy. Forty minutes into the drive she saw a sign for the fabled Forest of Fontainebleau and its prehistoric cave drawings. She had always been intrigued by the spooky tales of the ancient forest. Also, when she was in college during a summer program in the south of France, she had had to choose between an excursion to the prehistoric cave writings of Chauvet-Pont-d'Arc and a trip to Basque Country in the Pyrénées Mountains. She had chosen the latter, but after hearing about the prehistoric drawings from her classmates, she had regretted missing the caves. So, in a sudden sense of adventure and self-inflicted dépaysement,[12] she took the opportunity to rectify a bit of her past and drove into the woods of giant elms and pines.

She arrived at the famous artists' village of Barbizon and drove down the long Grand Rue, which wound for about a mile past ancient stone houses where Jean-François Millet and Théodore Rousseau used to drink and paint. Most of the historic buildings were now converted into art galleries, inns and cafés. She stopped at a café where she found a brochure about the town and the surrounding forest. The owner of the café drew her a map and she headed out to explore the trails. She parked where the café owner had indicated and read the brochure. The Forest of Fontainebleau was sixty-five square miles of woodlands with mysterious gorges and rock formations, several of which she could see from the side of the road. According to the brochure, the geological past of the forest remained a mystery. Until the 1830s it was known only as one enormous white spot on the map of France.

---

[12] The feeling one gets of not being in one's own country.

No one had attempted to enter the ancient *Forest of Heather*. Even criminals who had escaped the royal prisons were deterred by legends of mysterious inhabitants who haunted the forest. According to lore, the *Black Hunter* – accompanied by a pack of vicious dogs – guarded the forest, frightening away visitors, leaving the flora and fauna untouched.

She got out and started up the nearest beaten path. But the mystery of the caves was soon heightened by the difficulty in finding them. The forest canopy darkened the trail, but she persevered and finally found the large boulders engraved with busts of Millet and Rousseau. The hike turned spookier as she entered the area of the cave drawings. Plaques in the Neolithic Goddess Cave described the cave writings dated about 11,700 years ago from the third interglacial stage of the Pleistocene through the Iron Age. Some drawings struck a remarkable resemblance to medieval art. Other patterns were reminiscent of the designs found at Ireland's famous Neolithic site at Newgrange. Some drawings looked similar to those left by the Bronze Age Hittite civilization near Ukraine.

In the damp morning air, she heard a branch snap nearby, breaking the silence and sending a chill over her whole body. It might have been a deer, but something told her not to linger. She hurried back to her car and resumed her drive to Burgundy. After an hour she arrived in the pinot noir wine region.

Louise reached a crossroads near Auxerre with the town of Chablis to the East on her left, and Les Fontaines Salées on her right. She continued south toward the historic town of Beaune, passing a small billboard advertising the annual Film Noir Festival. A few miles before Beaune, she turned right and continued down a winding stretch marked by signs indicating she was on *La Routes des Grand Crus*. She reached the village of Pommard and turned onto Ruelle Richebourg then continued to the rental cottage LaFontaine had arranged for her. It was a newly refurbished farmhouse on a small nineteenth century vineyard. The setting seemed peaceful and authentic, ideal for her undercover status. Louise parked and left her bags in the car. The sign on the front door of the large main structure read *Ouvert* so she entered. A cherubic boy played with a wooden train near a towering Christmas tree.

"Attention, mon ange," said his mother who appeared to be in her mid-thirties. She gently moved him away from the tree as he giggled. She smiled upon seeing Louise, her large brown eyes and angelic face matching that of the child.

"Bonjour! Bienvenue," she said in singsong French.

"Bonjour! Je m'appelle Karen Baker." The child's giant eyes gazed at her from under a mop of blond hair and he smiled shyly. Louise continued speaking in French. "I booked your cottage?"

"It's nice to meet you. My name is Magali." She went to an antique desk and handed a form to Louise. "Please fill this out. The cottage is ready, so you can check in right away."

"Génial, merci."

"You speak French very well. Are you here on holiday?"

"Actually, I'm on hiatus to write a novel." Louise gave her the new passport.

"A novel! What is it about?"

"It's a mystery novel, I think."

"Your mystery is a mystery." They laughed and Magali looked at the paperwork. "Americaine! Maybe you will write the Great American Novel?"

"I'll settle for an adequate French novel. I'm a French teacher by profession."

"Ah, mystery solved about why you speak French so well." They laughed again and Louise realized Magali was very perceptive. "Allez, mon petit chou. Let's show our new friend her lodgings." The little boy walked over and took Louise by the hand. "He likes you!" Magali said.

"Comment t'appelles-tu?" Louise asked the boy's name.

"Je m'appelle Luke!"

"Bonjour, Luke!" They walked outside, the gravel crunching as they made their way to Louise's rental car and she opened the trunk to get her bags.

"Would you like help?" Magali asked.

"No, thank you. I travel light."

"Yes, it looks like it!" They walked to the enchanting stone cottage with periwinkle shutters. "This used to be a farmhouse, but we updated everything so you will be very comfortable," Magali said. "You must return in the summer for the sunflowers." She pointed to some pots containing with yellow flowers. "Fortunately, these winter jasmines love the cold."

Magali opened the door and the wood burning in the fireplace gave Louise warm chills. "This morning, I turned on the heat and started the fire for you. There's plenty more firewood."

"This is exquisite. Thank you."

Magali pointed toward the kitchenette. "You have everything you need. Here's a welcome basket with tea bags, water, even some snacks. After you've settled in, please feel free to come for a wine tasting."

"I'd love to. Thank you. I'll see you both soon."

Magali went to the door, but little Luke stood looking up at Louise with a big pucker on his lips and his cheeks puffed out. "Ah! He wants some bisous."

Louise gave him a kiss on each cheek, but he remained there puckered up. Louise was confused.

"We do four kisses here," Magali explained pointing to her cheeks. Louise repeated with another kiss on each cheek. Luke was satisfied and they left.

Wasting no time, Louise plopped onto the down-filled chair in front of the fireplace. She took out the map of France and began plotting her itinerary. First, she would explore Les Fontaines Salées or the *Salt Springs* where Almasi had sent Todd Mayer to research holistic cures. She cross-checked her notes from the library and learned that it was located at the geological crossing of two fault lines that allowed deep wells to rise across the salt and granite rocks. The resulting spring water with temperatures of about 60 degrees was very mineralized and slightly radioactive.

The first resourcing of the waters was done around 3,000 BC during the Neolithic Stone Age. The area had become a religious cult center where the devout and ailing would flock to be blessed at the source, bringing offerings, some of which were on display in the museum. What remained now were ancient ruins, with no access to the medicinal benefits of the springs.

She stretched out on the bed and drifted off to sleep. The unfamiliar ring of her new cell phone woke her.

"Allô?"

"Bonjour, ma belle!"

"Big Steve, is everything okay?"

"All good. Did I wake you?"

"Yes. I must have dozed off."

"Okay, go back to sleep. Just checkin' up on y'all."

"How's it going over there?"

"There's a party going on up in here." Big Steve turned up the music, and Louise could hear whoops from the customers.

"Sounds like fun."

"Well, get yo' ass back home!"

"I hope to soon. By the way, there's a package arriving so keep an eye out for it." She related the events of the last couple weeks, leaving out the details about her mother, to satisfy Big Steve's curiosity. They truly missed each other. She had to end the conversation, as not to get too emotional. "Don't forget, watch for that package. Ciao."

"I'd rather y'all arrive back here than the package, but I will keep my eyes peeled. Ciao, bella."

She hung up and noticed the cell phone battery had run low. She took the charger and adapter out of her bag and plugged it in. She observed that, as these phones were becoming more commonplace, this "plugging in" would become a ritual, like the morning toilette. She unpacked, brushed her teeth, and checked her hair. She put on the faux fur coat and new boots she had picked up at the Sonia Rykiel boutique in Paris and walked to the house for a wine tasting.

"Bonjour!" Louise said to no one and everyone.

"Bonjour, Miss Karen!" Magali replied. "Bien installée?"

"Yes, I'm all settled in nicely," Louise said in French. "I even took a little nap."

"Would you like to try our Premier Cru?" Magali offered. "I was just about to taste it."

"I won't say no to a Premier Cru."

Magali poured the plum-red liquid into a large wineglass, and Louise held it up toward the window, the truest light source. Magali spontaneously went into her wine tasting spiel. "Pommard is famous partly because the name was easy for foreigners to pronounce. We produce only red wine, 130,000 cases per year, a third of which was Premier Cru, making it the second biggest area of production, after Beaune.

"It has such a lovely clear light color."

"Oh, excuse me, it is habitude to give the description. But you sound like you know wines."

"I took a wine tasting course before this trip, but I'm definitely an amateur. Please, go on."

Magali surprised her with the depth of additional information. "The lovely clear color you mentioned is because of the thin skins and low levels of phenolic compounds of pinot noir grapes. That makes pinot noir mostly medium-bodied, low-tannin wines that can often go through *dumb phases.*"

"Dumb phases?" Louise thought perhaps her understanding of French was lacking.

"Yes, *dumb*! It has uneven and unpredictable aging, like an adolescent. It is a difficult variety to cultivate and transform into wine. *Pinot* or *pine* alludes to the grapes having tightly clustered, pinecone-shaped bunches. *Noir* as you know means *black,* the French term for the red grape. The pinot noir grapes' tendency to grow in tightly packed clusters makes them susceptible to rot and requires diligent canopy management."

"Thank you. Your knowledge of wine is impressive." Louise plunged her nose into the glass and inhaled deeply. "Ooh, there's a lot going on there. Very complex."

"Bravo," Magali agreed, as if praising her son. "When it is young, the wine made from pinot noir grapes tends to have red fruit aromas of cherries, raspberries, and strawberries. But as the wines age, pinots have the potential to develop vegetal and barnyard aromas that can contribute to the complexity of the wine."

Louise contemplated the term "barnyard odors" as she took a sip, aerated it in her mouth and then chewed. Magali joined her in the ritual and Louise followed her lead by swallowing as opposed to spitting it out.

"Thank God you drank it," Louise said. "I didn't want to spit it out. It's delicious."

"I'm glad you like it. Our family is very lucky to have a Premier Cru. It has taken many decades to acquire these hectares."

"You are the viticulturist?"

"Yes, my brother grows the vines and I develop the wine formulation." As if on cue, the front door opened, and Luke squealed.

"Oncle Matthieu!"

"Bonjour, les enfants!" A tall, burly farmer type stomped his feet and beat his shoulders against chills brought on by the rush of warmth. He gave a primal grunt. Little Luke imitated the grunt with a teeny growl, and even Magali joined in.

"Les Trois Ours," Louise said, drawing Matthieu's attention like Goldilocks.

"This is Karen, our new lodger," Magali said.

A spectrum of expressions crossed Matthieu's face, from alarm to confusion, ending with a welcoming smile. Louise made a mental note of the odd countenances.

"Bonjour! Bienvenue!" he said, shaking her hand. "I'm Matthieu."

"Bonjour, it's nice to meet you, *uncle* Matthieu."

His unaffected demeanor belied his matinee-idol chiseled jawline, blue eyes, grey-blond hair, and overpowering physique. A French Joel McCrea. Louise stared up at him far too long.

"You are just in time to join us in the tasting," Magali said.

"Ah! You are tasting the Premier Cru."

Magali poured him a glass and, holding the glasses by the stems they clinked, striking the tops for maximum chime. At the same moment, Luke banged together two of his trains in a head-on collision making a verbal crashing sound effect.

"Alors, les racines?" Magali asked Matthieu. Louise realized they were talking business about the vine roots, so she put down her glass and went over to play with Luke.

"The trains went boom!" Louise said in French.

"Oui, boom!" Luke repeated, crashing the trains together.

"May I try?" Luke gave one of the trains to Louise and they reared the trains back then crashed them together in slow-motion, lifting them up into the air, making explosion sounds.

"C'est la catastrophe," Magali huffed.

"La catastrophe!" echoed Luke. In any language, Louise suddenly felt she was eavesdropping. Apparently, there was a catastrophe at the vineyard.

"Allez, Luke, dodo," Magali said, picking the boy up. "Naptime so I can prepare dinner, mon amour." Magali took Luke to his bedroom leaving Louise alone with Matthieu.

Louise resumed sipping her wine at a loss for conversation, while Matthieu added logs to the fire. Magali's return cut short the awkward silence.

"Will you be joining us for dinner, Karen?" Magali asked.

"Oh, I don't want to trouble you. I can go to Pommard."

"The first night of your stay we invite you as our guest for a welcome dinner. Breakfast every day is included with your room. Otherwise, you can explore the restaurants in the area or if you have lunch or dinner here, I just add it to your bill." Magali gave Matthieu a look suggesting he make Louise feel welcome.

"Yes," Matthieu said. "Tonight, you should have dinner here. Magali makes the fabulous wine and cooks the most delicious food. I just grow the crops."

"Well, then, I accept. Is there anything I can do to help?"

"Absolutely not," Magali said.

"Okay. I'll go take a quick tour of the town before dinner."

"À toute à l'heure."

Louise left and headed to the village on a mission to meet someone knowledgeable about local lore, in particular about Les Fontaines Salées. What better place for local lore than a local bar?

EIGHTEEN

January 4, 2002

Terracotta rooftops of Regency-style houses, miniatures of the imposing Château de Pommard flanking the west side of the town, clustered around an old stone church belfry. The peaceful vista of vineyards and the ivy-covered Château de la Commaraine at the entrance of town made it difficult to imagine anything nefarious taking place anywhere near there.

Louise drove down Rue de la Refene to the Place de l'Eglise in the town square. The church bell tolled 5 o'clock as she parked and crossed the cobblestones to a quaint inn that boasted a gift shop and a pub. She entered the shop and browsed souvenirs, spotting a trinket for Luke. She paid and walked through to the adjacent pub.

The barman greeted her. "Bonsoir!" He was polishing a wine glass and motioned for her to sit anywhere. She chose the barstool in front of him. "Qu'est-ce que je vous sers, mademoiselle?" Calling her *mademoiselle* at her age could be taken as a compliment.

"Je vous laisse choisir." Louise let him surprise her.

The barman whistled merrily as he put down the standard wine glass and picked up a larger one. He had a grown boy look with a crop of wavy brown hair and smiling hazel eyes.

"Allemande?"

Albeit pleased he had guessed her nationality to be German, she had to confess. "Américaine."

"Alors, pour la belle Américaine, je propose…" He took a pinot noir Premier Cru off the shelf and placed the balloon glass in front of her. He splashed a plum-red ribbon of wine into the glass, which settled into a tantalizing pool. The large glass had a decanter-like effect giving the wine greater contact with oxygen. Holding the stem, Louise swirled it and studied the *legs* as the wine ran down the sides. She stuck her nose in and breathed deeply, her wide eyes expressing her approval of the earthy bouquet.

"À vôtre santé." She raised her glass.

The barman raised his own glass up from below the bar. "A vous, a nous, a nos amours, qu'ils durent toujours." Their glasses clinked in F-sharp. They sipped, aerated, and chewed, swallowing only after fully tasting the wine.

"Delicieux." Louise held out her hand and introduced herself. "Je m'apelle Karen."

He shook her hand. "Jules."

She relaxed into another sip of the exquisite wine. "Excellent millesime," she said praising the vintage.

"Bravo!" He wiped the bottle top and put the cork back in. They continued chatting in French. "You know wine," he said.

"I took a wine-tasting lesson before my trip here." Louise omitted that she owned a bar herself, with a well-stocked wine cave.

"It must have been an advanced class."

She quickly changed the subject. "So, what is the one place one must absolutely visit in Burgundy?"

"Vous-voici!" He waved his hand indicating the bar.

Louise smiled and continued playing tourist while speaking perfect French. "What about Les Fontaines Salées?"

He raised an eyebrow. "A beautiful *jeune femme* like yourself with no maladies, pas la peine."

"Les Fontaines Salées is only for sick people?"

"It used to be a destination for the ailing long ago. The Gauls believed the divinities of Les Fontaines had the power to heal." The barman paused before continuing. "Little known fact, Arthur Riothamus spent many years there." His eyes twinkled cannily.

"King Arthur?" Louise said.

"Ahh," Jules pushed out his bottom lip, impressed. "You know your wines and your legends." A lone customer at the end of the bar pretended not to listen with his nose in a book sipping a snifter of brandy. But the mention of Les Fontaines Salées pricked up his ears. He was older, in his seventies, Louise estimated. He motioned to the barman for the tab. As soon as Jules gave him the bill, he tossed some cash on the bar, got up, and walked toward the exit. As the man passed Louise, he stopped and said, "*Evitez dis pater.*" Then he left.

"Allez, bonne soiree!" Jules shouted after him. "Don't pay attention to him," Jules told Louise. "He is an excellent customer, but a lousy tour guide."

"He said *stay away from dispatay*?"

Jules corrected her. "Two words: *Dis Pater*. The old people of the region tend to be very, how you say, *superstitieux*. They believe in the old mysticism of Les Fontaines Salées, and they are very frightened of it."

"It sounds fascinating."

"It has a fascinating past," Jules said, continuing with a practiced air. "There are two ruins carbon-dated to around 3000 BC. One of the ruins is an open-air temple and the other a necropolis."

"Burial grounds?"

"Oui. But there are also the remains of a huge circular wall, about a hundred meters in diameter. A symbol of the sun or moon. So, Romans arriving would have immediately recognized their god *Dis Pater* represented by this circle."

"Dis Pater," Louise echoed.

"Another temple shaped like this," with his fingers he made an inverted T, "also contained a sacred basin where artifacts of *ex votos* were discovered."

"Ex votos, the symbolic offerings?" Louise was pleased she was tracking with him.

"*Exactement.* The offerings were made of stone, metal, or wood. They were related to healing and represented the ailing body parts, heads, hands, feet, and phallus." He covered his mouth in mock embarrassment. "Excusez-moi."

Louise extended her index finger from her glass, giggled and sipped her wine. "Please, go on."

"The bubbling salt-water springs were a healing sanctuary of Celtic worship. The Celts believed that the bubbles rising to the surface of the water were the essence of deities. But it was actually helium, which, when inhaled, increased the pitch of the voice, giving it the chipmunk effect. Imagine the ancient vast underground caverns filled with helium and Celtic druids conducting their secret meetings, speaking in bizarre voices, dumbfounding their constituency.

Louise laughed at his cartoonish depiction. "You said King Arthur was there?"

"Ahh oui. There are many questionable tales of King Arthur: the location of Arthur's battles, his birthplace, his parentage, his ethnicity, and his very existence. However, few have ever questioned if *Avalon* was real, in the way that they question if *Camelot* was real. No one has ever found Camelot. But, the discovery of coins dating from the fourth century within the basin of Les Fontaines Salées could be considered proof of Avalon, as described by the author Geoffrey of Monmouth in the 11th century."

It had been a while since Louise had indulged in the Arthurian legend. "Wait," she said, "I always get confused by the timeline. King Arthur was fifth century AD, inspired by ancient Celts from the Iron Age 700 years BC."

"Exactement."

"Then the Templars were twelfth-century knights, *inspired* by King Arthur."

"Precisely. The formation of the Knights Templar came hundreds of years after King Arthur, but their philosophy and ideas of honor were based on the legend of King Arthur and his knights. They made a vow of *taking the cross,* hence the red crosses sewn into their tunics. Anyway, since the late twelfth century, it had been widely accepted that Avalon was an otherworld, according to that fifth-century legend of King Arthur, like heaven in Christianity, or a nirvana, or a mythical paradise. A concept, rather than a physical place."

Jules sipped his wine then continued, "A similar concept of paradise was the Celtic Yniswitrin – or Isle of Apples – most closely associated with the town of Glastonbury in the county of Somerset in England. Glastonbury was a kind of physical embodiment of the Concept of Avalon. But there never has been a physical place called *The Isle of Avalon* anywhere in Britain. The word Avalon in ancient Celtic and Gaelic means *apple tree goddess.*"

Louise's head was spinning, partly from the wine she had consumed and partly from the thrilling facts and figures the barman seemed to possess. "There is an ancient town of Avallon right here in Burgundy, n'est-ce-pas?" Louise asked.

"Bull's eye!" Jules said. "Think about it. After the Gallic Wars in the second century A.D., the Roman Conquest added on to the Celtic site of Les Fontaines Salées. Then in the fifth century, as the Roman Empire was collapsing, about the time that Arthur Riothamus was in Burgundy, workers built the Christian Chapel of St. Jean-Baptiste on the site of the open-air Temple of Les Fontaines Salées."

Now Jules had lost her. "I don't understand," Louise said.

Jules blushed a bit. He forgot that when he revved up about the history of the region, he tended to get too complex. "This was an extraordinarily optimistic addition at that site considering the power-struggle between the colonizing Germanic tribes. Armies were ransacking their way through Gaul, leaving smoldering buildings and bodies in their wake. But those atrocities had no effect on Les Fontaines Salées. Christians were confident their new chapel would survive. Les Fontaines Salées became a magnificent example of a Roman spa, with hot and cold baths, gymnasium, wrestling arena, and beauty parlor."

"What happened?"

"The Dark Ages happened. We have little idea of how things were after the Romans left. Emerging out into the light again in the fourteenth century, it was a long time before anyone recorded any reliable information. There was only spoken lore and archaeology. But Arthur Riothamus was at the mouth of that tunnel in the middle of the fifth century. The springs are an important time capsule of the period having collected many artifacts. Not only were the mineral waters a mecca for their healing powers, but also the water had a high concentration of salt that was collected and processed by evaporation and traded. The extraction of valuable salt continued until the fourteenth century when monks buried the site so that the townspeople had to use the Church's salt store and pay a salt tax rather than help themselves to what had always been available to them at Les Fontaines Salées. The wells drifted into distant memory and then were forgotten altogether. That is how they remained until Les Fontaines Salées and all its beautifully preserved artifacts were rediscovered in the twentieth century."

"Aren't they near Vézelay?" Louise asked.

"Oui, the ancient village near Les Fontaines Salées was originally named Vezeliacum, after a wealthy Roman who had built a villa a few kilometers away from the springs. The small village that grew up around Vezeliacum became one of the most important places in medieval Christendom. By the Middle Ages, churches had been built up the sides of the hill creating a walled town now known as Vézelay, just 16 kilometers from Avallon. It is thought King Arthur lived in Avallon around 470 A.D. tending his wounds at Les Fontaines Salées. The land was said to be spiritually charged and a whole community of Romano-Celtic women practiced at the healing basin dedicating a shrine to the goddess Diana. The site which had been used for healing and worship since Neolithic times would have been the ultimate, ancestral Celtic experience for King Arthur."

"Are you theorizing King Arthur died at Les Fontaines Salées? Wouldn't that make it *the* Avalon?"

"That is the legend. In that area you will also find many depictions of Coquilles Saint Jacques along the road. That's how you know you are on Santiago de Compostela."

"Saint James Way, the annual pilgrimage route?"

"Yes, which began during the time of the Templars."

"What about Dis Pater?" Louise asked, as if she were at a Socratic lecture.

"It is also, how you say, symbolique. According to legend, the first century Roman consul Cicero derived the name from a contraction, the Latin *dives* for *wealthy*, and *pater* for *father*. Dives Pater is *Father Wealth*. It refers to the wealth of precious stones below the earth. Like Pluto, Dis Pater became associated with the underworld because the wealth of the earth – gems and precious metals – were considered the domain of the Greco-Roman underworld. The Gauls believed they were descended from Dis Pater, a tradition handed down by the Druids. That is why they computed every season by the number of *nights* and not the number of *days*. For birthdays and the beginnings of months and years the day followed the night.

Louise was like a child listening to an academic bedtime story. "So, Dis Pater, the Roman god of wealth and the underworld, comes from Celtic lore?"

"That's right," Jules said. "But beware, the goals of Dis Pater are lurking behind countless lies and deceptions."

Louise looked at her watch and remembered dinner. "How much do I owe you?"

"Zat dependz," Jules said in English. "Will you be back?"

"Absolutely."

"Zen eet eez on zee house."

"Formidable. Merci." Louise shook his hand and left.

The words, "Beware, the goals of Dis Pater are lurking behind countless lies and deceptions," echoed as Louise drove through the ancient forest back to the vineyard. The glass of wine, coupled with jetlag, seemed to play on her vision, mysterious figures seeming to gambol in the shadows.

NINETEEN

January 4, 2002

"Bonsoir!" Magali greeted Louise.

"Bonsoir!" Louise was relieved to be back in the warm family setting.

"Ça a été?"

"Yes, Pommard is so picturesque," Louise said in French. "And the people are very friendly."

"Bonsoir!" Matthieu entered with Luke on piggyback and placed him in his booster chair.

"Bonsoir!" Louise said. She took the small gift out of her purse and placed it in front of Luke. "Cadeau."

"A gift? Qu'est-ce qu'on dit?" Magali told Luke.

"Merci!" Luke gingerly took what appeared to be an antique brass disk out of the small paper bag and turned it over in his little hands. Just as Louise expected, within a minute, Luke figured out the moving parts and flipped out the lens.

"That's a magnifying glass!" Magali exclaimed. "Do you know how to use it?" She mimicked holding a magnifying glass in front of her eye.

Luke peered through the loop, making his large eye appear even bigger. Then he pulled back, startled by the change in vision and they all laughed.

"Allez, à table." Matthieu pulled Louise's chair out for her and touched her back, giving her an unexpected frisson. She sat and he brought over a large bowl of tossed mixed greens with a simple dressing of Dijon mustard, fresh lemon, salt, and pepper. "All from our greenhouse and garden. Even our own mustard seeds."

"La pièce de résistance." Magali set a white serving bowl in the center of the table. "Coq au vin, made with our own red wine."

LaFontaine had been right about these accommodations, Louise through to herself.

"Bon appétit," they said in unison.

Louise tried the tender chicken braised in rich red wine sauce with button mushrooms and onions. "Delicious."

"I'm glad you like it."

"Have you had this farm long?"

"Our great grandfather acquired this parcel of land when our family first settled in Bourgogne in the nineteenth century," Matthieu said. "He bought it along with another parcel of Chablis."

"Chablis is the diamond among rubies," Louise said, quoting her research about the region.

"That's right!" Magali said. "Chablis is the only white burgundy grape."

"How many hectares do you have, if I may ask?"

"It's hard to say, exactly," Matthieu replied. "We have increased the domain little by little over the generations. But it's barely large enough to exploit at a profit."

"Would expanding more help?" Louise asked.

"Yes, we need to expand. But it's not easy," Matthieu explained. "You need liquid assets to purchase quickly when something comes on the market, which is usually due to some financial difficulty or other misfortune."

"What a business, having to wait for someone's misfortune to have your own good fortune, n'est-ce pas?" Magali added.

"It sounds like a natural cycle," Louise said, her banker's instincts kicking in. "I mean, you're trying to develop the region while at the same time support local growers to keep the traditions alive. Right?"

"Yes, but it feels like a war of attrition," Matthieu grumbled.

Magali raised her wineglass. "Allez, à votre santé!"

"To your health," Louise repeated.

"A la santé des vignes," Matthieu added.

Louise's natural curiosity inspired her next inquiry. "The vineyards look bare," Louise said. "Is that normal?"

"It is completely normal this time of year," Magali said. "In the winter, the vines are dormant. Matthieu has been worried about some issues we have been having…"

"Magali…" Matthieu gave her an ominous look. "It is bad luck to talk about the vineyards. The reputation is the most important asset a terroir has."[13]

"Given this meal and the wine, I can assure you that your reputation is intact as far as I'm concerned," Louise said.

Magali spilled another bit of news. "Unfortunately, the inspector said we must cure the affected crop, or our bank will call the loan," Magali said. "My brother avoids the truth sometimes, as he is a proud man like most farmers."

"Ça suffit, Magali." Matthieu said, bristling.

Louise could understand why. This information was shocking. LaFontaine must have had a reason for referring her to this particular gîte, and the bank could be it.

"Is it a local bank?" Louise asked.

"Yes, we have had a line of credit with them for decades to get through the less prosperous vintage years," Magali explained.

Matthieu got up and brought his plate to the sink. "Allez, au lit, mon petit." He picked Luke up and carried him off.

"Good night, my cabbage," Magali said to Luke then turned to Louise. "My brother is a proud man, as are most farmers. But even more so for viticulturists."

"I hope the issue with the bank will sort itself out. It's hard to believe such a world-class vineyard would ever have to struggle."

"It's the unexpected costs," Magali said. "The inspector gave us an estimate for the treatment of the disease, and we won't be able to afford it if the bank calls the loan. We might be forced to sell."

Louise was now convinced the banker's behavior was suspicious. But she didn't want to alarm Magali so instead tried to console her. "Do you have family who could help?"

"Luke is the last of our lineage."

"Perhaps you can find an outside investor?"

"This community looks down on any kind of outside influence."

"Maman!" Luke cried from his bedroom.

"Excuse me." Magali put her napkin aside. "I need to tuck in my son."

After Magali left, Louise got up to clear the dishes, but Matthieu returned and stopped her. "Please, you are our guest." He took the plates from her hands.

---

[13] Terroir is a French term that refers to the environmental factors that affect a crop's observable structure.

"It is a pleasure for me to help," Louise insisted, resuming her clean-up efforts. "It's like meditation for me."

"Cleaning is a meditation?" Matthieu asked.

"Let's just say, teachers are glorified housekeepers." She had almost said barkeepers.

Matthieu laughed. "I have never thought of it that way. But, yes, it is a constant challenge to keep order."

"It's amazing how I already feel at home here."

"That is the intention of the gîte concept," Matthieu said. "This region is fiercely protective of its community."

"I'm sorry about the problems you're having with the vines. Is it something you can explain in layman terms? I promise to keep it confidential."

"You mean you won't write it in your novel?" Matthieu dried his hands and they both picked up their wineglasses.

"I'll change the names to protect the innocent," Louise said, and they clinked glasses.

"Did you know that some believe the reason we clink glasses is to fulfill the fifth sense of sound?"

Louise actually found that very interesting. "Ah yes, I see, sight, smell, taste…what about touch?" Louise asked.

"I'll show you. He raised his glass pointing out the color. "First you have sight, look at the color." Matthieu took a deep sniff of the wine to demonstrate and Louise eagerly followed along. "Then the nose." He spun the wine in the glass. "Aerate to allow the wine to open up." He sniffed again. "Now, second nose." He raised a finger in warning. "Now here is where it's gets physical. Chew the wine then spit it out while blowing out of your nose." He demonstrated, taking a sip and chomping his teeth as though chewing. Then, he spit the wine into the sink making a slight grunt.

"You spit so gracefully," Louise said. "I didn't know that was even possible."

"Allez, you are among friends."

Louise tried simultaneously spitting while blowing out of her nose with disastrous results. Red wine trickled from her nose as she bent over the sink, coughing and laughing. Matthieu turned on the water, allowing her to rinse and then handed her a towel.

"How embarrassing!" Louise said, her eyes watering.

"It happens all the time." Louise tried to clean a spot on her blouse.

"Allow me." Matthieu wet the corner of a clean towel and held the dry corner of the towel on the inside of her blouse and blotted the top of the blouse with the wet corner. His hand brushed her skin and Louise blushed. "Excusez-moi." He then put a pinch of salt on the stain. "Voila. Good as new."

"Is everything okay?" Magali asked, sweeping back into the room as if catching two amorous teenagers.

"Everything is fine," Louise said, as her skin flushed with warm sensations. "Matthieu was teaching me how to spit out the wine while blowing out of my nose and…" Louise showed her the water spot.

It was way too detailed an explanation and Magali laughed wholeheartedly. "It is not the first time and it won't be the last. It takes some practice."

It was time to temper the moment. "Well," Louise said, looking at the clock. "It's late and I should go rinse this out." Louise put her coat on.

"I'll walk you to your cottage," Matthieu said. "It's perfectly safe outside, but it takes time to get used to the darkness."

Louise felt her skin flushing again. "Thank you for the delicious dinner, Magali."

"It was our pleasure." Magali handed Matthieu a lantern. "Bonne nuit, dormez bien."

Louise welcomed the chilly air and looked up at the starry sky. "You can see the Milky Way!"

"Yes, there's the big bear," said Matthieu, pointing. "And right there is the little bear."

"In English, we call them the Big and Little Dippers."

"Ah, oui! I can see how that would be."

Louise opened the cottage door. "I think I'll light a fire."

"Would you like me to do it for you?" Matthieu offered.

"Yes, thanks."

Matthieu came in and took three small logs from the woodpile and made a teepee in the fireplace. "What are your plans while you're here?"

"I'd like to check out Beaune and Dijon."

"That is a good place to start." Matthieu placed some pinecones underneath the logs for kindling, lit a long wooden match and got the fire going.

"I'd also like to tour a vineyard or two," Louise said. "Are there tours of your vineyard?"

"I can give you a tour if you like."

"Yes, I'd love some insider information on how the vineyards work."

"You sound like a stock trader," Matthieu observed.

"It's for my novel."

"What is your novel about?"

"It's a mystery. But I don't want to say yet."

"An unsolved mystery." He put his hands in his pockets and headed toward the door. "Tomorrow morning, I start working very early and could give you a private tour for some real insider information."

"That sounds perfect."

"Bonne nuit, a demain."

"Bonne nuit."

TWENTY

January 5, 2002

Her eyes opened reluctantly to a sliver of sunrise that had trickled through the almost impenetrable shutters. In a state of torpid arousal, her dreams of stallions and cockerels, roused by new surroundings and a strong male presence, faded into her subconscious. She extended her extremities to get the blood circulating and realized the actual sound of horse hooves and a rooster crowing must have prompted the wild dreamscape. She got up and cracked open the door.

"Vous savez monter à cheval, non?" Matthieu sat atop a horse holding the reins of a second horse in his hand.

"Yes, I know how to ride."

"Allez, work before food."

"Give me a minute."

Louise brushed her teeth and got dressed in jeans, a cashmere turtleneck, and boots. In the mirror she spied a soupçon of her natural blonde roots. She put on her cashmere béret pulling it down over her ears, then borrowed the Barbour coat hanging on a hook by the door and went outside.

"What beautiful horses!" She petted the neck of her designated horse. "I don't recognize the breed."

"They are Russian Dons," Matthieu replied.

"Oh, I've never heard of them."

"Allez, montez."

Louise got on the sturdy horse and trotted alongside Matthieu.

"Very noble," Louise said.

"Life in Russia demands a universal horse," Matthieu said. "They are superb under the saddle and make good carriage horses as well."

"He almost looks like a racehorse."

"Russia is not known as a country of equestrian sportsmen and gentleman riders, like England. The Russian Don is well rounded, equally equipped for racing as for hard practical work."

"A Renaissance horse," Louise said.

"Ah, oui!"

"How did you happen to get Russian horses?"

"Russian wine wholesalers. Our international sales are significant. In-kind trades are taxed at a lower rate, and since 9/11, there are greater restrictions on cash transactions. One of our Russian clients shipped in horses to barter with."

"Très intéressant."

"Allez!" Matthieu kicked his horse into gear and they took off at a gallop through the undulating vineyards. Louise's horse knew where to go, so she leaned forward and enjoyed the scenery. Clouds smudged pink across the blue horizon and the frigid air met the dewy warmth of the earth, creating a steamy haze.

They veered left and cut across the estate. Louise saw a fast-approaching stone barrier, but the horses weren't slowing, so she braced her knees, feet firmly in the stirrups, prepared to use her legs as shock absorbers. Then the horses floated over the obstacle and landed gracefully with minimum impact. They rode a little further then stopped near a stone shed and tethered the horses. Matthieu gathered tools from the shed and explained his work. The "insider information" that "Karen" wanted for her "novel" had begun.

"It is important to prune even through the winter." Matthieu tossed three logs into an old steel barrel placed sideways on a cart. He wheeled it to a row of vines, placed some dead sticks under the logs and kindled a flame. Using special clippers, he began pruning.

"How do you know what to cut?" Louise asked.

"I cut only the longest dead stray vines," Matthieu explained, discarding the stems in the fire. "From a botanical standpoint, we are dealing with a vine in the truest sense of the word. If it is not pruned, it will grow without stopping. Pruning now helps the vine to grow even stronger in the spring-time." He pointed to the trunk of the venerable plant. "Different winegrowing regions have different pruning styles. Of course, the essential tool for pruning is the *secateurs*." He opened and closed his pruning shears like a tiny raptor. The single-handed clipper, about eight inches long, appeared well worn but sturdy.

"Those look antique."

"These have been in my family since the late 1800s when they were new. They are a fine example of the way things used to be made—solid and durable." Matthieu pointed to one of the wide crescent-shaped blades. "This blade is replaceable." He pointed at the specific moving parts. "This spring, safety clip, blade, and pivot are original and still work perfectly. Just a couple drops of oil and a touch with the sharpening stone keeps them fully functional."

"If only humans were that maintenance free," Louise quipped.

Matthieu laughed in reply. He checked the wires that the vines were attached to, then clipped off a small shoot. "The shoots attach themselves to these wires supporting the vines. Workers called *tacherons* are hired to remove the shoots." He waved Louise closer. "Here, you can see each pruning technique. It may seem simple, but it requires a great deal of practice and an expert eye. The person pruning must select which canes and buds to cut, and which will bear the harvest."

"Can I help?" Louise asked.

"Yes, stand near me to gather the trimmings and put them in the fire." He thrust a handful of freshly cut shoots toward Louise. She was taken off guard and fumbled. But with a juggler's reflexes, she grasped Matthieu's hand and caught the shoots. The warmth of his hand steadied hers. She darted an apologetic look at him and realized he was watching her silently. His smoldering eyes, the flame having long been extinguished, seared the scar tissue of her heart. His gaze tested her well-tempered spirit long ago shatter-proofed by lost love. Habitually, Louise looked to a person's right eye, as it was the closest to the soul. But, for some reason, she considered his left eye where she saw an icy rage. Something dark was stored deep down within his psyche.

"The fire serves as a heat source too," Matthieu said. "That is why you will often see plumes of smoke rising in the vineyards in winter." He continued to work nimbly as Louise gathered the shoots and tossed them into the fire. She stopped to warm her hands over the flames. "Ah, j'ai failli oublier." Matthieu reached inside his jacket and took out a small thermos and two stackable tin cups. He handed the cups to Louise, and she held them as he poured hot coffee into each cup.

"My hero!" Louise drank the delicious French brew.

"Pas mal, eh?" Matthieu smiled.

"Not bad at all." The sun cleared the horizon, its rays increasing the ambient temperature. "It's magnificent here."

After about two hours they finished pruning a good-sized section of the vineyard. "Ça suffit pour aujourd'hui." Matthieu picked up and wheeled the barrel. "I try to do about 200 square meters every morning. My back is getting too old to do more."

"Do you hire workers?"

"In summer there are students who need the work, and I am happy for the low-wage labor."

"So, where are the diseased vines?"

"We will go there next." They got back on the horses and trotted across a road to an enclosure. "These are called *clos*, which are walled-in vineyards, usually for ancient vines."

They dismounted and hung the reins over the stone wall of the enclosure. The morning sun cast a golden hue over vineyard that was beautifully framed by the opening of the clos like a painting. Louise followed Matthieu down one of the rows to where a section of the vines had been covered by a tarp.

Matthieu lifted the corner. "C'est horrible," he muttered as though seeing his own child suffering.

"Does the tarp keep the disease from spreading?"

"Wishful thinking. These things find a way of spreading."

"What are you looking for?"

He pointed to a dark blemish on the vine. "According to my research, this particular disease, in this region doesn't make sense."

"I don't understand."

"This strain is from a completely different region that wouldn't be anywhere near here. It's almost as if it were...planted."

"Is that possible?"

"With the GMOs and so-called designer agriculture these days, who knows?"

"Will you be able to salvage the vines?"

Matthieu suddenly remembered that Louise was a guest. "I'm sorry, you should not have to deal with this. It's just that the timing is unfortunate. You booked our cottage in the off-season, and we weren't expecting you. And this just happened in the past week. I apologize if this is ruining your stay."

"Not at all," insisted Louise. "Don't forget, I'm writing a mystery novel. This is quite a fascinating mystery." She could tell by his look that her words were insensitive. "I would love to help you solve it. Can you explain it to me?"

"The bank sent an agricultural inspector who discovered the infection in this small area of our Premier Cru grapes. I have been researching it on my own and it appears to be a new disease caused by a Botryosphaeriaceous species identified in Bordeaux and in other French vine-growing areas. This disease is referred to as 'black dead arm' or BDA, for the cankers caused on the grapevine. Symptoms range from leaves showing discolorations to complete vine wilting. Here we have discolorations so it's in the early stages."

"What's the cure?"

"It is complicated and requires professional treatment."

"Which is expensive."

"Unfortunately, yes."

A gentle breeze wafted the scent of breakfast their way. Matthieu looked at his watch. "Mon dieu! You must be famished."

"I could eat."

They got on the horses and headed back to the lodge. It was only 9:00 a.m., but the day already felt long and productive as Louise sat down to breakfast.

"Alors, Karen, croque-madame ou croque-monsieur?" Magali asked.

"Croque-madame, s'il vous plaît." Magali served the French equivalent of a grilled cheese sandwich but with ham and béchamel sauce on the inside and covered with crusty melted cheese. Topping it with an over-easy egg changed it from a croque-monsieur to a croque-madame.

"Luke and I gathered the eggs this morning."

"You can definitely work up an appetite on the farm," Louise said, eating with gusto.

"You are a true gourmand," Matthieu said.

Louise ate properly with a fork and knife in the European manner. However, being left-handed, she held the knife in her left and fork in her right hand.

"Quelque chose ne va pas," Luke said, holding his magnifying glass and looking at Louise's hands.

"Je suis gauchère," Louise said.

"Karen writes with her left hand," Magali explained. "Opposite of the way you write. So, that's why she holds the utensils the other way."

Luke took his fork and knife and tried to imitate Louise to adorable results.

"What is on your agenda today, Karen?" Magali asked.

"I'm going to do a quick tour of several places to get an overview of the area in search of inspiration."

"May I make a suggestion?" asked Matthieu.

"Please do."

"An excellent way to tour Burgundy is by boat."

"By boat?"

"Ah, oui," seconded Magali. "Burgundy is laced with canals that were dug for transportation. The canals have locks every mile or so, allowing boats to climb over the hills."

"Yes, there are actually two canals that bisect Burgundy with many branching off. The Canal de Bourgogne is a 200-mile engineering master-piece of the pre-Industrial Revolution. It flows from Auxerre Southeast past Dijon. The other is Canal du Nivernais which links two of France's great rivers, the Seine and the Loire, in the town of Vermenton. That is the one I recommend you explore first. If you like, I can accompany you," Matthieu offered.

"No, that won't be necessary." Matthieu appeared rejected so Louise added, "Can I take you up on your offer next time? I tend to follow my instincts better alone and taking my first tour on my own would be better for my creative writing."

"Of course," Matthieu said.

Louise finished her café au lait and picked up her dishes. "May I help clean up?"

"Absolutely not," said Magali, taking her plate. "You already helped Matthieu enough this morning. Please, go enjoy your inspiration tour."

"Thank you for the delicious breakfast." Louise gave Magali four cheek kisses, now that they had grown familiar enough to do so. She did the same to Luke, but when she turned to Matthieu, he walked out. Louise looked at Magali. "Did I say something wrong?"

"He's very protective. I think he would have preferred you to let him take you on the tour."

"That's very sweet, but I can take care of myself. Besides, what danger could there possibly be?"

Magali suddenly spoke in accented English, "Just be careful. There's a lot of mystery in our history."

"*Mystery in our history*," Louise repeated. "I'll have to write that down."

Satisfied with her little rhyme, Magali went back to speaking French. "Perhaps Matthieu will explain someday. It is not my place. Just beware of people you don't know. It's best to associate only with people to whom you have been introduced."

"Thanks for the tip."

TWENTY-ONE

January 5, 2002

Louise decided that renting a boat and skippering it herself would offer greater discretion and different opportunities than exploring Burgundy by car or guided boat tour. She went back to her cottage and searched the Internet for the geographical location of the canal Matthieu had suggested. Then she changed into Wellies, got in the car and headed north.

She made a call on the mobile phone. "Hi, Charlie."

"Hello, mademoiselle Baker. How's France?"

"There's not much to update you on yet. But I am pursuing a couple of leads and following my gut instinct."

"Take your time. It's better to assimilate slowly."

"That's my thinking too. In a few days I might have something more substantial." She saw the freeway signs to Vermenton. "Sorry, gotta go, this is my exit."

She hung up and turned off. On Matthieu's advice, and what she found on the Internet, she would take a tour of Canal du Nivernais in Vermenton. which was close to Vézelay, the ancient village near Les Fontaines Salées.

She arrived in Vermenton and stopped at a bicycle rental shop. After speaking to the owner, she learned of a local fisherman named Clément who might have a boat for rent on the River Cure. She hitched the rental bike to the back of her Peugeot and drove a short distance to the marina. She walked down the dock where she met a scruffy type with dark hair and olive skin.

"Clément?"

"Oui, c'est moi," he replied. Despite his burly ruggedness he was jovial and easily enticed by a pretty woman.

"Bonjour. The owner of the bicycle shop in town said you might have a boat for rent," Louise said in French. "I would just need it for a few hours."

"Navigatrice solitaire? What if you have engine trouble?"

"Je sais bricoler." Louise dropped some nautical terminology persuading him she could handle mechanical issues.

"Okay," he agreed, "Five hundred Euros now, and I refund you 200 Euros when you return the boat the way you found it."

"Deal." Louise handed him the cash.

"Here are the keys and a map of the canals." He handed her the key to the 1982 Inland Waterways Cruiser, which had a champagne cork as a float, and the dogeared map.

"Parfait, merci." She loaded the bicycle and supplies onboard. Her mental compass was set to head south. But she took off north from Clément's dock to explore the locks Magali had mentioned. The boat wasn't what she was used to on the island. But driving it was easy enough once she'd mastered the sluggish response to the steering. She piloted along a bucolic stretch of the Canal du Nivernais, weaving in and out of the River Yonne. She passed the village of Cravant with its vineyards, cherry orchards and timber-framed houses. After about thirty minutes she turned around and retraced her trip back past Clement's dock and continued south.

She scanned the map for points of interest along the River Cure. Starting from the tributary at Cravant, it flowed past waterfalls, forests, limestone cliffs, and caves, to the medieval town of Vézelay. A mile downriver perched atop the high riverbank was the enchanting 14th century Reigny Abbaye with a stone refectory and a 17th century dovecote. Feeling hunger pangs, she took out the Brie and cornichon baguette that she had picked up in town and rummaged around the small galley to find a corkscrew and a wineglass. In addition to the well-appointed galley, two separate cabins and two heads made the 32-foot boat a comfortable river cruiser. Steering with one knee, she popped the cork of a Chablis and washed the sandwich down with the rich buttery white wine.

She approached the town of Lucy-sur-Cure, the site of Château du Chastenay, an 11th century château with a mystical past that piqued her curiosity. It had been constructed over a network of underground grottos at the intersection of the two symbolic roads, the Via Agrippa and the Christian pilgrimage route of Saint James's Way. But the water became too shallow to continue by boat a couple miles short of the Château du Chastenay. She tied the boat up to an empty dock, unloaded the bicycle and slung her bag across her back. She pedaled down the cobblestone streets and spotted symbols of scallop shells indicating Saint James's Way. Several homes had scallops sculpted over doorways or forged into iron gates. A sign pointed to the hamlet of Beugnon and she turned left.

Her forensic accounting experience had taught her to follow her instincts to solve a problem. When she came to a small gothic chapel, she stopped and read the plaque. In 1494 the monks of the nearby Reigny Abbey attempted to evict the Lord of Arcy, Claude d'Aullenay, from their land in order to retake the mineral springs. However, d'Aullenay made a counteroffer to exchange the village of Lucy-sur-Cure for the springs. The monks accepted, and the hamlet of Beugnon with its chapel came into being.

With the large scallop shell sculpted over the door, it was easy to imagine Knights Templars stopping there for food and shelter. The chapel's simple architectural elements combined gothic and early Renaissance from Lombardy, Italy, with three external buttresses supporting three ribbed arches and the vaulted nave inside. There was a well-worn baptismal font near the altar crowned with another scallop shell. These were distinctive signs that the chapel had been a coaching inn on the Saint James's Way.

Louise sat at a wooden pew and took in the calming atmosphere of the medieval structure. Sensing nothing else of interest there, she returned to her bicycle. Just as she started to ride away, two gentlemen came out of an adjacent cottage. One man entered the chapel and the other got into a Peugeot and headed in the direction of the Château du Chastenay. Louise decided to follow his car but lost sight of it when he turned onto Route 6 and sped off. She made a mental note of the license plate in hopes of finding it in the village.

She pedaled two miles along the road bordered by prehistoric cliffs toward Lucy-sur-Cure and the hamlet of Val-Sainte-Marie, where the Château du Chastenay was located. She searched for the Peugeot to no avail until she arrived at Château du Chastenay. Something drew her attention upward where she saw a woman watching her from the window, but then quickly disappeared. Louise left the bike on its kickstand and entered the foyer, the walls of which were adorned by symbols and paintings. She touched the smooth surface of one of the symbols.

"They are hermetically sealed into the walls," a man said in French. Louise turned and recognized the man in the Peugeot. "These are formulas for the transformation of lead into gold," he said, indicating the images on the walls. "That symbol represents the Philosopher's Stone, the mythical alchemical substance capable of turning base metals, such as mercury, into gold. The alchemists living here created the resin providing the airtight conditions to preserve the formulas."

"That's amazing," Louise said. "Actually, I was hoping to take the tour."

"We are closed." The man was elegant, around eighty years old with salt-and-pepper hair, classic features, and stately attire. He had a permanent wide-eyed expression that made him appear on constant alert. "But I'd be happy to show you around," he said, offering his hand. "My name is Gérard."

Louise shook his hand. "It's nice to meet you, Gérard. My name is L...Karen."

"Le Karen, or Karen with a K?"

"Karen with a K," Louise replied, recovering with humor. "Le slip of the tongue." The phrase *le lapsus de langue* worked in French or English.

"Shall we?" He held the door open for her, and they entered the next room. "This chamber is the only one open to the public. It is the Tower of Saint-Jean where you will see several allegorical figures sculpted above the porticos of the sages."

"There is a scallop symbol," Louise said.

"Yes, the Château du Chastenay was a known pilgrim refuge on the Saint James's Way to Santiago de Compostela. The Knights Templar once occupied this château to guard pilgrims on their way along the dangerous roads to Jerusalem. But it mainly served as a commune for medieval alchemists." He pointed to a series of portraits on wood. "These paintings represent the typical life of the saint on the path to divine wisdom."

"Was there a reason they congregated here?" Louise asked, recalling the barman Jules' talk of mystical energy in the area. "Is there something about this region that attracted the alchemists?"

"Good question," Gérard said. "The château was built over an ancient cave system that seems to have attracted humans from the beginning. It was originally conceived as a Faraday shield."

"I'm sorry, I don't understand."

"The château was constructed as an enclosure to block electric fields to aid in the joining of earthly and celestial forces. These grounds are known to be exposed to powerful telluric currents believed to have beneficial effects such as curing depression or fighting fatigue." Gérard raised his hands and moved his fingers like leaves blowing in the breeze. "Some can feel vibrations."

He motioned for her to follow him to the next chamber, which, she gathered, was closed to the public. On the wall hung a portrait captioned as Gibaut d'Arcy, builder of the château.

"Le Château du Chastenay has remained in the same family since 1086 without interruption, something that is very unusual in France. My father inherited it from my grandfather, the Count of Varende, in the 1960s.

"You are Gérard de la Varende?" Louise asked.

"Oui, c'est moi," he replied.

"Excuse me for not recognizing you. I did some research but never found any photos of you."

"I don't like photos." He resumed the tour. "My father believed that a *higher power* insisted the manor belonged to him, inspiring him to research his family tree. That's how he discovered his Burgundy roots permitting him his rightful inheritance. After he took over the château in the 1960s, he completely restored it."

"Your wife lives here with you?" Louise asked rather clumsily. But she was curious about the woman in the window.

"No, I am divorced."

"There was a woman in the window when I arrived."

"A woman in a white nightgown?"

"I'm not sure."

"When my father recovered the château, he had no doubt that it would be haunted. From the very first night, strange noises echoing throughout the château woke him several times. There were muffled cries, wings flapping, and odd sounds, like the draining of giant siphons. Being an aficionado of the occult, he was accustomed to living with the supernatural. But he never learned the actual source of the muffled cries or the bizarre noises that echo here at night. Visitors are welcome to attend the short presentation about the Templar, Pythagorean, and alchemy symbols found throughout the château. However..." He paused and looked at her ominously with those wide eyes, "we don't talk about the woman in white."

"I'm sorry."

"No need to apologize." He spoke candidly. "We probably don't talk about her because her identity remains a mystery. But the myth is that a woman discovered a hidden treasure and had her tongue cut out to keep her from talking about it. It is believed that she was a direct descendent of a family of Scottish origin. She was adored by the local peasants, and nothing could make her leave her home, not even her death." He smiled puckishly.

"Perhaps she continues to guard the treasure she discovered."

Louise was a bit chilled by the idea she might actually have seen a ghost, but she played it cool. "Perhaps a higher power insisted the manor belonged to her," Louise said.

"Is that why you came here? The paranormal phenomena?"

"Actually, I'm not really sure why I'm here."

"Your instincts led you here, did they not?"

"Yes, exactly."

"We were expecting you."

"We?"

"My neighbor, Kathy Gibbons, is a renowned hypnotist and claire-voyante. Kathy says the manor overflows with energy. She has felt the distinct presence of a very unhappy Italian woman in an upstairs chamber. Personally, I don't believe that the manor is haunted. Everyone knows that all old buildings make creaking noises when the wood and the pipes settle."

"Why were you and Ms. Gibbons expecting me?"

"Ms. Gibbons had a premonition that you would arrive."

"Moi?" Louise looked around thinking he must be joking.

"Yes, she was quite specific about your appearance and your name would begin with a K or an L."

The conversation was closing in on her and she wasn't prepared for it. In a bit of a panic she looked at her watch.

"I'm sorry but I need to leave before it gets dark. Is it okay if I come back tomorrow? I am very interested in seeing the caves."

"We are counting on it."

She darted out to her bicycle and bolted down the road. Within fifteen minutes, she was back on the boat. There had been no other boats on her cruise down the river, and now in the dusk, she felt very isolated. But her sense of security increased with every knot as she pressed the throttle forward to accelerate. Suddenly the engine sputtered and chugged to a stop. She could tell from the sound that something had interfered with the fuel line. Still spooked by the conversation with Gérard, Louise acted quickly. Upon closer inspection of the engine, she saw the fuel line had been cut. She recalled seeing a supply box stored near the corkscrew she had used earlier. She rummaged through it and found a spare fuel line. She hurriedly replaced the damaged hose just as she heard another boat rumbling downstream. She was sure the timing was intentional, so she did some of her own strategic timing.

The approaching boat sidled up to her. "Vous êtes en panne d'essence?" the skipper asked. He was average-looking in his forties, stocky with very short hair and wire-rimmed glasses.

"Yes, I must be out of gas," she replied in French.

The man held up a fuel can. "Permission to come aboard?"

"Yes, thank you." As he drifted closer, Louise had enough time to finish connecting the replacement fuel line. He coasted alongside her boat and was about to tie up to hers when she went to the helm, turned on the engine, and jammed the throttle forward at full speed. The thrust of her boat forced the man to stumble and fall backward. He got to his feet, jumped to the helm and started after her. But she had gotten enough of a head start that he was soon out of her rearview.

As she pulled up to Clément's dock her heart was still racing. She parked and gathered her belongings as Clément tied up.

"Alors, ça a été?" Clément asked cheerily. But he picked up on her distressed state. "Quelque chose ne va pas?"

"It's nothing." Louise showed him the damaged fuel line. "Luckily, you had a spare, so I replaced it."

"Who did this?" Clément climbed aboard and assessed the cut fuel line.

"I'll pay you for the damage." Louise reached into her bag for more cash.

He looked up and shook his head, "No, Merci."

"Please, I insist," she said in reply. The methodical exchange and Clément's sympathetic attitude were calming her down.

He finished looking over the rest of the boat and changed the subject away from money. "She's true to her name, Denrée Rare."

"She is truly a rare commodity," Louise agreed. She wanted to keep the conversation going to stabilize her state of mind. "I was going to call my boat Denrée Rare. But she already had a name."

"Oh? What is your boat called?"

"Serendipity."

"Good name. Don't change it."

"That would be bad luck. Your boat brought me good luck."

"It was our pleasure, Denrée Rare and me." Clément smiled and handed the cash deposit back to her. "Leave the bicycle onboard and I will return it to my friend," he added. "It's the least I can do."

"Merci beaucoup." They shook hands and Louise left.

On the drive back, Louise pondered the boating encounter. The fuel line was cut. Or was it? It could have just split and the boat that approached WAS just coming to help her. But, instinctively, she was determined to keep an eye out for anything unusual on this mission in Burgundy. She was no longer on an island, protected under an assumed name.

She was livid and terrified that she might still be the target of outside forces, nefarious entities who wouldn't mind her conveniently dead, both for what she knew and just plain revenge. The cut line must have been an attempt of some kind, but for what? To kidnap her? To kill her? And who might be pursuing her? The next thought chilled her more than even the ghost she saw. Has the BCCI Black Network finally caught up with her?

TWENTY-TWO

January 5, 2002

Louise arrived back at the gîte to freshen up before dinner. When she took off her cap, she saw her blonde roots sprouting noticeably. *I could open a salon with what I've learned maintaining this look*, she thought. After a quick retouch, she rinsed and dried her hair, then put on a knit turtleneck black dress with her Doc Martins and went over to the main house.

"Bonsoir!" Magali said.

"Bonsoir!" Louise said, giving Magali double cheek kisses. She bent down to give Luke two cheek kisses.

"Quatre bisous!" Luke said.

"You forgot, four," Magali said, pointing to her own cheeks.

Louise gave Luke two more kisses. "Voilà." Luke giggled and ran to his toys. "That smells divine," Louise said. She had stayed in five-star hotels that didn't have this level of cuisine.

"Châteaubriand," Magali said. "Matthieu's favorite."

"Is this a special occasion?"

"We are having a small celebration. Matthieu was able to get a six-month extension on our loan."

"Congratulations!"

"Merci," Matthieu said as he entered with a bounce in his step. He gave Louise four emphatic cheek kisses. "You made it back in one piece."

"Yes…" She refrained from adding *barely*, and simply admitted her feeling of relief, "It's great to be back."

Matthieu seemed genuinely pleased to see Louise. His mood was expansive, and he suddenly realized that their guest had only been in a couple of rooms in the historic dwelling. "Would you like to see the rest of our home?"

"I'd love to."

"Allez, Luke, on fait le tour." Matthieu picked up Luke and led Louise into the next room of the split-level house with high-beamed ceilings, terracotta floors, and lime-washed walls. "The earliest parts of the house are thirteenth century, and the main house was built in 1656 of timber and stonework. Over the years, the family has amassed all these furnishings and antiques." Luke poked at the piano in the large salon furnished with comfy sofas.

"It's charming."

Matthieu opened the French doors to views of the sloping vineyard in the last light of the day. The sun had set, but a bluish hue remained over the landscape. Matthieu pointed to a separate structure. "We converted that barn into my house. The bedroom upstairs used to be a hayloft. We won't go over there. It's messy."

"Le bordel," Luke said.

"Allez, mon petit," Matthieu said as he picked up Luke. "Where do you learn words like that? We don't say that." But he couldn't help but laugh himself. He led Louise back to the kitchen, where she saw an opportunity to help and started to set the table.

"No, Karen," Magali protested. "You have done enough of Matthieu's work."

"I don't like being waited on," Louise said, spying another task. "Shall I slice the bread?"

"That would be fine," Magali conceded.

Louise placed a crusty baguette on the heavy woodblock cutting board and began slicing it on the bias.

"Your technique is formidable," Matthieu said.

"Merci."

"However, here is a little trick." Matthieu gestured for the knife. "May I?" Louise handed him the knife and he moved close to demonstrate. "Instead of cutting back and forth, you start with the tip of the knife on the top of the bread then glide it forward. Let the sharp blade do the work. Plus, it slices without tearing or crushing the crust." He handed the knife back to Louise. This time, she did not fumble and deftly repeated his technique.

"Yes, that's much better," Louise said, genuinely surprised.

"You are a natural at bread slicing," Matthieu teased, resting a massive hand gently on her shoulder. His touch was comforting. Their eyes met, this time both less guarded, reading into each other's stormy pasts. A smoldering flame in Matthieu's right eye hinted of passion. The left eye remained unpromising. Louise's gaze promised nothing while leaving room for everything.

"À table les enfants!" Magali said.

Luke tried to move his booster seat from the chair next to Matthieu. "Oncle Matthieu, you sit next to your wife." Everyone laughed as Matthieu placed Luke's booster seat back on his chair.

"Karen is not Uncle Matthieu's wife, Luke," Magali said, winking at Louise. "Yet."

Louise felt the blush rising inside her and changed the subject by raising her glass. "To the bank!"

"To the bank!" they echoed.

The irony of her own toast was not lost on Louise. "Bon appétit," she added before cutting into the perfectly presented Châteaubriand. As they enjoyed the meal in silence – always a sign of great cooking – Louise considered that visiting their bank seemed the next logical step in her attempt to connect the dots. There could be a corrupt lender taking advantage of the tribal nature of the residents. She had seen it before with BCCI. It was far too easy for greed to poison the well of good intentions.

"Speaking of your bank," Louise said, breaking the silence. "I'm considering buying a small property here, maybe a summer home in the area."

"How exciting!" Magali said.

"Could you refer me to someone at your bank?"

"Our accounts are with Le Crédit Agricole," Matthieu said.

"Will you be purchasing a vineyard?" Magali asked.

"I don't know," said Louise. "My mom has a green thumb. But, I don't."

"The reason I ask is because Le Crédit Agricole is sometimes called the *Green Bank* due to its ties to farming," Magali explained. "It has been our family bank since the 1800s."

"Do you like Le Crédit Agricole?" Louise asked.

"We used to love them," said Magali.

"Used to?"

"The bank was part of many government subsidy programs during postwar reconstruction and mechanization of farming," Matthieu said. "But when they started consolidating all the regional banks, things changed. It was when Crédit Agricole went public in 2000 that we began to have problems."

Louise was surprised by this bit of information. "Going public usually means more transparency and oversight," Louise said. "Which should be good for customers."

"Maybe it's just a transitional thing," Magali said. She momentarily wondered how this American teacher knew so much about banking.

"I'll make an appointment with them," Louise said.

Changing the subject, Matthieu asked, "Did you take the boat tour today?"

"Sort of," replied Louise. "I rented a private boat in Vermenton and went up the Canal du Nivernais as you suggested. Then I turned back south down the Cure River. There's so much to see, and I'd especially like to visit the Grottes d'Arcy-sur-Cure."

Matthieu's demeanor suddenly returned to its former intensity. "Do not go north by yourself," he warned.

"Why? What's in the north?" Louise asked.

"Just, promise me, if you go near Auxerre, you will allow me to accompany you."

Louise almost shot back with the usual, *I can take care of myself.* But as she glanced up, she could see Matthieu's concern and after the events of today, she had to acknowledge that he was probably right. "I promise," is what came out of her mouth.

It was an easy promise to make because her goal for the next day would not be to go north, but to return to the Château du Chastenay and continue her discussions with the owner, Gérard. She was also very curious about the underground caves on the property. After her brief visit to the caves in the Forest of Fontainebleau, she wanted more than ever to explore the caves of Arcy-sur-Cure. She tried a new gambit to cut Matthieu's intensity.

"There's something about this area," Louise added. "A sort of mystical spirituality."

"Yes, there are many historic healing meccas," Magali said. "And of course, the Saint James Way."

There it was again, the Saint James Way. The path to redemption. Magali got up and began clearing the table.

"Dessert and coffee?" Magali offered.

But Louise now knew she needed to continue the journey.

"Not for me," she said. "I have to get an early start tomorrow." Louise brought her dish to the sink and bid her new family goodnight.

She went to her cottage and turned on the computer to do some research on the Caves of Arcy-sur-Cure. She learned that they were an archaeological site of national interest and designated an historical monument. The underground network had formed over millennia from natural acids in the rain. The remains of almost all the stages of human evolution had been discovered there, dating back more than 250,000 years. The most ancient were bone fragments and bone tools used by Neanderthal man dating to 60,000 years ago found in The Hyena Cave. Neanderthals, who had disappeared about 30,000 years ago, were followed by Cro-Magnons, who differed very little from modern man, and were responsible for the cave paintings. Cro-Magnons were essentially hunter-gatherers who used tools and weapons, dyes, pestles, hearths, and lamps, all of which were discovered 30 centimeters deep in the prehistoric soil of the caves.

Exhausted, she turned off the computer and fell asleep.

January 6, 2002

Wasting no time, the next morning Louise had a quick croissant and café au lait in Magali's kitchen, then drove to the Château du Chastenay arriving by 10:00 a.m. Wanting to get her own first impression before meeting with Gérard, she ventured into the Caves of Arcy-sur-Cure alone. The setting of the caves was like a science fiction film. The millennia of natural acids in the rain had fashioned fantastic shapes and sculptures into the calcareous rock, transforming the caverns into weird rooms of cathedral proportions. Louise noted the well-marked whimsical names given to the formations, such as *The Ball Room* and *The Fairies' Washing House*. Some held religious connotations including *Coquilles St. Jacques*.

But the drawings were the most fascinating. According to her research the night before, they were carbon dated to about 33,000 years old, making it the second oldest decorated cave in the world after Chauvet-Pont-d'Arc. The Great Cave contained over one hundred and forty engravings and paintings of animal art rarely found in other decorated caves, including mammoths, bears, oxen, horses, a rhinoceros, bison, a bird, a big cat. The handprints, eight in all, were quite distinctive and eerie. Most of the handprints seemed to be from an adolescent or a small female. It was believed that the artist made the handprint by putting red ochre paint in her mouth, placing her hand on the rock, and spitting it out in a spray to create the negative image.

It was tempting to leave her own handprint in the ancient line of human ancestry. But instead, she relaxed into a meditative state to take in the energy. She suddenly felt a presence, reminding her of the encounter she had while locked in the Paris catacombs.[14] She opened her eyes half expecting to see Sri Sri Ravi Shankar, but only saw the cave bathed in a golden luminosity giving it the appearance of a medieval painting. Louise checked her watch that indicated she had been meditating exactly thirty minutes.

She heard a clicking sound and turned to see a dog wagging its tail. The dog, which appeared to be a Basenji hound mix with short brown and white fur, floppy ears, and a curly tail, stared up at her and tilted its head. He must have belonged to Gérard, the owner of the château, and was allowed to wander the familiar grounds. Louise put out her hand for him to sniff, and he put his paw in it. She left the cave and walked back to the château with the dog following. She saw Gérard's Peugeot parked outside and entered.

"Bonjour. Is monsieur de la Varende here?"

"Un moment, s'il vous plaît," the front desk clerk said. She disappeared through a door and returned after a minute. "He will be with you shortly."

"Thank you."

Louise perused some of the many books and publications on display that Gérard de la Varende had written. She opened one and found an extensive biography of the author. She read how he had been a combatant for France-Libre at the age of twenty, and then a French intelligence agent during the French Indochina war. He had been taken prisoner by the Japanese in 1945 and placed in a forced labor camp. After inheriting the domain du Chaste-nay he devoted his life to making the estate an exciting tourist attraction, even opening the caves to researchers.

"Mademoiselle Baker! How good of you to come back." The elegant octogenarian approached as energetically as a young doctoral student and couldn't help but notice that Louise was reading up on him. He shook her hand and then pet the dog. "Good boy, Perceval."

Louise recognized the name as yet another Arthurian reference. "Perceval? Like King Arthur's Knight who saw the Holy Grail?"

"Oui, bravo! In Old French *percer val* means to pierce the valley. The twelfth-century chronicler Geoffrey of Monmouth used it in his Arthurian

[14] From the author's first novel in the Louise Moscow series, *Foliage: An International Banking Spy Thriller*

tales."

This was the second allusion to old Geoffrey that Louise had heard since she arrived in Burgundy. She wondered if Gérard and the bartender Jules spent nights swapping tales, as her host guided Louise to the alchemy displays.

"My grandfather, Marie Charles Gaston Mallard de la Varende, was a Maltese Knight in the Legion of Honor and a descendent of the Knights Templar."

"Are there any heirs to carry on your legacy?" Louise asked.

"My son, François, is a count by birthright. But he does not care about his title or nobility. A count without money is practically worthless."

Gérard waved a hand over the display of the alchemy equipment. "I inherited the manor and the caves in 1968, along with much debt. My birthright was disputed, and I spent over twenty-five years fighting for it, living like a monk on about five francs per day."

Louise was finding this new information fascinating but couldn't help noticing the old man get a little angry when describing this part of this history. "But I leveraged my stature as a Count and finally in 1990, I recovered my property rights. That is when I opened the doors to researchers and the community. It is because of my stubborn madness that the hundreds of prehistoric drawings over 30,000 years old have seen the light of day." He seemed relieved to have gotten that last bit into the conversation.

Louise wanted to diffuse Gérard's ire. "I just visited the caves and saw the drawings, amazing. It's quite a legacy."

"Perhaps. But it would be difficult for my son to take up the torch from such a whimsical father who has sacrificed everything to keep his heritage alive. Especially now with these new challenges."

"New challenges? You mean, the Woman in White?" Louise had to remind herself that she saw a ghost.

"No. This is something else. For years, the clairvoyant sensed forces only from past lives, like the Woman in White you mention. But now she feels someone is trying to interfere with my inheritance again. She said you have been sent here to help."

Louise was a bit skeptical, but her curiosity was piqued. "What did the clairvoyant see?"

"It's not what she saw. It's what she *heard*."

"Like voices?" Louise asked.

"No music. A song *Tira Lira*."

"The Italian song?"

"She thinks it's symbolic," Gérard explained. "Maybe *tirelire*, in French."

"Piggy bank?"

"Yes, banking," Gérard said.

"But, I'm just a retired schoolteacher writing a novel," Louise bluffed.

Gérard looked bemused. "The psychic was sure this would be of interest to you," he said. "Perhaps for your novel?"

Louise wanted to put this line of inquiry on ice. "It sounds interesting, but..."

"May I make a proposal?" Gérard said.

"Of course."

"Over the years, I have allowed many researchers to explore the caves and other historic artifacts on the grounds, which has been mutually beneficial. Since your arrival was foretold, I feel a need to grant you full access to the company history and records as research for your novel."

Louise sensed an opening. "It's an intriguing plotline," Louise countered. "But I would need access to all the documents from the legal proceedings of your claim to this estate as well."

"No problem. We are fastidious record keepers."

"This is exciting," Louise said in earnest. "Would you mind if I took a quick look right now?"

"No time like the present." Louise and Perceval followed Gérard to a large salon that served as his business office. It was tidy and sparsely furnished, with a heavy antique oak desk and leather chair. He used his index finger as a pointer running up and down a wall of metal filing cabinets until he found L-M-O then P just below it. "Voila, it will be archived under *Procès*." He pulled the drawer out revealing a series of thick file folders. "Here it is, the official court docket with the transcriptions, as well as my notes that I kept during the entire proceeding." He hefted the first two folders out and hauled them over to the desk putting them down with a thud. He continued to take out folders, lining them up, side by side in an order only he understood. He leafed through the first folder. His index fingers now serving as drumsticks, he tapped out an emphatic rat-a-tat. "Voila!" He took out a multiple-page outline. "This is the summary by date of the proceedings. You will find it to be an excellent narrative of the arguments. The rest of the files are in chronological order."

Even though Gérard had boasted about his record-keeping, she wasn't expecting so much material. "Were there any official notarized documents issued, such as damages awarded, or a release of liens on the property?"

The old caretaker appreciated his guest's thoroughness. His finger led him to the contents of another folder. "Here is the final writ removing the trustee and returning administrative powers to me," he said handing her the file.

Louise leafed through the docket, separating pages out creating staggered piles, careful to keep them in the order in which Gérard had filed them. Her old banking instincts kicked in intuitively and she found several names that immediately caught her eye. Louise pointed to a legal pad on the desk. "May I?"

"Of course." Gérard handed her the legal pad and an antique fountain pen from its matching holder. "I will leave you to your research. If you have any questions, use the phone over there to call the front desk and they'll notify me to return.

Louise dug in. She noted the name of the trustee and the party contesting the ownership. Having had some experience in property law because of her dealings with wealthy clients at BCCI, Louise knew that, unlike English-speaking countries, which used a system of Common Law, France had a system of Civil Law based on a two-hundred-year-old code. The *Code Civil* or Code Napoléon of 1804 stipulated the rights and obligations of citizens, the laws of property, contract, inheritance, etc. Based on the principles of Roman and customary law, the Code Civil remained the cornerstone of French law. Out of the 2,281 articles of the *Code Civil*, nearly 1,200 had kept their original version. She found the information she was seeking and called for Gérard to come back to the office.

"French law applies," Louise said immediately as he walked into the room, "regardless of whether the owner is a French citizen or a foreigner," Louise said, pointing to a passage. "Look, it is cited here, '*Article 544 of the Civil Code, Property owner has the right to use and control things in the most absolute manner provided this use and control are not prohibited by the law.*' That means there are limitations to what a property owner can do with his property. In France, assets pass immediately to the decedent's heirs, regardless of whether there was a will. The heirs are deemed to own the assets from the moment of the owner's death. The most important practical consequence of the French forced heir-ship law is that the children or parents of the deceased spouse become co-owners at the first death. Even if the surviving spouse retained the right to lifetime occupation, he or she wouldn't be able to dispose freely of the assets. For instance, if the surviving spouse wished to sell the estate, the consent of all the inheritors would be required. So, when your father inherited the estate, he would have needed the consent of his brother to dispose of it."

She pointed to a name on the document. "Conversely, your uncle who filed this claim wished to sell the property. Therefore, a trustee placed the contested estate under administrative control until the ownership was resolved. The documents say that your uncle had a purchaser already lined up. That purchaser was working with a bank, Crédit Agricole."

Gérard was impressed and wondered what kind of novel this school-teacher was writing. "Yes, we use Crédit Agricole for our line of credit. Lately, they have been putting pressure on us, sending inspectors, trying to claim that some of the tourism creates liabilities that make our loans risky, and raising our interest rates. This has also resulted in higher liability insurance rates."

"That's very interesting," Louise said, taking careful notes of all names and their positions at companies of all parties involved, including a Crédit Agricole account manager, Yves Renard. "This is incredible stuff, right in line with my story notes." Louise was so used to Karen's cover that she was considering actually writing a novel. "I'll schedule a meeting with Crédit Agricole. Without mentioning you, of course."

"I trust you," Gérard said.

Louise looked at her watch. "I must go, but I will let you know what I find out."

"Thank you."

They exchanged four cheek kisses, then Louise made sure to bid farewell to her guide dog Perceval with a head scratch and got back on the road.

On the way back to the vineyard Louise, dialed the number for the Crédit Agricole Beaune branch on her mobile phone and scheduled an appointment with a certain Yves Renard to open a bank account. Then she made a call to Charlie.

"Good morning, Charlie."

"How are you Karen?"

"Is Patrick with you?"

"Yes, we're on speakerphone."

"Hi Patrick. I have an idea and may need to use all the funds in that checking account. But it's just temporary. I'm going to open a checking account at a local bank, which I'll be able to access."

"Ah, yes, good strategy for infiltrating the bank," Patrick was quick on the uptake.

"Exactly," Louise said.

"Do you need more funds?"

"I've been paying everything with the credit card you gave me. But I did withdraw some cash and I will probably transfer the entire $50,000 to the new account. I'll reimburse you for anything I spend over the $50,000."

"Don't worry about that. I'll have my client transfer more funds to make sure everything is covered," Roblot said.

"Thanks, I'll talk to you soon."

Louise hung up just as she arrived at the vineyard. She went straight to her cottage to work on her computer without distractions.

She fell asleep early, the exertion of the trip finally catching up with her.

TWENTY-THREE

January 7, 2002

Her visibility was hindered by the mist, but the horse led the way. Louise pitched forward, riding bareback, clutching the mane, her body rocking with the pace. Her spirits soared as she jockeyed faster and faster, following the whisper of Jean-Philippe's voice, but the words he uttered were confusing.

"Karen? Karen?"

She awoke from a paralyzing slumber. The dream state had suppressed laughter and tears, both of which now burst forth in stifled sobs.

"Karen?" Matthieu repeated from outside.

She calmed down, her throat relaxed, and she felt her heart rate show back to normal. She wiped the sleep from her eyes. "Oui?" she managed to say.

"Breakfast is ready."

She threw the covers aside, the cold snap fully awakening her. She got up and opened the door without thinking of her usual sleepwear – or lack thereof – and saw Matthieu on horseback. The horse shuddered in response to Matthieu's involuntary leg clench upon seeing her in shape-revealing tank top with matching panties with mussed-up hair and ruddy cheeks.

Matthieu looked her up and down. "Tu viens?" he muttered.

"Oui, j'arrive." Louise finally noticed what the stupefied Matthieu was taking in and closed the door. Then, she smirked remembering the French expression, *J'arrive*, held the same sexual double entendre as English, *I'm coming*. She shrugged, knowing she would never have gotten anywhere in life without pushing the boundaries of decorum. Besides, it had been a couple of months since Captain Robert had called and she had a tremendous appetite for Matthieu's intensity. But, right now, she had to get to the bank.

She hurriedly dressed, putting together business casual attire wearing a burgundy knit pencil skirt, black turtleneck, charcoal Wolford thigh-high tights, and Sonia Rykiel Mary Janes. After brushing her teeth, she combed her hair to match her passport photo. She grabbed her bag and went to the main house.

"Bonjour!" Louise said. Wood burned in the fireplace, and an appetizing breakfast was set out on the farmhouse table.

"Bonjour," Magali said. "Bien dormi?"

"Yes, I slept *too* well."

Suddenly Matthieu's voice boomed too loudly from the table. "It was difficult to wake you!"

Louise eyed him warily. "A lot of dreams," she confessed.

"Tu as fait de beaux rêves?" Luke asked.

"Yes, very good dreams. There were horses and flowers."

"And puppies?" asked Luke.

"Yesterday I met a very cute puppy," Louise said. "His name was Perceval."

"Like from King Arthur!" Magali said. Louise couldn't help but chuckle to herself at yet another reference. Luke ran to his toys and came back wearing his plastic helmet and brandishing his little plastic Excalibur.

"Allez, à table mon ange," Magali said. "Finish your breakfast. We are going to the market in Beaune today."

"Would you like to drive into town together?" Louise asked, finishing her café au lait and bringing her dishes to the sink. "I have an appointment at Crédit Agricole this morning. With an account manager, Yves Renard."

"Yves Renard is our account manager," Magali said.

"What a coincidence!" Louise was not entirely surprised.

"You go on ahead without us," Magali said. "I have some things to take care of here first."

"Okay, merci for another incredible meal." She meant it.

Louise left and Matthieu followed her to the car, opening the door for her. "Thanks." Louise felt his intensity, so she got in and lowered the window to let him talk.

"How was your trip yesterday?" Matthieu asked.

"It was very interesting."

"Yes, you just happened to get an appointment with our bank manager the next day. That *is* very interesting."

Louise distracted him with a more enticing subject. "Would you mind taking me on a tour up north tomorrow?"

His attitude immediately changed from suspicious to dutiful, "À votre service." He gave a salute as she drove off.

When Louise entered the bank, all eyes were on her. Even in her more conventional attire, she stood out at the rural bank where everyone in the community knew each other. Banking there was deeply rooted in tradition, with the first local banks having been set up by town elites and farmers playing a minority role. But that had all changed with the Act of November 5, 1894 by the Minister for Agriculture to promote lending to small family farms and paving the way for the creation of Crédit Agricole's local banks. The *Green Bank* thrived, and by 2001 had gone public, listed on the Paris Euronext Stock Exchange under the name Crédit Agricole S.A.

A front desk clerk greeted Louise. "Bonjour. Comment allez-vous?"

"Tres bien, merci," Louise replied in her faultless French. She wanted to signal that she wasn't a lost tourist. "J'ai rendez-vous avec Monsieur Renard."

"C'est de la part de?"

"Karen Baker."

"Un moment s'il vous plaît."

Louise sat in the lobby with sterile furnishings and flipped through an issue of Santé Magazine. She was pleasantly surprised by the quality of the articles in the Crédit Agricole publication. Fifteen minutes later, a pasty but well-dressed gentleman in his forties greeted her.

"Madame Baker?" he put out his hand and introduced himself. "Yves Renard."

She was face to face with the very man named in Gérard's legal documents who had attempted to illicitly sell the Château du Chastenay on behalf of Gérard's uncle.

"Monsieur Renard. Thank you for meeting with me," she said in French, shaking his hand.

"Please follow me."

Renard led her to a small office with a glass wall and door, providing no privacy or confidentiality. He motioned for her to take a seat in front of his desk. "You are interested in opening a bank account with Crédit Agricole?" He asked, looking at her through rimless glasses.

"Yes, I'm thinking of buying a summer home in this area and would like to have the funds readily available when the time comes to make the deposit for the three-month waiting period."

"You have done your homework," Renard observed.

"Yes, I'm a schoolteacher, so I am used to homework."

Unimpressed, he began to explain the process anyway. "It is fairly straightforward. As you pointed out, once your loan is approved, you make a ten percent down payment, there is a mandatory seven-day cooling-off period and then a ten- to twelve-week waiting period. How much were you thinking of spending on your vacation home?"

"Well, I have set aside 25,000 US dollars for the down payment, plus whatever costs to make any necessary updates, up to 50,000 US dollars total."

Seeing an opportunity, he began to warm up to her. "There's a lot you can do with that kind of money," he said. "Loans up to eighty percent of the property value are generally permissible. With a ten percent deposit, you can leverage a mortgage to acquire a very special property. This is an exceptionally opportune time to buy right now."

"That's good to know. Would you be able to refer me to a local realtor?"

"Of course." He pressed his fingertips together making a fleshy steeple. "Leave it to me to assist you every step of the way." His spongy pale complexion and beady eyes completed the picture. "Will you be depositing the full amount today?"

"I don't see why not." Louise reached into her handbag and pulled out her wallet.

Renard picked up the handset and pressed the call button. "Oui, madame Baker will be opening a premium checking account today. Please prepare some temporary checks for her." He opened a drawer and took out several forms and handed them to her. "Please fill these out. Also, I'll need to make a photocopy of your passport and one other form of identification."

"Of course." Louise opened her wallet. "Will my passport and driver's license work?"

"That's perfect. I'll be right back." He took the IDs and walked out of the office, leaving her alone. She seized the opportunity to scan his office for any clues. A framed photo on the desk of what appeared to be Renard with his wife and two young daughters on holiday somewhere in the south of France was the only personal item. Hanging on the wall was a small, framed corporate portrait of Renard with the title of *Branch Manager* emblazoned below. Looking closer, she noticed something on his lapel, a kind of pin that reminded her of a Rotary Club insignia. But she didn't recognize it.

Renard entered, handed her the photo IDs and sat at his desk. She effortlessly completed the application from memory, including her new social security number, and handed the document to him.

"Merci," he said, looking at her expectantly. In response to her quizzical look, he said, "Would you like to deposit the 50,000 euros now? That gives you the premium checking account, which includes a one-point-five percent annual interest rate and free checking."

"Oh, sorry. Yes, of course." She opened the checkbook and filled in the amount of 50,000 euros, signed it, and gave it to him.

He examined the check, "Ahh..."

"Is there something wrong?" Louise feared she might have accidentally given him a check drawn under her real identity from her Cayman Islands account. She looked at the checkbook to verify that it was indeed drawn on the JP Morgan Chase New York City account of Karen Baker.

"Not at all," he replied. "I just noticed this is drawn on a JP Morgan Chase account, which usually requires quite a large minimum balance."

Louise reminded him what every banker should know. "No, that was JP Morgan. After the merger with Chase Bank, they no longer require a million-dollar minimum balance and have a much broader clientele now."

"Ah, yes, now I remember," he said, in a way that indicated he did not. Renard handed Louise a short stack of checks. "Here are a few temporary checks." Reading her application, he said, "You have given a local address in Pommard and a permanent address in Arlington Heights, Illinois. Would you like your new checks and documents sent to the Pommard address?"

"Yes, please. I will be there for at least a month. I'll provide my new mailing address if it changes."

He regarded the address. "This is a lovely vineyard."

"You know that place?" Louise asked.

"Yes, it has been in the same family for many years." He stood to walk her out.

"They are wonderful hosts and the property is charming."

"Excellent wines too," Renard said.

"Well, thank you for your help," Louise shook his hand.

"I'll call you as soon as I have news about the loan," he said. "It should come through fairly quickly. À très bientôt."

"À bientôt."

When Louise got on the road back to the vineyard, she felt a crick in her neck and overall fatigue. The meeting at the bank and her recent adventures by boat and bicycle had left Louise tense and achy. As she drove up, the vineyard appeared deserted, with Magali and Luke at the market, and Matthieu working in the fields or meeting with wholesalers.

She parked and went to the cottage to change into yoga clothes. Stepping outside into the fresh air and picturesque views produced a visceral reaction. Nature's beauty offered the promise of something, a sense of hope. Her mind wandered to the most positive and uplifting person she had ever known, her mother. Mary's revelation to Louise just weeks ago had given her new respect for her mom. Mary had refused to let an unspeakable horror defeat her. She had made a new life, buffered by the love of an honorable man, finding dignity and grace. She was a fighter.

Louise fell forward landing on her hands and kicked effortlessly up into a handstand, for a new perspective. She came back down into plank pose, arms extended, straight back and legs aligned. She bent at the elbows, lowering her body, then lifting her head and chest into a cobra pose. She lowered her head and drove her hips upward, straightening her arms and legs, making an inverted V in downward dog. She continued, doing three sun salutations, each with a slight variation, using different poses to open each chakra. She finished in tree pose, her left foot pressing against her right inner thigh, hands together at her heart.

Sensing a presence, she gazed through relaxed eyelids. On the immediate horizon she made out the silhouette of a man on horseback wearing a weathered Barbour coat and a wide-brimmed hat. Her memory defaulted to the quixotic moment when she had first met Jean-Philippe, like a vision, briefly obscured by her scarf billowing in the breeze. A cloud of dust rose from the pulverized granite of the Paris Tuileries Gardens as his horse reared to a sudden stop.[15] Louise lingered in the memory while Matthieu waited at a distance, patiently sharpening the antique clippers. She relaxed into standing pose and he rode closer.

"Impressionant." Even from under the hat, Matthieu's azure eyes pierced her soul.

---

[15] From the author's first novel in the Louise Moscow series, *Foliage: An International Banking Spy Thriller*

Normally, Louise looked people straight in the eyes. But looking into his triggered anxiety, like the dream of falling and then startling awake. She felt the blood rush to her face.

"Were you watching long?"

"Long enough to know that you have a black belt in yoga."

"There are no belts in yoga. It's not a competition."

"That's too bad. Because if it were, you'd be winning."

"There's no winning or losing, either. It's about balance." Louise said, waving him down. "Here, I'll show you."

"I could never do that." Matthieu came down, placing the reins on the fence post and his hat on his horse.

"Just give it a try."

"Couldn't I just watch you?"

"Come on." Louise guided him to stand next to her, facing the vineyard. "Breathe. Tune into your breath. Know that you are perfect as you are. Try a simple mountain pose. Stand with your feet slightly apart and press the palms of your hands together in front of your heart."

Matthieu did as he was told. "That's it? Yoga is so easy."

"That's right! Now reach your arms up over your head like a tree." Matthieu followed instructions. "Extend your hands upward, tilt your head back, looking up. Feel the stretch in your spine." Matthieu groaned. Louise moved behind him and gently placed a hand on his shoulder. "Now, bend forward at the hips." He bent down his arms reaching only to his knees as he grunted. "Breathe," Louise coaxed.

"As you can see, I'm not very flexible."

"I've seen worse. Bend your knees a little and just ease into it. Don't force it." She moved her hand up his spine until she reached his neck. She applied gentle pressure coaxing his spine to lengthen. "Let the weight of your arms and head do the work."

Matthieu instinctively placed the palms of his hands on his knees and lifted his head. "Are we done yet?"

"Good! You're doing a half forward bend!"

"I'm doing what?"

Louise placed her hand under his chin. "Press the palms of your hands against your knees and reach your head up, extending your spine." She stood alongside him and moved her hand down his spine until she reached his outer thigh. "Feel the stretch here in your glutes and outer thigh."

"Oh, la la," Matthieu teased.

Louise backed off. "Oh, I'm so sorry!"

Matthieu straightened up and turned to her. His eyes were glistening. "It's okay, I like yoga." He put his hands on her shoulders and massaged gently. Her slight build dwarfed by the grizzly bear of a man, she wanted to roll into a fetal position so as not to be devoured. His eyes took on a stormy cast, jostling her, and she bailed on the lesson.

"Will you take me to Auxerre tomorrow?" Louise asked pulling away.

His eyes darkened. "Why do you want to go to Auxerre?"

"You said not to go north without you, so I suspect there is a plot line to explore there."

"If you insist on going to Auxerre, I will take you."

The sound of car tires crunching on the driveway drew their attention to Magali arriving home. She parked and took Luke out of the child seat in the back. He ran to Matthieu, carrying a small container with air holes.

"Oncle Matthieu, look at my escargots!"

"They look delicious!" said Matthieu. Luke's expression combined horror and disgust. Then he giggled.

"The escargots are his friends," Magali said.

"Quelle déception." Matthieu winked. Louise contemplated the undertones of the French term for *how disappointing*.

"Allez, ma lutine!" Magali picked up Luke. "Let's bring them inside."

"It is time to get them drunk," Matthieu said, taking groceries from the car.

Louise wasn't sure if she had heard correctly. "Get who drunk?"

"The escargots! It is part of the preparation." Matthieu waved a hand over his domain. "We tried to harvest snails here ourselves, but it was too much work. So, we let the professionals scavenge for them in our vineyards. In turn, they give a share of the harvest to us for free."

Louise helped Matthieu carry the groceries. She was grateful for both Magali's timely arrival and a decided shift in the situation.

"You mean, we could eat the snails right from your vineyard?"

"That's what we *are* doing. But there is a lot of preparation. We have no idea what the snails have been eating so they could be toxic. The harvesters put them through a ten-day cleansing period, controlling what they eat." They entered the kitchen and put the groceries away. "Now for three days, we feed the snails only water or wine until they finish digesting any sand or dirt before we eat them. It's during those three days that they become Luke's little friends. Would you like to see?"

"Sure." Intrigued, she hesitantly followed Matthieu down the staircase to the cellar. "The first person to eat an escargot must have been very hungry," Louise joked, nervously.

Matthieu didn't react to her joke and was diligently back in teaching mode. "Empty escargot shells have been found at prehistoric sites throughout the Mediterranean," Matthieu said. "They were a luxury food for ancient Greeks and Romans." They entered the cellar where Magali and Luke were tending to the snails. Matthieu picked up one of the snails and showed it to Louise. "The escargot of Burgundy, *Helix Pomatia*, are considered the best. They are plump and tender and a good source of protein, minerals, and vitamin C." He put the snail back into a five-gallon, food-grade bucket with small holes drilled into it. "Like any livestock, snails need water. You must refill it frequently."

"That's my job!" Luke said, placing a canning jar fitted with a vacuum-controlled base filled with water in one of the buckets. "This is my bucket."

Louise noticed an old clay pot inside the bucket. "They have a little house in there."

"It's the escargot château!" Luke said.

Magali filled a similar canning jar with wine and placed it in another bucket. "We keep a separate bucket for the adults and make pre-marinated mollusks using wine instead of water, like the Romans." Magali placed a lid on the bucket. "Because a snail can lift five times its own weight, we cover them to keep them from organizing an escape." Magali went over to another bucket. "These have already undergone the three-day fasting period. Now, they need to be de-slimed." She filled a jug with water at the utility sink, added salt and vinegar, and poured it into the bucket. "We cover the snails with this mixture and soak them until they release all their slime. In four hours, they will be ready to go."

"We will set them free!" said Luke.

"That's right, mon ange. They will go to paradise," Magali said. "Will you join us for the special dinner tonight, Karen?"

The gourmand in Louise couldn't believe her good fortune. "It sounds delicious!"

TWENTY-FOUR

January 8, 2002

Louise's long black hair swirled into vortices over her ears, sapping her powers and deafening her to rational thought. Muffled voices failed to penetrate the vacuum. No matter how hard she concentrated, she couldn't make out the words. She invoked her dream rule: when the nightmare was too scary, she let go, stopped fighting, and allowed the monster to take control. Aroused by the danger heightening her senses, she finally awoke.

"Karen, we're waiting for you." Matthieu's disembodied voice sounded different, erudite, the antithesis of the farmer role, and definitely altered from their previous wake-up encounter. It combined many personas, from Gary Cooper's everyman to the suave but self-deprecating Cary Grant.

"Karen. Vous dormez?"

"I'll be there in a minute," Louise managed to say. Hearing him walk away she sat up and groggily checked her watch, 7:30 a.m. It wasn't exactly late, but for her it was tantamount to oversleeping. With the persistent jetlag and agrarian lifestyle, she wasn't quite her usual self. The garlic-laden escargot the night before had also given her strange dreams. She dressed comfortably layering a long slouchy black V-neck sweater over a black cotton turtleneck and black leggings. She put on her Dr. Martens and went to the main house.

"Bonjour, les enfants!" Louise said. "That smells good!"

"Maman made pain d'épices!" exclaimed Luke.

"I thought you would like to try an old specialty of Burgundy," Magali said.

Louise devoured the dense spiced bread, still warm from the oven and topped with crème fraîche. As her taste buds were being aroused, she swore that after this was all over, she might open a restaurant with Magali. She washed it down with a revitalizing café au lait. Matthieu interrupted her food revelry.

"Alors, we go north today?" he asked.

"Yes, I'd love to visit Vézelay on the way to Auxerres."

"That is quite a lot for one day. We'll take the scenic route and see how you feel when we get to Vézelay."

"I'll drive," Louise said, taking her dishes to the sink.

"Why don't I drive?" Matthieu said. "It will be quicker since I know my way around." Louise couldn't argue with his reasoning.

"Bonne journée!" Magali said as they left.

Louise walked toward the family's Peugeot 306 station wagon. But, Matthieu walked on, opened the wooden door of the old stone coach house and disappeared inside. A minute later Louise heard a rumbling then, through a dust cloud, Matthieu emerged in a 1964 Mini Moke. Louise had a flashback to Jean-Philippe's four-wheel-drive Citroën Méhari. In similar fashion to that off-road vehicle, the mechanical parts of the 1960 Mini Cooper had become the four-wheel-drive Mini Moke.[16]

"Allez!" Matthieu waved for her to get in. "Now I'll show you *my* Burgundy!"

Louise soon realized she was seeing an entirely different side of Matthieu. He was suddenly talkative and engaging, pointing out the historic highlights as he drove. After about an hour driving northwest through Saint-Brisson National Forest they reached the castle of Chastellux-sur-Cure rising out of the forest.

"It looks like a fairy tale!" Louise said. They drove past groves of oak, beech, and chestnut trees and large conifer plantations of Christmas trees. "This is near where I took the boat."

"That's right!" Matthieu said, continuing his guided tour. "This is the Morvan forest. The River Cure used to be part of the transportation system. Logs from this forest were shipped to Paris to keep the capital warm."

"Very interesting." Everyone really knew their history around here.

Matthieu looked at her and saw that she was serious. "I find you interesting," he said as they drove through the pretty village of Domecy-sur-Cure.

Louise was about to reply to Matthieu's compliment when another one of her senses were triggered. "That smells wonderful!"

"Wild garlic grows all along the banks of the river."

---

[16] From the author's first novel in the Louise Moscow series, *Foliage: An International Banking Spy Thriller*

"It's making me hungry."

"We'll stop here. Magali prepared a picnic basket for us." *Where does Magali find the time*, Louise thought. Matthieu veered off the main route and drove through a village. "This is the town of Pierre-Perthuis. named after a rock that forms a natural arch."

"It looks medieval."

"It was built in the tenth century." Matthieu parked on the right bank of the River Cure and took the picnic basket from the back. They hiked up a path to the top of the arch and sat dangling their feet while snacking on baguette sandwiches of brie and cornichons. Louise thought they would be perfect for the lunch menu at her fantasy Magali's Café.

"Pierre-Perthuis is old French for pierced rock."

"Oh, I see, it's actually a giant rock," Louise observed.

"The hole in the rock was worn through over thousands of years by the river."

Louise looked across the valley below, feeling the great void of the arch just beneath her. "It's magical."

"It's a very special region."

"It makes me want to do a handstand!" Louise found a flat space and kicked into a handstand. Matthieu instinctively jumped up, throwing her off balance. She came down landing near the edge, but Matthieu reached out in time and pulled her close to him.

"I almost fell."

"Your heart is beating very fast," Matthieu said.

"Yours is beating very slowly."

"I'm tall. My blood has more distance to travel." Being in his arms felt perfect. They held still for a minute, his heartbeat piercing a hole through hers.

They got back on the road and drove about ten minutes.

"Here we are," Matthieu announced as they approached Vézelay. The tower and basilica rose high above the town on the hill. "As you can see from here, the basilica is a masterpiece of Romanesque architecture. It is also close to Les Fontaines-Salées on your itinerary." They made their way up the hill to the village. "Vézelay and its Basilica of Saint Mary Magdalene have been the center of the pilgrimage since the Middle Ages. It used to be a Benedictine abbey."

"How do we get up to the basilica?" Louise wondered aloud.

"We have to park and walk up."

"We need more time to explore here. Let's go to Auxerre and come back," Louise said, making Auxerre the priority of the day.

"I agree." Matthieu drove down from the village and got back on the autoroute.

As they approached the city of Auxerre, Louise sensed Matthieu's pleasant disposition growing stormy. She had always been very sensitive to other people's moods whether they realized it or not. Over the years she had trained herself to be tactful because most people won't admit uncomfortable mood swings, no matter how obvious. Louise usually kept her perceptions to herself until the other person was ready and willing to discuss it. That had just played out with her mother's confession last month in New Jersey.

Louise saw a sign for a vaguely familiar culturally historic site, Via Agrippa, and tried to draw out his inner tour guide.

"Is that the same Via Agrippa I think it is?" Louise asked, breaking the silence with her impressive memory of college Geography 101.

"Yes, well done!" Matthieu sounded like a professor. "Auxerre used to be a Gallo-Roman city called Autissiodorum. Via Agrippa was one of the main Roman roads during the first century. It crossed the Yonne River right here. In the third century, Auxerre was the seat of a bishop and a provincial capital of the Roman Empire. It became part of France under King Louis XI in the fourteen-hundreds."

"Where are we going?" Louise asked, intrigued.

"You'll see." They approached a trio of imposing churches perched above the Yonne River. Matthieu drove through the steep, crooked streets past ancient timber and stone buildings through a gateway to the heart of Auxerre Old Town. A fifteenth century clock tower with an ochre and gold colored sun- and moon dial displayed the time, two o'clock.

"We should hurry if we want to finish today's tour." He drove a few blocks and parked on boulevard Vauban. They got out, and Matthieu paid the small entrance fee as they entered the museum. He walked straight to a display of a small Cretan limestone sculpture less than three feet tall.

"This is The Lady of Auxerre," Matthieu said reverentially. "The sculpture is from the seventh century B.C. when Greece was emerging from its Dark Age."

"It says this is a replica, and the original is at the Louvre," Louise pointed out.

"Yes, in 1907 a Louvre curator, Maxime Collignon, discovered the original in a storage vault right here. I find it interesting because it is believed to be a votary[17] rather than the Goddess Persephone herself. Her right hand touches her solar plexus and her left remains stiffly at her side. See how she still has the narrow waist of a Minoan-Mycenaean goddess, and her stiff hair suggests Egyptian influence. The Early Archaic style was the first stage of Daedalic Greek sculpture. Its style is based on a simple formula, which remained dominant for about two generations before evolving into the Archaic style. Her hint of a smile is often characterized as the *archaic smile*, secretive, knowing and serene."

Louise was thrown by Matthieu's knowledge of ancient art. "You said it's Greek, but was found here?"

"Correct. The provenance is unknown, and its mysterious arrival here gave it some notoriety in the press at the time."

"She's beautiful."

Matthieu looked at Louise as though he just realized she was there. "You are beautiful."

Louise pretended not to hear. "You know a lot about archeology."

Suddenly it was about Matthieu. "I know a lot about archeology and even some anthropology. I have a PhD from the University of Bourgogne in Dijon and used to be an archeologist for the Musée du Châtillonnais. Have you heard of it?"

"No, should I have?"

"You are in for a very special treat!"

He led her out hurriedly and they got back into the car. Matthieu spoke animatedly as he sped down the national route toward Dijon.

"Celts were fascinated by mineral springs." All over Burgundy, magical springs bubble continuously out of the earth. There are many springs dedicated to deities, almost all of which are gods of healing and fertility."

It was as though he hadn't been able to talk to anyone for years and just needed someone to listen. Louise was happy to be his therapist at this point. Besides, the subject of mineral springs was starting to get really interesting. But Louise could hardly catch her breath. Between this new gregarious side of Matthieu and his knowledge about archeology, anthropology and mineral springs, she started to wonder if something, or someone had led her to him.

---

[17] A devoted follower, adherent, or advocate of someone or something.

"Did you know that the goddess Sequana is associated exclusively with the source of the Seine?" Matthieu was still talking. Louise nodded, but had no idea what it meant. "Most other gods, such as Borvo, gave their names to sources in many regions like Bourbon-Lancy, Bourbon-l'Archambault, Bourbon-les-Bains, the Springs of Borvo at St. Moré. But Sequana is associated only with the Seine."

"I didn't know that."

"Do you know what ex votos are?"

Suddenly Louise got a chill at hearing the words of both LaFontaine and the barman Jules. "Religious offerings?"

"Exactly. The ex votos have great charm as *objets d'art*, but they also tell fascinating stories of the pilgrims, their health problems, and their sense of gratitude. They are a wealth of knowledge for archeologists and anthropologists. The idea was to place a little effigy of the ailing body part, such as an ear, foot, leg, lung, or head into the pool for Sequana to work her magic. Ex votos of women with large bellies, or couples entwined together, or swaddled babies suggest Sequana's function as fertility goddess. The Sequana finds are in the Musée Archéologique in Dijon. But many fascinating ex votos discovered in other wells and springs can be seen at the museum in Châtillon-sur-Seine."

"Where you used to work as an archeologist?"

"Oui, the Musée du Châtillonnais that houses the amazing Treasure of Vix."

"Treasure of Vix?" Louise wondered if it could be the long sought-after ex voto that LaFontaine had alluded to.

"You'll see."

They arrived in the town of Châtillon-sur-Seine, which, as the name indicated, was on the River Seine. Matthieu turned onto a country lane and parked. They walked a short way and entered through the gate.

"Et voilà, we are now in Paris!" Matthieu pointed to a sign that designated the location to be the source of the Seine River.

"Isn't Paris 240 kilometers from here?"

"Yes, but in 1867 the city of Paris sequestered this land surrounding a Celtic healing shrine called *Sequana's pool.*"

They descended a hill to a garden then followed the little stream until they came to a pool.

"The museum in Dijon has many objects from excavations here in this boggy pond, which was once a ritual bathing pool." They crossed over a small stone bridge and came to a grotto with layers of moss covering bulging stones forming a cave with two alcoves. At the center between the alcoves was a sculpture of a reclining nymph.

"This grotto was built in 1868 under Napoleon's orders. But, during Celtic times in Burgundy, this site was a major destination for pilgrims coming to cure their ailments. More than 1,500 coins and ex votos of stone and wood have been found here, dating to at least 150 BC. Would you like to visit the museum?"

"Is that where the Treasure of Vix is?"

"Oui. Follow me." They walked back up and entered the museum. "This is the Abbey of Notre Dame. It used to be a Cistercian monastery before being transformed into a museum." Matthieu explained. "The light airy spaces display the exhibits to perfection." They gravitated to the center where a huge bronze vase stood. "This is the centerpiece of the Musée du Châtillonnais."

"It's so pristine, it looks like new," Louise said.

"In 1953, a tomb from the sixth century B.C. was discovered near Vix, in northern Burgundy. The skeleton of a thirty-year-old princess wearing jewels including a massive gold torc was uncovered in the tomb. This Vase of Vix also in the tomb is the largest piece ever found from the Celtic period." Matthieu pointed to a section of the vase. "This sculpted frieze and Gorgons' heads on the handles with snake-like legs is a recurring theme in Burgundian sculpture. How these magnificent objects found their way to such a remote place is a mystery. The village of Vix is the highest navigable point on the Seine. It's thought that the Celtic chieftains who controlled it received such gifts possibly from Cornish tin traders coming from Britain on their way to the Adriatic. There is still so much to discover on the site."

"You have a great passion for archeology."

Lights flickered indicating the museum was closing. "Allez, we should get back," Matthieu said.

"Thank you for the beautiful adventure."

"It is only the beginning." They went out to the car.

"Oh? Where to next?"

"I'm doing some investigating of my own, if you recall, of my vines. I'm coming back here tomorrow, and you are welcome to join me. It should be very interesting."

Matthieu opened the car door for Louise, but instead of getting in she leaned against it and slipped her arms around his waist. There would be no hesitation this time. His bearlike physique, chiseled jawline, and salty grey blond hair made him irresistible. She kissed his receptive lips and he slid his tongue into her mouth just enough to taste the tip of hers. Opening wider, she flicked her tongue along his teeth with a hunger that was heightened when her teeth clicked against his. He pressed against her at just the precise spot to weaken her. But she squirmed away into the car seat. Matthieu got in and pulled her to him, but she pushed back. Trying to ground the electricity in the air, Louise almost pleaded.

"There's just so much I need to understand." Louise touched his temple. "In here."

"What would you like to know?"

"Why did you give up a career in archeology that you clearly loved so much?"

Matthieu started the engine but left the parking brake engaged. Before hitting the clutch, he leaned over and put his forehead against hers. "You seem to have your own secrets," he said, pointing to her temple.

"I'll tell you mine if you tell me yours," she bluffed.

He put the car in gear and drove. "I was working as an archeologist for the Musée du Châtillonnais in 1990, when I met a language student from England, Jo. We were going to be married."

"She broke your heart?"

"She was murdered."

A sense of dread rushed over Louise. It was an unexpected plot twist. "What happened?"

"She placed an advertisement in a local Burgundy newspaper, offering English lessons. A man contacted her, she went to meet him, then disappeared. On May 17th, 1990, her body was found in the Yonne River. She was naked and had been raped, beaten, and strangled. The crime remains unsolved."

"That's horrible," was all Louise could muster to say. "Were there any suspects?"

"A major suspect was the convicted serial killer known as The Beast of Ardennes."

"A serial killer?"

"His real name is Michel Fourniret."

"I'm so sorry." She touched his hand and he jerked the steering wheel while slamming the brakes and pulled over to the side of the road. It was obvious that this part of his life was still sensitive. His eyes were now gray in the colorless gloom and she cautiously placed her hand on the door latch.

"Promise me you will not do anymore *research*," Matthieu growled, the storm clearing from his eyes, leaving tears in its wake. He closed his eyes letting the tears drop. "Not without me."

She let go of the door handle and brushed the hair from his brow. "I promise to be careful. That's the best I can do."

He lowered his head and Louise held him tightly. His giant arms enveloped her, and she felt the shutters of his sobs as he cried into her sweater.

"It was my fault," he said. "If only I had not been away on an excavation, she would not have been alone."

"It was *not* your fault."

"Yes, it was! I should have known!"

"How could you have known?" His anguish seemed to go deeper than heartbreak or survivor's guilt. It evoked an unpleasant memory for her, when the Chief Financial Officer of the BCCI London office after learning that the criminal activity was more than just money laundering and pyramid schemes, but also murder.[18] Louise would never forget his look of horrified remorse.

"Everything will be okay," Louise said.

He put the car in gear and headed back down the road. All the charm of the day had vaporized, leaving the debris of shattered souvenirs, ruined in an instant. They drove in strained silence, but her mind raced.

"I'm sorry for the way I have been acting toward you," Matthieu finally said. "I have lived here all my life and never thought something like that ever could happen." He glowered at the beams of oncoming headlights in the inky darkness. "The murderer, Fourniret, is still out on the streets, and now they are harassing us."

"They?" Louise asked, but Matthieu didn't respond.

He pulled into the driveway, the fireplace burning inside the main house cast a warm contrast to cold reality outside. Matthieu walked Louise to her cottage.

---

[18] From the author's first novel in the Louise Moscow series, *Foliage: An International Banking Spy Thriller*

"Thank you for today," Louise said emptily. He moved closer, his lips brushing softly against hers, their tongues playing, but with less enthusiasm than before. The pressure of his weight aroused her, but his un-dried tears reminded her of his tortured soul. She broke away, with little protest by Matthieu. "See you tomorrow. Get some sleep." Louise kissed his cheek then retreated into her cottage and closing the door with the sound of finality.

PART III
ALL ROADS LEAD TO BELGIUM

TWENTY-FIVE

January 9, 2002

Sleep was not an option. There were too many clues to ignore. First, both Vladimir and LaFontaine had pointed her to Burgundy. Second, the ominous warning of *Dis Pater* from the man at the bar in Pommard. Then the clairvoyant's visions at Château du Chastenay. And now Matthieu's tragic revelation. Louise booted up her laptop and waited for it to connect to a satellite signal, praying that the Internet would yield information to connect the dots. She opened the Netscape web browser and typed in the Yahoo search engine. After a few attempts with different wording in French, she found shocking headlines about the English student, Joanna *Jo* Rogers.

On the morning of May 17, 1990, police found a body floating in the Yonne River. According to news reports – and confirming what Matthieu had told her – Jo had placed an advertisement in a local newspaper, offering English lessons. Investigators learned that a local man had responded to Joanna's ad by phone and was interested in hiring her to teach his teenage son. They arranged to meet at 7:00 p.m. on May 16 at the town square in Auxerre. Joanna was never seen alive again.

According to the comprehensive article Louise had found on the Internet, the authorities conducted a bungled investigation. The police cordoned off a small section of land close to where the body had been found and began searching for clues. However, investigators ignored a large portion of the surrounding area, most of which had been trampled by police, emergency personnel, onlookers, and vehicles. The secured area became accessible to the public just hours later, and the following day, children on a field trip further trampled it. Had there been any evidence, it was likely lost due to the contamination of the crime scene.

The body was taken to a nearby hospital for autopsy and her identity was confirmed. Joanna was twenty-two years old, from Gloucestershire, England. She had enrolled in a modern languages work-study program at

Leeds University and had taken a position as an assistant English teacher at a secondary school in the nearby town of Auxerre. At the time of her death, she was only one week away from completing her bachelor's degree.

Online court records included a scan of her autopsy report. It revealed that Joanna had been drugged, tied up, raped, beaten, and strangled before being dumped into the river. The medical examiner determined that her body had been in the water only several hours, indicating that it had been discarded in broad daylight. Referring back to the previous article, police still could not find any witnesses. They believed that whoever murdered Joanna was probably familiar with the area and resided in the immediate vicinity. Yet, police were unable to produce any suspects.

Louise found some additional information in another article. Joanna's parents, Edward and Paula, hired an attorney to assist them in gaining access to information about the case from the Auxerre police. Their expectations were quickly shattered when they realized how inadequately the case had been handled. Most shockingly, the reporter of the article revealed, was that their daughter's murder was not an isolated case. Apparently, seventeen other girls, ages sixteen to twenty-two, had gone missing or had been found murdered in Auxerre. Most of the cases had also been grossly mismanaged, completely ignored and even discarded. The reporter theorized that high-level officials intended to cover up the fact that Burgundy had an unusually high murder rate.

With this new information, Louise got in the car and drove to the bar in Pommard. She sat on the same stool of the busy pub and waited for the bartender, Jules, to notice her. She saw the old man sitting in his usual spot at the end of the bar nursing a brandy and reading a book, but he did not acknowledge her.

"Qu'est-ce que je vous sers?" Jules said robotically while drying a wine glass. Then he looked up from his work and saw her. "Ahhh! Mademoiselle Karen! Vous revoilà!"

"Bonsoir, Jules. Une bouteille de pinot noir Grand Cru, s'il vous plaît."

"Une bouteille? Un jour de fête, ou un jour de deuil?"

"Un peu des deux," Louise replied that she was both celebrating and mourning.

He eyed her with a boyish charm and a magician's agility as he placed a large Burgundy glass in front of her. He presented the bottle of the Grand Cru, then expertly uncorked it and poured a small amount for her to taste.

"Alors, I thought you had forgotten me," Jules said.

"Jamais." Louise swirled, sniffed, sipped and nodded.

He poured 150ml into her glass. "Are you hungry?"

Louise realized she hadn't had dinner. "I'm famished."

"Would you like to try the spécialité of the house?"

"That sounds perfect."

He dashed off and Louise continued to swirl the ruby liquid then picked up the glass by the stem to observe the color. Through the mirror behind the bar she noticed the old man watching her. She gave him a subtle nod and his face twitched with a half-smile. Jules returned and placed a steaming plate in front of her.

"Voilà, le boeuf bourguignon. Bon appétit."

"Ça a été rapide, Merci!" Louise was grateful for the fast service after the long emotional day. She enjoyed the roast beef smothered in rich red wine gravy which paired perfectly with the pinot noir. They certainly could cook in this region. After she had eaten it all, Louise tore off a bit of baguette crust, tossed it onto her plate and pushed it around with the fork and knife to soak up the last of the sauce, making the perfect bite. She washed it down with the last sip in her glass. It was now around 10 p.m. and the restaurant started to empty of locals, whereas in Paris the dinner rush would just be getting started. However, Jules seemed in no hurry to get rid of Louise, patiently drying wineglasses, then refilling hers.

"Ça a été?"

"It was delicious," Louise said. "Can I offer you a glass?"

"How can I refuse?" Jules reached for a Burgundy balloon glass and poured himself some.

"Can you pour a glass for the gentleman at the end of the bar?"

"Inspecteur Ducard? He's more of a brandy drinker at this hour."

Inspector? Louise was now insistent. "Please, offer him some wine so I can pull the worms from his nose." The French expression, thought to come from a deformation of the Latin word *verum* for truth, which was similar to the French word *vers* for worms, combined with the English expression *to worm a secret out of somebody*, had gracefully mutated into *pulling the worms from one's nose.*

"Let's give it a try." Jules took the bottle and another large glass. He placed it front of the old man who looked at Louise. She tipped her glass to him, he nodded, and Jules poured the wine. The inspector came and sat next to Louise.

"Santé." He raised his glass, which Louise clinked. "Inspecteur Gérard Ducard," he said, offering his hand.

"Enchantée, inspecteur. Je m'appelle Karen Baker."

"Américaine?"

"Oui. I'm a teacher on hiatus doing research for my novel," she continued in French.

"Your novel?" Ducard asked.

"Yes, a mystery set in Burgundy."

Deducing where she was headed, Ducard guzzled the whole glass of fine wine and got up to leave. "Good luck."

"Do you have to leave so soon? I'd love to interview you for a character in my book."

"I don't do interviews," he said tersely.

"Well, I hope to see you here again."

"Bonne soirée," he replied and made for the door.

Louise looked at Jules who gave her a foreboding look. "Law enforcement has had a tough time over the past couple years."

"How so?"

"The botched investigation of the serial murders in Auxerre ten years ago had been mostly forgotten until recently."

"What happened recently?"

"The confession of the bus driver last year and now the serial murders in Belgium seem to be stirring things up here."

"That's it!" Louise said, absentmindedly.

"Pardon?"

"I heard about the serial killer in Belgium. It made international news not only for his gruesomeness, but also for the police incompetence." She took a sip of the wine and looked Jules in the eyes. "Do you think they're connected?"

"I am just a humble barman," he said. "But there are many conspiracy theories."

"Come on, you must know as much as anyone. What about that English girl?" Louise snapped her fingers feigning to remember. "Jo...?"

Louise could see by Jules' expression that she had found the right topic to turn on the information spigot. "You mean Joanna Rogers," the barman began. "Jo's murder was another investigation that was bungled from the beginning. The crime scene was a forensic disaster and the French police withheld so much information that the British government had to do an independent inquiry. They found that French coroners had ignored critical evidence discovered on the crime scene, prompting a second autopsy that revealed several bite marks on Joanna's body. From a forensic standpoint, bite marks are vital clues that can reveal information about the killer because teeth…" He bared his teeth and chomped.

"Of course!" Louise finished his thought. "Bite marks are unique like fingerprints and can be matched to dental records."

"Indeed." *What kind of novel was the American writing?* Jules thought. "The revelation shocked Joanna's parents who couldn't comprehend how something so obvious and important could have gone unnoticed. Also, during the British autopsy, medical examiners obtained…" Jules paused a beat, "…sperm samples. It took forensics two years to analyze the samples, the results of which led to a genetic print. The DNA evidence was one of the biggest clues in the investigation, and the parents hoped that it would lead investigators to the killer. However, investigators refused to call for DNA tests of the local male population."

"Inspector Ducard refused?"

"Non! Ducard pushed for an investigation of men with criminal records, but he was denied. The family had to take matters into their own hands, distributing leaflets offering a reward to anyone with information into Joanna's death. They received some interesting responses."

"What kind of responses?" Louise was riveted as Jules filled in the gaps of her previous Internet research.

"The family members of three other women murdered in Burgundy between 1987 and 1990, Isabelle Laville, Danielle Bernard, and Sylvie Baton, responded to the leaflets. Their families were angry because they also felt that the investigators had been mishandling the cases. Joanna's parents presented the new leads to the French authorities. However, for some unknown reason, the investigators failed to pursue the tips. Because of Joanna's parents, approximately thirteen more unsolved murders and disappearances in the Auxerre area over the last thirty years became public. Investigators never told Joanna's parents about the spate of murders, two of which occurred within months of Joanna's death."

"Scandalous." Louise was truly shocked and pressed him for more. "You mentioned a bus driver confessed last year?"

"Yes, in December 2000, Émile Louis, a sixty-eight-year-old retired bus driver for a special needs school, confessed that he had raped and murdered seven pupils between 1977 and 1979. When the girls first began to disappear, the police had interviewed Émile, because they knew he had a history of sex offenses and the cases had some similarities. Many of the girls were either mentally handicapped, or, like Joanna, far from home. However, the police disregarded him as a suspect and instead reported the girls as runaway cases. Émile continued to drive female students to and from school..." Jules paused again for speculative effect, "...probably continuing to rape and kill them indiscriminately. He would not be considered a suspect again until he confessed two decades later."

"How could that happen?" Louise asked.

"It gets worse. Émile was caught because his daughter found items in his house belonging to several of the victims. During his confession, Émile told authorities that he had buried the girls near the Yonne River. Only the skeletal remains of two girls were ever recovered. Then, not long after his admission of guilt, Émile changed his story claiming that he had been pressured into giving false testimony. He insisted that a nebulous ring of prominent local authorities had routinely abducted, abused and killed girls."

"But he knew where the bodies were, so he was convicted, right?" Louise asked.

"They could not charge Émile with the murders because under French law, the statute of limitations to charge someone for murder was ten years after the commission of a crime. Instead, they convicted him for kidnapping, for which there is no statute of limitations."

"But he must have been Joanna's killer, right?"

"Non! Émile could not have been directly responsible for Joanna's death. At the time of her murder, he was serving a prison sentence for sexually assaulting a minor. However, a private investigation by Christian Jambert clearly established that Émile was linked to all the women."

"Who is Christian Jambert?" Louise asked.

"Christian Jambert was a former police officer who quit to become a private investigator. After conducting a thirteen-year investigation, Jambert believed that Émile was affiliated with a sex ring operation that prostituted, abused, and murdered many girls in the region.

Jules was on a roll. "At first, the authorities ignored Jambert's theories, but an incident in 1984 led them to reconsider the idea that there was indeed a sex ring in the area. In January 1984 someone found a nineteen-year-old girl wandering the streets of Auxerre in a confused state. When the police questioned her, she claimed that she had been held captive in the basement of a nearby house where she had been sexually abused and tortured. The girl's testimony led the police to the home of Claude and Monique Dunand, known friends of Émile Louis. When they searched the house, they found another girl in the cellar, naked and suspended from a ladder by her wrists. For fifteen years they had been luring local handicapped girls to the house, locking them up, feeding them dog food, and then inviting guests who repeatedly raped and tortured them. However, there was no indication that any of the girls were murdered."

"Mon Dieu," was all Louise could mutter.

"Claude Dunand eventually received a life sentence in 1991 for kidnapping. His wife, Monique, received two years as accessory to the crimes. Dunand has always maintained that politicians and other influential people were involved but refuses to name them. The police discovered a list of at least fifty clients rumored to include several French notables who paid to torture and abuse captive girls. The police handed the list over to the Auxerre Courthouse. However, the list mysteriously disappeared from a courtroom and has never been found. It was not the only document that went missing. There were more than one hundred murder and missing-person case files from between 1958 and 1982 that vanished from the courthouse. The court ledger documenting the investigations also vanished. It became clear that Auxerre Courthouse either had a serious management problem, or someone was trying to cover up the crimes."

"Sounds like a conspiracy web," Louise offered. "Did Jambert find the perpetrators?"

"Jambert felt almost certain he knew who was behind Burgundy's rash of murders and missing person cases, and he was sure that Émile was one of the primary culprits. However, he also believed that Émile was only one of many involved in the crimes. Jambert kept meticulous notes and diaries concerning the cases, along with the evidence he collected over the years. In 1997 he prepared to present his findings during a new inquiry. But he never got the chance to reveal what he had worked so hard to prove. In August 1997, just several days before the start of the inquiries, someone found Jambert dead in the basement of his Auxerre home. An autopsy revealed that he had died from a single gunshot wound to the head. Investigators claimed that Jambert had a history of depression and the official cause of his death was suicide."

"How frighteningly convenient." Louise was getting that sense of dread.

Jules poured the remaining wine into their glasses. "That is why Inspecteur Ducard is a tortured man."

"I don't understand."

"Before Jambert became a private investigator, he was Ducard's partner on the police force."

"Inspecteur Ducard was Jambert's partner?"

Jules nodded yes. "This is why he spends his retirement drinking."

"Will he be back here?" Louise asked, looking at the bar tab.

"Inspecteur Ducard? He's here almost every evening. He usually reads before dinner."

"What does he like to read?"

"Detective novels mostly," Jules replied.

"Is he an honest detective?"

Jules took his cue. "As honest as the day is long." Suddenly they were both at Rick's Café Americain in Morocco, as Jules threw his hands up and then wiped a serving tray exactly like Carl the waiter, portrayed by Hungarian actor S.Z. "Cuddles" Sakall.

"Bravo! Casablanca is my favorite movie!" Louise left enough cash to cover the bill plus a hefty tip. "Thank you, Jules. À très bientôt."

"À votre service."

TWENTY-SIX

January 9, 2002

The next morning, back at the vineyard, Louise rushed from the bathroom to answer her ringing mobile phone. "Allô!"

"Mademoiselle Baker?" The caller asked.

"Oui, c'est moi."

"Bonjour. C'est Yves Renard du Crédit Agricole à l'appareil."

"Ah, oui, bonjour!" Louise was a little thrown getting a call from the Crédit Agricole manager.

"Your loan documents are ready," Renard continued in French. "Would you be able to come and sign them today?"

"I can be there in half an hour, okay?"

"Ça marche, À tout à l'heure."

Louise hung up, grabbed a quick café in Magali's kitchen and a half hour later was waiting in the lobby of the Crédit Agricole bank that catered to both humble farming community and wealthy viticulturists alike. It was a far cry from the gleaming BCCI Paris headquarters where she used to coddle affluent clientele. Renard impassively greeted Louise and escorted her to his office.

"I have also arranged for you to meet with the real estate agent today," Renard said.

Louise was actually impressed. "That's wonderful!"

Renard handed her documents to sign with the nonchalance of a bistro server giving her l'addition. *The greedier the man, the blanker the expression,* Louise thought. To Renard, she was just another gullible foreigner eager to part with perfectly good cash for a piece of the dream. "I'm a little nervous."

"You have nothing to worry about. I've been doing this for thirty years," Renard assured her.

"You've been with Crédit Agricole for thirty years?"

"I've been with Crédit Agricole for five years, but I have many prior years' experience in banking."

"Here in Burgundy?"

"No, I'm from Belgium." Louise suppressed any reaction, her silence prompting him to try to impress her. "I was with the Chase bank in Belgium for ten years, then Banque Almasi."

"Oh, that poor monsieur Almasi."

Renard quipped, uncharacteristically, "Bankers never die; they just lose interest." Louise hesitated, then laughed, despite the poor taste of the joke.

"Still using that old joke, Renard?" a statuesque blonde woman said from the doorway.

"Ah! Here she is." Renard stood to greet her. "Mademoiselle Baker, this is Charlotte Perreaux. She will take you around to see some properties today."

Charlotte had giant blue eyes and heart-shaped lips. "It is nice to meet you." She shook Louise's hand firmly while studying her closely. "It's a funny coincidence. Something just came on the market, and I have a premonition you'll love it."

If this was a sales tactic, Louise was buying. Charlotte's intensity made her credible and likable. "How soon can I see it?"

"I'll make a call." Charlotte took out her mobile phone and input the number. "We might be able to go there right now. I'll meet you outside." Charlotte waved to Renard and left.

"Thank you so much," Louise told Renard. "Charlotte seems great." She finished signing the documents.

"You're quite welcome." He took the documents. "Bonne journée." They shook hands and Louise left.

Charlotte smiled as Louise came out to meet her. "The owner is home and will let us visit right now."

"That's great! Should I follow you?" Louise asked.

"I'll drive." They got into Charlotte's Mercedes-Benz G-Class.

"I didn't know Mercedes made this body type. I've never seen it in the U.S." Louise had indeed been away from the States for too long.

"I believe it's only available in Europe. It's good to have four-wheel drive around here." She sped off accelerating with ease.

"It feels like a very luxurious Jeep," Louise said appreciating the ruggedness.

Charlotte agreed and touted its advantages. "It's sometimes referred to as the *Wolf*. It was developed as a military vehicle for the Shah of Iran. I've heard there is a grey market for these in the U.S. with the basic model going for six figures. This one is much less, of course." Charlotte merged onto route A6 south.

"Is the property very far?" Louise asked.

"It's only about 20 kilometers south of here, right on the cusp of Burgundy." As they continued, the landscape became more bucolic with pastures and orchards interspersed among the vineyards. "This house is very special because it's literally right in the middle of a peach orchard."

Louise grinned. "Would I have to become a peach farmer?"

Charlotte laughed. "No, you would not own the orchards. It's a small parcel of land that happened to stay independent of the orchards. So, you get the best of both worlds." Their chat made the drive go quickly and they were soon passing soft rolling hills.

"It's beautiful. What river this that?"

"It's the Saône River. This area is Côte Chalonnaise named after the town of Chalon-sur-Saône. Being on the river made the town an important trading center of the Celts in Gaul and later by the ancient Romans, with wine being one of the commodities traded along the river." Louise had always been impressed with how well the French knew their history. It made up for how few could manage basic English. "More than twenty thousand Roman amphorae have been found in graves in this area."

Now it was Louise's turn to impress. "Are those the long narrow ceramic pots?" At the museum Matthieu had explained the amphorae were ideal for the transport and storage of olive oil and wine. The pointed base allowed it to stand upright when embedded in soft ground and also concentrated sediments from liquids.

"Bravo! You have been learning some of the local culture." Charlotte began a convincing sales pitch. "There's so much history here. In the 1980s, this region began producing higher-quality wine and experienced a renaissance. As the price of Burgundy wine increased, the Côte Chalonnaise developed a reputation for consistent quality at a lower price than some of the better-known villages of Burgundy. It led to a sharp increase in the price of wines, which brought an influx of investment to this area."

They passed rows of mature peach groves, still bare from the winter. Charlotte turned onto a gravel road that was a long driveway ending at a charming stone cottage. "This house was built in the 1600s. You're so fortunate that it just happened to go on the market. I've known this house all my life and absolutely adore it."

"Don't you want to buy it?" Louise asked.

"Believe me, I would. But I must be practical. My young daughter is in school, and my husband works in Dijon."

They walked up to the garden with a long narrow stone swimming pool at the end of which water trickled from a scallop shell. Steam rose invitingly from the crystal-clear lagoon.

"I feel like a swim!" Louise said.

Suddenly an older gentleman was upon them. "The scent of peach blossoms, lavender, and herbs is wonderful in spring," the man spoke with an Italian accent. He pointed up. "These two ancient cork trees provide shade in the summer."

"Ciao, bello!" Charlotte said, exchanging many cheek kisses. "Giorgio, this is Karen. She's looking for a summer home, so of course I had to show her your place."

Giorgio had a soft manner. His silver hair and slight stubble gave him an aging-movie-star elegance. He wiped his hands on a rag. "It is nice to meet you, Karen." They exchanged four cheek kisses. "Please come in. I apologize for my appearance. I'm trying out a new pigment on the sitting room walls." They walked into the cottage with centuries-old stone floors, worn antique furniture covered with vintage textiles, and picture frames without pictures.

"Giorgio and his wife Irène have been restoring this house for over ten years," Charlotte said.

"It hadn't been occupied in eighty years when we bought it," Giorgio added.

"Giorgio is a genius at using the resources at hand. He painted the rooms with local pigments."

"Yellow, ocher, red, green." Giorgio walked them through. "I even painted some of the lampshades, lest they look too bare."

"It's perfect," Louise said. "What a treasure."

"We were living in Paris when I saw a listing in the paper that said, *Ruin for Sale.*" Giorgio laughed. "Irène thought I had lost my mind."

"You've done an incredible job restoring it," Louise said.

"It is a never-ending project. We believe that a house should never be finished. When the house is finished, you die."

"May I ask why you are parting with it?" Louise inquired.

"We are moving back to Paris," Giorgio said. "It is too much work for us now. Can I offer you some lunch?"

"Well…" How could she refuse? It seemed everyone in Burgundy either knew history or cuisine, probably both. Before Louise could answer, Giorgio began plating sliced fresh mozzarella di bufala and homegrown tomatoes. He walked over and brushed his hand across a bushy basil plant by the door, pinching off a few white flowers that were trying to sprout and discarding them outside. He snipped a stem and plucked off a few leaves that he stacked, rolled, sliced into a chiffonade. He drizzled balsamic vinegar and fresh olive oil, then a pinch of fleur de sel and cracked pepper, and sprinkled the chiffonade over all. Giorgio placed the beautiful ceramic platter in the center of the large wooden farm table, alongside a bowl of crusty sliced baguette. He quickly set the table with mismatched flowery plates and utensils.

"Asseyez-vous," he said, indicating the chairs.

Louise sat, taking in the beautiful presentation, simple, fresh, and magnificent. "It looks delicious."

Giorgio served them red wine poured over ice in cobalt tumblers. "Tchin tchin," he said, raising his glass.

Louise had gone to the bank under the pretext of buying a vacation home for her investigation. But now she was seriously wondering if this house was in her stars.

"Is the house on the market yet?" Louise asked.

"We're still deciding," Giorgio said. "But I wanted to let Charlotte know we were thinking about it."

"Well, if you decide to sell, could you call me first?"

"Of course," Charlotte replied. "Karen is a referral to me by Yves Renard at Crédit Agricole," she informed Giorgio.

"Renard in French means *fox*," Giorgio said. "Let's just leave it at that."

Charlotte winked at Louise. "For all of Renard's faults, he sent us Karen."

"Cheers to that." Giorgio got up and refilled their glasses. "Just watch your *derrière*, Karen." To which Charlotte giggled.

"Why?" Louise asked. Charlotte and Giorgio both rolled their eyes. Giorgio made the universal sign of putting a key between his lips, turning it, and throwing it away.

"He is, how you say, a bit louche," Charlotte said.

"Shady, sournois, like a rat," Giorgio said. "Un petit mesquin."

"He's a dirty old man," Charlotte concluded.

"Pervert," Giorgio said. They laughed but Charlotte picked up on Louise's concern.

"Just keep him at arm's length," Charlotte advised. "You may have noticed I don't give him the bisous."

"Yes, keep far away," Giorgio said.

They switched to a more pleasant conversation and after lunch, they bid Giorgio farewell. Charlotte dropped Louise off at her car and she headed straight home.

Trying to avoid Matthieu, Louise darted into her cottage. That evening she planned to stake out Inspector Ducard and needed to do more research. She turned on her computer and sifted through articles on Usenet, cutting and pasting data to a proliferating Word document. Most of the leads into serial killings fizzled out, except for one article about Joanna's parents who had looked into the French investigation of a truck driver, Thierry Villetard, in prison for sex crimes. He had lived near the school in Auxerre where Jo taught. But there was not much else about him on the Internet.

Louise freshened up, wet down her hair and parted it on the side creating a retro look. She put on the Myrna Loy pencil dress in burgundy crepe rayon – burgundy in Burgundy – with a notched neckline and small rounded collar, dark hose, and her Mary Janes.

She drove to the pub in Pommard, hoping to arrive before Inspector Ducard.

TWENTY-SEVEN

January 9, 2002

"Mademoiselle Karen!" Jules greeted her.

She sat in her usual spot at the bar. "I had a craving."

"Assiette de fromages?"

"You read my mind." He went to fetch the cheese plate leaving her lost in thought. There was a definite pattern with the serial killings. Also, the former Monte Carlo Chief Superintendent of the Urban Police Division, M. Patrick Roblot, believed there were connections to the banking world, perhaps some kind of dark network involved in thwarting the police.

Jules returned with a plate of local cheeses and fresh sliced baguette. "Voilà!" He presented it to her, pointing to each cheese as if he were in a Michelin-starred restaurant. "Start with the king of cheeses, Epoisses. It is excellent with this white Burgundy from Côte de Beaune." He showed her the bottle then poured her a glass.

"*White burgundy* sounds like an oxymoron."

"The diamond among rubies," Jules said.

Louise spread the semi-soft cow's milk cheese on the bread, bit down into the creamy crusty delight, and sipped the wine.

"Exquisite."

Jules pointed to the next cheese. "Try this Bouton de Culotte goat cheese with your *oxymoron*." He pointed to the last cheese. "But wait for your next glass of wine to try this Morbier. It goes great with a pinot noir."

Louise spread the goat cheese on the bread and bit into it. "Sublime."

Jules rushed off to serve some new arrivals, leaving Louise gorging on cheese, bread, and wine, comforted by the earthy flavors. She made a mental note to add this to the menu of Magali's dream Café.

Jules returned and quipped, "Les émotions, ça creuse." The French expression literally means *emotions hollow out the stomach*, making you hungry.

Louise gave him a look of guilty pleasure. "True. Let's just say I've had an eventful day." She took another satisfying bite and finished the white wine.

Jules poured a glass of pinot noir. "For the Morbier."

She cut into the cheese and ate a chunk, sans bread, chasing it with the red wine. "Heaven."

"Fit for an angel," Jules said.

Louise laughed. "Bartenders are gods among men."

"Bartenders are gods?"

"Think about it," Louise expounded. "Maybe God isn't omnipotent. Maybe he's just been around so long, he knows everything."

"Un Jour Sans Fin!"

"Bravo!" Louise might have known she couldn't put one over on Jules. He caught the film quote from Bill Murray in *Groundhog Day*. She craved some more information about him. His boyish good looks made him both disarming and approachable. "Are you married?"

"Yes, I have a lovely wife and a beautiful daughter," he confessed.

"Lucky women," Louise said.

Jules looked at his watch, and, like clockwork, Inspector Ducard entered. He acknowledged no one and walked directly to his usual seat at the end of the bar. He cracked open his book and read intently. As expected, a glass of wine appeared in his line of vision. Unexpectedly, a book slid into his view. It was *The Maltese Falcon* by Dashiell Hammett, but the French version, *Le Faucon De Malte*. The haunting eyes of the *femme fatale* on the cover glared up at him.

Ducard raised his eyes and saw Jules looking at him from behind the bar, then turned to see Louise sitting next to him. In her Myrna Loy dress and her black hair parted on the side reminiscent of the woman on the book cover, from Ducard's reaction, Louise's version of the *femme fatale* had an immediate effect.

"May I join you?" Louise asked in French.

He nodded yes and picked up the book. "*Le Faucon De Malte* en français."

"Cadeau," Louise said.

"No, I couldn't possibly accept this." He pushed the book toward her. "It is very rare."

Louise pushed the book back to him. "J'insiste."

"Where did you get this?"

"I found it when I was at university in Paris. While I was packing to come here from Chicago, this dress inspired me to bring the book along. I finally had a chance to read it. So, now I pass it on to you."

Ducard was at a loss for words. He had seen his share of the worst of mankind and it had hardened him. This act of kindness made a chink in his armor. "Merci," was all he could muster.

"You're welcome." She turned to Jules. "A bottle of champagne, s'il vous plaît."

"Avec plaisir!" Jules said, filling an ice bucket.

"What are you reading?" Louise asked Ducard.

He closed the cover of the book, revealing the French bestseller, *Les Rivières Pourpres.*

"The Crimson Rivers," Louise said aloud in English, recognizing the author's name on the cover. "That's the latest Jean-Christophe Grangé crime novel. I've been meaning to get a copy."

Taking the book with both hands he presented it to her. "Cadeau," he said.

"But you're still reading it."

"I have already read it twice. Please take it. J'insiste."

"Thank you," Louise said. The champagne cork popped, perfectly timed. "Three glasses please. One for you too, Jules."

By the second bottle, they had discussed life, love, and family. Ducard was warm, charming, and intelligent. Around ten-thirty, the place had mostly emptied out. Jules turned up the stereo when the song *In a Sentimental Mood*, the Sarah Vaughan version, came on.

"I love this music," Louise said. The familiar refrain brought back old memories of her father, yet it sounded so fresh and new. "Inspector Ducard, you remind me of my father. I detect that, like him, you are very stoic, very enigmatic, but deep down, a softy."

Ducard gave a crooked smile and raised his glass. "He is a wonderful father too, that is clear."

"Thank you," she said, clinking his glass, truly touched by the double compliment. The conversation and champagne had both fortified and emboldened her. "Sooo," hesitating, "what's your theory about the unsolved murders in Auxerres?" Louise immediately regretted blurting it out so clumsily. Ducard glared at her. "I'm so sorry, I didn't mean to bring up a sensitive subject."

He looked at Jules, then back at Louise. They both could tell his anger was brewing and thought he was about to walk out. But then something remarkable occurred. His entire demeanor softened – as though he were mulling something, and then made a decision – right before their eyes. He was ready to get something off his chest.

He took a deep breath, then exhaled. "I was a senior detective in Auxerre when the murders happened." The first sentence almost sounded sentimental. "Even the good cops couldn't do anything to stop the killers."

"*Killers*?" Louise took the tone of a therapist. No acting class could have given her the skills to remain in character of Karen. She thought of Marlon Brando's technique, she wasn't acting, she just was. "Wasn't it a serial killer?"

"Serial *killers*," said Ducard. "They are still kidnapping, raping, and killing."

"Still?" Louise asked. "Do you have proof?"

"Proof? What good does proof do? We had overwhelming evidence. But the judge threw it away."

"What kind of evidence?" Louise, in her tipsy state, was interrogating Ducard as if he were the perpetrator.

Ducard didn't notice. "Follow the trail of death. The primary suspects, Michael Fourniret and Monique Olivier, the couple who were committing abductions and serial murders in Auxerre, fled to Belgium. Suddenly, there are serial killers in Belgium. There is no such thing as a coincidence."

Louise was stunned. Michel Fourniret was the same name that Matthieu had mentioned. "How long ago was that?"

"Very recent. In 2000 Fourniret and his wife Monique Olivier were arrested in Belgium. Fourniret confessed to kidnapping, raping, and murdering nine girls over a period of fourteen years. His wife, Olivier, admitted that she sometimes picked up young women for him in their car with their baby son in the back. Olivier also confessed she had been present at the murder of a young woman in Auxerre in 1990."

"The English girl, Joanna?" Louise asked.

"Oui," he confirmed, his eyes filled with anguish. "But then, Olivier withdrew her statement, claiming to have made it under pressure from an investigator.

"Were you working on those older cases?" Louise asked.

"My department didn't get involved until the cases were deemed runaways. But, even when we were involved, we were met with great resistance. Finally, my partner and I resigned in protest."

"But you continued to follow the cases?" Louise asked.

"We had to," Ducard said.

"What do you mean?" Louise asked.

"The public was outraged over police incompetence," Ducard explained. "We were sure there was obstruction of justice. Not only did we want justice, we needed to do our due diligence in case we were implicated. But it was too big for us. There were so many perpetrators reaching all the way to Belgium"

"The Fourniret case." Louise proclaimed, as if she was coming up with the title for Karen's fake novel.

"Oui. But also, witnesses testified to having seen a white van in several missing-girl cases. Investigations led to an unemployed Belgian electrician with criminal history, Marc Dutroux."

"Was there any evidence against him?"

"Just follow the money. Even though he was living on welfare, he owned several houses. His own mother insisted he would very likely commit a crime again. But he was released. Then there is the botched investigation in Belgium."

"Like the botched investigation in Auxerre?" Louise said.

"Worse. Police set up cameras outside Dutroux's residence, but they only recorded from 8:00 a.m. to 6:00 p.m. As though it was banker's hours!" Ducard's pent-up frustration became manifest. "Then a police officer came to inspect one of his homes, accompanied by a locksmith who said he heard girls yelling. But the officer insisted the sounds were coming from outside.

"Now, get this." Ducard's voice was rising. "They entered the house, but the officer did not investigate thoroughly enough to find a door to the basement dungeon behind some boxes. He also found videotapes, but the police didn't watch them because they didn't have a VCR." He repeated for emphasis, "They didn't have a VCR! It wasn't until weeks later that they finally watched what was clearly evidence, showing Dutroux actually constructing the dungeon in his basement. They raided the house again and found the two girls inside had died of starvation."

"Quelle horreur." Louise was truly disgusted.

The once taciturn Ducard now couldn't stop telling his story. "In August 1996, Dutroux was finally arrested. But just when they were making progress on the investigation, the judge in charge was dismissed and replaced by someone who only focused on dead-end leads. Several prominent people involved in the investigation died under suspicious circumstances."

This information struck Louise as more KGB style tactics with key witnesses turning up dead. But she remained silent to allow Ducard to continue.

"Marc Dutroux was eventually convicted and sentenced to life in prison. But he testified that he had kidnapped the girls to supply a larger organized pedophile network. Those claims were never investigated."

"A network." Louise said, trying to follow.

"As far as the authorities were concerned, the case of the missing girls ended with Dutroux," Ducard explained. "The conspiracy theories started when authorities actively sabotaged the investigation to cover up evidence of an elite pedophile network. The public became aware of Dutroux's claims that he was part of a sex ring that included high-ranking members of the police force, politicians, influential businessmen, and judges in Belgium's court system. He also claimed that he had a partner who helped source girls from Eastern Europe. But then, the judge in charge of investigating the claims, Jean-Marc Connerotte, was dismissed on the grounds of conflict of interest because he attended a fundraising dinner for the girls' parents."

"It was quite the scandal," Jules added. "The judge's dismissal and the end of the investigation resulted in a massive protest called *The White March*. Two months after Dutroux's arrest, 300,000 people marched in Brussels, demanding reforms of Belgium's police and justice system.

Ducard resumed. "On the witness stand Judge Connerotte broke down in tears when he described the bulletproof vehicles and armed guards needed to protect him against shadowy figures determined to stop the truth from coming out. Police told him that murder contracts had been taken out against the magistrates. Connerotte testified that the investigation was seriously hampered because people in the government were protecting suspects. He believed that the Mafia had taken control of the case.

"A seventeen-month investigation by a parliamentary commission into the Dutroux affair produced a report in February 1998, which concluded that, while Dutroux did not have accomplices in high positions in the police and justice systems, as he continued to claim, he benefited from corruption, sloppiness, and incompetence. Public indignation flared up again in April 1998 after Dutroux escaped."

"Escaped?" *Stranger than fiction*, Louise thought.

"Oui. While being transferred to a courthouse without handcuffs, Dutroux overpowered one of his guards, took his gun, and escaped. Police forces in Belgium, France, Luxembourg, and Germany were on an all-borders alert and he was caught a few hours later. The Minister of Justice, the Minister of the Interior, and the police chief resigned as a result. In 2000 Dutroux received a five-year sentence for threatening a police officer during his escape."

Jules shook his head. "The Dutroux case was so infamous that a third of Belgians with the surname Dutroux applied to have their name changed."

Ducard continued. "In 2000 Fourniret and his wife were arrested in Belgium. The saga continues here because all the events in Belgium reopened old wounds of the unsolved cases."

"Can I ask you another question?" Louise asked.

"Why not?" Ducard emptied his champagne glass. He signaled to Jules who poured him a brandy.

"Do you know the account manager, Yves Renard, at the Beaune Crédit Agricole?"

"Oui. He's not a local," Ducard replied without hesitating. The drinks had loosened tongues. "With the Crédit Agricole merger, corporate types were put into the regional branches. This is not uncommon. But I refuse to bank with non-locals."

"I'm staying at the gîte of Matthieu and Magali Mersault," Louise revealed. "Renard is the Mersaults' banker at Crédit Agricole. They sent inspectors to check on Mersault's vineyards, and they found some diseased vines. Matthieu suspects foul play."

Ducard looked at Jules, who raised his eyebrows. "This is very interesting. If the bank determines that the vineyard is at risk, they can raise their interest rates or even call the loan," Ducard observed. "It could ruin them."

"Exactly. I made an appointment specifically with Renard under pretext that I needed a loan to buy a summer home here. He told me that he was previously with the Chase Bank in Belgium and had also worked at Banque Almasi in Monte Carlo." Louise said. They fell silent for a moment, digesting it all.

Ducard's police instincts were kicking in. "What kind of novel are you writing?" he asked.

Louise was taken aback for a second, and then sputtered a reply. "It...it was going to be a mystery novel. But now it's turning into a spy thriller."

Ducard noticed the hesitation and was suddenly very intrigued. "You seem very familiar to me."

"You seem familiar to me too," Louise said, bumping shoulders with him. She was hoping her playfulness would diffuse his line of questioning.

"Not just on a spiritual level," Ducard continued. "You look familiar to me."

She tried a different dodge. "I get that a lot. I have classic American features."

"No, it's something else. You speak French so well. You lived in France?"

Louise had used up all the excuses she had prepared for this line of questioning. Given her recent discoveries about her mother, she went off script and improvised on her faux past. "My mother lived here briefly," Louise said. "She went to school in Dijon, training to be a simultaneous translator."

Jules tried to help lighten the now-heavier mood. "Like Audrey Hepburn in *Charade*!" he said.

"Exactly," Louise said. "But she didn't finish. She never told me what happened exactly, but it was bad." Louise emptied the champagne glass. Jules refilled it. "Anyway, she spoke to me in French as a child, so I had a pretty good head start before school. Then I got my degree and became a high school French teacher. A family inheritance gave me a little financial freedom, and it has always been my dream to own a place in Burgundy, France."

"What does your mother think of that?" Ducard asked.

"She was against me even coming here."

"Giving you the seedlings for your novel," Ducard said.

"Yes, a mystery novel set in Burgundy."

Suddenly, Ducard became distracted by a customer who had gotten up to leave. Louise turned to see a mysterious figure watching them in the obscurity before exiting.

"Who was that?" Louise asked.

"Probably no one. But you should be careful."

"You're the second person to tell me that," Louise said.

"Oh?" Ducard said.

"Matthieu Mersault made me promise not to go to Auxerre without him."

"Good idea," Jules said. "That is one big angry man. He will protect you."

"Yes. If anyone wants to find the culprits it is Matthieu Mersault," Ducard said. "Did you say that Renard had also worked in Monte Carlo?"

"Yes, he transferred from there to Beaune," Louise said.

"Isn't that interesting, inspector Ducard?" Jules said.

"It is very interesting," Ducard said, finishing his brandy and getting up to leave. "Well, thank you for the champagne and the book." He placed the cherished gift under his arm and gave Louise four cheek kisses. "See you soon?"

"Yes, I'll see you both after I get back from a short trip," Louise said.

"Where are you going?" Ducard asked.

Louise didn't mean to pause, but it definitely gave her answer some weight. "Belgium."

Louise drove home carefully. She had had too much to drink but getting Ducard to open up was worth it. She focused intently on the dark road, not noticing the car that was tailing her. As soon as she arrived back at the gîte, she picked up her mobile and made a phone call.

"Hey, Michael." Her friend and confidant expressed gratitude for her call. But even in her multiple drink condition, Louise was all business. "I need a few background checks."

"Are you okay?" Michael asked. "You're slurring a little."

"Champagne."

"Ah. Don't do anything I wouldn't do," Michael teased.

Louise buckled down. "I'm using my serious voice right now. Background checks. Grab a pen."

The message was received, and he prepared to write. "Okay, I'm ready. Who do you want me to check out?"

"Yves Renard, Michel Fourniret and Monique Olivier, Marc and Lelièvre Dutroux, Michelle Martin, Bernard Weinstein…"

The names rang an alarm bell for Michael. "Wait a minute," Michael interrupted. "Why are you asking for background checks on serial killers?"

"Also, do a check on Matthieu Mersault," Louise said. "That's it for now."

"That's it for now? Who the hell is Mersault? How do you know him?"

"I'm staying at his family vineyard. They're great people, but something seems off about him." Louise gave Michael the relevant coordinates of the gîte.

Michael took it all down. "What's the connection?"

"That's what I need to figure out. Right now, they are all somehow tied to Belgium. See if there are any links at all between them. I'm heading to Auxerre tomorrow, then Paris and Brussels."

"What the hell are you getting into over there?"

"Just following leads."

"Leads, she says. Every time you follow leads, I want to call Interpol." Michael emphasized what he said next. "Okay, be careful. And give me a call when you get to Paris."

"Okay, thanks."

As soon as they hung up, Michael received a text from Jean-Philippe. "Doesn't anybody sleep in France?" he wondered aloud. He called him back immediately and heard the familiar voice on the other end of the line.

"Jean-Philippe, what's happening?"

"You may want to come back here. My contact at the retreat may have something."

"What is it?"

"There are two new Russian guests and he heard them mention the *Maltese Falcon*. Did the FBI find anything any COMINT about that?"

"No, but I'll check again and let you know," Michael replied. "Now get some rest." Michael was about to say goodbye, but Jean-Philippe had more.

"Wait, that's not the only reason I called," Jean-Philippe said. "We also heard the Russians use the term *Ruby Red*. Do you have any COMINT on that name?"

Michael froze at the mention of Louise's code name. Now the heat was on. "I'll catch the next flight." Michael's spring-into-action mode was in the red zone. He was about to hang up, when he remembered something. "Are you still there?"

"Yes?"

"Louise just called to say she is following a lead, leaving tomorrow for Paris then Brussels. Should I tell her to back off?"

Jean-Philippe was momentarily paralyzed, first hearing Louise's name, and then realizing he had to make a call on her safety. "No, let her go. She may disrupt our investigation. But trying to stop her might be even worse."

TWENTY-EIGHT

January 10, 2002

Bam! Blinding red and white stars burst in the blackness, then pain. Her head throbbed. She winced in anticipation of the next blow, but it didn't come. Only the ache at the point of impact remained, slowly spreading over her brain until it reached the nape of her neck. She tried to open her eyes to make out her surroundings, which appeared to be a dungeon. Hands tied above her head, the weight of her body creating a searing pain in her right shoulder.

"Karen." The voice was quiet, gentle, kind, concerned, and seemed out of place. "Karen!" The voice was more urgent. Louise moved her legs, trying to stand to relieve some of the pressure on her arms, but she was paralyzed. She pushed as hard as she could, causing her body to jerk, waking her. Pain shot through her shoulder, her arm was excruciatingly numb and tingled. The nightmare faded and a wave of relief washed over her. She sat up, shaking her right arm to get the circulation flowing, after the dead weight of her body, lying on it for hours, had cut it off. Burgundy had not been good for her dream state or for her liver.

"Karen, le petit déjeuner est prêt." It was Matthieu calling her to breakfast.

"Water," Louise said to herself. She walked to the little fridge and took out a bottle of Evian, filled a large glass, and drank the whole thing.

She went to the door and opened, groggily waving for Matthieu to enter. He did so reluctantly, noticing her state, not sure she realized what she was doing.

"Ça va? Tu as la gueule de bois?" he asked.

"J'ai la tête comme une citrouille," Louise said, bemoaning her hangover symptoms: a mouth as dry as wood and a head like a pumpkin. The French often compared the head to spherical vegetables. A pumpkin in this case not only for the shape but also to express the size of the head feeling swollen.

She'd been spending enough nights at the bars in France to know the expression well.

"Drink water," Matthieu advised.

Louise showed him how much of the Evian she already had drunk. Instead of pouring more water into the glass she drank straight from the bottle. Matthieu went to the bathroom and found some aspirin. He handed her three.

"Tiens."

Louise looked at the tablets. "Just two," she said.

"No, take three," he urged. She didn't argue and swallowed all three with another swig of water. Matthieu, ever a gentleman, politely moved to the door. "I'll let you get dressed."

"Wait," Louise said, dismissing his prudishness. She grabbed fresh lingerie from the drawer and went to the bathroom. "Today, I'll follow you to Auxerre," she said through the closed door. "Then I'll continue on to Brussels."

She came out wearing the fresh underwear, ignoring Matthieu's attempting-not-to-look eyes, and proceeded to dress and pack a bag. She was on a mission, despite the hangover. "We'll have to save Vézelay for another time. I need your help in case something goes wrong in Auxerre."

"What are you up to?" His gaze focused, staring directly at various dressed and undressed states of her taut yet supple curves.

"We'll talk over breakfast." They walked to the main house, Louise still wobbly, held onto Matthieu's arm.

"Bonjour!" they all said.

"Bien dormi?" Magali asked, looking skeptically at Louise.

"Café," Matthieu suggested.

"Oui, s'il vous plaît," Louise said, holding her hands like a bowl to indicate a big one.

Magali placed the bowl of coffee in front of Louise. "Lait?" she asked. Louise shook her head yes, and Magali poured the warm foamy milk. It was good to be at her breakfast table. "Sucre?" Louise nodded again sleepily.

"Karen fait dodo," Luke said, ever observant.

Louise drank sleepily at first. Then the coffee seemed to transform her instantly. Her eyes popped open and she looked at Luke in an almost cartoonish way. "Much better!" Luke giggled.

"We haven't seen you in a couple of days," Magali said.

"Vous nous avez manquée!" Luke said.

"I missed you too!" Louise replied. "I've been very busy working. But I'll be back again soon."

"Are you going away?" Magali asked.

"Just for the weekend to visit some friends. Matthieu is going to take me on a tour of Auxerre, then I have to stop in Paris and Brussels."

"Matthieu is going the whole weekend too?" Magali asked, with a pronounced enthusiasm.

"He's just accompanying me to Auxerre," Louise replied, before Matthieu had the chance. "We'll take two cars so I can continue on to Paris."

"Ça marche pour moi," he said. "I have an appointment in Auxerre then have to get back here."

"An appointment?" Magali asked.

"Oui, I am taking some samples of the vine fungi to a botanist in Auxerre."

"Oh, good idea," Magali said.

"That is a good idea," Louise agreed. She finished yet another *Magali's Café* breakfast and put her dishes in the sink. "Let me go back to the cottage to make a call and finish packing. Matthieu, will you be able to leave in about half an hour?"

"I'm ready when you are."

"Bonne journée," Louise said, giving Luke and Magali cheek kisses.

Louise finished packing the essentials in her overnight bag. The weather was still cold enough for the leather bomber jacket and boots, which was a nice change from tropical attire. But she'd also been away long enough to look forward to her kaftan and flip-flops as soon as this was all over. She threw her bag into the Peugeot just as Matthieu pulled up in his Mini Moke and rolled down his window.

"Let's meet at the Auxerre Crédit Agricole on Rue du Temple," Louise said. "Do you know that one?"

"Yes, it's the main branch," he said. "Do you have an appointment?"

"Not really. But I have a plan."

They took off and Louise blasted French pop tunes. *If you can't beat 'em, join 'em*, she thought. In an hour and a half, she pulled into the parking lot at

80 Bis Rue du Temple in Auxerre. From under her black turtleneck, she pulled out the necklace that held a diamond ring, Jean-Philippe's family heirloom. She removed it from the chain and put it on the ring finger of her left hand, then rifled through her purse for a piece of paper and pen. She wrote something down and waited until the Mini Moke pulled up. They got out and Louise put her arm around his waist as they walked toward the bank.

"Just follow my lead," she said.

As they entered, Louise pulled him closer to leave no doubt that they were romantically attached. The curvature of her body, which he had still been thinking about, fit perfectly against his thigh. He went with it. Louise checked out the two different tellers, one working diligently and the other chattering with another employee. Louise approached the one who was busy working.

"Bonjour," the teller said.

"Bonjour, we have an appointment with Yves Renard," Louise said in fluent French.

The teller smiled and politely replied in French, "I'm sorry, there is no Yves Renard here."

Louise took the piece of paper she had written on out of her purse and read it aloud, "*Yves Renard, account manager.*" She flipped the note around to show her. "I was told that Monsieur Renard used to work in Brussels and could help me set up a Belgian bank account. I'll be working there this summer and need an account for my paycheck."

"Do you already have an account with Crédit Agricole?" the teller asked.

"Yes."

"You can use your French Crédit Agricole account in Brussels."

"Are you sure? We're getting married in Brussels this summer, so we need everything sorted out before I leave." Louise hugged Matthieu, flashing the ring. He looked down at her affectionately, then kissed her a little longer than she expected.

The teller appeared rattled that the inquiry was beyond her depth of knowledge, but she was determined to solve the problem.

"We have another account manager from Brussels who might be able to help you," she said. "I'll get him for you."

"Wonderful, thanks."

Louise turned to Matthieu. "You take direction well."

"I like the direction this is going." His eyes were green-grey now. She could almost hear his thoughts and steadied herself.

"Bonjour," said a middle-aged man, neatly dressed in a dark suit and purple Hermès cravate. "I'm Charles Ausseil. I understand you are inquiring about an account in Belgium?"

"Yes," Louise replied. "However, your colleague pointed out that if I already have an account with Crédit Agricole here in France, I could use the same one in Belgium. Is that correct?"

"Of course. The Carte Bleue works at most ATMs around the world. You can use it to withdraw cash and make deposits at the ATM. You can also make purchases, just like you would with a credit card."

"Oh, that's great!" Louise said.

Ausseil typed on the computer. "If you like, I can see what kind of account you have. What is your account number?" Louise handed him her checkbook and he looked up her account. "You have a premium checking account so there should be no problem."

"So, I don't need to open a separate account in Belgium?"

"It's really not necessary," Ausseil assured her. "If you need any assistance while you're in Brussels, I can refer you to one of the account managers there." He wrote a name on the back of one of his business cards and handed it to her.

"Perfect!" Louise took the card, *mission accomplished.*

"Show him my card and let him know I referred you."

"Thank you so much," Louise said, shaking his hand.

"You're welcome. Bonne journée."

They walked outside, and Louise put Ausseil's card in her wallet. Matthieu opened her car door for her.

"What are you up to?" he asked.

"Just a little investigating. Shall we go see the botanist?"

"Sure." Matthieu went to his car. "The botanist is at the University of Burgundy, Auxerre campus. Follow me."

They drove to the campus located on the banks of the Yonne River. They parked and Matthieu took a small cooler from the back seat and they entered the building.

"When I was an archeologist in residence here, I became friends with a colleague who is a Paleoethnobotanist. He studied everything from fossilized to living algae, fungi, lichens, mosses, ferns, conifers, and flowering plants.

Then he started specializing in vine sciences and has a lab here."

"Naturally."

"Yes, it is a growing business in Burgundy and getting quite competitive." They passed several laboratories and continued out through another door.

"He wasn't in the lab?" Louise asked.

"His lab is not inside." They went down a path and reached a greenhouse. He held the door for her, and they entered.

"Matthieu!" A jovial man in a white lab coat greeted them.

"Bruno!" They gave each other cheek kisses. Matthieu seemed emotional. "It's great to see you, mon ami."

"It has been too long," Bruno said. His attention turned to Louise. "Bonjour." They exchanged cheek kisses as well.

"This is Karen Baker," Matthieu said. "She is our guest staying in the gîte."

"Lucky you," Bruno said.

"Yes, I'm very lucky," Louise said.

"I was talking to Matthieu," Bruno said. "But, yes you're lucky too. You have wonderful hosts." Bruno's ever-shifting attention turned to Matthieu's small container. "Les voilà!" he said, taking the cooler and placing it on a lab table among some potted plants. He opened it and took out one of the samples. "Let's have a look at this fungus. How can you tell if a mushroom is deadly?"

Matthieu and Louise shook their heads.

"By the autopsy!" They laughed, more at his delivery than at the old joke. "Excellent work getting these samples, Matthieu."

"Well, I used to be a scientist," Matthieu quipped. "Which has come in very handy in my viticulture work."

"No joke. Samples must be selected and collected properly to minimize the chances for false-negative results," Bruno said. "Sampling particular sections of the vine at certain times of the year can greatly increase the reliability of disease testing." He picked up one of the shoots and pointed at the tips. "For example, to test vines for grapevine fanleaf virus, shoot tips should be collected for testing no later than the spring. That virus is heat sensitive, and its concentration in vines becomes very low during summer, making detection less reliable."

"Hence the carrying cooler?" Louise noted.

"Exactly," Bruno said. "Proper handling and transportation of samples is important. In general, samples should be delivered to the testing lab as soon as possible. If the samples have been exposed to excessive heat or drying, or if they are stored for too long, it will not be possible to get reliable results."

"I just collected these this morning," Matthieu said.

"Perfect." Bruno went over to a high-powered microscope and briefly examined the sample. "It looks active and should test very accurately. Biological indexing is a valuable test, particularly for viruses. These tests require greenhouses or field plantings, which are rarely offered by commercial labs and are more often found at research institutions." Bruno smiled proudly. "That makes us very special."

Louise and Matthieu watched as he took an extract of the test vine fungus and rubbed it onto leaves of another plant growing in the greenhouse. "Some grapevine diseases can be identified easily in the field by visible signs of the pathogen. For example, the appearance of the powdery mildew fungus on the surface of infected leaves and fruit is quite characteristic, which is what Matthieu has here. Some diseases, such as crown gall, are characterized by abnormal plant growth."

Bruno pointed to the leaf that he rubbed the fungus on. "A few diseases are identifiable only through controlled inoculations of healthy indicator plants. Within several weeks, if a virus is present, it will move from the fungus buds to the indicator plant, causing infection and diagnostic disease symptoms. Although these tests are labor intensive and time consuming, they are very useful if the grapevines are valuable and a high level of confidence in the diagnosis is needed."

"It's good maintenance to have the grapevines tested regularly, which I do," Matthieu told Louise. "That makes it even more suspicious that the inspector would find this fungus. Bruno will help me figure out if the virus was intentionally planted and the best way to treat the plant."

"Plus, it is an opportunity for me to write new academic studies," said Bruno. "Publish or perish!" His attention was again drawn away as he brought a specimen over to the microscope.

"Well, thank you for the fascinating tour of your lab," Louise said. "Can I buy you both lunch?" Bruno was completely consumed by his new project.

"Bruno?" Matthieu asked.

"Oh, sorry, I was distracted. This is a very interesting case and might affect other plants, so time is of the essence." He stopped working to shake

236   LORRAINE EVANOFF

Matthieu's hand and give Louise cheek kisses. "Thank you for the offer of lunch. Next time?"

"Of course, I look forward to it."

"Matthieu, I might have something for you sooner than later," Bruno said. "I'll give you a call, mon pote."

"See you soon, my friend," Matthieu said.

As they walked back to their cars, Matthieu made a recommendation for lunch. "There's a little café just up the river," he said. "Follow me."

They crossed the bridge over the Yonne and parked on rue Saint-Pèlerin. Louise opened her car door just as a black sedan drove by. The driver caught her eye.

"What the hell?" Louise said, taking a good look at the car and making a note of his license plate.

"What is it?"

"Nothing, just a feeling."

They entered a cozy restaurant with a giant brick wood-burning oven behind a polished copper-topped counter over which hung shiny copper kettles. Antique paddles adorned white stucco walls, under the exposed-beam ceilings. Given that they were still in Burgundy, Louise assumed the cuisine would be as charming as the décor.

"Bonjour, messieurs-dames," the owner sing-songed. She filled their water glasses and left a basket of sliced baguette and two menus on the table. When she returned, Louise ordered the salad with warm goat cheese toasted in the wood-burning oven. Matthieu ordered the côte de boeuf with fried potatoes. Louise picked at a slice of baguette and was lost in thought.

"Is something wrong?" Matthieu asked.

"I'm just trying to remember where I saw that man before."

"What man?"

"Do you ever get that strange feeling that you're imagining or seeing things?"

"Around here? All the time. There's a lot of ancient history and strange energies. Speaking of which, Karen, why did you ask the banker about Belgium?"

A tinge of guilt came over Louise, hearing her false identity uttered by a man that she felt so close to now. "Your account manager in Beaune worked in Belgium before."

"How do you know that?"

"He told me." Things started to become clear to Louise. Now that she was pulling on this thread, she could see the pattern unraveling. Everything pointed to Belgium.

The owner placed their food on the table. "Bon appétit."

Louise cut into the goat cheese on toast and took a bite. The combination of textures and flavors—warm, creamy, savory, and crusty—with fresh buttery lettuce and Dijon mustard dressing was pure comfort. The high-quality food was delivered once again.

Louise suddenly came to a decision. "Matthieu, if the bank threatens you again, tell them that you have found the money to cure the diseased plants."

"But we don't have the money."

"You have a six-month extension on your loan. That gives you time to get it. Either way, you'll have it. I promise."

They finished lunch, and Louise ordered a *café noisette*, espresso with a dash of steamed milk, giving it a hazelnut color. Louise sipped and stared into the dark liquid, deep in thought. Then her eyes shot up at Matthieu's grey-green tempests.

"I remember where I saw him," Louise said.

"Who?"

Her movement was sudden, swift and with purpose. "Sorry, but I really need to get to Paris." Louise put cash on the table and got up. Matthieu followed her.

They walked out and Matthieu opened her car door. She gave him a hug and kissed him tenderly on either side of his lips, feeling the warmth of his breath. "See you in a couple days."

Louise dialed Charlie on her mobile phone, pressed the speaker option and placed it on the dash, before accelerating onto Route A6 north toward Paris. It was 3:00 p.m. for her, morning for him. He picked up on the second ring.

"Hi, it's Louise. Is Patrick still with you?"

"Yes, he's right here, you're on speaker phone."

"Patrick, I forgot to ask you a question that came up while I was chatting with Frédéric LaFontaine."

"Did he have any new information?" Patrick asked.

"Well, not exactly. But he mentioned something about the fire in Almasi's building that conflicted with your report."

"Oh?"

"LaFontaine mentioned that the police restricted the fire brigade from entering the building for forty-five minutes so they could search for the intruders that they believed were still there. Were your Urban Police Divisions officers the first on the scene?"

"Yes, we arrived at 5:30 a.m." Patrick said checking his notes. "The fire department was allowed access at 6:15 a.m."

"Right. So, who informed you that the intruders were still there?" Louise asked. There was an awkward silence as Patrick tried to clear his mind. "Patrick, are you still there?"

"It never occurred to me before," Patrick said, his voice trembling slightly. "When I arrived on the scene, one of my officers said that the CPD chief was already there when they arrived. He ordered them to search for the intruders." After another awkward silence, Patrick was audibly angry. "That filthy Dupont was at the scene before the fire was even reported to authorities!"

"You're referring to the chief of the Criminal Police Division, Paul Dupont you mention in your report, correct?" Louise asked, making sure they were understanding each other.

"That's correct. He interfered with my investigation every step of the way."

"That's a serious allegation," Louise said.

"You found the smoking gun, Louise," Patrick said. "Dupont was at the crime scene before the authorities were even notified. I knew he was trying to impede my investigation. And now I have proof, thanks to you!"

"There's definitely a pattern forming with all these cases," Louise murmured.

"What cases?"

"I'll get back to you on that." But Louise was reminded of some additional intel. "Oh, remember that camera pen you gave me? I captured some intriguing footage in Monaco. It could also be a smoking gun in the Almasi investigation, as Patrick put it."

After yet another admonishment from Charlie to be careful, Louise hung up and immediately called Michael. "What have you got?" she asked referring to the background checks she requested.

"Hello to you too," Michael rebuffed.

"Sorry, I'm driving to Paris and I've got you on speaker. Let's make this quick. Did you find anything out?"

"Paris you say?" Michael omitted the fact that he was already there. "I made a couple connections."

"Connections are good."

"Neither of Marc Dutroux's two wives, Michelle Martin and Lelièvre Dutroux, could have children, and both had teenage criminal records."

"What were the crimes?" Louise asked.

"Attempted kidnapping. Doesn't seem like a coincidence."

"Anything else?" Louise said impatiently.

"Your guy, Matthieu Mersault, he's an interesting one."

"How so?"

"He had a promising career in archaeology, and then his fiancée was killed in a famous serial killer case."

"This I know."

"Did you know she was pregnant?" Michael asked.

Louise paused. "This I did not know."

"Mersault didn't know, either," Michael continued.

"How do you know that?" Louise asked.

"No one knew. I found it in the coroner's report that was never made public. So, how well do you know this guy Mersault? You mentioned you're staying at his family estate in Burgundy?"

"Yes, I'm staying at a cottage on his family vineyard."

"Does he know that you're investigating him?"

"I'm not investigating him," Louise said. "I'm just doing my due diligence."

"Okay, banker lady. Can I do anything else for you?"

"Yes, actually, I need the background on Paul Dupont, chief superintendent of Monaco Criminal Police Division."

"Really? Why don't I pull Princess Grace's death certificate while I'm at it?" Michael wisecracked.

"You know you're my guy on this. Who else can do what you do?" The momentary pause on the speaker made Louise realize she'd hooked her fish.

"I'll see what I can find out," Michael said. "So, Paris, huh? To see Vladimir?"

"I'll probably need his help, if he's willing. This case is starting to ruffle some feathers."

"Don't make me come over there and save you, again."

"I'm hanging up now."

Louise reached the Boulevard Périphérique, a freeway around the periphery of Paris. She exited at Avenue de la Porte d'Orléans to Avenue du Général Leclerc and pulled up to the Hôtel Le Littré. She entered and approached the same twenty-something clerk at the front desk, hoping a room would be available.

"Bonjour."

"Bonjour, Madame."

"Sorry, I don't have a reservation. But I just need a room for one night. Is there anything available?"

The owner interrupted. "Bonjour, it's nice to see you again, Madame Baker. I think we can accommodate you." Louise watched him work his magic on the computer. "The penthouse is available but at the full rate. Is that okay?"

Louise thought for a beat. He didn't know her schoolteacher identity so it wouldn't be suspicious if she booked the penthouse.

"There goes the rest of my inheritance," she jested nonchalantly, as she handed him her new Crédit Agricole Carte Bleue. He processed the transaction and gave her a key.

When she got to the suite, she didn't even notice how spectacular it was because she immediately dialed her former paradise. Big Steve answered on the second ring, loud rap music playing in the background.

Louise used the same charming tone she just had in the exchange with the hotel owner. "How's it going?"

He turned down the noise. "Yo, woman! Where you at?"

"I'm in Paris, looking at the Eiffel Tower, thinking of you."

"I miss you too, mammy."

"It doesn't sound like it. Is there a party going on over there?"

"Just some homeys from the hood stopped by. Snoop is in the house!"

"Yes, I can hear your homey Snoop Dogg on the stereo."

"Girl, you need to get yo ass back over here. You missin' out big time! Snoop leavin' tomorrow."

Louise was a bit hurt that her familiar turf was getting along fine without her. Her association with Big Steve had always been a kind of mutual protection detail. Over the years since he had been her bodyguard while in hiding, known as Big Steve, she had learned about his struggles growing up.

He had described to her in detail about his childhood. When he was fifteen, he had contracted shingles of the brain after a rabid dog bit him. It had put him in a coma, which, he explained, seemed like heaven, where everyone was the same. God, with white beard and colorful eyes, spoke to him, "It's not your time." God showed him his arm and said his life is longer than his arm. The illness had caused him to speak erratically and too quickly, so he had to do speech therapy. The result was that his urban slang was even more pronounced as he tended not to enunciate.

The stories of his young adult years were extraordinary, growing up with Magic Johnson, his own cousin started the Crips in South Central Watts, home of Dr. Dray. Rival gangs the CC Riders in Compton, home of and Ice Cube, and the gang PyRules, a division of the Bloods, with Chris Brown. He had explained how it had started out with no weapons, just fist fights. But then big weapons arrived in the 1980s and it became a war zone.

Living in the hood had led to him doing some jail time. But Louise had always admired how he had turned his life around, serving to protect others with a big heart. Knowing the workings of the justice system, he became a powerful asset, which led to him working for top celebrities including Michael Jackson. Louise wouldn't be at all surprised if rap stars showed up to visit him. She was happy for him, even if she was a little jealous.

"So, everything is okay?"

"It's aaall good. Just worryin' about yo fine self."

There was a slight ache in Louise, the void of missing both Big Steve and her island. She wanted to end the call quickly. "Well, I'm probably going to be gone for another couple weeks. Call me if you need anything. See you soon."

"You sure y'all okay?" Big Steve wasn't ready to let her go.

"Éti, what is the one thing you know about me?" she asked, throwing in a dig on his fake name.

"That y'all can take care of yourself."

"See you soon."

She hung up and took out her laptop. She didn't need to connect to her satellite Internet, as the hotel had recently installed – for their high-roller clientele – a top-level ethernet system. She booted up and began her research to map out her trip to Belgium, starting with a visit to the primary crime scene. She wasn't sure if any of the houses where the serial murders had taken place were still intact. But a specific address appeared on a search, which led her to an article posted online. She found out from the article that Marc Dutroux had owned seven houses, four of which he used for his kidnappings.

A house in Jumet, where Dutroux had buried Ann Marchal and Eefje Lambrecks in the garden, was set to be demolished. An accomplice, Bernard Weinstein, had lived in that house for a while. Another house in Marchienne-au-Pont was where Julie Lejeune and Mélissa Russo had been held captive for a short time after their kidnappings. A third house in Sars-la-Buissière was where Lejuene, Russo, and Weinstain had all been buried after Dutroux killed them. The municipality petitioned to purchase that house to make a park with a monument commemorating the victims of the serial killer.

A fourth house at the address of the Route de Philippeville 128 in Marcinelle was the one most often cited in the media. All the girls had been held captive there in the basement and bedroom. The municipality seized ownership of that house because of the killings and the dilapidated state of the property. There were plans to raze it and create a garden with a memorial on the site.

Reading further, Louise noted an interesting disclosure. Under Belgian law the "procedure of compulsory purchase" meant an owner had a last right to visit a seized property. Dutroux would be allowed a final visit under heavy police guard. That property was about 70 miles south of Brussels, on the route from Paris. This would be the first place Louise would visit.

TWENTY-NINE

"You're getting warmer," the disembodied voice said. She knew he was there. But the closer she got, the further he slipped away. "Don't give up," Jean-Philippe said. "I'm right here."

Louise tried to say, "Where?" But it came out, *wuh, wuh*. Her lips quivered in frustration. She unconsciously rocked back and forth, the motion forcing her onto her back, eyes wide open in the darkness. She had fallen asleep! In a drowsy panic, she got up.

To sleep, perchance to dream. Lately the state of Louise's subconscious mind had been all about filling the void, distant-yet-vaguely familiar voices and ironic maiden-in-distress scenarios. She literally shook her head in an attempt to purge the notion. Her watch face glowed 10:00 p.m. Perfect timing to go to Silencio. She hurriedly dressed and ran to catch a cab.

Michael watched Louise from a taxi parked in the shadows. She was dressed to impress in black leather as she approached the bouncer guarding the entrance. This time she simply flashed him her charcoal-outlined emerald eyes, the bouncer nodded, and let her in without hesitation.

Michael paid the driver and walked to the entrance. The bouncer fidgeted with his walkie-talkie pretending not to see him.

"Hey, how's it going?" Michael asked, not even attempting to speak French. The bouncer stared at him lugubriously. "Is this some kind of nightclub or something? It looks pretty cool. Can I check it out?" Still no reaction, so Michael discretely flipped open his wallet and showed him the unmistakably official-looking FBI badge and ID. The bouncer impassively stepped aside, and Michael walked through the door.

He wandered down the corridor past the coat check girl and was soon confused by the multiple venues within the club. Not knowing which way to go to avoid being recognized, he slipped through the door into the lounge with live jazz and waited in the shadows. Staking out the hallway, he heard the approaching voices of two men speaking American English. He recognized Vladimir and Greg and stepped further into the shadows as they entered the lounge and continued to the next room. He followed unnoticed as they entered the fumoir. He stopped short and took a seat in the jazz lounge from which he could keep an eye on Louise. He knew she would have to cross this room to leave, it was an ideal spot to wait.

Louise had already made her way straight to the smoking room and was sitting at the bar. She ordered a *coupe de champagne* and a cigar. The barman snipped the tip, and Louise held it while he lit it for her. She amused herself, blowing smoke rings until her internal clock struck gold again. After just five minutes, Greg and Vladimir entered and took their usual corner booth.

These were the moments that Louise lived for, when the energy around her led the way and all she had to do was follow her instincts. It was strange and lucky karma, but it was also the result of Louise's habit of tapping into the instinct of her senses and profoundly connecting, and appreciating that connection, to the universe. Tracking down Vladimir this way was more fun and less awkward than the messy business of extricating a favor out of Greg. He was too kind and gentlemanly ever to cause her chagrin for rejecting his affections. Just like she wouldn't manipulate his affections to her advantage, however noble the cause.

Now it was a game of chicken to see who would blink. Louise enjoyed her cigar and champagne, and they enjoyed watching her. Seeing she had their attention she carried her drink over to their table.

"Can I borrow a match?" Louise asked.

"I use a lighter," Vladimir replied.

"Better still," Louise answered.

"Until they go wrong," Greg said.

Louise sat. "Sean Connery was the best James Bond."

"Who would argue with that?" Greg said.

"Perhaps a Russian," replied the Russian.

"That Russian gypsy catfight scene was absurd," Greg said, referring to *From Russia with Love.*

"Absurd but entertaining," Vladimir countered.

Louise puffed on her cigar that had gone out. "Now I actually do need a match." Greg flicked on his lighter before Vlad could even reach for a match.

"Thanks, Greg," Louise said. She blew a few more very satisfying smoke rings before handing the cigar to Greg. Wearing a family crest on the ring finger of his model-like hand, he nimbly took the cigar and puffed it as smoothly as James Bond himself. His gray hair and chiseled jawline were even more striking ten years after she had been with him. Vladimir picked up on her attention toward Greg and interrupted.

"It's nice to see you again, Louise," Vladimir said in Russian. "Or should I say Karen?"

"I wanted to thank you," Louise replied in Russian.

"It was a pleasure. For what?" Vladimir asked.

"For sending me to Burgundy. It's a beautiful place."

"Did you find what you were looking for?" Vladimir was actually interested in her reply.

"In fact, I found even more than I was looking for. But I need another favor."

"What's in it for me?" Vladimir asked.

Louise ignored any sexual innuendo and opted for sarcasm. "The satisfaction of helping your fellow man?"

"That currency is quite devalued where I come from," Vladimir deadpanned.

"Understood," Louise said, knowing that shaming or other negative means of persuasion would be useless on him.

"Hello, I'm still here," Greg said. "What are you guys talking about?"

Louise waved at the barman who brought over a tray with a bottle and three snifters. Vladimir and Greg both recognized the label of Privilege La Reserve du Prince. The cognac had a reputation for its unique history and exquisite taste. It was distilled from the personal stock of Jacques Boursaud's Pre-World War I vintages from the prime region of Cognac, Grande Champagne. Boursaud had built the largest stock of historical reserves over the course of fifty years, the youngest of which dated from 1914. At one point it had been hidden from the Germans during the invasion of France in WWII. Having escaped The Great War, the cognac received the surname *The Century Old Cognac*. Because of very limited and rare components, it could never be reproduced, and was priced accordingly at about $5,000 a bottle. It was intended to make an impression.

Vladimir eyed the cognac silently then looked sternly at Louise and then at Greg. In that moment, they witnessed something even more rare than the cognac, possibly a first ever for Louise.

Vladimir gave a toothy grin.

"What, no cigar?" Vladimir said. The barman balanced the tray with a juggler's skill, took a cigar from his breast pocket and handed it to Vladimir. "Now, this is my kind of party!"

Michael had been observing the conversation from the other room, while also enjoying the music. He had the distinct impression the party had been winding down, but now that the new bottle had arrived, he put up his feet and ordered another drink for himself.

By the second glass, Louise was sitting snuggly between the two men in the corner of the booth. The conversation had taken off and never stopped. They had caught each other up on their current lives and reminisced about old times.

Louise looked at her watch. "Merde! It's 1:30 in the morning. I gotta go." She tried to push her way out of the double bear hug.

"Where do you think you're going, little one?" Greg said.

"I'm driving to Brussels in the morning," she said, elbowing a passageway out.

"Brussels?" Vladimir said. He gently placed both hands snuggly around her slim waist and sat her back down. He fixed his regard on hers, the emerald of her eyes picking up the green in his hazel eyes. "What's going on, Louise?"

"Karen," she said defiantly. She had no idea why she spit out that name so intuitively.

Vladimir corrected himself. "What's going on, Karen?"

"What do you care?" Louise said, knowing very well from the look in his eyes that he did care. She was livid, like the time they had angry sex after Louise accused him of murdering her friend Diana.[19] "I'm fed up with your calloused spy routine working by the KGB playbook. Let me go."

"Hello!" Greg interrupted again. "I'm still here! Come on, talk to me. Vlad, as a friend, this is not cool. Louise, we have enough of a history that you know you can trust me."

"Of course," Louise said. "Greg, I trust you completely."

"And me?" said Vladimir. "You don't trust me?"

"Not completely."

---

[19] From the author's first novel in the Louise Moscow series, *Foliage: An International Banking Spy Thriller*

"What else do I have to do for you to trust me? If it weren't for me, you wouldn't have made it out of BCCI alive. You were a target of their black network."

Louise was stunned. "The black network is still around?"

"Follow the money," Vladimir said blithely. "The black network works with whoever pays top dollar.".

"*Works* with?" Louise asked. "As in, it still exists?"

"There will always be a black network," he said. "They evolve, go where the work is."

"They're everywhere," Greg said. "BCCI's thugs accosted me right in the lobby of the Hilton Brussels to discourage me from a legitimate deal."

"Yes, I know," Louise said.

"You *know*?" asked Greg.

"Yes, I learned some things in the process of the trial, when that whole thing went down," said Louise. "For instance, I learned about your work as an arms dealer." She saw the look of shock on Greg's face. "Don't worry. Everything checked out. Even that business has as few honest dealers." She looked at Vladimir. "You, on the other hand, walk the line between legitimate and corrupt."

Vladimir narrowed his eyes. "Nothing is ever black and white, no matter how much you Americans like to believe it is."

"Okay, so fill me in on the gray area. What did you mean when you said to *follow the money*? I need a more specific answer."

"All right," replied Vlad. "You say you're going to Brussels? Here's a clue: you're on the right track."

"By following the money," said Louise. "But I'm still flying blind here."

"Old corporate money," Vlad said. He could see the wheels turning in her head, trying to pick the lock, find the right combination. Vladimir refilled their glasses with the fine Cognac. "Have one more drink with us, and I'll give you another clue."

They picked up their glasses and Louise finished half her glass in one gulp. "Okay, I drank half. Tell me and I'll finish."

Vlad leaned in and spoke to her in Russian. "What name do you think of when you think of big American money?"

Louise smirked. There were many answers but really just one. "You mean like the Rockefellers?"

Vladimir smiled a second time, clinked her glass, and they drank. Louise slammed the glass down a little harder than planned. Michael had been patiently enjoying the music and beautiful women when the sound caught him off guard. He reached for his firearm but saw Louise crawling safely out of the booth and this time the guys let her go. He followed far enough behind her and headed back to the hotel where he got a room at nearby more affordable hotel.

THIRTY

January 12, 2002

The next morning Louise was energized by Vladimir's intriguing albeit cryptic clue. Before she hit the road for Brussels, she rang room service for a continental breakfast and logged onto the Internet to do more research. There was a new online encyclopedia called Wikipedia, that had just launched in 2001. She typed in Rockefeller and found that the most relevant to her case was David Rockefeller. David had joined the Chase National Bank in 1946, a bank that was associated with his family, and was chaired by David's uncle, Winthrop W. Aldrich. Louise knew from banking history that Chase National Bank was primarily a wholesale bank, dealing with other prominent financial institutions and major corporate clients, such as General Electric, which had, through its RCA affiliate, leased prominent space and become a crucial first tenant of Rockefeller Center in 1930, commonly known as 30 Rock.

Louise also knew that the bank was closely associated with the oil industry, having longstanding connections with its board of directors to the successor companies of Standard Oil, especially Exxon Mobil. Chase National Bank subsequently became the Chase Manhattan Bank in 1955 and shifted significantly into consumer banking. Cross referencing, Louise came across an article mentioning something intriguing that occurred around that same time. The first Bilderberg conference was held at the Hotel de Bilderberg in Oosterbeek, Netherlands, in May 1954.

The particulars of the conference were also available. Exiled Polish politician, Jozef Retinger, initiated the conference over his concern about the growth of anti-Americanism in Western Europe. The goal of the international conference was to promote a better understanding between the cultures and foster cooperation on political, economic, and defense issues. The conference was to be an annual private meeting of approximately one hundred and fifty people of the European and North American political elite, experts from industry, finance, academia, and the media. The guest list was to include two attendees from each nation, one of each to represent "conservative" and "liberal" points of view. Fifty delegates from eleven Western European countries along with eleven Americans attended the first conference. One of the prominent Americans at that first meeting was David Rockefeller.

The information Louise found was interesting, but nothing seemed nefarious or related to her case. Finally, on Usenet she found a lead – the 48th Bilderberg meeting was held in Brussels, Belgium, in June 2000, at the Château Du Lac Hotel in Genval. Upon further scrutiny, she found someone who had infiltrated the meeting and posted photos. One of the photos showed Ekram Almasi clearly attending the meeting at the hotel. The photographer had even timestamped it by putting a newspaper in the foreground, showing the date. That date was six months before Almasi's murder. She was satisfied with the lead she had found but miffed at Vladimir's obscure clue. Why didn't he just say Bilderberg?

Louise tossed her overnight bag into the back of her rental car and took off north on Route A1 for Belgium, the land of mussels and fried potatoes or *moules-frites*. Michael had already checked out of his hotel and was waiting in his rental car outside. Years of investigations had programed him with patience to wait as long as it took to solve the problem. He took off following several car lengths behind her.

Three hours later, about fifty miles south of Brussels, she took the exit for the municipality of Charleroi and followed her map toward Route de Philippeville 128 in Marcinelle. She wanted to see for herself the place where multiple murders of young women in four homes within a ten-mile radius could have taken place. The route to Sars-la-Buissière through magnificent bucolic countryside was befitting its name meaning boxwood hedge, with creatively sculpted topiaries adorning both private estates and humble homesteads alike.

But the landscape changed drastically as she entered Sars-la-Buissière, a desolate village lying in a bleak landscape. Only the sound of a lone villager pickaxing away rubble alongside a dump of rusting trailers and cars broke the silence. All other inhabitants had gone away or were shuttered inside their red brick homes. At first glance of the slag heaps – relics of coalmines from a time when the region of Wallonia was a booming industrial heartland – it was easy to see how the gruesome trade of Dutroux might have gone unnoticed. The entire population of less than a thousand worked several jobs to get by. Every car parked on the street seemed to be for sale at "a bargain."

Louise parked at the only establishment that appeared to be open, Bistro L'Embuscade. She entered and sat at the worn wooden bar, the top of which was inlaid with red brick. She smiled and spoke fluent French to the female proprietress.

"Bonjour. On est bien tranquille ici," Louise said, remarking on how quiet the town was.

The owner replied in nasally Belgian French "Here as elsewhere in Belgium, people like to keep to themselves. What can I get you?"

"Café au lait, s'il vous plaît.," Louise said, continuing in French. "I had to stop for petrol and thought I'd refuel myself too," Despite the frigid welcome, Louise wasn't backing down from engaging in conversation. "I just drove in from Paris." Making a point of being from France worked in her favor. According to her research, the Dutroux affair had exposed the animosity between the French-speaking south of Belgium and the Flemish north. Although the wealthier Flemish communities to the north had been careful not to rub it in, the undercurrents were clear. The serial killer Dutroux was from Wallonia. Not from Flanders.

A lone customer finished his espresso and got up to leave. "Merci, Natalie, bonne journée," he said in the same nasally French.

"Bonne journée, François. À demain," Louise now knew the owner's name, Natalie.

"Nice place," Louise said.

"Are you a journalist?"

"Not exactly. I'm a novelist." Louise was getting more and more comfortable with that cover story.

"As I was saying, we don't meddle in other people's affairs around here." She waited for milk steamer to stop screeching before adding, "And we don't appreciate a lot of questions."

"You're right. Sometimes in the midst of writing I get a bit too curious. I just drove a few hours alone and felt like conversation." Louise gave a friendly smile as a kicker.

Natalie placed the white porcelain cup and saucer in front of Louise. "What do you want to know that hasn't already been splashed across the newspapers?"

"To be honest, I'm interested to know how it was possible for the killings to go on right under your noses?"

"Why don't you ask the police and authorities? They were to blame for the failure to act earlier against Dutroux. Even the Flemish King Albert was unable to unify the country when we needed him most. The parents begged for help during the search of Julie and Melissa, both French-speaking families. He did nothing. Suffice it to say, he was not invited to their funerals."

"Do you believe if something like this had happened in the north the King would have been more responsive?"

"Évidemment!" Natalie had a chip on her shoulder and understandably so.

"Julie and Melissa." Louise softly repeated the names of the girls without surnames, like a saturnine celebrity couple. "What about the local government?"

"The corruption has been going on for many generations." Natalie indicated the bistro with a wave of her hand. "This place has been in my family since the 1930s and is the only reason I'm still here after many people have moved away. My mother still talks about when thousands of Italians came to work in the coalmines in the 1950s and '60s and many have remained."

Louise's thoughts raced to her own mother and the look on her face when she remembered horror she had survived.

"Like an ambush!" Louise said, catching on to the name of the restaurant.

"Exactement! That's how my mom came up with the name *L'Embuscade*. This area was ideal for organized crime to exploit, with the open borders of the European Union and funds pouring into regional coffers of Southern Belgium. The roads and trains provide easy access to the ports of Rotterdam and Antwerp. Charleroi is a known European narcotics hot spot with rampant gun crimes. Dutroux had easy access to organized crime networks there, distributing his pornography and operating an international trade in teenage girls to a steady stream of clients as far as Eastern Europe."

"You don't believe Dutroux was acting alone?"

"Of course not. The only good that may have come out of this horror was the world starting to understand the links between Dutroux and organized crime and the entire Belgian political class. Ordinary people here have known about it a long time."

"Which is why people like to mind their own business," Louise concluded.

"The underworld keeps to itself. As long as we ordinary people don't make waves, we are left alone."

"What about politicians? Haven't any elected officials tried to clean up?"

"It is impossible for an honest politician to succeed here. The greatest Belgian political mystery is the unsolved murder of André Cools, from Liege in Wallonia. He was shot dead at his home in 1991, many believe by political rivals working with the Mafia, because he had threatened to clean out the political rot. The investigation into the Dutroux murders has been linked to Italian mafioso, Mauro di Santis, who was also on the wanted list for the André Cools murder."

"But he's untouchable," Louise said.

"Alas, yes."

Louise checked her watch. "Well, thank you for talking to me, Natalie. What do I owe you?"

"Consider it a blessing from Sars-the-Accursed."

"Au revoir, bonne journée."

Louise walked back to her car and drove another 10 miles toward Charleroi. The words *Sars-the-Accursed* echoed in her mind. The sobriquet for Sars-la-Buissière was a stain left by a few evil souls on villagers who just wanted to be left in peace. As she approached the infamous address at Route de Philippeville 128, there was no mistaking the haunting sight of the crumbling red brick house, overgrown with ivy and shrubs. A gateless chain-link fence with a poster bearing the innocent faces of Julie and Melissa barricaded the small yard. There was nothing left to see there. All that remained was the shell of malevolence moved on. Louise continued on to Brussels with Michael still tailing her.

With Dutch and French as the official languages, most residents of Brussels spoke French. As the headquarters of the European Union and the political seat of NATO, modern Brussels had become the unofficial capital of Europe. This had brought a distinct cosmopolitan air with many shiny new office buildings, coexisting alongside the cobbled streets, splendid cafés, handmade lace, world-famous chocolate, local beers, and graceful Art Nouveau architecture that had long made Brussels a must-see destination. Louise was in college the last time she visited and had forgotten how charming the city was. Like many European cities, Brussels had suffered significant damage from air strikes during World War II, but its canals and many historic structures remained.

She drove southeast on the Avenue Louise, a major thoroughfare and one of the city's most prestigious streets. She followed the map to the main Crédit Agricole located in the residential village of Watermael-Boitsfort. The small suburb was only five square miles, more than half of which covered by the Sonian Forest. The town was still largely rural, but since being linked to Brussels by railway in 1854, it had become a fashionable bourgeois neighborhood.

Louise parked and fed the meter. Slightly disoriented in the unfamiliar country, she realized something that could have been considered an omen. Her internal international banking clock had failed her, and she had forgotten the banks closed for lunch. It had been worth the stop in Sars-la-Buissière to talk with Natalie, but she would have to wait forty-five minutes for the bank to reopen. She found a café nearby and ordered moules-frites.

While she waited for the meal, she read some local history written on the menu. Although the French had long laid claim to the fried potato, it was a Flemish manuscript from 1781 that first cited something resembling French fries or *frites*. When no river fish was available during winter, local Flemish cooks would slice potatoes into the shape of small fish and fry them. Belgian farmers were some of the first in Europe to embrace the potato soon after it had arrived in Europe from the New World in the sixteenth century. Mussels, cheap and plentiful, were another Belgian staple, originally considered food for the poor. They had long been paired with fried potatoes at the country's famous fry shops, known as *friteries*. In Belgium, steamed mussels and fried potatoes went together as naturally as fish and chips in England, and burgers and fries in the United States.

The moules-frites arrived and she enjoyed eating with her fingers, as was customary, using an empty mussel shell as tweezers to pluck and eat the bivalves. But, in a second omen, Louise noticed a definite air of distress in the restaurant. She listened in on some of the conversations but made out only the occasional *quel horreur* and *mon dieu!* She paid the tab then walked across the street to the Crédit Agricole, checking her watch as the bank was to open in minutes.

The doors opened and the staff resumed their post-lunch duties. As soon as the teller removed the *closed* sign, Louise was first at the window. She greeted the teller and handed her the business card she had received form the branch manager in Auxerre, with the name of the Brussels branch manager, Luc Legrand. The teller gave Louise a perplexed stare. Louise took this as a bit of a challenge and returned the teller's stare, upon which the teller blushed, trying to hold back tears. Softening, Louise became concerned.

"Is something wrong?" Louise asked in French.

"Forgive me," the teller said, composing herself. "Monsieur Legrand was killed last night."

Shocked, all that Louise could think of was *The Banker's Grave*. Collecting herself, she asked, "What happened?"

"We don't know. There is an ongoing investigation." The teller remembered her professional duties. "I'm sorry. Perhaps there is someone else who can help you?"

Louise needed to focus on the mission now more than ever. "I had hoped to meet with a wealth management expert."

"Of course." She pointed to a chair in the waiting area. "Please have a seat, and someone will be out shortly." Louise waited for about five minutes until a man in his forties, wearing a grey suit and an unremarkable tie, approached her.

"Boujour, I'm Bertrand Brunel." Louise stood and shook his hand. "Please follow me," he said somberly, and led her to his office.

"Thank you for seeing me on such short notice," Louise said, taking a seat in front of his desk.

"Of course," he replied. "How can I help you today?"

"Well, I was referred to Monsieur Legrand by the manager of the Beaune branch, Yves Renard."

Brunel looked startled. "Yves Renard?"

"Yes," Louise replied. "He's my account manager in Beaune. I wanted to see about placing some of my deposits into a higher interest-bearing account."

Brunel stared as though trying to make sense of something.

"Is there something the matter?"

He squinted. "May I look up your account?"

"Of course." Louise handed him her checkbook.

He typed on his computer. "Yes, I see, premium checking account, 1.5% interest."

"Correct. I'm leaving those funds in there for six months to establish my credit for the purchase of a house in Burgundy."

"You would definitely benefit from moving the funds into a higher interest, short-term investment account. Perhaps three months with automatic renewal."

"That's what I was thinking," Louise said.

Brunel entered all the details into his computer. "I'll be right back with your paperwork."

While he was out, Louise looked around the office. It was a similar sterile décor, with Brunel's corporate photo on the wall like Renard's. A detail stood out on the portrait as plain as day. On his lapel, Brunel wore the same pin she had seen on Renard's portrait, a badge with two crossed swords. Louise made sure her face remained composed when Brunel returned and handed her the documents and a pen.

"Please sign here and that should take care of it."

Louise signed and stood to leave. "Thank you for your help."

"If you need anything else, please contact me any time." He handed her a business card. "Do you have any other questions?"

No time like the present, Louise thought. "Actually, I'm curious about the pin on your lapel in the photo. Monsieur Renard wore the same pin in his portrait. What is the significance?"

"We were both part of the 4th Regiment of Chasseurs à Cheval that was re-created as the regiment of reconnaissance of the 1st Belgian Corps."

"You were a knight?"

He gave a demure smile. "Mounted rifleman. After the reorganization of the Armed Forces in 1993, the regiment of mounted rifles was reduced to a Squadron. That's when Renard and I left to work in the private banking sector. Monsieur Renard struggled. He was a competent banker, but he was forced to resign from our branch."

"Forced to resign?" Louise asked.

"Nothing was ever proven, but he was accused of fraud."

"What kind of fraud?"

Brunel was taken aback slightly by the line of questioning and chose his words carefully. "Falsifying client records. The bank has zero tolerance of even the slightest misappropriation and found that Monsieur Renard might have been collaborating with a fraudulent assessor."

Louise used bank terminology to make the conversation chummy. "An assessor making misleading property valuations?"

"I'm afraid so," he said.

"Thank you for your candor." Louise shook his hand, and he escorted her to the door. "What is the quickest way to Château Du Lac Hotel in Genval?"

"It is very easy, only about twenty minutes away. Continue east on Chaussée de la Hulpe and it will become route N275 south. Stay on that route to Genval."

"Thank you again. Au revoir."

THIRTY-ONE

January 12, 2002

The location of the June 2000 Bilderberg conference, Château Du Lac Hotel in Genval, was a popular vacation destination. Modeled after a Rhineland abbey, the ivy-covered white brick hotel with its single lighthouse tower reflected serenely in the lake surrounded by Belle Epoque homes. Louise parked and entered the hotel to look for more information on its intriguing history and found a display near the lobby in three languages. It was originally built on mineral springs as a spa in 1906 due to the renowned quality of its mineral water. In 1934 John V.B. Martin acquired the château and ran it as the Indian Tonic production plant. Over the next decades, the Martin family transformed the old factory into a convention center and five-star hotel, becoming the Martin's Château du Lac.

The sprawling resort was the sort of place that made Louise's palms sweaty. Any place where people prowled for celebrities was kryptonite to her. Yet, there she sat in the lobby, reading the French political magazine, *Le Nouvel Observateur*, doing her own prowling. Michael lingered out of sight reading the same plaque Louise had just read, trying to figure out what trail she was on.

"Qu'est-ce que je vous sers?" the waiter asked Louise.

"De l'eau chaud avec du citron, s'il vous plaît." A moment later, the server delivered the simple recipe. She squeezed three lemon wedges into plain hot water and took a long drink. It was one of those household remedies that worked. Whether psychosomatic or real, she immediately felt her liver release toxins from the night of drinking cognac. Sipping soothingly, she almost missed the drama playing out before her eyes.

At the other end of the lobby, two men were having a heated discussion while a tall, beautiful, teenaged girl passively stood by. One man looked like he could have been from Eastern Europe, ostentatiously dressed in Gucci loafers and designer jeans with his linen shirtsleeves rolled up, revealing hairy forearms. The body language of the other man with red hair indicated he was guarding the girl. He abruptly took her hand and brusquely escorted her out of the hotel. After what Louise had learned about the serial murders, these older men fighting over a teenaged girl was suspicious enough for her to want to follow.

Louise left cash on the table and went out to her car. She pretended to look through her purse while keeping an eye on the red-haired man leading the young woman to their vehicle. Louise got in her car and waited until they took off before putting it in gear and following at a safe distance, with Michael not far behind. They headed southwest of Lake Genval for about forty minutes until the driver slowed and turned down a lane to what looked like a private château that was open to the public. Louise waited for a minute, then turned into the treelined lane and drove through a dovecote entrance gate. She pulled into the pulverized gravel parking area of a seventeenth century château made entirely of stone with two Rapunzel towers.

Michael had stopped on the main road, knowing that Louise had successfully found the same chateau that Jean-Philippe's agent had infiltrated. He felt assured that she was on the right track and could count on her to call him and confirm her whereabouts. He left to meet Jean-Philippe at his monastery in the Sonian Forest nearby.

Louise waited in her parked car until the man got out of his car, opened the passenger side door and escorted the young woman to the back entrance. Louise got out and entered the front door of the main building. There was no one at reception, so she scanned one of the colorful brochures, marketing the château as a Catholic center, like a monastery, but for lay people to attend spiritual retreats. According to the brochure, in addition to the main château, an old mill and an old farmhouse had been converted into guesthouses. There was also a chapel and a Marian shrine. There was a picture in the brochure of the couple-in-residence who oversaw the place, the wife managing the accommodations, and the husband maintaining the buildings and grounds. Louise rang the bell, and the wife emerged.

"Bonjour! Bien venue," she greeted Louise in the same nasally Belgian French as the café owner in Sars-la-Buissière.

"Bonjour." Louise smiled, then inquired in French, "Do you have any rooms available? I've been exploring in the area, and this place looks wonderful."

"Yes, of course," she replied. "How many guests?"

"Just me," Louise said, handing her a passport and credit card. Until then, it hadn't occurred to Louise that she, a woman of a certain age traveling alone, might seem odd. She had been living such a sheltered independent life exiled in paradise, it sometimes came as a shock to see herself in the eyes of strangers. A French expression popped into her head, *vieille fille*, which translated literally to *old girl*, but colloquially it was the term for *spinster*. Even though it was an obsolete concept, Louise felt self-conscious now checking in alone.

"How lovely for you to take time for yourself."

"Yes, it will be nice to have some alone time."

"Eh, oh, cocotte!" a man shouted from the back.

The groundskeeper's wife put her hands together and looked to heaven then back at Louise. "Lucky you!" She came from behind the desk and handed Louise a heavy antique skeleton key. "Here's your room key. My name is Ferdinande and that is my husband, André. Do you have any bags?"

"I'll get them later," Louise replied.

"Follow me." Ferdinande headed down the darkly lit hallway toward a heavy wooden door that was ajar, silhouetting André holding a rake in one hand and a basket in another.

"What's taking so long?" André asked in the nasally French.

"We have a new guest," Ferdinande replied.

They took a path down to the back of the property and Ferdinande pointed to the converted mill, now a guesthouse.

"The second door is your room. Follow me and I'll show you the grounds." They walked toward a pond, and Ferdinande pointed to the chapel. "There is a service in the chapel at 7:00 every morning that you are welcome to attend." She indicated an outdoor shrine, a semi-circle of manicured hedges enclosing a raised bed of various plants, and a row of candles on wire stems, completing the front of the circle, all surrounding a statue of the Virgin Mary on a pedestal. "At the Marian shrine, the votive candles are free for you to light and offer blessings."

The sudden blast of a gunshot startled Louise.

"What was that?" Louise asked.

"Oh, that is Father Gregory. As you can see, our property sits precariously over a marsh. Even the word *Brussels* from old Dutch *Broekzele* means *home in the marsh*. The slightest erosion can destabilize our parish."

Louise saw a monk in full cassock, the traditional long black robe buttoned up the front, with a wide sash around the waist, over a white collared shirt and black pants.

"Is that Father Gregory?" Louise asked.

"Yes. Monks and nuns often stay here and volunteer to help with the property. Father Gregory has taken it upon himself to help with our gopher situation."

Louise watched the monk, who appeared to be on the young side of his thirties, sitting near the lake doing his five decades of the rosary prayers. To her amazement, he interrupted his prayers, took a revolver from his cloak and aimed it at one of the nearby gopher holes, waiting. A superfluity of nuns walked by, saw the monk with a weapon, and hurried away in the other direction. A gopher popped its head up out of the hole, and the monk fired off a shot with a marksman's precision, eviscerating the little critter. The monk resumed his five decades of the rosary prayers. The presence of nuns and the devoted groundskeepers notwithstanding, Louise speculated the center might be more than just a religious sanctuary.

"Thank you, Ferdinande," Louise said, after they'd both turned away from the scene. "I'll go get my bag and leave you to your work."

"Dinner is at 19:00 hours in the main hall."

"I'm looking forward to it."

Louise walked through the garden past the Marian shrine. As she approached the parking area, she noticed an idling black sedan that looked familiar. She backed against the wall to keep out of the driver's line of vision and rummaged in her bag for the piece of paper. As she suspected, it was the same license plate number she had seen in Auxerre. The driver was the mysterious man she had also observed leaving the bar in Pommard. Even as a shiver of fear was warning her, it also reassured that she was on the right trail. Louise waited for the car to drive off before retrieving her bag then went to her room.

Louise settled in, and the phone was in use again.

"Hi, Charlie."

"Louise, where are you?"

"Belgium. Just outside of Brussels."

"You are in a different city every day," Charlie observed. "That probably means you have some news."

"There have been some major developments, which I won't go into now. But if my suspicions are correct, I'm closing in on something really big."

"Big, as in setting up an arrest?" Charlie asked.

"Big, as in international conspiracy."

"Should I alert the local law enforcement, or our people in the region?" Patrick asked.

"Not yet. I won't make any moves until I have something actionable. I'll be in touch soon."

Charlie offered the usual, "Okay, stay safe," and hung up.

Louise changed into her yoga clothes. The showiness of her limber and lithe body contorting in different ways always brought all kinds of characters out into the open much like insects from a house on fire. One time on the island, when it was only her and Big Steve on the beach and not another soul for miles, a speedboat pulled out of nowhere. The boat full of young male divers had been checking her out with high-powered binoculars and maneuvered in for a closer look. Louise laughed at the simple idiocy of the crew and invited them to the bar for drinks, with Big Steve as protection, of course.

Louise walked to the garden and found a prime spot, away from the target range of the armed monk, who seemed to have finished the gopher hunt for the time being. She sat on the grass in lotus pose, the chilly air invigorating her, and went into a meditative mindfulness. As she breathed and repeated her mantra, her senses were both heightened and impervious to distractions.

During this state, a realization came to her. It was about the recurring dreams she'd been having. They were all about danger, and voices calling to her. What were the dreams trying to tell her? She recognized that most of the voices sounded like Jean-Philippe. Was he trying to send her a message? She needed to adjust her pose to open chakras.

Sitting on her knees, she leaned forward and placed her elbows on the ground and clasped her hands together creating a cradle for her head. She brought her legs up into a headstand while silently repeating the affirmation, *I am love and light*. The crown chakra, or *Sahasrara*, symbolized by a circle and a thousand petals, like a lotus flower, was the seventh chakra, located at the top of the head. The crown chakra is considered the gateway to the cosmic self or the divine self, to universal consciousness. Doing headstands allowed the crown chakra access to the utmost clarity and enlightened wisdom.

Louise felt the energy stimulated around the crown of her head. Remaining in the headstand, she opened to a wide-legged pose, pushing out through her heels. She bent her knees and pressed the soles of her feet together, opening her knees wide while keeping her toes pointing upwards. She brought her knees together, keeping her bottom slightly back, like sitting in a chair. She crossed one thigh over the other and wrapped one calf around the other in eagle pose. The various headstand poses helped to stimulate and activate her crown chakra.

"Impressionnant," Father Gregory said.

Louise focused her eyes and saw the legs of the monk. As she held the pose, she observed the gun in his right hand, cupped below his left hand, which was holding the rosary beads that draped to the left of the crucifix and hung down in a loop. Keeping her legs crossed, Louise bent at the waist and lowered her feet to the ground. She extended her hands up, tilting her face toward the sky, her back to the priest. Uncrossing her legs with her feet in place she pivoted 180 degrees to face the priest. She brought her palms together in front of her heart. "Namaste."

"Amen," the monk replied.

"Did I distract you from your work?" Louise said, assessing the firearm. It appeared to be antique with a 6-inch octagon barrel, a mottled gray patina and walnut grip.

"Excusez-moi," he said diffidently, slipping the gun inside his robe. "It is not exactly God's work. But it seems a necessary evil." He offered his hand. "I am Father Gregory."

"Hello," Louise said, shaking his hand. "I'm Karen." She nodded toward the now-concealed weapon. "Interesting form of charisma."

"Even monks have past lives," he said. "But these days I mostly practice the rosary."

"As you can see, I practice yoga and meditation."

"The Holy Rosary is also a meditation about the chief mysteries of the life, death and glory of Jesus Christ and of His Blessed Mother. The fifteen principal virtues serve as a mantra."

"The fifteen mysteries of the Holy Rosary," Louise rejoined.

"You know your rosary."

"There is no shortage of mysteries in a lifetime," Louise said, evoking a silent blessing for her mother.

"If you do not have rosary beads, it is perfectly okay to count with your fingers, which frees the mind for meditation. You do not have to be a Christian to understand this freedom."

"It's not that Christianity is limiting," Louise said, nearly under her breath. "But I prefer Om to prayer." She was looking for a way out of this discussion and noticed an embroidered patch on the left shoulder of the monk's habit. "That is an interesting badge."

"It is the emblem of the Congregation of the Fathers of Mercy."

"Fathers of Mercy?" Louise asked.

"That is why I am here." Father Gregory pointed to the Marian shrine. "To bless this shrine of the Blessed Mother. That is why I recite the five decades of the rosary every day."

"Is that why you're also wearing your full habit?" Louise inquired.

"Precisely. Our Founder, Father Rauzan, adopted this black Roman cassock from the secular clergy. This badge with the emblem of the congregation, *the Return of the Prodigal Son*, is always worn on the upper left side of the habit. Each member is required to undertake mental prayer and an examination of conscience twice a day."

"I also try to devote myself to daily meditation."

"You have many spiritual gifts, I see. We are happy to have your special presence at the shrine of the Holy Mother."

"Thank you," Louise said. "Will I see you at dinner?"

"Yes, I will be giving the blessing."

"I look forward to it."

"As do I," Father Gregory replied with a gracious bow of the head. "Forgive me, but I must resume my duties." He walked away with a forthright stride. Louise wasn't sure if Father Gregory was a legitimate monk, given his proficiency with his weapon, but he seemed to have his back story down pat, whoever he was. She resumed her yoga routine while contemplating the many mysteries in her life, keeping her eye on Father Gregory.

The monk approached the Marian shrine and tended to some of the greenery, then walked into the chapel. Louise extricated herself out of a yoga pose and walked over to take a look at the Marian shrine. She knew of official pilgrimage sites such as Lourdes in France, which had Marian shrines that marked the miracles ascribed to Mary, the Blessed Mother of

Jesus. But the shrine located here appeared to be symbolic, which was commonly found in silent retreat centers away from the chapel and residence. Louise took one of the long votive candles from the wicker trug and placed it in a holder in front of the Holy Mother's image. She lit the candle and, as she had been taught in another lifetime, crossed herself in silent prayer.

Having established her devotion, she wondered about the looming Rapunzel towers on the grounds. She went to the back of the château and stealthily tried to enter one of them, but the door was locked. She contemplated her next move and decided to go back to her room and her trusty mobile phone. Several messages and texts from Michael awaited her. The next text she sent to him was simple and to the point. F O L I A G E.

Michael immediately rang her phone, but as it was on silent in respect for the retreat atmosphere, it just buzzed in Louise's hand.

"Hello, Michael."

Michael went to full decoy mode even though he knew exactly where she was. "Where the hell are you? I've been trying to reach you."

"I'm at a retreat in Brussels and have my phone on silent," Louise said. After a back-and-forth on the importance of keeping the phone with her at all times, Louise got to the point. "I'm getting very close to something and I'll text you my exact location after I hang up. If after that text you don't hear from me precisely 24 hours from now, get a team of the local authorities over here."

"Why can't I mobilize something now? I don't want you to take unnecessary risks."

"I need to stay undercover and not arouse any suspicions, or certain suspects might escape."

"Could you at least tell me who you think these people are?" Michael asked.

"I have no idea yet. But I'll keep you posted." She hung up and texted Michael the location of the retreat.

THIRTY-TWO

January 12, 2002

Arnaud's red hair was disheveled as he riffled through Annabel's chest of drawers. She watched subserviently as he frantically gathered only the essentials for a short trip.

There was a change of plan and they needed to leave the retreat and the secrets inside this strange tower. The bodyguard-for-hire, who was assigned to protect the violin prodigy, Annabel, at any cost, was clearly earning every cent at this point. The spat with his contact at the Château Du Lac Hotel in Genval had set Arnaud off. He knew it was time to move his merchandise or everything he had worked for over the past 16 years would vaporize.

"Are we going away?" Annabel asked.

"Yes," Arnaud replied, but he immediately saw the anxiety on Annabel's face, so he improvised. "We're going to see Evelyne!" Her expression instantly changed to excitement. "Come now, finish packing your things. We're leaving tonight."

Annabel began meticulously folding and packing her overnight bag. Arnaud left, locking the door behind him, and made his way down the stairs. He heard someone jiggling the outside handle to the Rapunzel tower door and held still for a moment listening until the intruder gave up and walked away. Was it that idiot groundskeeper or his equally meddling wife? He decided not to check. Who else would even know someone was here?

He continued down the stairs and unlocked the internal door leading to the main château. Once in the kitchen, he prepared a plate of very plain food, a country pâté with crackers, and a glass of milk. He carried the meal back to the tower and bolted the door from the inside. Instead of going upstairs, he set the meager meal on a side table, took out his keyring, and opened another heavy door below the staircase. It creaked open, lighting a pathway into a damp gloomy dungeon. He turned on the lantern that sat outside the door and hung it over his forearm, picked up the plate and glass of milk, and entered. The heavy door closed with a thud, the latch catching.

"Evelyne, it's time to eat," Arnaud said.

He crept to the back of the cell, the lantern exposing a dingy wood frame with a mattress covered in tattered bedding. In the corner, a half-naked girl hung by her wrists from a ladder. When she saw him, her crystal blue eyes widened in terror. With her disheveled mass of platinum blonde hair and full red lips, Evelyne, the daughter of Annabel's former tutor, was still stunningly beautiful. However, it was clear that she was now emotionally and physically diminished. He removed the gag from her mouth, but she made no sound. Tears flowed from her eyes as she stared in horrified dread at the monster.

The décor of Louise's room with a canopied bed and a stone fireplace was sumptuous. But it was icy cold, so Louise freshened up with a birdbath in the sink instead of a shower. She pulled together a tasteful outfit, wearing her burgundy knit pencil skirt with a cream cashmere turtleneck and black leather boots. Her dark hair, black eyeliner, and burgundy lipstick tied the look together.

She walked to the main dining hall that was still empty of other guests. There was a long medieval wood table surrounded by high-backed uphol-stered chairs, set with candelabra and full dinner service. A fireplace large enough to walk into burned in vain to warm the cavernous space. Louise pulled her turtleneck up to her chin and helped herself to the red wine that was set out for the dinner guests. She stood by the fireplace watching the flames.

"Bonsoir!" Ferdinande entered carrying a tray of plated salads and breadbaskets.

"Bonsoir!" Louise continued in French, "May I help?"

"You have already helped by serving yourself a glass of wine." Ferdi-nande placed the tray on the table and distributed the salads and bread evenly around the seats.

"The wine by the fire is very pleasant," Louise said.

"À vôtre santé! Make yourself at home. The other guests will be arriving shortly." Ferdinande straightened a few place settings and hustled back out to the kitchen.

Father Gregory and three nuns entered.

"Bonsoir, mademoiselle Karen," Father Gregory said. "This is Sister Paula, Sister Anne, and Sister Monika." The nuns bowed their heads. "They are here on a silent retreat."

"Bonsoir," Louise said, bowing her head in turn.

Another couple entered, chatting quietly in Russian. The man was tall, with graying dark hair with a prominent proboscis, the woman also brunette, statuesque with short cropped hair. Everyone found seats around the table.

Ferdinande returned carrying a tray of the main course, distributing the plates first to the women then to the men. "Bon appétit," she said before dashing off to the kitchen.

"Let us pray," Father Gregory said.

They bowed their heads as Father Gregory recited the traditional grace with no embellishments.

All replied, "*Amen.*"

Ferdinande reentered with more bread and Louise used the etiquette of waiting for others before eating to ask, "Will anyone else be joining us? When I arrived, I saw a man and a young woman enter through the back of the château." Louise noticed the Russian's exchange a look.

"Oh, you must be thinking of the owner's son and his niece. They live on the premises, but usually dine in private." Ferdinande dashed off again.

"Praise be to the chef," Father Gregory replied.

"Amen, and bon appétit," Louise seconded. "You have a refreshing sense of humor, Father."

"Humor is tonic to the nonbeliever and comforting to the hopeful," Father Gregory said.

"Cheers to that," Louise said, drinking more pinot noir.

"You are American?" the monk asked.

Louise took his question as a subtle jab for asking the nosy question about the guests. "I was just trying to be polite." She shrugged in mock embarrassment.

"This Ruby Red is as stupid as that idiot male nurse," the woman said to her companion in Russian. Louise showed no sign of understanding, but she felt the blood rush to her face. Did they really know her by her code name, *Ruby Red*? She glanced at Father Gregory to see if he showed any signs of complicity, but his expression gave nothing away.

The Russian coolly turned to Louise and asked in French, "Where are you from in America?"

"Chicago," Louise replied. "But I've been traveling around Europe for over a month." She babbled, hoping the conversation would open him up so she could assess if the Russians really knew who she was.

"Where have you been to so far?" he asked.

Louise saw an opportunity. "Mostly Burgundy, but I've taken side trips to Paris and Monte Carlo." Bingo. The Russian blinked when she said "Monte Carlo."

Recovering, he said to Louise, "Excuse me, my wife wants me to translate for her." He turned to his companion and said in Russian, "That confirms it, she's here investigating the murder of the Israeli banker. It's time to move the Maltese Falcon," he continued in Russian. "Make an excuse to leave."

Ferdinande's husband, André, entered and tried to build the fire higher in an ever-futile attempt to bring the ambient temperature up a couple of degrees.

The Russian woman shivered and said in broken English, "Excuse me, I forgot my sweater." She got up and walked out.

"Is everything okay?" Louise asked the Russian.

"She'll be fine," he replied. "She's rather thin blooded for a Russian," he joked.

"André, mon amour," Ferdinande asked her husband, "could you also check the heat in the guest rooms?" She looked apologetically at the visitors. "This old château is beautiful, but there is no central heating."

This was Louise's only chance to excuse herself and go after them as they tried to get away. She shivered and said, "I'm chilly too. Please excuse me while I go get a jacket."

She rose from the table and exited the grand salon in time to see the Russian woman walking up the staircase to what Louise assumed was their suite in the main château. She headed down the shadowy hallway toward the back exit and opened the door, letting it swing wide. She pressed herself against the wall in the shadows allowing the door to close to give the impression she had gone out.

She made her way back into the château and looked for an entrance into the rear Rapunzel tower. Turning a corner that led to another hallway, she stayed in the shadows searching for the tower door. She surmised with the guest rooms upstairs, the rooms on the ground floor were common areas or servants' quarters. She passed a chamber with the door ajar that had four single beds and a simple chest of drawers. She also passed a reading room with well-stocked bookshelves, comfortable armchairs, side tables, and reading lamps.

At the end of the hallway, she could see the curved wall of the Rapunzel tower with a large wooden door. Historically, these flanking towers protruded from castle allowing defenders to fire along the length of the wall, making an attack difficult. Although the original purpose of the towers had been defense, they could also be used for storage and imprisonment.

Louise approached the door and assessed the old lock. Her fascination with these older security methods began when she lived in Paris and found the secret room in her apartment.[20] She started taking note of various medieval doors then bought the fascinating book *Lock & Key* by Stephen Tchudi. Locksmiths from the fourteenth through seventeenth century were skilled metalworkers, the best of which became internationally famous. However, this lock was a simple warded lock invented by the Romans and was based on projections built inside the keyhole. The projection would block a wrongly-shaped key from turning the lock, but it didn't look difficult to pick. Louise tried her room key and although the shank was long enough, the bit was too short to trigger the projection. She took her metal nail file from her purse and held it at an angle against the key to extend the key lever. It took several tries and determination, but she finally got the internal mechanism to tumble. She pushed down on the handle and entered the tower.

A staircase spiraled clockwise down the right wall. Another bit of trivia entered her head as she assessed the situation. In medieval castles staircases were deliberately built clockwise to diminish the ability of right-handed attackers to properly swing their swords. Below the staircase was a wooden door that Louise assumed was a storage cellar. She ascended the staircase to another heavy wooden door with the same kind of warded lock. She tried the handle, but it was locked. She crouched to look through the keyhole. Inside was dark except for the light of a single lamp. She could make out a well-appointed room with stone floors covered in French Aubusson-style rugs.

---

[20] From the author's first novel in the Louise Moscow series, *Foliage: An International Banking Spy Thriller*

The French Royal style queen-sized bed was covered in warm quilts and ample pillows. There were comfortable chairs, and burning wood crackled in the stone fireplace.

Louise tried to open the lock, using the same skeleton key-nail-file method. She froze when she heard someone moving on the other side of the door. Looking through the keyhole again, Louise saw the same tall blonde girl from the hotel on Lake Genval. She looked frightened at the sound of Louise's key in the lock.

"It's okay," Louise said. "I'm here to help you. Can you open the door?"

"It's locked," the girl said.

Louise hurried to pick the lock, but in her panicked effort, she didn't hear the person come up behind her until it was too late.

Louise squirmed, the sharp pain of the knife blade penetrating her shoulder.

"No!"

Her own cries awoke her from the nightmare to the real-life horror. She realized the searing pain was not from a knife, but from her arms being bound over her head as she dangled from a heavy wooden folding ladder. She straightened her legs and stood to alleviate the pressure on her arms and shoulders. The darkness dissipated as her eyes adjusted to the dim light of a single lantern revealing a dank squalid dungeon with stone and dirt floors.

The pain in her shoulders eased only to bring her attention to her throbbing headache. She gently pressed the back of her head against the wall to detect the injury at the right side of her skull. Having been knocked unconscious meant she would likely have a concussion. To remain conscious, she tried to wrest herself loose or tip the ladder over so she could lower her arms. But the ladder was bolted to the wall. She screamed again, trying to alert anyone. Another scream echoed, but she wasn't sure if it was her own.

"Is anybody there?" Louise asked. The sound of nearby whimpering startled Louise, the anguish conveyed by the sobs redoubling her fear. "Who are you? Where are we?"

The clang of a heavy door elicited a blood-curdling scream from the other soul in the room. But the sound was completely absorbed by the dense, solid-stone walls.

"Shut up, Evelyne!" a man snarled.

The glow of his lantern silhouetted him, an evil filament within a surreal golden sphere. The face belonging to Evelyne became visible as he approached her. It was a young woman who appeared to be physically handicapped. Her wide blue eyes and bulbous red lips were animated under a shock of platinum blonde hair. She sat on the ground in a scooting position, one leg bent in front of the other, cowering against the wall to Louise's right, utterly helpless. From the torn rags she wore exposing most of her skin, it was clear she had been the object of all kinds of abuse, including sexual. She raised her good arm in pitiful defiance against her offender. The captive girl was of no interest to him now, except to demonstrate to the immobile Louise of what he was capable. Holding the lantern in his right hand, he grabbed Evelyne's hair in his left hand and kicked her shriveled legs.

He turned to Louise, raising the lamp to reveal himself, in a display of dominance. His expression was devoid of compassion or concern for being identified. Louise recognized him as the red-haired man she had followed from the Château du Lac resort in Genval. He raised his right hand to his head, plucked a single hair, and rolled it in his fingertips. Louise scrutinized his behavior, a combination of narcissism and trichotillomania, the impulse to literally pull one's hair out. His eyes were empty and sadistic, instinctively causing Louise to squirm helplessly.

"You are a little old for my taste, but still very pretty." He clutched her face in his sweaty hand and lowered it to grab one of her breasts. She could see where this was going, so just as he was about to grab her between the legs, she spat at him and screamed at the top of her lungs. He clasped his hand over her mouth, but she bit him until she felt his flesh give. Pulling back in agony, he backhanded her across the face. The young woman also screamed, so he went over to her and knocked her out with one punch. Then he returned to Louise and punched her lights out too.

Moments later, when Louise regained consciousness, her head and jaw were on fire and she could taste blood in the corner of her mouth. She fought to remain awake.

"I told you not to hurt her, Arnaud," a voice said. It was familiar, but distant, so Louise thought she was dreaming again.

"They wouldn't shut up," Arnaud barked. He was in full process mode. This wasn't his first violent rodeo. He began giving orders. "Take her down and bring her upstairs."

The familiar voice belonged to the shadowy figure who now untied her from the ladder and carried her out, leaving Evelyne behind. Louise passed out again.

When she came to, she was in a room like the one she had seen through the keyhole with French Royal décor and a warm fire. She lay comfortably on the bed and opened her eyes to the vision of Matthieu, eliciting happy relief.

"Matthieu," Louise said. "I had the most horrible dream."

Matthieu wore the same tortured expression he had the many times they talked. There had always been something amiss about him. As she fully regained consciousness and felt the pain of her injuries, she realized that Matthieu's expression was more than sorrow or regret. It was helplessness.

"I'm so sorry, Louise." It was the first time she had heard him say her name.

"My name is Karen," she said, reflexively.

"Karen Baker from Illinois is dead," Matthieu said.

"How did you know?"

"They know everything," he said. "You can disguise yourself and change your name, but your handwriting is undeniable. There were rumors and intel that you had emerged from wherever you had been hiding. It was just a question of when you'd slip up. You filled out that loan application, now they know all about you."

"And I know all about the crime syndicate that apparently you are a part of!" Louise struggled to sit up while attempting to roundhouse punch him. "Let me out of here!"

Matthieu held her down and tried to calm her. "I *am* going to get you out of here! But you must do as I say."

"Jean-Philippe said the same thing ten years ago," was all she could manage to say. Louise was in a tailspin, woozy from the beating and distraught by her identity being revealed. But she remained defiant. "There's no way I'm falling for that again."

Louise pushed him away, freeing herself from his grip. He made no effort to re-engage. She sat up, nearly blacking out again, and turned to face him. "How are you involved in this, Matthieu? Don't you realize they are holding women as prisoners here? Your fiancée was probably murdered by these same people."

"That's the point," he replied. "These people have implicated me. I am also their prisoner."

"What the hell are you talking about?"

He struggled with his emotions as he tried to explain his predicament. "When I met Jo, we fell in love and got engaged. I had a dream job as an archeologist in the most prestigious institution in the country. Then one day, an outsider came into a prominent dig I was on, claiming he was a fellow archeologist. It was Arnaud, the man who beat you. He was working for a shadowy prostitution ring as an enforcer. His assignment was to recruit me back into the ring by blackmailing me. During one of my excavations I had found a relic, an ex voto, that I stupidly kept, to give to Jo as a wedding gift. Being a contracted archeologist on a sponsored excavation, keeping the antiquity without reporting it would be considered a high crime. Arnaud had the evidence and could have destroyed my career. But I still refused to return to the ring."

"What do you mean, *return* to the ring,'" Louise observed, shocked into full attention.

"While I was in school, I did things I'm not proud of," he explained. "It was easy money in those days, and I was a perfect candidate. Girls would just gravitate to me." Louise could see why, even in his forties Matthieu was endowed with movie star good looks. Matthieu continued, "I invited the girls to what they called *recruiting parties* and that's as far as my involvement went. The girls would be pulled into the same prostitution ring, usually unwillingly. After graduating, I tried to disappear into a high-profile career. But they caught up with me. After I refused, they seemed to back off."

The next part of the story was clearly difficult for Matthieu. "While I was away on a dig, they took Jo. They raped, tortured, and killed her, and had evidence to make it look like I was a suspect. They came to me, during the worst loss of my life, and told me they'd frame me for Jo's murder unless I signed over the family vineyard to them. But there was a flaw in their extortion. I pointed out that French law doesn't allow the sale of property without approval by all immediate family members. Of course, that put my sister and nephew in jeopardy. So, I offered to give them a portion of the profits, which became a better deal for them. They continued to threaten to hurt my family if I ever went to the police. So, in essence, I quit my career to protect the only remaining people who mattered to me, Magali and Luke."

Louise's expression oddly changed from horror to epiphany.

"That's it!" she exclaimed, the pieces coming together.

"What?" asked Matthieu.

Louise fought through the haze to think out loud. "You said someone is using private background checks to blackmail people in all professions."

"Yes," Matthieu said. "The network goes very high up. It is not just sex trafficking. They incriminate and blackmail all kinds of people in positions of power, including politicians and bankers.

"Like Yves Renard," Louise said.

"Exactly. Any person applying for a job or a bank loan that requires a private background check can be targeted. There are corrupt insiders with access to the background checks who search for anything incriminating to be used in this blackmail scheme."

"It all makes sense," Louise was starting to make the connections. "Just like you, most people have things in their past that they don't want made public. The only thing I need now is proof. If you help me, I promise to protect your family. In the meantime, we have to help the girls being held prisoner here."

"You don't understand," Matthieu said, with that twisted look in his eyes.

"What?"

"These are very powerful people," Matthieu explained. "The young woman in the upstairs room, Annabel, has been raised from a baby for a Eugenicist marriage."

"Eugenicist marriage?"

"Annabel was kidnapped as a child. She was targeted even in the womb, as it was obvious from her parentage that she would become a stunning beauty. When she was born, she was kidnapped and turned over to Arnaud whose assignment was to keep her a pure virgin, give her the best education, and then when time was right, market her to the highest bidder as a *Maltese Falcon*."

"What do you mean Maltese Falcon?" Louise asked.

"Maltese Falcon is a code name specifically for this kind of trade. It's symbolic based on the annual tribute payable to the monarchy on All Saints' Day, November 1st, *one falcon*."

"The annual payment was a Maltese Falcon?"

"Yes. They use the term as a code specifically for Eugenicists seeking these kinds of pure women. They were scheduled to deliver the girl last November 1ˢᵗ to a Russian billionaire, but after 9/11 everything changed. Many lost all their fortunes and others made money. The original buyer could no longer pay, and Arnaud put the message out that she would go to a new highest bidder."

"Who was the highest bidder?" Louise asked.

"The two Russians that were here at the château."

"I have to get those girls out of here." Louise tried to get up but was weak.

"You cannot help them," Matthieu said, his eyes driving home the truth. "These people are dangerous. I'm going to get you out of here. You just have to trust me."

"I'm not leaving without them," Louise said.

"Then you will never leave," Matthieu said. "You must follow my lead if you want to stay alive." They heard someone approaching. "Lie down, pretend to be unconscious."

The door opened. "Let's go," Arnaud said.

Matthieu lifted Louise up to a sitting position. "Allez, on your feet," Matthieu said, slapping her. Louise pretended to wake up. She could see Arnaud clearly now, bloated and doughy with brittle rusty hair that had been thinned out by his hair-pulling tic.

"What are you waiting for?" Arnaud puffed. "Get her the hell out of my room!"

Matthieu took Louise by the arm and stood her up. She teetered, dizzy from the near concussion. He stabilized her.

"Come on," he said, pulling her with mock forcefulness toward the door.

They went down the staircase, and Louise saw that they were in the other flanking tower. The heavy wooden door leading outside was open, and she could see the secluded loading area behind the château. The same black sedan was idling just beyond the door. As Louise reached the ground floor, the rear window of the sedan rolled down, the dome light revealing the Russian couple in back and the man behind the steering wheel. Even in the obscurity she could tell the driver was the same man she had seen at the bar in Pommard, in the car in Auxerre and who had approached her on the boat. He was part of the sex trafficking ring.

"Let's go!" the Russian said. Louise knew if she got into that car, she was doomed. She pretended to trip and convincingly fell flat on her stomach.

"What the fuck is she doing?" Arnaud shouted.

"She has a concussion," Matthieu said, going along with Louise's stall tactic.

"Pick her up and carry her!" Arnaud growled. "I think she tipped somebody off. That fucking French agent she was working with, Jean-Philippe, is onto us. This place will be under lockdown any minute!"

There was an uncharacteristic panic in his voice, but he still noticed Louise's response to his words. She couldn't help herself. When she heard the name Jean-Philippe, her eyes opened wide and she rolled onto her back, giving herself away. Arnaud raised his hand and plucked a single hair from his head, twirling it in satisfaction like a Bond villain. He moved closer, looming over her.

"Oh, look who's suddenly okay." He looked down on her. "Yes, Jean-Philippe has been staking out this place the whole time. And from what I know about your past with him, he didn't come back to save you before, and he will not save you now."

While Louise had been unconscious, her eyeliner had smudged and formed a smoky black outline that intensified her green eyes as she glared up at him. The last of the haze from Arnaud's beating had miraculously lifted, and the accumulated fury inside her raged. She kept cool outwardly, as her attacker smirked like a deranged Grinch.

The side effect of years of yoga training was her incredible strength. Her core contracted, her abs flexed, and her quads clenched all the muscles she had built up. With a slight adjustment in position, that Arnaud did not notice, she was able to cross her arms, creating a battering ram. She sprang up and cold-cocked him directly under the chin, forcing him backward. He stumbled into the wall then pulled a gun from behind his back and aimed it at her.

"Bitch! Get in the fucking car. Now!"

Like a bizarre cinematic special effect, everything seemed to slow down for Louise. The realization that Jean-Philippe had been around over the years since the trial – possibly even knowing where she was but had never come for her – flipped a switch in her psyche. There was nothing left to lose, no one to pine for. She was the master of her destiny.

"Go fuck yourself, fat pig," Louise snarled.

The fat pig snorted what sounded like laughter and came closer, aiming the gun right between her eyes. Louise stared at him, not flinching.

Suddenly, the internal tower door flew open.

"How rude," Father Gregory said, pointing his revolver at Louise. "You didn't finish your dinner."

Time froze as Louise, Matthieu, and Arnaud assessed the situation. The dramatic stand-off intensified as Father Gregory slowly pointed his gun away from Louise and at her attacker.

"I'll kill her!" Arnaud yelled, flailing his gun frantically.

Matthieu came out of his stupor and pounced just as Arnaud fired. Like a bloody ballet, he leaped in time to take the shot that was intended for Louise. Simultaneously, Father Gregory unloaded his weapon on Arnaud. The monk's aim was true. Arnaud died a coward's death, shot through his least vulnerable spot...his heart. He was gone instantly, while Matthieu lay motionless, still breathing, but bleeding heavily.

"Go!" The Russian shouted, and the black sedan sped off.

Louise moved quickly to help Matthieu as Father Gregory tended to the last rights with Arnaud.

"What are you doing?" Louise nearly screamed.

Calmly, Father Gregory finished over the corpse, and came over to help Louise with Matthieu. "All souls," he said, "however damaged, deserve prayer before passing to the next world."

One more mystery was finally clear. "So, you're a real monk?" Louise asked.

"Guilty," he offered. "Even monks can work for Interpol."

"Interpol?" But she was interrupted by Ferdinande and André.

"Oh, mon dieu! What happened to monsieur?" Ferdinande shouted.

Father Gregory was now in charge. "Monsieur is dead, and this man is badly injured. He is losing blood and needs to get to the hospital. André, call an ambulance!" The groundskeeper ran off.

Matthieu was pale and losing consciousness, as Louise applied pressure to his wound.

"Matthieu, stay with me," she pleaded. "Luke needs you to teach him how to prune the vines."

Father Gregory held Matthieu's hand. "Do you have any last confessions?"

"Hang on!" Louise said. "He's not going to die!"

"He might still have something to confess?"

Louise knew he was right and moved her face close to Matthieu's. "Is there anything you can tell us about the murder of Ekram Almasi?"

Matthieu's voice was barely above a whisper. "Almasi?" he said. "They killed Almasi…" His was now ashen from blood loss. "The caves, search the caves…" He lost consciousness leaving Louise stunned by his words. She snapped out of it when André returned armed with a Tabatière Rifle. Although it was antique, it appeared polished and well maintained, ready for just such an occasion.

"Le SAMU arrive!" André announced.

"We must go," Father Gregory said.

"What about those girls?" Louise said. "They are still in danger and I'm not leaving without them."

Ferdinande had been absorbing the conversation. "You and Father can go," she told Louise. "André and I will take care of monsieur until the ambulance arrives."

"Thank you," Louise said.

Father Gregory rummaged through Arnaud's pockets. "The Russians will be returning with back-up. They already paid for Annabel. We'll take the girls with us. They will be safe where we're going."

"How are you involved in this?" Louise asked.

"I'll explain later." He found the room keys in Arnaud's pocket and they ran to the other tower and up the stairs to retrieve Annabel. When they opened the door, she appeared frightened, but seeing Father Gregory calmed her.

"Hello, my child."

"Hello, Father," she said. "Is it time for the wedding?"

"There will be no wedding," Father Gregory said. "This is Louise. We are taking you home." Although Annabel remained composed, she was clearly emotional.

"Everything will be okay now," Louise said, putting an arm around her shoulder and helping her down the stairs.

Father Gregory used the key to open the door below the stairs. They could hear the girl crying and he recited a blessing that seemed to calm her. He helped her to her feet and out of the room. She walked with a limp that appeared to be from a partial paralysis on her left side, possibly a birth defect. Still, she was stunningly beautiful. Her blue eyes sparkled back to life when she saw Louise. Then she saw Annabel and they both screamed.

"Evelyne!"

"Annabel!"

They fell into each other's arms. They became excited children again. Evelyne turned to Louise.

"Are you an angel?" she asked, tears of joy running down her ruddy cheeks. It was obvious that she was only physically handicapped, and despite the traumatic stress, was a very bright girl. All she wanted, all she needed, despite her torture and abuse, was a safe reunion with Annabel. But still, the thought of what the girls had been through repulsed Louise, now the avenging angel.

"Yes," said the Father. "An angel has come to save you."

They returned to the other tower as the medics lifted the unconscious Matthieu into the ambulance. Louise waved off medical attention, as the adrenalin and her natural protective instincts had made her pain from injuries vanish.

Louise turned to Father Gregory. "I'll drive."

THIRTY-THREE

January 12, 2002

"Where are we going?" Louise asked.

"Just follow the signs toward Brussels," Father Gregory said.

Louise gunned the accelerator, glimpsing her rearview mirror to check on the girls. Annabel was incredibly calm and poised. She comforted Evelyne who rested her head on Annabel's shoulder. Evelyne was not just sucking her thumb. She had crossed her index finger over her thumb, fitting both into her mouth.

"Why didn't Ferdinande and André report Evelyne to the police?"

"They had no idea she was there. Neither did I. Arnaud was very private. He never allowed anyone to enter that wing of the château. I have been stationed here tracking his movements."

"On whose orders?"

"You'll see very shortly."

A half-hour later, Louise pulled into the Sonian Forest and arrived at a fourteenth century monastery. She parked, and they led the girls through the front entrance where a nun met them.

"Welcome, children." Her demeanor calmed the girls as she led them down a hallway to the nuns' quarters. Louise and Father Gregory followed.

"They will be safe here," Father Gregory said. "Let's get them situated, then we can meet with the others and discuss our plan." Louise was too confused to argue. They arrived at a dormitory where several sisters welcomed the girls. Louise knew they were finally safe and turned to leave, but Annabel gently took her hand.

"Thank you," Annabel said. She hugged Louise and Evelyne came over to hug Louise too.

"You are safe now," Louise said reassuringly.

They left and Father Gregory led Louise down the cloister to the other end of the abbey.

"How long have you been working for Interpol?" Louise asked wanting to know if he worked with Jean-Philippe.

"God sent us here on a very important mission," Father Gregory said cryptically. "We could not turn away from our obligation." With that he opened the antediluvian door, and they entered the expansive meeting room of the chapter-house. Around the long table, about two dozen monks, seated and standing, were in intense discussions. Everyone stopped when Louise entered. A familiar face rose from the table to greet her.

"Hi Louise," Michael said.

"Michael?" Louise was in a state of confusion. "How did you get here?"

"Brothers, please welcome our guest, Louise Moscow," Michael announced. Those seated stood, and all bowed their heads to greet Louise. Some approached to shake her hand. They were gracious and seemed enthusiastic to meet her. One monk was particularly overwhelmed and enveloped her in his cloaked arms.

"It is an honor to meet you finally," Father Timothy said. "Please forgive me. I'm a hugger."

"The honor is mine," Louise said awkwardly. "Thank you for taking in those poor girls."

"Mission accomplished," Father Gregory said. "But there is much more that needs to be done."

"Which is why we have gathered here." The authoritative but familiar voice startled Louise.

The monks parted like the Red Sea to reveal the source. In a kind of Hitchcockian optical illusion, the room seemed to widen then narrow as Louise focused her eyes on what she thought must have been a hallucination.

"It's wonderful to see you, Louise," Jean-Philippe said, rising from his chair. Dressed in full Roman cassock, he had blended in with all the other monks until that moment. Now, he stood out like a god among men. Louise remained frozen, confused.

She made her way through the monks to the head of the table until she was face to face with Jean-Philippe. She raised a hand, Jean-Philippe didn't flinch. She gently touched his cheek.

"It's really you," Louise said.

Jean-Philippe opened his arms as though to say, *yes, it's me.* The other monks funneled out of the room, with only Michael and Father Gregory remaining.

This feels like a dream," Louise said, staring at Jean-Philippe.

"It's no dream," Jean-Philippe said. "You found me." She leaned into him, and he wrapped his arms around her. "I knew you could do it, Lulu." He stood back to look at her. "I like your hair." Then he felt her biceps. "And you're so *musclé.*"

"And you. Of all places to find you, this was the last place I would have considered. Are you really a priest?"

"Yes, it's official," he replied, pulling a chair out for her. Please, let's sit down." He sat at an angle from her and took her hand. "I had to go undercover." He indicated his cassock. "This allowed me anonymity, and the Fathers of Mercy took me in. Adapting to this cloistered lifestyle came very naturally."

"As much as I hate to admit it," Louise said resignedly, tears welling in her eyes, "this holy life suits you. This allows you to continue to work for Interpol along with Father Gregory?"

"Precisely. We have been investigating the ring behind all these disappearances of young women in Europe for many years."

Michael chimed in. "Louise, your investigation uncovered clues leading to the same chateau that Father Gregory had infiltrated. But your approach tied together more missing links."

"Yes, it looks like the Burgundy serial killers are connected to the Brussels serial killers," Louise said. "It's a truly evil ring."

Jean-Philippe elaborated. "This network seeks out the most depraved souls and feeds their sickness. They provide young women to corrupt elite at a high price. In exchange, these sadistic serial killers get to keep the girls that are deemed beneath the wealthy clients' standards."

"Thanks to Charlie, I acquired video evidence and I was also able to tie up some lose ends in Patrick's investigation. Both should be enough evidence to re-open the Almasi murder case."

"Yes, Michael told me." Jean-Philippe said.

"As usual, you have gone above and beyond expectations," Michael added. "But this is a long game, Louise."

"That's correct," Jean-Philippe said. "We have been working together while you have been in hiding. This network is so secretive that it has taken many years to infiltrate. Just tracking down the organization behind the Maltese Falcon trade and finally planting Father Gregory at the château took three years. After tonight our cover will have been compromised, but two girls have been saved. The death of Arnaud will only create a vacuum that will soon be filled with another corrupt soul. We will pick up where we left off in a long-drawn-out war with only incremental victories."

Louise remembered Matthieu' words, *the caves*. "Actually, I think we can do better than that. We have to talk with Matthieu as soon as possible."

"The patient will make a full recovery," the doctor said. Louise, Jean-Philippe and Michael followed him to Matthieu's hospital room, which was guarded by a police officer. "You can visit with him briefly, but then he will need his rest." The doctor left and they closed the door.

"Tu as bonne mine," Louise said, taking Matthieu's hand.

"Merci," Matthieu replied, the color and a smile coming back to his face. "It's good to see you, Louise."

"This is FBI agent, Michael Fuentes, and you know who Jean-Philippe is," Louise said. "I told them you could help us."

Matthieu explained that he had been doing his own investigating of Arnaud and the crime ring ever since Jo's murder and the blackmail. "After they killed Jo and threatened my family," Matthieu said, "I had no choice but to keep paying them from the vineyard profits. But it couldn't go on forever, so I had to take matters into my own hands. For months I followed Arnaud, tracking his movements. When you turned up at our vineyard, I knew there was more to you than you let on. When I realized that you were going to Belgium, I followed you. Imagine my horror when you led me to Arnaud. I confronted him and he told me he knew who you were because of the background check the bank did for your loan."

"So, you were there to rescue me?"

"Yes, of course. These people are evil."

"After you were shot, you mentioned the *caves*," Louise said. "What did you mean by that?"

"Just a few months ago, Arnaud's trail led me to secret caves. That is where they hold their terrible…meetings." Matthieu became upset and his heart monitor spiked.

The nurse opened the door. "I'm afraid you'll have to leave, so he can rest."

Louise leaned over Matthieu and asked, "Can you tell us where the caves are?"

"Impossible," Matthieu said. "The only way is to show you."

The gurgle of underground mineral springs seemed to taunt the nubile beauty whose whimpers could be heard in a bizarre orchestration that echoed in the caverns. Lying on a massive granite slab, only a small swath of cloth provided the girl the slightest modesty. A man dressed in a Celtic Gora cloak, the hood concealing his visage, held a large primitive artifact resembling a snake above his head and chanted in ancient Gaelic.

"That could be the mythical ex voto. It is said to be in the shape of a phallus," Matthieu whispered to Louise. The doctor had released him after a week recovering in hospital and he had led them to these caves. "The serpent represents the cyclic nature of life due to the annual shedding of its skin. It was important to the Druids and is depicted on much Celtic jewelry. Druid's were also known as 'Adders' and it's possible that the story of St. Patrick ridding Ireland of snakes refers to the Druids." They stood in the obscurity of the vast cave network, surrounded by the French version of a SWAT team waiting silently to raid the ring's secret ritual.

"That is a common misconception," said Gérard de la Varende, also present. "The notion that the long-sought relic considered the holy grail of healing is a phallus is misinformed. The custom of the phallus is a remnant of the Catholic Church fertility cult in classical antiquity from Isernia in Southern Italy. The true Celtic holy grail ex voto of healing is a symbol of female fertility."

His words gave Matthieu an epiphany. "That makes sense!" The group shifted in silent unison as Matthieu's relatively loud whisper threatened their concealment. The ritual chanting ceased, and the cave fell silent as the gathering listened for intruders. After a moment they resumed the ceremony.

Matthieu explained his outburst. "Every sacred Celtic shrine in Burgundy celebrates female fertility and all the relics are to the Goddess Diana. The ex voto of healing is *not* a phallus. It is a *vulva*."

"That's correct," Gérard agreed. "The Sheela-na-gig."

"Yes!" Matthieu said. "The female fertility figure, carved in stone, stands with an open mouth, her legs wide apart, holding open her vagina. The vulva is the main door, the mysterious divide between life and nonlife. There were many found near the holy wells in Ireland."

Louise interrupted him. "While it's refreshing to hear men so comfortable discussing the vagina, may I remind you that we are here to thwart a murderous cult?"

Suddenly a strange noise shook the caverns. It sounded like a large siphon followed by gurgling water. They watched from the obscurity as another man wearing a Gora cloak thrust a large wooden lever downward causing searing steam to engulf the sacrificial altar. The girl screamed as the vapors threatened to scald her. Several other cloaked men joined the chant as the master of ceremonies placed a heavy gold torq around the neck of an elderly man seated upon an ornate throne embedded with precious stones.

"That's the source of the mysterious sounds in my château," Gérard realized aloud. "This whole time it was these clandestine gatherings beneath the Château du Chastenay. Perceval tried to lead me here several times, but I never wanted to venture into this densely overgrown part of the forest."

"Perceval?" Michael asked.

"Gérard's dog," Louise replied. The sound of the water gurgled louder.

Matthieu cut in. "After following Arnaud, he finally led me here, where I have been secretly observing their rituals. If they knew I had found it, they would certainly have killed me. It is a gruesome practice. I only saw this ritual once before, with every pump of the well, the heat increases, and the steam eventually burns the girl alive. That is why I followed you to Belgium. I knew you were dealing with dangerous people. During my archeological research, I had only read of this ancient sacrificial *Dis Pater* ritual, but never imagined it would still be in use."

Stupefied by Matthieu's choice of words, Louise repeated what the bartender Jules had said. "*Dis Pater's goals lurk behind countless lies and deceptions!*"

"Exactly!" Matthieu said. "In fact, this cult has taken the name of *Dis Pater* precisely for that reason. They have mastered the art of deception, remaining in constant state of flux, morphing, disappearing and reappearing where least expected.

"They call themselves Dis Pater?" Louise asked.

"Yes," Matthieu confirmed. The *Order of Dis Pater*."

Dis pater means *Father Wealth*," Louise added.

"Yes, they use this symbolism in their rituals," Matthieu said. "That gold torq, and the gems on that throne, are very symbolic of the Dis Pater underworld. The ritual serves more as an initiation than any kind of actual healing. But these gatherings represent large sums of money to the crime ring from desperate wealthy souls. The caves are so secret the individuals gain access only wearing a blindfold and partake in what they believe are healing rituals. That was Todd Mayer's fatal mistake. Trying to impress his boss, Mayer made the reckless decision to invite Almasi to these secret caves for treatments. He was able to convince Almasi using the connection to gemstones. But as soon as Almasi realized the situation he was doomed. They threatened Almasi at the Bilderberg conference last year. But he was too ethical and would not play along, so they had no leverage against him. They had to do away with him."

"They must have been keeping this place a secret for hundreds of years," Gérard said. "It is the perfect secret hideaway."

"That also explains why you have had to fight so hard to keep the château," Louise said. "This place is on your land and is worth a fortune to the crime ring." The sound of the siphon resumed, and the girl screamed.

"Not anymore," Jean-Philippe said. "We have these vermin surrounded and this place is about to be fumigated."

The signal was given by Jean-Philippe, who no longer wore his cassock and was now on a different mission. He and Father Gregory, both in street clothes, watched alongside Michael as a squad of French Gendarmerie descended upon and then quickly overpowered the unsuspecting criminals.

The passenger door of a black sedan opened, and George Moscow stepped out. The driver, a beefy security guard in a dark suit and government-issued sunglasses, opened the back door. He held out his hand for Mary Moscow, who descended the vehicle and looked around in a daze. George put a protective arm around her shoulder and led her past the blinking lights of the squad cars and gendarmes placing people in custody. Mary couldn't take her eyes off a stunning teenaged woman sitting inside the open back doors of an ambulance. A medic placed a warm blanket over her shivering bare shoulders and examined her for visible injuries. The girl looked up and locked eyes with Mary, a mirror image of her older self.

Mary pulled George closer as he coaxed her forward through the thick forest to the entrance of the cave network. The dawn was just piercing the darkness of the witching hour. The security guard carried a torch to light their way into the tunnel. Louise held a lantern and greeted her mom with a reassuring hug.

"I know this is difficult, mom," Louise said. "But Dad and I are right here with you."

It had been Louise's idea. After saving the girls from the Maltese Falcon sex ring, she had called her father, George Moscow, and told him a version of what Mary had told her that December night, which seemed like three years ago instead of just three weeks. In 1962 when Mary was 20 years old and doing an internship as a simultaneous translator in Dijon, she had been captured by a sadistic ring that sounded too similar to the *Dis Pater* ring to be a coincidence. George agreed that they needed Mary's testimony as a witness and therefore they would need her to go identify the caves.

Back in the present, Mary still could not articulate her feelings. Coming face to face with her worst nightmare, after all those years of working to forget it, had her head spinning. She stood silently in the obscurity of the cave, closed her eyes and crossed herself. Louise had seen it many times throughout her life, Mary's inner-strength pose.

Suddenly Mary opened her eyes like she had seen a ghost.

"What is it, Mary?" George asked.

Mary breathed in deeply then froze. Then she coughed convulsively.

"Relax, mom. Take a deep breath."

But Mary waved her off, nodding her head up and down. "This is the place," Mary managed to choke out. "I can smell it." Her blue eyes were now filled with resolve. She grabbed the lamp from Louise and forged ahead into the dark chasm, their shadows playing against the walls, like shadows of the past. As Louise and the others followed, eventually the light from all sources allowed those shadows to fade.

Louise looked at her dad. "She's going to be okay."

"I should say so," George said, allowing an expression of relief to cross his face. But then his inner cop emerged. "Let's get her testimony before she – like she always does – starts forgiving and forgetting."

EPILOGUE

January 15, 2002

Jean-Philippe looked out of place walking down the Avenue Princesse Grace in Monte Carlo dressed in full cassock, black Saturno hat, sunglasses, and carrying a rosary in one hand with a large crucifix in the other. Women gazed and men nodded respectfully.

"The idea of going undercover is to *not* attract attention," Louise said.

"The things of God are hidden in plain sight," Jean-Philippe said, paraphrasing Proverbs.

"Do you have a bible passage for everything?"

"Having wisdom and understanding is better than having silver and gold." Proverbs again.

"Aaaa-men," Louise concluded, hoping it would end the Sunday school class.

They entered the Monte-Carlo Beach Hotel overlooking the Mediterranean. A smiling Frédéric LaFontaine greeted them.

"Mademoiselle Moscow!" They exchanged cheek kisses.

"Frédéric, thank you for helping us organize this meeting," Louise said. "This is Jean-Philippe…"

Frédéric gave his signature jovial laugh. "Monsieur de Villeneuve needs no introduction," LaFontaine said, shaking hands. "It is an honor to meet you."

"And you as well," Jean-Philippe said. "This is FBI agent Michael Fuentes." They shook hands then traversed the lobby and continued out the back toward the bungalows facing the sea.

"Charlie is with Patrick Roblot and his wife in the bungalow," LaFontaine said. When they reached the proper bungalow, they knocked on the door and there was Charlie. Louise hugged her protector warmly.

Charlie hugged Louise back then greeted the others. "Please come in," he said, introducing everyone. "Louise, you've met Patrick Roblot. This is his wife Lisette. Louise exchanged cheek kisses with the Roblots. "And this is the Undercover Monk himself, Jean-Philippe de Villeneuve."

"Father, thank you for coming," Roblot said shaking hands.

"It is a joyous day." Jean-Philippe said.

"And FBI agent Michael Fuentes," Charlie said.

"Yes, bravo on a job well done," Roblot said. "We are very interested to hear all about it."

With the introductions concluded, Louise took over the meeting. "Please, let's all sit down, and I will go over the details of the case with you."

Charlie and the Roblots were aghast as Louise recounted the investigation, and the headshaking news about how Almasi had stumbled into the sex ring due to Todd Mayer's reckless ambitions.

Michael added the information that they had acquired in a debriefing with Matthieu after they raided the cave and arrested the leader of the Dis Pater ring that went back over 100 years.

"Unfortunately," Louise concluded, "because of the vast network involved in this ring, this is still an ongoing investigation. So, all of this information is top secret."

"Understood," Roblot said and Lisette nodded in agreement.

"We thought you would also be happy to know," Louise continued, "that Paul Dupont and other Monaco officials have been arrested on corruption charges."

Roblot's eyes opened wide. "I knew all along Dupont was dirty!" Lisette put her arm around her husband's shoulder.

"We are so grateful," Lisette added. "This has been very trying for Patrick."

"We have more news," Louise said. "Which concerns you too, Lisette."

"The joyous occasion I was referring to," Jean-Philippe added. He stood and motioned to the lockout door leading to the adjacent bungalow. "Please, come with me."

Jean-Philippe knocked three times, then two more times. Father Gregory opened the door from the other side, and they entered. The two young ladies, Annabel and Evelyne, were sitting on the sofa, talking quietly when they saw the others. Somehow, Mrs. Roblot immediately recognized Annabel and gasped.

"Elizabeth!" Mrs. Roblot said in a throaty but restrained voice. Annabel stood, looking confused as the Roblots approached.

Charlie whispered to Louise, Michael and Jean-Philippe. "How did you know it was Roblot's lost baby?"

"Cross referencing," Jean-Philippe explained. "This criminal element was very fastidious about keeping records. Apparently, Lisette had a baby in 1985 that was kidnapped at about two months old while she visited family in Brussels. The case was badly bungled, evidence was compromised, and leads weren't followed. The baby was never found. Annabel was groomed for service as a dutiful wife in high society. Proof of her *provenance*, for lack of a better word, would have been required by her *purchaser*. A search of Arnaud's living quarters produced photocopies of original hospital birth records and duplicates that were made after the abduction and forged with her new name."

"Evelyne was taken fairly recently and easily identified herself as the daughter of Annabel's tutor," Louise explained. "We hope that you can help rejoin her with her family."

"Of course," Charlie replied. "Patrick and I will do everything we can to insure her complete recovery and reunion with her loved ones."

Louise watched as the family tearfully reunited. "We will leave you now to let you get reacquainted."

Lisette hugged Louise. "This is a new beginning for everyone. Bless you all."

They said good-bye and Louise gathered with the men outside for a final farewell.

"Thank you for booking the bungalow for me," Louise told LaFontaine. They exchanged cheek kisses.

"It was my pleasure," LaFontaine said. "I'll be in touch soon. Perhaps I can take you on another boat tour?"

"That would be wonderful," Louise said, genuinely enthusiastic. After the others said good-bye, Michael and Jean-Philippe lingered. Louise took out her room key and they walked her to the bungalow.

"I'm tired," was all Louise could think to say. It was hard to keep up appearances in the face of Jean-Philippe's stoicism and Michael's possessiveness.

"You know where to reach me," Michael said, giving her a kiss on the cheek and gracefully bowing out.

"Thanks Michael," Jean-Philippe said. Michael shook his hand and walked away.

"Well, it was wonderful to see you again, Jean-Philippe," Louise said. But just speaking the words brought up emotions, which she choked back. His eyes penetrated her soul further weakening her resolve to remain dignified. But then she recognized a familiar look of anguish in his left eye, reminiscent of Matthieu's.

"Would you like to come inside?" She offered, trying to give him an opportunity to get whatever bothered him off his chest.

"Yes, please." She unlocked the door and he followed her in. The stunning sea view notwithstanding, Louise sensed Jean-Philippe's intensity and closed the drapes to help put him at ease.

"Is there something wrong?" Louise finally asked.

Jean-Philippe took the envelope that his father had given him out of his robe and handed it to her. She opened it a read.

"A notice from the General Directorate. French Intelligence is investigating the purchaser of the Stradivarius violin you sold 10 years ago? Whom did you sell it to?"

"It was the friend of a close acquaintance, a Russian oligarch. I did my due diligence to make sure that the payment was clean. But it's appears the authorities suspect money laundering."

"Do they expect you to forfeit the payment?"

"No, the statute of limitations has long passed. But they are expecting me to cooperate and provide any information about the sale." Jean-Philippe moved closer and took Louise's hands, placing them in a prayer position. Her heart quaked at his touch. "This is your domain, Lulu. Can you help me through this? I will have to come out of hiding, at least temporarily."

Louise didn't hesitate. "Of course. Anything at all. I still have all the corporate records." He seemed to visibly relax. Their proximity unleashed a fury of passion, drawing them irreversibly toward the inevitable. Her openness was like a gravitational pull and they fell into each other's arms. His tongue entered her mouth like a satisfying bite of food after a long fast. Their chests heaved from their racing hearts as he dropped his cassock revealing his muscular body. Her clothing slipped off easily and they were on the bed in seconds. Her openness was so complete that he only had to enter her for a moment when they both reached a kind of divine detonation that had only happened to Louise once before.

They remained entwined, their heart rates returning to normal and Louise drifted off to a deep slumber.

She awoke alone, covered by the blanket. She looked at the clock on the nightstand where she found a note from Jean-Philippe. It simply said, "À très bientôt, mon amour."

April 2, 2002

Back at Château du Chastenay, there were more hugs for Louise, this time from Gérard.

"You saved my life's work," he said. "My son will have the resources to take over the business now because we were awarded damages by the bank."

"What about the caves we discovered? Will you open those up for research and tourism?"

"For now, it is still a crime scene. Perhaps I'll keep the mystery of the strange noises unsolved."

Louise bid him good-bye and continued on to the vineyard.

There was a hint of spring in the air as Magali and Luke prepared escargot for dinner and Matthieu set the table. At the sound of Louise's tires on the gravel, they all ran out to greet her.

"Bonjour, Karen!"

"Bonjour, Luke!" Louise gave him four cheek kisses.

"Bonjour, Louise," Matthieu kissed her cheeks too.

"No, oncle Matthieu, c'est Karen!" Luke said, correcting his uncle. Louise knelt to his eye level to explain in French.

"My name is Louise too."

"Karen Louise?" Luke asked.

"Why don't you just call me Lulu?"

"Lulu! Lulu!" Luke skipped away, and Magali approached for welcoming cheek kisses.

"Bonjour, Lulu! It is good to have you back home."

"It's wonderful to be back."

"You're just in time for dinner. We have fresh escargots." They went inside and Magali opened a bottle of champagne. She poured three glasses and they raised them. "To your health!"

"À la vôtre," Louise said.

They clinked and sat around the table as Magali served.

"Thank you for saving our vineyard," Magali said. "We are so grateful to you."

"Yes, I heard the bank is paying to cure the vines."

"Bruno's analysis of my vine fungus provided the evidence the police needed to get a search warrant," Matthieu said. "They seized diseased plants and other incriminating items from the assessor's home, and he confessed to the scam with Renard."

"The bank refinanced us with a low interest thirty-year mortgage," Magali said.

"All is right with the world again," Louise said. "By the way, Matthieu, there was something I didn't understand about the Shee… shee…" She reached into her purse and took out a piece of paper. "Ah, yes, the Sheela-na-gig. It's hard to keep track of the timeline." She read her notes. "The name comes from Celtic origins around 600 B.C. However, the relics didn't show up until the 12th century?"

"That's part of the mystery," Matthieu explained. "Until relatively recently, the symbol was considered evil because of its perceived sexual nature. Therefore, most of the Celtic artifacts were destroyed."

"So, the image of the open mouth and…" Louise stopped at *la bouche ouverte* not wanting to say *vulva* in front of Luke.

"La bouche ouverte," Luke repeated. He looked through the lens of his magnifying glass that Louise had given him, enlarging his big eye. "Comme l'escargot château."

Everyone stopped talking and looked at Luke. They all got up from the table, Magali took Luke in her arms, and they rushed to the escargot cellar. Luke still held the magnifying glass and Magali set him down by his bucket with the old pottery inside it.

"Luke, montres-nous *la bouche overte*," Matthieu said. Luke picked up the ancient clay pot that was now empty of escargots after the harvesting for dinner. To their amazement, Luke turned the pot upside down and showed Matthieu some embossed patterns through his magnifying glass.

"Les voila," Luke said, pointing at the markings and offering the magnifying glass.

Matthieu looked, then opened his mouth wide in amazement. He finally spoke. "It never occurred to me to look at this pot from this angle."

"What is it?" Louise asked.

"This is the artifact that I stole from one of my digs and the origins of all of my troubles. But what is incredible is, at the time I found this object, I carbon dated it back to the Iron Age."

"So, it is Celtic?" Louise asked.

"Yes. But my error was thinking it was just another ex voto and didn't seem very important. Having the symbol of the Sheela-na-gig makes it extremely rare, if not one-of-a-kind."

"So, I'm guessing it shouldn't be kept in an escargot bucket," Louise said.

"It should be in a museum," Matthieu said. "In fact, it could be the long sought-after holy grail of healing ex voto."

"L'escargot château!" Luke said reaching for the relic.

"Allez, on y va, Luke, au lit." Magali picked Luke up. "We'll get you another escargot château." She carried him off to bed leaving Louise alone with Matthieu. They went back to the kitchen and Matthieu poured more champagne. They clinked glasses.

"What an amazing day," Louise said. "Do you really think this could be the long-sought-after ex voto?"

"Even if it is," Matthieu speculated, "I'm sure it doesn't have any magic powers. But it is an amazing museum piece."

"Perhaps if you return it to the excavation company where it was found, they will be lenient. You could even return to your work as an archeologist."

"It's possible. It seems I have come full circle. The harassment has stopped since Arnaud's death and Renard's arrest." Matthieu picked up the ancient Sheela-na-gig. "Maybe I should get back into doing archeology. Thank you, Lulu." She liked the way he pronounced her real name.

"And your recovery is still on track?" Louise asked.

"Yes, they were able to replace the bit of artery the bullet tore away. The doctor said five more minutes and I would have been a goner. I have a slight limp, but I'm getting better every day."

"Boiter, c'est sexy," Louise said, teasing him about his limp. Matthieu blushed and she was delighted to see that old troubled look in his eye was gone. "Well, I'm happy for you. There's still so much to discover here."

Matthieu changed the subject. "Speaking of which, I heard we are going to be neighbors!"

"Yes! I am now the proud owner of that little house in Chalon-sur-

Saône. I just came from the bank."

"Congratulations!" Magali said, returning to the kitchen. "Will you be moving in soon?"

"Yes, but first a trip back to paradise."

"Do you have to go back into hiding?" Matthieu asked.

"No! After the raid and the Roblot's reunion, I went back to New York and Washington to testify to the various agencies. They decided that, due to the evidence I provided in the Almasi case, I would no longer have to worry about the Black Network." Louise went on to explain her situation. It wasn't 100% iron clad, but with Michael's name on her phone, she was ready to report anything suspicious. She told Magali and Matthieu the whole story of Karen. In a sense, this was her last day as a schoolteacher from Chicago.

"When is your flight?" Magali asked.

"In the morning," Louise replied. "Have you looked over the paperwork I sent you?"

Magali smiled coyly. "Oui," she said. "But I still don't understand why you are willing to finance a café for me?"

Louise just laughed. She had decided to make her dream café a reality. "A toast," she said.

"A vôtre santé!" Matthieu and Magali said simultaneously.

"That's a great name for the restaurant!" Louise said.

"Cheers!" Luke said in English. They all laughed.

Magali added, "To Louise Moscow...AND Karen Baker!"

Louise felt unsettled during the long journey back to the island. When she was staring at the business end of Arnaud's gun, she had had an epiphany that she was her own lover and had momentarily broken her obsession with Jean-Philippe. But she hadn't figured on that subsequent impromptu reunion.

They had to spend a lot of time together while preparing the case for Interpol and she helped him with the investigation of the violin sale. But their heated affair had to end abruptly when Jean-Philippe forthrightly confessed he was returning to the monastery. He said he would always love her, but was devoted to his higher love of God, something he couldn't explain and had to let play out.

On her side, she knew the competition was now ultimate, but she vowed to try on more time to connect to his soul. She felt that destiny coming. In Burgundy. In France.

The small aircraft landed, and Big Steve greeted her at the tiny island airport.

"Welcome home!" Two words had never felt better. She spied Big Steve at the tiny terminal and heard the booming greeting, like music to her ears. His hug seemed to last for days. As they made their way to the dock, Louise did her best to catch him up. They arrived at her old friend, *Serendipity*, and Big Steve placed her bags onboard.

"Get in, I'll drive," Louise said taking the helm. Big Steve was barely seated when Louise pushed the throttle and took off over the crystal blue waters with the wind in her hair. Soon, the towering thatched roof of the Tiki bar and the swaying palm trees appeared like a mirage in a deep blue Sahara. Had it been four months or four years? Tears welled in her eyes.

Louise approached the dock smoothly, and Big Steve jumped out to tie up. She stepped ashore, her feet back on solid ground, steadying her spirits. Big Steve carried her bag and they entered the Tiki bar. The white walls with blue and green tropical décor had never looked so inviting.

"Welcome home, Lulu." He watched her take in her surroundings.

"It really is great to be back."

Not missing a beat, she started rearranging chairs and straightening tables to her preference. Big Steve waited silently until she suddenly stopped working transfixed by Max's painting hanging on the wall. It was a majestic image of Diana with her Mona Lisa smile. Her pose evoked the Statue of Liberty, and in the background were subtle images of the American and French flags.

"It's beautiful." Louise became emotional from fatigue and jetlag. "I'm going to take a nap." She went to her bungalow, undressed, and fell asleep as soon as her head hit the pillow.

Just around sunset, Louise woke from her nap refreshed. The sea air had already done wonders for her and she relished dressing in the simple bikini and sarong. She walked out to the beach and took on the western view, with the sun slowly sinking into its watery night. It reflected in her green eyes like celebratory fireworks. She made her way back to the Tiki bar.

"There she is!" Big Steve shouted.

There was a rousing chorus of "SURPRISE!" as many of the regulars, sprinkled with the divers of the day, had come to participate in the homecoming. The drinks began to flow, and Louise was served her first tropical libation in months.

Big Steve went to the terrace and raised his glass. "Lulu, I want y'all to meet some friends of mine."

Louise put her glass on the bar and turned to Big Steve. In the twilight, Louise spied another boat at the dock, not a diving charter, but a luxury yacht.

"Oh, now I see what's going on," she teased. "You were 'surprising me' so you could have friends over for a party."

The gaggle of guests parted, as if they were the Red Sea. Louise looked up from her drink to see the silhouette of a familiar superstar and Big Steve made the introduction.

"Lulu, I'd like you to meet my homie." He grinned as he saw Louise's eyes open wide. "Louise Moscow, meet Snoop Dogg."

Big Steve turned up the music, and Snoop Dogg kissed her hand. Louise's soul swelled back into island time and she raised her glass. "Now this is my kind of homecoming!"

She awoke the next morning, not as much hung over, as wholly satisfied. Captain Robert had been part of the celebration crew, but things had changed for Louise since the encounter with Jean-Philippe. Knowing she would only be back on the island temporarily, she had paperwork inside her bags transferring the Tiki Bar to Big Steve and would eventually have to tell him the news.

She leisurely strolled to her private beach for some much-needed yoga and meditation. The freedom to walk straight from bed barefoot to the beach was hard to beat. As she sat in lotus pose, silently repeating her mantra, her thoughts sifted down and settled. Suddenly, a moment of clarity hit her like a lightning bolt. She opened her eyes and looked at her watch, which indicated she had done exactly thirty minutes of meditation.

It was words echoing in her mind, a much-loved passage from a special book. She went back to her bungalow and opened her closet. She reached way back and found it was still there, in a hermetically sealed case, the ancient manuscript. The words were contained in this book. She brought it out to the beach along with her laptop computer. Reclining on the cushions of her chaise lounge she began to re-read the words that seemed to have new meaning:

> *Perched safely on the cliffs of Thera, high over the southern Aegean Sea, her screams of anguish were heard by no one as she witnessed the massive wave wash away the entire civilization.*

Louise had read the manuscript many times since first discovering it in a hidden closet of her Paris apartment almost ten year ago.[21] She had always intended to explore its meaning if she ever had the opportunity. The writings contained many clues mapping out a geographical region yet to be confirmed. Up until then, she had been off the grid for her own protection. But in light of recent events – she had been cleared from her exile, she had property in France, and she was free to roam the world again.

She booted up that same laptop from the mission, the CIA had let her keep it – after they had erased the memory, naturally –turned on the satellite Internet and did a quick query of the Lost City of Atlantis. On Usenet she scanned several theories, but one from Marina Mylona, Tourism Officer of Marketing at the Cyprus Tourism Organization stood out:

It's been long-rumored that the lost city of Atlantis was located just off the coast of Cyprus.

Louise lay back and gazed upwards at the cloudless blue sky.

"Cyprus," she muttered to herself.

END

---

[21] From the author's first novel in the Louise Moscow series, *Foliage: An International Banking Spy Thriller*

ENDNOTES

- Murderpedia, Juan Ignacio Blanco, Website: http://murderpedia.org/male.M/m/maher-theodore.htm
- Justice: Crimes, Trials, and Punishments, By Dominick Dunne, Feb 25, 2009
- Death in Monaco by Dominick Dunne December 1, 2000 12:00 am
- Wikipedia: Law enforcement in Monaco
- Wikipedia: Ted Maher
- Wikipedia: Camino de Santiago
- Wikipedia: Georges André Malraux
- Wikipedia: Marc Dutroux
- Gouvernement Princier, Principauté de Monaco, Website: http://en.gouv.mc/Government-Institutions/The-Government/The-Ministry-of-State/The-Minister-of-State
- Understanding A Course in Miracles, Website: https://understandacim.com/
- Lordsandladies.org/medieval-monastery.htm
- Wikipedia: Fathers of Mercy
- Richard Clarke: "Against All Enemies, Inside America's War on Terror" by Free Press, a subsidiary of Simon & Schuster
- Newsweek: Time For The Grand Finale, By Meg Greenfield, Aug 18, 1991
- Giza Death Star: 1991-2011: The BCCI Scandal 20 Years Later, By Joseph P. Farrell, Apr 13, 2011
- Goldseek.com, 9/11 & Gold, Money and Power, By Darryl Robert Schoon, Aug 20, 2012
- The New York Times: Russian Money-Laundering Investigation Finds a Familiar Swiss Banker in the Middle, By Timothy L. O'Brien With Raymond Bonner, Aug 22, 1999
- Spy Museum: Language of Espionage
- Marlow Yachts Limited, Inc.

- Jon Stewart, 2004
- Caminoways.com
- GlobalCom Satellite Phones
- Chicago Tribune: The French Connection, By Mary Daniels, Sept 24, 1989
- BBC News World Edition: NYC Out of the Ashes, By Peter Gould, Dec 21, 2001
- The Italian, or The Confessional of the Black Penitents, By Ann Radcliffe, published 1797
- Burgundytoday.com
- Independent: Billionaire Who Blew Whistle on Russian Cash Scandal is Killed in Monte Carlo, By John Lichfield, Dec 4, 1999
- The Guardian: The Strange Case of Edmond Safra, By Andrew Anthony, October 28, 2000
- The Safra Dynasty: The Mysterious Family Of The Richest Banker In The World, By Carrie Hojnicki, June 7, 2012
- Aubert de Villaine
- Intowine.com
- Trans-D Digital Blog, Mar 2, 2015
- Office De Tourisme, Beaune & Pay Beaunois
- Airbnb.fr
- Bourgogne-wines.com
- The Telegraph: Burgundy Canal Journeys, Aug 9, 2017
- Crédit Agricole Group
- Irene and Giorgio Silvagni
- Independent: Joanna Parrish, By Cole Moreton, Sept 12, 2015
- Lodi Wines California
- Privilege La Reserve du Prince Cognac
- Bilderberg.org
- Time: What to Know About the Bilderberg Group's Secret Annual Meeting, By Josh Sanburn, Jun 9, 2016
- LaLibre.be: De Sars-la-Maudite à Sars-la-Buissière, By Sophie Lebrun, Feb 23, 2004

- Independent: A Country Brought Low By Horror, By Sarah Helm, Sept 10, 1996
- Sacred-Destinations.com
- The New York Times: Ex-Chief of BCCI to Be Extradited to US for Trial, By Stephen Labaton, Jan. 10, 1994
- Independent: BCCI Men Jailed and Ordered to Pay Dollars 9bn: Former Chief Executive and Founder of Collapsed Bank Sentenced in Their Absence, June 15, 1994
- The Washington Post: Former BCCI Official Naqvi Sentenced to Prison By Sharon Walsh, Oct. 20, 1994
- Mbgmindfulness: OM: What Is It & Why Do We Chant It? By Sam Saunders.
- Medievalchronicles.com

Made in the USA
Columbia, SC
25 August 2020